W9-AZD-031

Dear Reader,

I'd barely finished writing the last of my marines trilogy when gamblers and showgirls started agitating me for their stories to be told. Never let it be said that I'm not an accommodating woman. I planted my rear in that seat and started to write. And now, with the hard work behind me and *the end* finally typed, it is my pleasure to present to you the first of two books featuring long-legged women who make their living dancing in a lavish Las Vegas revue.

Sounds pretty glam, right? Go tell it to Treena McCall. She's worked hard to get where she is, but the past year has left her scrambling to hang on to her spot in the chorus line. Her sole aim is to pass the upcoming annual audition and gain the security of employment for another year.

Then professional poker player Jax Gallagher comes to town with his sexy eyes and private agenda—and their lives are suddenly turned upside down. He isn't the man she thinks he is. She isn't the woman he expected. He came to Vegas planning to rob Treena blind, only to have his heart stolen by *her*.

Figuring out how two people can forge a future from a relationship founded on lies was a wild roller coaster of ups, downs and loop-de-loops for me. I hope you enjoy the ride.

Susan Andersen

Also by SUSAN ANDERSEN

HOT & BOTHERED

Susan Andersen

skintight

MIRA®

ISBN 0-7394-5561-3

SKINTIGHT

This book is dedicated, with love, to:

Meg Ruley
for being the best,
the greatest,
the most fun agent
a girl could ever have

My sister Rogue Authors
Victoria Alexander, Patti Berg,
Stephanie Laurens and Linda Needham
for laughter, commiseration,
friendship and shared meals

and to
Styx
for warm fur, a great purr and stupid pet tricks

Prologue

Jackson Gallagher McCall set his drink down on the tiny cocktail table in front of him as a group of show-girls, clearly ready to party, strolled into the Las Vegas casino bar where he sat. *How about that? Ask and ye shall receive.*

This must be his lucky night; his target was right in the midst of things. He watched her wild tangle of pale red curls gently shift against her collarbone and spill over her shoulders to float out behind her. It had been a bitch trying to pick her out in *la Stravaganza,* the lavish revue he'd attended a short while ago in the hotel showroom. All the dancers on stage had killer bodies, seemed to be within an inch or two of each other in height, and wore heavy makeup and identical costumes. They either had matching wigs or the exact same lavish headdresses, give or take a plume or three.

He didn't doubt for a minute it was the same group, however, for while they'd replaced all that theatrical greasepaint with the regular kind of makeup women wore, a few of the dancers were still in the skimpy costumes he'd last seen on stage in the final act.

Not *her,* though. He looked her over from head to foot, and decided it wouldn't be a hardship to seduce his way into this one's house. Not with that body, clad now in tall, barely-there sandals, peach-colored hip-hugging slacks, and a matching top, the entire back of which consisted of nothing more than a few skinny criss-cross straps. She had a bawdy laugh and a mouth that was now curved up on the left side in a slight, knowing, closed-lips smile. It was a look that said this woman had probably forgotten more tricks than most women ever learned.

And the same I'm-gonna-give-you-the-hottest-night-of-your-life crook of the lips he'd seen in the professional head shot his old man had sent him to show off the woman he'd persuaded to marry him.

The woman who would become Big Jim McCall's widow practically before the ink was dry on the marriage certificate.

One

"Happy birthday, girlfriend!" With glasses raised, a multitude of female voices echoed the toast. Someone added, "So, which one is this, anyhow—your thirty-second?"

Treena McCall looked at the group of women ringing the tables they'd shoved together to accommodate everyone and felt the corner of her mouth turn up. "My thirtieth," she corrected smoothly, although it was actually her thirty-fifth. That was a fact she'd just as soon forget, but the ache of muscle strain in her left calf due to a simple high kick in the final number made it tough to do.

Her friends hooted. "Sure it is," someone agreed with friendly sarcasm. A dancer named Juney nodded and said, "And this makes *how* many thirtieth birthdays you've celebrated?"

"Oh. Well. If you're going to be picky..." Her lip crooked up a little higher yet. "The truth is, I've decided to quit adding numbers and go straight to the alphabetical system...which I suppose makes me thirty-E. Tell you what, though, Juney. If you don't go there on mine, I promise to stay away from the subject on *your* next birthday."

"Deal."

"In any case—" Julie-Ann Spencer leaned forward from down the table to say "—I guess you won't be dancing the Crazy Horse Show for La Femme anytime soon."

There was an instant silence, since everyone knew Julie-Ann's remark—although offered in a friendly enough tone—wasn't made in the true spirit of comradery.

"Bitch," Carly murmured in Treena's ear, then raised her voice. "Is *anyone* at this table besides you still under twenty-five, Julie-Ann?" Rude catcalls greeted her question, and Carly gave the young woman a pointed glance. "Then I guess no one but your perky little self qualifies for the Crazy Horse."

"And that is sure as hell La Femme's loss," Eve said.

"Idiots don't know what they're missing," Michelle agreed.

But if Julie-Ann's intention had been to cast a pall over Treena's mood, she'd accomplished her mission. For not only would she never dance in the Crazy Horse, she'd be damn lucky if she passed the mandatory annual audition two weeks from now in order to keep the job she already had. Those eleven months off with Big Jim had cost her. His rapidly escalating illness had allowed her time only to take infrequent dance classes, and that sort of hit-and-miss practice simply wasn't sufficient for a Las Vegas showgirl to stay in shape. In little less than a year, she'd gone from being dance captain of the troupe to barely keeping her spot. Thirty-five might be the prime of most women's lives, but for a dancer it was nearly over the hill. There was nothing to look forward to but the slippery slope on the other side.

Age hadn't been something she'd given much thought to until she'd come back to the show, for the end of her career had always seemed far, far in the future. But as much as she'd like to ignore the way her career seemed to be hurtling toward its final destination faster than a Japanese bullet train, she'd awakened this morning to the realization that she was officially thirty-five. She knew that once this train got into the station, she'd have no choice but to get off. Unfortunately she wasn't even close to realizing her backup dream—that of someday opening up her own dance studio.

No sense dredging up the fact right this minute, however. It only served to exacerbate the itchy feeling of recklessness that had been building in her all day.

She heard a low, sharp exclamation from a male throat and an accompanying high-pitched feminine yip, but even as she turned to see the commotion going on behind her, her bare shoulder and back were suddenly drenched with a shower of melting ice. With a startled shriek, she jumped to her feet.

"Omigod, Treena, I'm sorry," said their waitress Clarissa, who was already bent down on one black fishnet-stockinged knee, righting the empty glasses on her tray.

"No, the fault is mine," said a smooth, deep voice. A tanned, long-fingered hand cupped the waitress's elbow and assisted her to her feet. "My apologies. I should have made sure no one was coming before I got up out of my chair."

As soon as the cocktail waitress regained her footing, he turned to Treena. She had a quick impression of height, wide shoulders, and tousled, sun-streaked brown hair before the man whipped a handkerchief from the breast pocket of a black jacket she'd bet a week's pay had been fashioned by some brand-name, high-priced designer. Reaching out, he used it to gently blot the moisture from her shoulder.

"I'm sorry," he said, taking obvious care not to touch her with anything but the linen square as he daubed under her hair. He fished a dripping cube from her curls with his free hand, and his dark eyebrows met over the strong thrust of a nose that had clearly been broken at some point in his life. "The only saving grace here is that she was carrying empties when I tripped her up. Turn around. Let me get your back."

He spoke with such impersonal coolness that she automatically about-faced, and found herself staring at her friends who were all watching with varying degrees of wide-eyed or raised-brow fascination as he efficiently mopped the moisture from her back. That was when her own compliance hit her.

She wasn't docile by nature, and if he'd made even a single attempt to touch her in an inappropriate manner, she'd have cut him off at the knees so fast he would've been four foot two before he knew what hit him. She was used to deflecting that sort of bullshit from Stage Door Johnnies who thought because a woman danced topless in the final show of the night she was fair game for their wandering hands. But this man's flesh didn't touch hers at all. She felt him only as a heat source through the rapidly dampening handkerchief sliding over her skin.

"There." His voice sounded like a low rumble in her ear, and his hand dropped to his side. He stepped back. "It's not perfect, I'm afraid, but the best I can do under the circumstances."

Turning to face him, she found him standing closer than she'd anticipated. She stepped back only to bump into her chair, and it rocked up onto two legs. When she reached out to steady it, she knocked off her purse. "Oh, for—"

They both stooped down at the same time, their fingers tangling as each reached for the small leather envelope. He relinquished it to her, but pinned her in place with his vivid blue eyes and murmured low enough so only she could hear, "The young woman who's young enough to dance for the Crazy Whatzit you ladies were talking about? Trust me—she doesn't look half as good at twenty-five as you do at thirty-E." His mouth crooked.

She should have been miffed at his eavesdropping but instead, a small whoop of delighted laughter exploded up from her belly. She looked at him, squatting in front of her with his faded jeans stretched white over his widespread knees, his silk T-shirt beneath that lightweight designer jacket nearly an exact color match for his sky-blue eyes, and felt something she hadn't experienced for a long, long time—attraction. Pure, animal, man-woman attraction. Her lips curved into her unique one-sided smile and she rose to her feet. "Thank you. That's possibly the nicest birthday present I've received today."

He rose, as well, and stood looking down at her. "Listen," he said slowly. "I don't supposed you'd consider—" With a shake of his head, he cut himself off and, combing a hand through his disheveled hair, he stepped back. "No, never mind. Of course you wouldn't."

"What?"

"Nothing. It's too presumptuous."

Treena shrugged, but her heart skipped like crazy and only through sheer force of will did she stop herself from demanding to know what he'd been about to say.

Then he dropped his hand to his side, raised his lean jaw, and said, "What the hell. Would you consider joining me for breakfast tomorrow morning? I understand they have an excellent dining room here."

The reckless itch that had been agitating for expression all day urged her to snap up his invitation. *Go on,* whispered a little devil sitting on her shoulder. *Live a little.* It was her thirty-freaking-fifth birthday. She might as well get something out of it.

Exactly, the tiny red-horned demon agreed. *You could stand a little fun in your life.*

She wasn't a young girl who acted on her every impulse, however, and the truth was her husband had only been buried four months earlier. So even though she wanted to say yes, she wrestled the temptation into submission and opened her mouth with every intention of politely but firmly declining his offer.

But Julie-Ann beat her to the punch. "You might want to make that for brunch, big guy—or possibly lunch. Our Treena's getting up there in age, you know, so she requires a bit more beauty rest than she used to."

Tilting back her head in a way that displayed her smooth, youthful throat to its best advantage, she laughed as if she'd just let him in on a huge inside joke.

Rebelliousness rose in Treena's chest as she turned to stare at the twentysomething dancer. What on earth was her problem? Julie-Ann had taken over Treena's position as dance captain. Couldn't she be content with that? Instead Treena's very existence seemed to aggravate the younger woman. Well, to hell with her. She turned back to the man. "What's your name?"

"Gallagher. Jax Gallagher."

His voice reverberated along her nerve endings. "Well, Gallagher, Jax Gallagher, I believe I would like to have breakfast with you."

His smile deepened, showcasing his straight white teeth and the creasing lines that fanned out from the corners of his incredibly blue eyes. "Yeah?"

"Yeah. But Julie-Ann's right—I'm not the young woman I was yesterday, and we old ladies do need our rest. So would you mind terribly if we made it for ten o'clock? Or if you have something else going and are pressed for time, perhaps nine-thirty."

"Ten o'clock would be great." He offered his hand.

She grasped it, amazed at how energized his long, slightly rough-tipped fingers made her feel. She had first, second and third thoughts about the wisdom of meeting him in the morning, but she merely said, "I'm Treena McCall, by the way."

"Pleased to meet you, Treena." His fingers slowly released hers and slid away. "Would you like me to send a car to pick you up?"

"That's not necessary. I'll meet you in the dining room."

"Very well. Until tomorrow, then."

"Yes," she said, as he took a step back. "Until then." She watched as he turned and strode from the open concept bar, stopping only long enough to say something to Clarissa and drop some bills on her tray. Then his long legs took him up the aisle that ran between the craps and the blackjack tables. For a moment the sounds to which she'd long ago become so accustomed she rarely even heard them anymore—the clatter of silver dollars hitting trays, the constant ringing of bells, and the competing, clashing tones and beeps of the various electronic slot machines—saturated her consciousness. When Jax disappeared into the depths of the casino, she turned back to her friends. For a second she merely stared blankly at them. Then she pantomimed a scream.

Juney, Eve and Michelle screamed for real. Jerrilyn, Sue and Jo drummed their fingers on the table and grunted, "Whoo! Whoo! Whoo! Whoo!" as if she'd just scored the winning goal at a pro-ball game. Her best friend Carly lounged back in her chair, one slender arm draped across the chair back, and grinned up at Treena. "Way to go, girlfriend! Now, *that's* what I call a birthday present."

Julie-Ann sulked, which should have felt like sweet vindication to Treena, considering what a pain in the butt she'd been ever since Treena's return to the show. Instead her adrenaline rush bottomed out and, looping her purse strap back over her chair, she dropped into her seat. She gave her friends a cocky smile, just as if she'd scored herself—as Carly had said—an exceptional birthday gift.

But deep inside, she wondered what on earth she thought she was doing.

Jax leaned back in his seat at a linen-draped banquette table in the hotel dining room the following morning and turned a little pink packet of artificial sweetener end for end between his fingers as he kept an eye on the entrance. He thought he'd played things rather well last night, but still he found himself laying bets as to whether or not Treena would actually show.

Tripping the poor cocktail waitress had paid off even better than he'd anticipated. He didn't ordinarily like to involve innocent people in his private agendas, but in this case it had been necessary. He'd watched Treena enough the past few days to know a straight pickup wasn't likely to work. He didn't know what she was getting out of the nondating, all-work-and-no-play widow act he was sure she was putting on, but a good gambler nevertheless always went with the odds. So he'd created his own opportunity and assuaged his conscience by making sure he compensated the waitress with a very generous tip for her trouble and any embarrassment he'd caused her.

Particularly for the embarrassment. He'd spent too much of his youth learning more about that state of mind than any kid needed to know. Humiliation might not kill you, but it could sure as hell make you *wish* you were dead, if only momentarily.

But he didn't want to think about that, so he focused

on the couple of minutes spent getting up close and personal with Treena McCall. He stilled the packet between his fingers midflip as he reflected on those few brief moments.

His reaction to her had caught him by surprise. He'd noticed the shift in her mood when Julie-Ann made such a production out of her age, and he hadn't hesitated to use it to his advantage.

But he sure as hell hadn't expected to feel such an instant connection when her golden brown eyes lit up and she'd let rip with that full-throated laugh once he told her nothing short of the truth: that she looked ten times better at thirty-five than the decade younger Julie-Ann. The small surge of lust he'd felt at catching her scent and feeling the soft brush of her pale red curls across his knuckles was no big surprise. But that momentary flash of *I know you* he'd experienced just because she had a great laugh? What the hell was that all about?

Just then the object of his thoughts strolled through the dining room door, and he tossed the sweetener packet back into the little silver holder in the middle of the table and straightened. Draping his arm along the back of the leather upholstered banquette, he adopted a casual, friendly pose as he watched her speak to the hostess, then turn to follow the young woman as she wove through the dining room toward his booth.

She caught him watching her and flashed him that lopsided smile. Jax smiled back, aware of his heartbeat shifting into overdrive.

She was dressed in sleek, polished cotton beige pants and an olive-green top made of some slinky material that hung loosely, yet tantalizingly suggested the curves beneath.

So, okay then, most likely his attraction *was* about sex. And, hell, even if it wasn't, it really didn't matter. Treena McCall was a means to an end. She had something that belonged to him. Something he needed if he planned to stay alive.

Which he did.

So he'd do whatever it took to get it back.

Two

Treena had come *this close* to not showing up. She'd talked herself into keeping the breakfast date only by administering a few pithy lectures about the rudeness of standing up someone who'd been nothing but nice to her. Yet even as she followed the hostess into the heart of the restaurant, she was tempted to turn around and head back to the 'burbs. She really did need to run a few errands before her dance class at noon.

Then she looked up and saw Jax staring at her from the banquette, and all her reservations melted like so much sugar on the tongue.

Man, she didn't know what it was about this guy, but *something* sure grabbed her attention. She didn't think it was his looks, because he was hardly your standard babe material. The man was certainly no troll, but neither did he qualify as knock-your-socks-off gorgeous. His nose was a little too big, his jaw a little too long. All of his features taken individually, in fact, shouldn't have added up to much. But somehow, put together, they formed an appealing whole that worked. Plus, he was fit, which as an athlete she appreciated, and there was an intensity in his vibrant blue eyes that she could feel clear across the room.

He rose to his feet as she approached the table, and she found herself at an eye level with his collarbone. With a little start, she realized that he was so much taller and wider than she was that she felt almost petite. It was a rare sensation. Since most choruses in Las Vegas shows had height minimums of at least five feet nine inches, she'd never considered herself one of those pocket Venus types.

His height caught her by surprise only because she'd worn heels last night instead of the strappy little flats she'd shoved her feet into this morning. Giving him a discreet once-over, she judged him to be roughly six foot four or five, and close to two hundred and twenty pounds of solid muscle.

Treena smiled as the hostess told them to enjoy their breakfast and headed back to her station. "Good morning," she said and wondered what she should offer in the way of a physical greeting. After a hesitation, she thrust out her hand. They didn't know each other well enough to exchange a hug, much less a kiss. Clearing her throat as his warm fingers wrapped around hers, she was struck by how downright pathetic she'd become at this. She used to be pretty good at small talk, but it had been a long time since she'd had a date and she was clearly out of practice. Her hand tingling, she slipped her fingers free and murmured, "I hope I'm not late."

"Not at all. You're right on time." He ushered her into the banquette then slid in across from her. "I was early."

Placing her small purse next to her hip she settled in, gazing at him across the narrow table. He either wore the same gorgeous jacket he'd had on last night or one just like it, paired this time with a gray silk T-shirt and black jeans. He looked confident and at ease, and she wondered if he acquired breakfast companions as easily as he had her on a regular basis.

"You know," she said impulsively, "I don't ordinarily accept dates from total strangers." She made a face. "And, gee, you're real likely to believe *that,* considering what an easy pickup I turned out to be last night."

"Oh, I believe it." His dark eyebrows met over the thrust of his nose for a moment as if puzzled by the fact. But just as quickly they smoothed out, and he handed her a menu, giving her a sober look over it. "You don't have the moves of a natural flirt."

Treena laughed out loud. "Thanks…I think."

"Maybe I should have said of someone on the prowl for a man. For a one-night-stan—that is, a pickup." He looked at her. "I'm making this worse, aren't I?"

She grinned. "Maybe we should move on to a new subject."

"Good plan."

"I'm guessing you're not from around here." She cocked an inquiring eyebrow at him.

"Actually, I lived here as a teen, but I've been gone for a long time."

"Is that what brings you here? Moving back to town?"

"No."

"Then you must be here on business. Or am I jumping to conclusions again? Are you on vacation?"

"A little of both. First I'm reacquainting myself with one of my hometowns. Then business."

"What is it that you do?" She waved a hand before he had a chance to respond. "No, wait, let me guess." She studied him. "Your jacket is exquisite. Armani?"

"Hugo Boss."

"Okay, expensive, fairly conservative, and you've got that great dressy-casual thing going by pairing it with those silk T-shirts. But the combination with jeans and—" she leaned sideways to peer under the table "—Nikes tells me you're probably not a CEO, am I right?"

"Definitely."

"Yet you strike me as being both brainy and perhaps a little…wild." She gazed at his sun-streaked brown hair, which, while far from long, was a little longer and perhaps just the tiniest bit shaggier than the average businessman would wear. "So, something in the arts, maybe? Are you a graphic artist?"

He shook his head.

"A painter or a photographer?"

He gave her a crooked smile. "The results of my forays into those fields were less than spectacular."

His smile did funny things to her libido, and she quickly racked her brain for more professions to divert her attention. "Are you a dot-commer?"

"Nope. Although I do have an affinity for computers."

"College professor?"

He laughed.

"I'm taking that as a no. The jacket would probably be tweedier anyway. So, let's see." She studied him. "You're tan. Of course, most people in this town are. Still, please tell me you're not a surfer boy." She smacked herself in the forehead. "Duh—not a lot of surf to be found in Las Vegas. Plus I haven't once heard you say 'dude'—so that's probably not the world's greatest guess. You don't *design* surfboards by any chance, do you?" Hadn't she heard somewhere that there was a convention of those guys in town?

Or maybe that had been snowboard designers.

Either way, he flashed her another white-toothed smile and said, "'Fraid not."

"Okay, I give. What brings you to Vegas?"

"Poker."

Her mouth dropped open. Snapping it shut, she reached over and smacked him lightly on the arm. "You cheat! You said you were here on business!"

"That is my business."

She stared at him, startled. "You're a professional gambler?" He raised an eyebrow at her, and she said slowly, "Okay. That's about the last thing I would have guessed." And the knowledge unsettled her a little, although she didn't know why. It wasn't as if she planned to marry the guy, so surely it was no skin off her nose how he made his living. He likely wouldn't even be in town long enough for them to *have* a relationship.

It shocked her to realize how curiously deflating that was.

Jax watched her withdraw slightly and wondered,

what he was doing. Honesty was *not* the best policy, and he'd determined he wouldn't go down that road after he had tried to accomplish his goal the honorable way and got shot down for his efforts. So fine. He wanted her to believe he was a high roller with money to burn, and unfortunately most people's conception of a professional gambler was something a little sleazier even though he'd been doing very, very well for himself on the pro circuit.

Until he'd fucked up in Monaco. But he only had himself to blame for that fiasco and this resulting predicament.

So he wasn't here to have a good time with the woman—yet that was precisely what he was doing. Seducing Treena McCall was the only way he thought he would get an invitation into her home and then be left alone there long enough to get his hands on the item that would get his pecker out of the wringer.

He didn't foresee his mission taking long. She was a showgirl, after all, and God knew his father had already proven she could be bought. But looking at her across the table, at that mass of curls and that mouth, he warned himself not to get cocky. Ego was what had gotten him into this mess in the first place. He had to be careful because, after watching her these past couple of nights and spending a little time with her this morning, his body was already starting to get ahead of itself, and he couldn't afford to let his dick rule his movements. Even if she wasn't at all what he'd expected.

He'd figured she would be dumb and greedy, not humorous and down-to-earth. Why the hell else would a woman like her marry a man ancient enough to be her father? He remembered life with his old man. His father hadn't exactly been Mr. Easygoing. But he was definitely rich.

"So are you in Las Vegas a lot, then?"

Treena's voice interrupted his musings, and he shoved them away to mull over later as he refocused his full attention on her. "No, this is my first time back in years. Since I left to attend college, in fact. I spend most of my time in Europe these days. Most recently Monte Carlo."

"As in the Riviera?"

"Yeah."

"Oh, my God." She sighed and planted her chin in the palm of her hand as she gazed at him with admiring wistfulness. "I can't even imagine. Except for a week Carly and I spent in Cancun three—no, God, it's been four years ago now—I've never even been out of the States."

"You're kidding me." He wasn't faking his amazement. He imagined she would have had the old man trotting her here, there and everywhere. In first class, wasting away the family fortune to such an extent that she'd had no choice but to return to dancing in a chorus line.

"I wish I were. Unfortunately, it's the God's honest truth. Pretty sad, huh?"

"You mean to tell me a nice Irish girl like you has never even made it back to the Motherland?"

She gave him one of those one-sided I've-seen-it-all smiles. "You think I'm Irish?"

"Aren't you? With that red hair and a name like McCall, I figured you had to be either Irish or Scottish."

She laughed and he watched a couple of businessmen at a nearby table turn to give her appreciative looks.

"By way of Warsaw, maybe," she said. "I grew up in a little Pennsylvania steel town I'm sure you've never heard of. And until about a year and a half ago, I was Treena Sarkilahti."

"So McCall is your stage name?"

"No, it's my married name. Was my married name. I'm a widow."

"Oh, man." He sat back, and to his surprise discovered chagrin was yet another thing he didn't have to feign—at least not a hundred percent. He'd honestly expected her to snap up the stage name excuse he'd offered and found it slightly shocking to hear the word *widow*. It conjured all sorts of sympathetic images he had no desire to feel. "I'm sorry."

"Me, too. He was a great guy."

If you have really low standards, he thought. But he stowed the bitterness that belonged to another time. It sure as hell wouldn't advance his agenda to dwell on it at this late date.

But even as he opened his mouth to literally charm the pants off her, she said, "You know, in a strange kind of way you remind me of him a little."

He stared at her in horror.

She laughed. "I know. Nothing like hearing a woman compare you to her dead husband, huh? Jim was a self-made man without a lot of education and you're smoother than he was. But all the same, you're…kind… like he was. And big like him. He was a real man's man."

Now he *knew* she was a liar. Kindness was not a word he'd use to describe his father. It sure as hell wasn't part of his own makeup, either.

Not anymore.

But a man's man—oh, yeah, Dad had been that all right. He'd lived to fish and hunt and play or watch every sport known to man.

He'd cared more about other men's opinions—even those of complete strangers—than about his own kid's state of mind. How many times had the old man towered over him, trying to get him to behave in a way that would garner the approval of his peers? A ghost of his father's voice whispered in disgust from a dark corner of Jax's mind.

"Choke up on the bat, Jackson, and keep your eye on the ball. Christ Almighty, boy, you swing like a girl!"

Treena touched the back of his hand. "I'm sorry," she said. "I shouldn't have brought him up."

Blinking the old memories away, he focused on his agenda. The old man had been right about one thing. He needed to keep his eye on the goddamn ball. Looking at the sexy redhead across from him, he silently cursed for allowing that little crease of worry to develop between her eyebrows. "How long has your husband been gone?"

"A little over four months."

"That's no time at all. Of course he's going to be in your thoughts." Leaning forward, he smoothed his fingers over the tips of hers. "Am I your first date since he died?"

"Yes. And I can honestly say I don't know what came over me."

That elicited a genuine smile. "Yeah?"

"Oh, yes." Color rose in her cheeks.

"Then I take back that 'not having the moves of a natural flirt' remark. If making a man feel like a million bucks is any criteria, you're a lot better at it than I thought."

She blinked at him. "Why you silver-tongued devil," she deadpanned. "Please. All this flattery is turning my head."

"Hey, pretend all you want," he said with a grin. "But I'm wise to you now. Letting a guy know you accepted his invitation against your better judgment—that's flirting, honey. That's effective flirting." Seeing her flustered gaze made him change the subject. "So," he said, "you have any kiddies at home?"

"No. We weren't even married an entire year. Big Jim had a grown son who was some kind of child prodigy math genius, but I've never met him."

"Why not?" He sat back, the better to absorb her explanation. This oughtta be good, he thought.

But she merely pressed her lips together as if she'd bitten into something that left a nasty taste in her mouth. "If it's all the same to you, I'd really rather not talk about him."

The old bitter sense of inadequacy swept over him, and he blessed the waitress who arrived to take their order. What the hell did he expect, he wondered as he ordered. He was never anything but an embarrassment to the old man, so did he truly think that would have changed because he'd been gone for years? He'd outgrown such unlikely hopes years ago.

It wasn't like he gave a rat's ass, anyhow. He'd left off looking for Big Jim McCall's approval half a lifetime ago.

Now he only had until the end of the month to charm his way into Treena's good graces and find the autographed baseball that had been his father's most prized possession. God knew that if anyone had earned ownership of that valuable little collectible, he had. And he meant to claim it through fair means or foul. Before Sergei Kirov set the dogs on him.

At the same time he had to reserve part of his concentration so he could win the Las Vegas leg of this poker tournament. Ideally he'd have the former all wrapped up before he had to worry about the latter. Even so, he found his shoulders tensing and he rolled them as the waitress flipped her order pad closed and walked away.

Then he relaxed. *You're thinking too much.* He'd built in plenty of wiggle room, and he didn't expect to spend much effort seducing one showgirl. He flashed Treena a smile, and watched one side of her mouth curl up in response in that kiss-me-daddy smile of hers.

Oh, yeah. It was just a matter of time.

Three

Treena was sweating her way through another interminable set of pliés when Carly suddenly appeared in front of her. "Hey," she said in startled greeting as she sank down, her knees turned out and her back erect. She surged back upright, ignoring her screaming quadriceps. "What are you doing here?"

"Are you kidding me?" Reaching out a hand to rest her fingertips lightly upon the barre, Carly pliéd in sync with Treena's next repetition. "You didn't come home from your class!"

She blinked. "They had an opening in the schedule here, so I took it." She often grabbed unscheduled time, and Carly knew it.

"Yeah, well, that would be fine any other day." Her friend waved the explanation aside. "But not after your date this morning. Like I could wait to hear? So, spill! How did it go?"

Memories of her date with Jax, which she'd been

firmly repressing in order to focus on her class and the extra studio time she'd finagled, washed over her. She smiled.

"Ooh, God, that good, huh?"

"Yeah."

"I knew it! There was just something about that guy—"

Treena paused mid-plié, throwing off their mirror-image synchronization, then resumed the rhythm. "That's exactly what I thought—that there's just something about him. But I can't seem to pin down what it is."

"Maybe I should have said there was something about you and him together, because chemistry would be my guess." Carly shrugged. "Does it really matter?"

"Yes. Why him, why now?" She looked at her friend. "The timing sucks—Big Jim's only been gone a short while. And Jax probably isn't going to be around for very long, anyhow. Turns out he's a professional gambler."

"No shit?" This time it was Carly who broke the rhythm. "That's the last thing I would've guessed. He doesn't have that shiny-shoed, greased-back-haired, mobster look that pops to mind when you hear the word *gambler.*"

Treena laughed out loud, tickled by the description since it so closely echoed how she might have described the profession herself before she met Jax. "He's part of the big poker tournament that's going to be starting over at Bellagio next week. Or maybe it's the week after— I'm not real clear on the time frame."

"Ah, that's different, then—he's legit. Not to mention big, built and in town for a while. And he obviously likes what he sees when he looks at you." Carly tilted her head to one side. "Considering he's the first guy you've accepted a date from since Big Jim, I'm guessing you like him, too. So I don't see the problem."

"I know, I know—there shouldn't be one. Maybe it's just...too soon."

"Aw, hon, it's not." Carly reached out and gave Treena's shoulder a quick, fierce squeeze. "You and I both know your time with Big Jim wasn't even close to what most would expect from marriage." She reached out to brush back a curl that had managed to escape the sloppy French twist Treena had screwed her hair into. "Besides, there's no rule that says you have to jump into this thing feet first," she said, her blue eyes soft with compassion. "You can take it as slow as you want. But I'd sure hate to see you blow this off entirely."

Treena smiled fondly at her friend. Carly's breezy don't-mess-with-me attitude, flawless figure, and spiky blond hair often fooled people into assuming she was a cynical die-hard party girl. Her friend might look like the last of the red-hot mamas, but in Treena's opinion she was actually the original free-spirited earth mother, nurturing and fiercely loyal. "Then you'll be happy to know," she said, "that I have another date with Jax after the ten-o'clock show tonight. I also gave him my phone number."

Carly whooped. "That's my girl!"

"Well, I'd hardly classify her as a girl," said a third voice from across the room.

Treena sighed and knew before turning around who she'd see. "Eavesdropping again, Julie-Ann?"

Irritation crossed the younger woman's face as she strode across the hardwood floor toward them, but she swiftly disguised it. "Trust me,' she said coolly, "your pitiful life is the last thing I'd find interesting. Overhearing Carly was strictly inadvertent."

"Inadvertent," Carly murmured. "My, what big words we know."

Julie-Ann ignored her, and said to Treena, "If you'd bothered to check the schedule you'd have seen that I have the studio for the next hour. I've been chosen to be part of a documentary on Las Vegas showgirls and I want to give them my very best." Then she looked her up and down and added with false sweetness, "Still, if you're not finished yet, please, feel free to share the space with me. I know you can use the practice."

Instead of bitch-slapping the little twit Treena smiled. Failing to react as predicted drove the younger woman up the wall more than anything. "Why, thank you, Julie-Ann. How very…kind. What do you think, Carly—you up for another hour?"

"Absolutely. I can't think of anything more lovely. We can always benefit from Julie-Ann's expertise, can't we?"

"Indeed." Whatever else could be said about the young dancer, Treena had to admit she wasn't stupid, and she watched in satisfaction as frustration flickered across her face at their acceptance of an offer she'd only tendered for the annoyance factor. Then she turned to Carly. "On the other hand, I've already done a class and put in the additional time Suse let me squeeze out of the schedule. And the babies are probably ready to climb the wall, waiting for you to get home and feed them."

"That's true." Carly flashed Julie-Ann a friendly grin. "Not to mention Treena has a date to get ready for. You remember what that was like, don't you, dear? I mean, it hasn't been that long since you've been out on one yourself, surely."

Julie-Ann smiled tightly. "You're so droll, Carly."

Treena laughed. "Isn't she?" she agreed and excused herself to pack up her dance bag. Carly strolled over to join her and the two of them said a breezy goodbye to the young woman and let themselves out of the studio.

The smile dropped from Treena's face the moment the door swung shut behind them. "What is the deal with that girl?" she demanded as they emerged onto the street. A blast of furnace-hot, dry desert heat hit them. "What on earth have I ever done to make her dislike me so?"

"Been a better teacher than she'll ever be."

She stopped dead and stared at her friend. "Say what?"

"You've got an easy way of instructing that gets the point across without making people feel like clumsy dolts. But when Julie-Ann compliments someone, you find yourself patting your back in search of the knife. And everyone is sick to death of hearing how she's done this, that or the other thing, each one more marvelous than the last, according to her. Hell, who knows, it may even be true. But when it comes to dance captain, the troupe liked you better, and she knows it."

"So, big deal. They like me better." She started down the street again. "Life's a trade-off—and as much as it pains me to admit it, she's a better dancer than I am these days. Can't she be happy with that?"

"No. The kid's got a killer competitive streak, and nobody gets to be better than her at anything."

Treena couldn't understand what it must be like to grow up in a world that allowed such behavior. She was raised in a steel town that was constantly downsizing. One counted oneself fortunate to have steady employment and certainly no one had the leisure of developing a superiority complex. They were too busy trying to earn enough money to put food on the table. "I just don't understand that," she admitted aloud.

"That's because you've got one of the best work ethics I've ever seen—I don't know anyone else in this business who's worked two jobs from the time they were old enough to land any kind of employment at all."

"My folks needed my contribution, and *I* needed those dance classes." Dancing had been the only escape she'd ever had—the single bright spot in a tungsten-colored world—and it had been worth every penny she'd scraped together. Her early classes had transported her out of that dreary town for one brief, shining hour at a time.

Her parents had never understood that. They still didn't. They loved her, but they couldn't understand why she didn't marry someone like Billy Wardinski next door and settle down to the kind of life they knew. Neither her two sisters nor the other girls in town had had a problem marrying young and cranking out the kids. It was simply the way things were supposed to be. Good Polish-American girls didn't run off to Sin City. And they sure as hell didn't wear next to nothing and do splits and high kicks on a stage.

"What on earth are you thinking about?"

She shot her friend a crooked smile. "How grateful I am that my folks only caught the eight-o'clock show that one time I got them to visit me out here."

Carly grinned. "Yeah, the costumes we wore in that show appalled them enough as it was."

"'Almost wore' is how Pop put it. Can you imagine his reaction if he'd seen me without my top? Never mind that I was thirty-two years old at the time. He probably would have dragged me home by my hair."

"Speaking of costumes—or sort of, anyway—did I tell you what Rufus did to my brand-new character shoes?" Carly launched into a story about her newest baby, an abandoned mixed-breed puppy she'd rescued from the side of I-15 near the California border. They chatted about him all the way to the garage.

Treena forgot Julie-Ann's enmity, her parents' baffled disapproval of her lifestyle and her own steadily growing financial and professional woes. Instead, her lips curved up, remembering the way Big Jim had once asked her if she and Carly had ever run out of things to talk about. Because the fact was they hadn't, not from the first moment they'd met more than eleven years ago, at an open audition for *la Stravaganza*. They'd simply clicked and their only real problem during the intervening years had been narrowing down topics for discussion.

When she was alone in her car a short while later with nothing to distract her, however, Treena's problems came crowding back in on her. She managed to ignore them for a while when she arrived home by launching straight into one of her periodic cleaning frenzies. Then she found the baseball atop one of the piles in her messy coat closet. Picking up the Plexiglas box in which it was ensconced, she sat back on her heels and gazed at it with disparate emotions.

The antique baseball had been one of Big Jim's most treasured possessions. It was a rare collectible, a 1927 World Series home-run baseball that his then-twelve-year-old father had snagged out of the air at one of the games and gotten autographed by everyone on "Murderers' Row," the famous New York Yankees lineup. It was worth a small fortune, but it was remembering Jim's pleasure in it that elicited the true surge of satisfaction. For him, the ball's value had lain more in its sports history and the fact that it was a family heirloom.

A greedy little kernel inside of her was anything but satisfied, however, and setting the case carefully back where she'd found it, she left the cramped space for another day's cleanup and backed out of the closet, firmly closing the door between herself and temptation. For what felt like the hundredth time, she rehashed the phone call she'd received a week ago from a lawyer named Richardson. He'd been authorized by an unnamed client to make her an offer for the ball, and the amount tendered had simply boggled her mind.

The prospect of all that money had been more seductive than anything she could ever remember. As Carly had pointed out earlier, she had worked hard her whole life, and even after she'd left home at eighteen, she'd continued working two jobs. She hadn't dropped the second one until she'd built up a little nest egg after landing the *la Stravaganza* gig at the Avventurato Resort

Hotel and Casino. Unfortunately, she'd used up most of her savings this past year, which made the kind of money the lawyer offered so hard to resist. All she had to do was sell that ball and her financial worries would be over.

The idea of failing the upcoming annual *la Stravaganza* audition really preyed on her. She detested that she was starting to lose something that had always been special to her, that she was approaching the end of a professional life she'd worked so hard to make a reality. Far worse, though, was the idea of being thrust back into financial insecurity. And a little voice kept whispering in her head that it didn't have to be come to that. The cushion Richardson had dangled in front of her would give her the start-up money she needed for her dance studio, and she'd have enough left over to see her through for several months while she got her business off the ground. She knew she could make a go of it, for as Carly had said she was a good teacher. It had therefore taken every bit of fortitude she possessed not to leap at his offer.

The only problem was she'd known Jim's wishes all too well. And he'd wanted the baseball to go to his son.

Her teeth clenched at even the fleeting thought of Jackson McCall, for she could wrack her brain all day and all night long and still never come up with a less deserving recipient.

Then she drew a deep breath and let it out. She'd not allow that lousy excuse for a son to ruin what had been a truly decent day so far. The last thing she needed between now and the audition was more stress, and she shook out her hands while practicing additional calming breaths. Her time and energy would be much more productively spent by concentrating on positive images like the memory of this morning's breakfast date with Jax and their upcoming one tonight. Gradually her tension began to dissolve, and she blew out a sigh. Things would work out.

Why waste time dwelling on a rat bastard when she could think about a really great guy instead?

Four

Jax felt great. His plan was proceeding according to schedule, the prospect of sack time with a Las Vegas showgirl was a promising glimmer on his horizon and he was up forty-eight grand from his original stake when he'd sat down to play a little poker at the five-thousand-dollar-limit table three hours ago.

Life was good.

He studied his fellow players. The woman to his right had a good, stoic poker face. So did the Asian man sitting in the small blind position. The guy next to him had been an All-Star pick for three years running, but while he might knock 'em dead on the baseball diamonds, he had two definite tells. His left eye narrowed slightly when he was bluffing, and he compulsively fanned open and snapped shut his cards when he had a good hand.

A good portion of the stack of chips sitting in front of Jax were courtesy of Mr. All-Star.

The cocktail waitress offered him a drink and he refused it with a smile. Catching a flash of red hair across the casino, he straightened from his slouch and craned to see over the crowd before he caught himself and relaxed his forearms, draping himself over the table once again.

It wasn't Treena. The woman whose hair he'd seen across the room didn't share the same pale flame shade of hers. Its deeper color had merely caught his eye for a minute and he decided that it was natural for Treena to be in the back of his mind. She was, after all, the object standing squarely between him and his goal.

The fact that his heart had begun to beat a stronger, more rapid rhythm merely meant he was a red-blooded guy. It would be a hell of a lot more unnatural if the thought of a sexy showgirl *didn't* rev his engine a little. He didn't mind admitting that he was looking forward to taking her to bed. But he also knew he wouldn't let pleasure get in the way of the program.

Realizing his concentration was broken, he cashed in his chips for the day, bought himself a club soda and took it over to watch the action at a nearby Gai Pow poker table. There was a decorative post not far away and he leaned his shoulders against it while he watched the action going on at the table.

"Where's my baseball?"

Shit. Jax dropped the foot he'd propped against the post and straightened with a lazy show of indifference. But if there was anyone who could bust his mellow mood, it was Sergei Kirov.

"I haven't got it yet," he said evenly, looking at the Russian. "I told you it would take a while."

"Tick tock," Kirov said. "Clock is counting down."

The two beefy men flanking him laughed as if he'd just uttered something witty, but Jax merely looked at him and thought, *You fucking freak.*

Sergei's appearance wasn't as startling in Las Vegas as it had been on the rest of tour. Black pompadours and sneering mouths were a dime a dozen in a city where one was just as likely to find an Elvis impersonator officiating at a wedding as a regular minister. The same look in Europe, however, had made the millionaire Russian stand out like a hooker at a Baptist wedding.

With anyone else, Jax might have written the affectation off as a ploy to psych out his fellow players. But Kirov was dead serious about paying homage to the late, great King of Rock and Roll. He had a passion for all things American from Elvis Presley to baseball. He also had the money to indulge in his obsessions. Jax looked at the tangle of gold chains that glinted in the V where Kirov's jumpsuit was unzipped nearly to his navel and shook his head.

"I want that ball," the Russian said.

"And you'll get it. But as I explained before, my dad's estate turned out to be more complicated than I anticipated." He didn't mention that the baseball hadn't actually been left to him. And he sure as hell wasn't about to bring up Treena's name. Rumor had it Kirov's money had its origins in the Russian mafia, and as much as Jax figured the showgirl for a scheming gold digger, he had no intention of seeing her injured—which was a distinct possibility if Sergei ever learned it was she who stood between him and the baseball. "I'll have it for you by the end of the tournament, just as we agreed."

"See you do," Kirov ordered. When he snapped his fingers his companions wheeled around and marched off on either side of him, looking like two black crows flanking a Russian Elvis wannabe in a glittering white jumpsuit.

Jax blew out his breath and sagged back against the post. He'd behaved like a rank amateur when he'd allowed Kirov to maneuver him into losing the baseball.

In fact he hadn't made so many dumb moves since he was a kid trying to be the athlete his father wanted. He shouldn't have even told Sergei about his dad's baseball in the first place. Never volunteering the details of his personal life was a code he lived by on the circuit, or had been until the night in Geneva when Kirov's eternal bragging had rubbed him the wrong way one time too many.

His response to it, however, had been all out of proportion. Yes, he had received bad news about his father, but it wasn't as if he and the old man had ever been close. Big Jim hadn't been around much when Jax's mother was still alive, and after her death Jax had futilely tried to please him. Life had been tough enough for a brainy kid who'd skipped three grades and didn't know how to interact with his older peers. He'd hoped that at least his dad would be as proud of him as his mother had always been. Instead, Big Jim had wanted him to be one of the "regular" kids.

It just hadn't been in the cards, Jax reflected bitterly. They'd fought over everything. It was no surprise he had jumped at a full scholarship to the school of engineering at the Massachusetts Institute of Technology when he was fourteen, and not merely because MIT was his university of choice. The bigger incentive had been the fact that it was about as far away within the continental United States as he could get from Big Jim.

It had been a good move for him, too. He'd been suffocating in Las Vegas, trying to fulfill his father's expectations. In Cambridge he'd discovered that it didn't matter if he sucked at organized sports. The other students appreciated his mathematical mind. And once away from his father's badgering he'd lost his perpetual clumsiness and gained more physical grace over the course of his three-year accelerated program than he could ever have imagined. After that, he'd avoided as much as possible going back to the environment that had made him feel like such a loser.

Of course he'd still been an adolescent in an adult world. When classes were over, it hadn't mattered if he'd dazzled his fellow students with his brilliance. They'd gone off to grab a beer; he'd headed back to the dorm to play video games. Yet their appreciation of his mind—not to mention that of the think tank that had snapped him up after graduation—had made him feel like a winner most of the time.

That was more than he'd ever been able to say of his dad. Which only made that night in Geneva that much harder to accept.

Jax shook his head. Thinking about it was a huge waste of time and energy. Yet, even as he stared blankly into the middle distance, he couldn't get the night that had set him on his current path out of his mind.

* * *

His father was dead. Jax shook his head to clear it, then read the letter from the attorney again, certain he must have misunderstood. Yet, not only did it state that his old man was gone, it explained that he'd passed away almost four months earlier. No one had been able to locate Jax right away to notify him—and for that he had no one to blame but himself, since he hadn't bothered to keep Big Jim and the Bimbo Bride informed of his whereabouts.

He set the letter carefully on the hotel desk then crossed the room to the courtesy bar. Digging out two mini bottles, he poured their contents into a glass. Not bothering to dilute it, he knocked back the drink, then poured another double and carried it over to the window. Sipping this one, he stared out the window at the Alps. The view that had knocked his socks off yesterday barely registered now.

He caught himself rubbing his chest, feeling as if he had a huge gaping hole where his heart should be.

Considering his estrangement from his father, the depth of his grief didn't seem logical and it sure as hell wasn't probable. His entire adult life had been built around logic and probabilities, so he was at a dead loss to understand the way he felt now. But the hole spread and the gnawing grief dug deeper until he experienced an inexplicable urge to howl.

Swearing, he grabbed his key card and headed down to the hotel bar in search of distraction.

Twenty minutes later Sergei Kirov walked into the lounge. Ordinarily, Jax went out of his way to avoid the

Russian, but he was on his fourth drink, no one else spoke English and he was desperate to avoid the emotions that had his stomach in a knot. He greeted the other man like a long lost friend.

Kirov swerved from the counter where he'd been heading and came over to the table. "Hello, Jax. It is unusual to see you in bar."

"Yeah, well, I got tired of my own company." He studied the other man, taking in his black denim suit with its white topstitching and the boldly striped black and white T-shirt beneath. "Lemme guess. The King's Jailhouse Rock period?"

"Very good." Sergei beamed his approval of Jax's keen eye. "Not everyone picks that up. You like?"

"Very cool."

"Thank you. Thanyouveramuch. I am best Elvis."

According to Sergei he was the best at everything. Jax bit back a smart-ass put-down, reminding himself that, in the scheme of things, the Russian was a minor irritation. "Whatever. So what have you been up to today?"

Kirov gave his order to the waitress who appeared then turned his attention back to Jax. "I finally—how do you say?—score the baseball card to complete my 1927 World Series collection."

Jax's heart lurched at hearing the pennant championship that had haunted his childhood mentioned, but he regarded the man across the table without expression. "I didn't know you were a collector."

"I have the best collection of all. Nobody has better. I own the official program of Worlds Championship series, the bat Herb Pennock used to win the fourth and final game, the New York Yankees team picture and every Pirates baseball card. I had every Yankee baseball card, too, except one. Today I buy rare Earle Combs card to complete my set." He smiled smugly. "Is most important collection in the world."

Jax had managed to shrug off Kirov's constant boasting in the past; he'd shrugged it off two minutes ago. He was no longer in the mood. Raising his drink, he looked at Sergei over its rim. "I own the first home run ball of the series." He took a sip.

Sergei stared at him. "Babe Ruth's ball? The one in third game that brought in three runs?"

"Yep. Signed by the entire Murderers' Row."

"I will buy from you." Kirov slapped both hands down on the tabletop. "Name your price. Sergei will pay."

"Oh, it's not for sale." In a far off corner of his mind he knew he was taking just a little too much pleasure in saying no. But it had been a crappy afternoon, so he'd grab his jollies where he could. "It has great sentimental value, don'tcha know. My grandfather caught that ball and when he died it passed to my father. Now the fucker belongs to me." Fresh pain stabbed deep and he killed off his bourbon.

To his surprise Sergei let it go and signaled the waitress. They had a couple more drinks. When the Russian suggested a friendly game of straight draw poker, Jax dragged his wandering attention back to the other man, grateful for a focal point that wasn't Big Jim's death. His inner professional whispered the number one cardinal sin of poker in his ear: never play when you're too preoccupied to give the game your complete attention. Hell, he never played cards with his competitors during off-hours, period. He flashed Sergei a big loose smile. "Sounds like a plan."

Five minutes later they were up in his room, clearing the small table by the window of everything except a deck of cards and the money from their wallets. Kirov carried significantly more cash than he and Jax crossed to the room safe, staggering once before he caught himself. When he turned back with the difference from his stash clutched in his hand, Sergei was standing at the desk, reading the letter from Big Jim's lawyer.

Rage rose in a bitter tide up his throat. "Put that down."

The Russian did so, carefully, then turned to him. "I am sorry for your loss."

He shrugged. "We weren't that close." He indicated the table. "Let's play."

He lost consistently. He had no business playing at all and looking down at his fifth hand, he had just enough functioning brain cells left to realize it was time to fold and call it a night.

Kirov, who had been talking nonstop, studied him across the table. "Is funny thing about fathers and sons," he said.

A red mist fogged his already cloudy mind. "I don't want to talk about my old man."

"Mine was old-time Communist. I didn't like him worth a damn but I wanted his approval anyway. How many cards you want?"

He studied his hand. He had to draw to an inside straight and that was never the most promising odds.

"Did you—how you say—chase your father's approval, too?"

"Seek. Seek my father's approval. And what's it to you? Are you gonna talk all night or play cards?" he demanded. Extracting the card that didn't fit his straight, he skimmed it across the table. "I'll take one."

He actually drew the card he needed to fill out his belly-buster straight draw. After Sergei dealt himself two cards, Jax tossed three one hundred dollar bills into the pot.

Sergei saw his bet and raised it seven thousand.

He counted his remaining cash. He didn't have enough and knew he ought to toss in his hand.

"Sergei is best poker player," the Russian crowed. "You may as well save your money and skip Las Vegas. I am going to win."

Shit. He didn't have enough left in the safe and he knew without asking that Kirov wouldn't allow him to leave to visit an ATM machine. "Will you take my IOU?"

"For ball."

What the hell, he thought blurrily. He had a good hand. "Gimme a piece of paper."

He wrote the IOU and tossed it into the pot. Then he turned over his king-high straight.

Sergei turned over four twos.

For a minute Jax thought he was seeing double. God knew he'd been having a tough time focusing. But then he realized he'd just lost his grandfather's World Series baseball. His gut twisted and he felt sick. Still, a bet was a bet.

Long after the Russian left, Jax remained at the table

thinking about losing the ball and wondering what difference it made to him. It wasn't as if he wanted the damn thing himself. It had been the frigging bane of his existence for as long as he could remember, a symbol of everything that was wrong between him and his old man.

So why the hell did losing it bite so deep? He assured himself it was merely because he'd been outmaneuvered by someone he didn't respect. It had nothing to do with the way he'd carelessly tossed aside a memento his father had put a lot of stock in.

That was his story.

And he was sticking to it.

Jax gave himself a shake. Enough of this trip down memory lane. He didn't want to think about things he couldn't change.

Maybe he'd cashed in his chips too soon. Because what he needed right now was the slick feel of a new deck of cards in his hands, the tink and click of a stack of chips sliding through his fingers. He needed to inhale the scent of green felt and nervous players.

The game had been his one constant companion for the past dozen or so years, and if there was one thing it had taught him it was that some days things just went to shit despite his best efforts.

But there was always another poker game.

"Hey, Treen," the dancer named Jerrilyn called from across the dressing room. "I heard some interesting news about your hot new beau."

Treena finished wiping greasepaint from her face,

then lowered the hand towel, aware that the backstage chatter had softened. In the mirror she saw the other woman walk toward her; then, before Treena could even swivel to face her, Jerrilyn bent down and met her gaze in the mirror.

"You missed a spot." Jerrilyn indicated a patch in front of Treena's left ear where a smear of stage makeup remained. "So, anyhow," she continued as Treena scrubbed at the splotch, "I've got a new honey, too. His name is Donny and he's a huge World Poker fan. I'm talking a guy who *lives* for the televised tournaments, if you can imagine such a thing." Shaking her head, she plopped down on the vacated stool next to Treena. "It's sure as hell lucky he's good between the sheets or we wouldn't have anything in common." Then she flapped her hand. "But that's neither here nor there. What I wanted to tell you is that when I was telling him about how you and Jax met last night and got to the part where you said, 'Well, Gallagher, Jax Gallagher, I believe I would like to have breakfast with you,' Donny went ape-shit. Did you know your boy Jax is part of the big poker tournament that's gonna be held over at Bellagio at the end of the month?"

"Yeah, he mentioned that this morning."

"Did he mention his ranking? Because apparently he is *big* on this circuit. Donny says he's probably one of the top five winners of the past couple years. And according to my guy, that equates to huge—and I'm talking *mega*—winnings."

"And he's a hottie, too," Michelle piped in from down the row of stools in front of the long lighted mirror.

"Um, um, um," Eve murmured and grinned at Treena. "Money *and* sex appeal. Sugar, I'm thinking you definitely hit the jackpot with this one."

"Did I tell you all about the television special I'm going to be in?" Julie-Ann asked.

"Ad nauseam," Carly said, strolling into the dressing area from the shower room. Reaching her station next to Treena's she dropped her towel and picked up a pair of silky undies from the countertop. She raised a brow at Treena as she stepped into them and adjusted the thong's fit. "So what are you going to wear on your date?"

Treena removed the nylon skullcap that enabled her to fit all her hair under the wig from the final act and rose to her feet. Fluffing out her curls with both hands, she strode over to the garment rack. She stopped in front of it and slid aside a couple of costumes that the wardrobe mistress hadn't yet collected for repair. Unhooking the hanger containing the cocktail dress she'd brought from home, she swung around and held the garment against her front for her friends to see. "What do you think? He indicated I should dress up."

It was an above-the-knee, empire-waisted, black-and-gold crocheted dress that was cut low in front. It had a slip-dress lining and tiny capped sleeves, and its bias-cut hem was finished with silky eight-inch knotted fringe that swayed with the least little movement. She raised an eyebrow. "Yes?"

"Oh, hell, yeah," Juney breathed, coming over to inspect the dress. "Where did you get this?" She fingered the fringe. "This is totally hot. I'm going to have to borrow it sometime."

"Whenever you want," she agreed. She'd gotten it when she and Big Jim had first gotten married, but she refused to dwell on that. She'd realized this afternoon that it had been ages since she'd anticipated anything the way she was looking forward to her date with Jax tonight—and she was damned if she was going to let guilt ruin her evening. She hooked the hanger back on the rack and returned to her station to get ready.

A few moments later Julie-Ann said admiringly, "It sure is nice the way you can just forget your husband's only been dead a few months."

Carly half rose from her stool. "Listen, you little bi—"

Treena reached up and halted her with a hand on her arm. "It's okay," she said quietly, and turned to Julie-Ann. "My husband has been dead for over four months," she said evenly, "and he was ill practically our entire marriage before that. I was faithful to him while he was alive, and I hardly think going out with another man now can be considered dancing on his grave."

"Of course not," Julie-Ann agreed with an innocent blink of her eyes. "That's what I said. It's nice that you can just forget all about him and have fun with another guy."

No guilt, no guilt, she reminded herself and returned Julie-Ann's saccharine smile with an equally insincere one of her own. "Isn't it?" she agreed, and turned back to finish applying her makeup.

Despite her best intentions, Treena knew Julie-Ann had introduced a faint niggle of unease into her anticipation. It disappeared, however, the moment she clapped eyes on Jax when she entered the main salon a short while later.

He straightened away from the pillar he'd been leaning against, his gaze frankly admiring her. "Yowsa," he said, stepping forward to meet her. "You look fantastic."

"Thanks. You're looking mighty spiff, yourself." And he was. Carly's description of big and built accurately described him in his pin-striped, double-breasted suit coat that stretched wide across his broad shoulders. Once again he was wearing jeans, but tonight he'd paired the two items with an elegantly knotted, subtly striped silk tie and a fitted royal blue dress shirt that accentuated the shade of his eyes.

"Thank you, ma'am." He ran his finger beneath the tie. "Believe me, this is strictly in your honor. I don't know who invented these things, but if you ask me they oughtta be shot."

She laughed. "Poor baby," she said without an iota of sympathy. "But you're a gambling man. I'll see your necktie and raise you the average bra anytime. You dragged that out for a special occasion? Try wearing something that digs grooves in your hide twelve to eighteen hours a day, every day of the week."

His gaze dropped to the wide scoop of her bodice where it culminated in a deep V between her breasts. "Not a particular problem for you tonight, I see."

Doing her best to ignore the sudden heat flashing through all her secret places, she shot him a grin. "Yeah, well, if only one of us gets to be comfortable, I vote it's me."

"That seems fair." He took her elbow and escorted

her out onto the street. The night sky was a rich midnight blue, and a balmy desert breeze whispered gently through the palms. "Now, this is more like it," he said in satisfaction. "I'm afraid I've lost my ability to adapt to triple-digit-degree weather." He looked from the neon-lit Strip to her tall-heeled, strappy sandals. "What do you think? Can you walk to the Aladdin in those things? I can always call for a car."

She made a rude noise. "Please. I can play basketball in these. Walking a few blocks is a piece of cake."

"If you say so," he said skeptically. "Forget the necktie and bra. If you ask me, *those* have gotta be the real torture device." Then his gaze rose slowly from his contemplation of her ankles, grazing her calves, her knees and her thighs, before continuing higher. His eyes were an intense and brilliant hue that pinned hers in place when they finally reached her face. "But I have to admit they make your legs look fabulous." He glanced down at the fringe that swung against the limbs under discussion. "Or maybe it's your legs that make the shoes look sexier 'n sin."

"Oh, man, you're dangerous, you know that? I can see I'm going to have to stay on my toes if I want to avoid getting swept right off my feet."

He arched a brow. "Like you don't come equipped with an arsenal all your own? What do you call those shoes, that dress, those lips? Honey, I have a feeling you were *born* loaded for bear. I'm the one who'd better stay on my toes here or I won't stand a chance."

His voice went flat on the last sentence, but when she shot him a questioning glance, he gave her a rueful smile and shrugged. "Sorry. Had a sudden flashback there to my geeky, gawky teenage years."

"Oh, sure," she said doubtfully. "Like I'm supposed to believe a big, good-looking guy like you wasn't overrun with more girls than you knew what to do with? You were probably captain of the football team, beating off perky little cheerleaders with a stick."

Jax couldn't stop his sudden bark of acrimonious laughter. "Captain of the football team?" he said, images of being a fourteen-year-old in an eighteen-year-old's world looming large in his head. "Hardly." When she just blinked at him, he admitted, "I gained my full height around the time I turned twelve, but I was in college before I developed the coordination to go with it. Hell, *regular* girls thought I was a nerd—never mind the most popular girls in school."

Arriving at the Desert Passage shopping center adjacent to the Aladdin Hotel, he looked down at Treena as he opened the door for her, taking in her pretty whiskey-brown eyes and mass of Pre-Raphaelite curls. "Believe me," he said drily, "I admired girls like you from afar."

She shot him a startled glance as they walked into the North Africa setting that hosted the shops and restaurants of Desert Passage. "Like me?" Stopping beneath the twilight-blue domed ceiling, with its streaky clouds of gold and pink, she laughed up at him. "Trust me, you wouldn't have admired me, from afar or otherwise. I wasn't part of the in crowd. I was the tall girl with the unruly carrot-colored hair who only wanted to learn to dance well enough to get out of town. And since the school I went to had a student body whose biggest ambition was to kick Lehigh Valley High's ass at football or be voted Homecoming Queen, Miss Popularity I wasn't."

So she'd been a misfit like him as a teen, he thought as the maitre d' at the Commander's Palace perused the reservation list, then summoned a waiter who led them to their table. Big deal. She'd sure as hell clawed her way to a better place since then, hadn't she?

Her little tease of a dress was a prime example of just how much she'd changed her image. If he didn't drag his gaze away from her breasts pretty damn soon, his pants weren't going to fit.

She had the prettiest tits he'd clapped eyes on in a long time. They were small, yet round and high, and the way her outfit's neckline flirted with her cleavage threatened to give him the granddaddy of all hard-ons.

Which was nuts. What was he, seventeen? He'd made a cold-blooded decision to check into the Avventurato rather than the Bellagio where the tournament would take place simply because Treena Sarkilahti McCall worked there and he'd needed the advantage of propinquity in order to carry out his plan.

He knew he could see her breasts buck naked five nights a week at the ten-o'clock show if he wanted. So what was the big deal about seeing them partially exposed now?

Something, he admitted grudgingly. There was just something about the sight of her pale smooth curves straining against black fabric that he could not ignore, game plan or not.

"This is lovely," Treena said, glancing around the

dining room with its green walls and harem-tent ceiling. "I've heard a lot about this restaurant but I've never been here before."

"I haven't been to this one, but I've been to the original in New Orleans. I thought you'd enjoy it."

"Oh, I will. I love eating out."

"Do you? And here I'd kill for a home-cooked meal." *So invite me over, sweetheart.* He gazed at her expectantly.

She merely gave him that knowing, one-sided smile. "Are you nuts? I'd eat in restaurants every day of the week if I could afford to."

"Trust me, it gets old." But he could see he was going to have to work harder than he'd expected to elicit the invitation he desired. He got down to some serious wooing.

But it didn't reap him the reward he'd hoped to harvest, and by the time he walked her back to her car, frustration was eating him alive. He could tell she liked him. They'd talked and laughed for two and a half solid hours. In fact, he'd had to remind himself several times that he wasn't there to have a good time. He'd redoubled his efforts after each reminder, but no matter how slickly he'd maneuvered the conversation, she hadn't extended an invitation to her place.

He had to work to keep his voice light when they arrived at her car. "This is for the birds," he said, when she'd opened the driver's door and turned to look up at him. "I don't like dropping you off in a big, empty parking garage. The next time we go out, I'm picking you up and delivering you back to your door."

She raised an eyebrow at him. "Assuming there is a next time, of course."

"Oh, there will be." He shot her a cocky smile. "You dig me. Admit it. You really dig me."

She gave him a cool-eyed up-and-down. Then she caved and flashed him a wide white smile. "I might dig you a little."

"No, you dig me a lot." He took a step forward, crowding her. "The way I dig you." The latter was a little too close to the truth for comfort, and he lowered his head purposefully. This seduction would come off the way it was intended, dammit—with one-sided precision, uncluttered by messy emotions.

He congratulated himself for kissing her exactly that way, with cool, calculated expertise. Plunging his fingers through her soft hair, he held her in place and treated her to a sample of his best work.

The only problem was, she treated him right back to some damn fine work of her own. Her lips were soft and supple and they clung to his. Then they parted beneath the press of his kiss, and when he took her up on her invitation and slid his tongue across her teeth and into her mouth, he discovered flavors that were dark and addictive. When she moaned, the sound seemed to have a direct line to his cock, and he pressed closer. Her legs parted as much as her snug little dress would allow, and he pressed his pelvis forward to fit his erection against the warm, sweet notch between her thighs. But it simply wasn't possible to get close enough.

Her hands slid up his chest, her arms wrapped around his neck, and those enticing breasts that had been provoking him all night long flattened against his chest. He groaned, finding himself suddenly unable to breathe.

He ripped his mouth free. *"God,"* he said, his chest heaving. He pulled her away from the open car door, slammed it shut and, wrapping his hands around her hips, hoisted her up onto the hood. Bunching the material of her skirt between his fingers, he eased it up around her waist, glancing in admiration at the skimpy scrap of lace he exposed for the second it took to knee her legs apart. "You. Are. So. *Hot,"* he growled. Then he stepped into the space he'd made for himself, plunged his fingers back into her curls and slammed his mouth over hers once again.

He couldn't get enough. Not of her taste, nor the elusive scent that wafted off her skin, nor the firm, warm feel of her in his arms. Holding her in place and oscillating his hips, he just about came unglued when the sweet mound he rocked against became damper and damper against his fly. He raised his head, his breath sawing in and out of his lungs, and stared down at her.

Her eyes were slumberous, the sexily shadowed lids heavy as she stared back at him, the clear honey color of her irises nearly swallowed up by her dilated pupils. Her lips were red and swollen from the pressure of his kisses, and as he watched she smiled lazily and slicked her tongue over the full bottom curve. He lowered his head to bite at the damp, plump lip.

"Ooh." Treena's head dropped back.

He sucked her lip, then let it go and kissed the corner of her mouth, the angle of her jaw, and then just beneath it. Kissing his way down her long, smooth throat, he smoothed his hand along her neck as he moved to her creamy chest and pressed his parted lips into her shallow cleavage. Then he cupped her breast in his hand, reveling in its warm weight as he kissed his way down to her nipple.

Reaching it, he pressed a gentle smooch on its rigid tip, then opened his mouth to suck the tiny morsel inside.

She inhaled sharply and thrust her breasts up for closer attention. Almost immediately, however, she slid her hands down to his chest and thrust him away. "Too much," she panted. "Oh, God, Jax, too much, too soon." She slid off the hood.

He begged to differ. He thought the time was absolutely right to lay her back and rip those little panties aside.

"Forgive me," she panted. "I've never—" A wild laugh escaped her and she shook her head, sending her soft curls floating in a wild nimbus around her head. "Oh, man, I can't believe what I was about to do in the middle of a parking garage." She sidled skittishly toward the car door.

An image of the two of them humping on the hood of her car flashed through his head. She had a point. This was hardly the place for his big seduction. He was stunned at how quickly he'd lost control of the situation.

Remember the plan. He sucked in and blew out a quiet breath. Staring at her, he licked his bottom lip, tasting a weak reminder of her flavor. "Take me home with you."

She was tempted; he could tell she was. But she shook her head. "I can't," she said, edging closer to the driver-side door. "I'm sorry—you must think I'm such a tease, but I just…can't. I've only known you a day." She pulled the door open and climbed inside.

He resisted swearing a blue streak and said mildly instead, "I'll call you," as she pulled the door closed.

She nodded, but started the engine without further comment. And the next thing he knew, he was standing in an echoing, concrete cavern, sporting a raging hard-on and the beginnings of an equally raging headache as he watched her taillights blink red before disappearing up the ramp.

"Shit," he said, thrusting his hands through his hair. *"SHIT!"*

God, he was a chump. Such a big agenda, and all he had to show for it was the need for a cold shower and the sound of his own voice as it bounced back at him off the walls.

His mouth tightened as it dawned on him that he'd just been played. "You must think I'm such a tease," he said in a vicious falsetto. His voice dropped back down into its normal register. "No shit, baby."

She'd sucked him in, turned him inside out, then left him twisting in the wind. Shoving his hands deep in his pockets, he stalked toward the elevator.

It damn well wouldn't happen again.

Five

Treena pounded on Carly's door. Excited barking immediately commenced within the condo and she winced, giving her wristwatch a guilty glance when her friend's voice called out with patent irritation, "Knock it off, already—I'm coming! Rufus, Buster, be quiet!" When the dogs continued barking she heard Carly's frustrated snarl and an exasperated, "Oh, for God's sake!"

The door whipped open.

Her friend's blond hair looked spikier than usual, and her face was scrubbed clean of all makeup. With her big blue eyes flashing fire, she opened her mouth to say something that Treena didn't doubt for an instant would be rude and to the point. But after a quick look at her, she merely said, "Whoa. Come on in." She pushed the two mutts dancing around her feet aside to make room.

"I'm sorry," Treena said, following them into the short entryway. "I know it's late."

"Forget it." Carly led the way into her colorful living room. "Have a seat. You want a cup of tea? Or a shot of tequila, maybe? Here, let me get Rags out of your way." She studied Treena as she swept a long-haired black cat off an overstuffed chintz-covered chair and dumped the feline on the floor. "I gotta say you look like you had a much more interesting night than I did."

"Oh, God." Treena laughed wildly and collapsed onto the chair. "I came *this close* to having sex with Jax Gallagher on the hood of my car!"

Her friend blinked. Then the corners of her mouth twitched. Then her incipient smile blossomed into a full-fledged grin. "Way to go, Treena!"

A three-legged cat leapt up into her lap, and she buried her hand in its soft gray-and-white fur. "This is not a good thing, Tripod," she bent her head to tell it sternly. "Tell your person that. I've known the man, oh, gee, what's it been now? *Twenty-four freaking hours!*"

Apparently Tripod didn't care. He circled twice, then settled down on her thighs. A second later, he butted his head against her hand to get her petting again and purred when she complied.

"Yeah, well, you're a guy. No one expects better from you," she muttered, then looked at Carly, who had flopped down on the couch across from her and was watching her with interest. "You, on the other hand, are another story. This *isn't* a good thing."

"Sez you. Sex alfresco strikes me as a very good thing."

"Alfresco my butt. This wasn't on a soft blanket beneath the desert moon, Carly. It was in the middle of a concrete parking garage!"

"Okay, not real romantic. Still, you get points for spontaneity."

"It was spontaneous all right. God, it was just totally out of control." And if there was one thing that fired Treena's determination, it was the need to stay in control. She still didn't understand what had come over her, but she felt like an idiot, not just for the way she'd gone crazy on top of that car, but for her inane chatter once she'd finally come to her senses. She cringed at the remembrance of sounding more like a junior high school airhead than a grown woman.

"Ooh." Carly executed a little wriggle of delight. "I love out of control." Then she sobered, shooting Treena an apologetic grimace. "But I'm sorry, Treen, I can see you're upset. It's just that it's been awhile since I've had sex of any sort, so it all sounds pretty exciting to me."

"Believe me, I understand," Treena agreed. "It's been a while for me, too."

Carly laughed. "Yeah, right. At least you were getting it on a regular basis before Big Jim got sick. I can't even remember the last time—" she broke off to stare at Treena. "What?"

Oh, shit. She blinked innocently. "What, what?"

"You had a look on your face. Now, I know Big Jim was too ill to do the hootchie-kootch for most of your marriage, but..." She hesitated, studied Treena's expression closely, then, eyes narrowing, asked, "Is there something you'd like to tell me?"

No. But this was her best friend, and outright lying didn't set well on her conscience, either. "We, um, never did the hootchie-kootch. At least not properly."

"What?" Carly laughed. "Of course you did. Big Jim was a sex machine before he got—" She broke off, looked at Treena. "He wasn't?"

"No. Look, it's kind of complicated. One of the first things that attracted me to him was the fact that he wasn't looking for a quick roll in the hay with a showgirl."

Carly nodded. "Sure, I get that. Lord knows we get enough of those kinda guys hitting on us."

"Precisely."

"Jim was different?"

"Very. Of course I didn't know at the time that he was in remission from his prostate cancer. He thought he'd beat it for good, but the downside was that the meds he was taking messed with his ability to have sex. I can't exactly claim love, or even lust, at first sight on either side. I liked that he wasn't all over me like so many of the hot-handed Harrys I'd met, and he probably liked the fact that his pals thought I was Grade A arm candy that he was screwing up, down and sideways. I mean, you bought it, and you're not that easily fooled."

"And that didn't bother you?"

"No. He cared a *lot* what his friends thought, and I think the mere idea of them knowing he couldn't get it up—or sustain an erection when he did manage to get one—was about the worst-case scenario he could imagine."

"But what about you? Didn't you wonder when he didn't make a move?"

She shrugged. "I thought he was just being a gentleman." And that was the truth, as far as it went. The deeper truth, however, was that she'd been relieved.

She wasn't about to admit that to Carly, however.

It seemed as if every woman she'd ever known—with the possible exception of her mother—adored sex. So perhaps the reason she'd understood Big Jim's reluctance to have his friends learn of his dysfunction was because she had a serious disinclination of her own to share just how lousy *she* was in the hootchie-kootch department.

She didn't understand it. She certainly loved the kissing and the foreplay. But when it came to the main event, she just didn't get the attraction, even though she liked an orgasm as much as the next woman. She'd even been known to help herself to one on occasion. She and the handheld shower massage were on very close terms.

But with men—well, she had a small…issue…with losing control, and apparently that was a prerequisite to attaining a guy-sponsored climax. So, as much as she hated to admit it even to herself, she was a bust in bed. One guy she'd slept with had gone so far as to tell her she was about as much fun in the sack as a cadaver.

"I can't believe you married the guy without sampling the merchandise. What was the attraction for you if it wasn't the sex?"

"He seduced me with his attentiveness." She laughed at the expression on her friend's face. "I know, I know, it doesn't sound like much. But believe me, given the way I was raised it was actually quite a lot. There was just something so great about being more to him than tits and ass. He actually listened when I talked. He noticed the things I liked. Paid attention to details. You've met my mom and pop. They're good people who love me without question. But they've had a rough life and were always too beaten down just trying to survive to fuss over things like birthdays or holidays."

"Oh, man, not Big Jim." Carly laughed out loud. "Your thirty-fourth birthday party will probably go down in infamy."

"Yeah, he made it one of the most special nights of my life—and he'd already found out by then that his cancer was back and had begun feeling pretty lousy. He did a *lot* of stuff like that for me. My favorite thing, though, has to be the way he made me laugh. I never knew how much fun everyday life could be until I met him."

"He was a sweetheart."

"Yeah. I know a lot of people think I married him for his money—and I can't deny it was fun not having to worry about finances for a while. But the real reason I married him was because he kept telling me how much he wanted to take care of me."

"That had to be a first for you."

Stretching out her leg, Treena nudged her friend with her toe. "I love that I never have to explain things to you. But, yeah, it was. I've taken care of myself for as long as I can remember, and Jim's wanting to give me a break was more seductive than all the money in the world."

"So how unfair is it, then, that instead you ended up taking care of him?"

She hated to admit it, but she'd thought the same thing herself, and more than once. They hadn't been married long before illness had begun ravaging Big Jim from the inside out. She was soon consumed with responsibilities once again. Whenever she'd had a moment away from his sickbed, she'd tackled a mountain of bills and watched as expenses mounted to the point where they'd finally sucked not only Jim's fortune dry, but her own savings, as well. The only thing she'd managed to hang onto was her condo.

But she merely shrugged, for when it came right down to it, no one had promised her life would be fair. "Yeah, well, shit happens."

"More often to you than others, for some damn reason. I'm confused, though, Treen. By the sounds of things you've been sex deprived for a long time now. So why didn't you take advantage of that sexy man wanting to jump your bones tonight?"

"I just—I don't know." A flash of the way she'd felt in that garage made her clamp her thighs together, and she rapidly pushed the resulting panic aside. Her chin inched up. "I've never been a one-night-stand sort of woman, I guess. Plus, I can't seem to get past the fact that I've known Jax for all of about ten minutes. I'm not ready for something that intense."

And perhaps she never would be. She thought about that all night long, as she tossed and turned and tried to reconcile the greedy sexuality she'd experienced those few brief moments on her car hood with the in-command-of-herself woman she'd always been. Unfortunately, she came to no conclusions. All that her restless self-questioning gained her was a sleepless night, and the vehement desire for a respite from having to think about Jax Gallagher at all.

Easier said than done, as it turned out.

He'd left a message on her machine while she was at Carly's and he called again the following morning. Uneasy over the possibility that the ringing phone might be him calling, she allowed the machine to answer for her.

"Treena, are you there?" There was a moment of silence, then his voice, deep and a little desperate, said, "Please, if you're there, talk to me. Don't leave me hanging like this. I've got a poker game scheduled in L.A. this morning, and I really don't want to get drummed out of it like some rank amateur. But I'm probably going to be because I scared you off or something last night, and now I can't concentrate for shit on the game."

She snatched up the receiver. "You didn't scare me. I don't scare." It was important he understood that.

"Glad to hear it. Then you'll go out with me tonight."

The way her heart jumped at the idea made her literally take a large step backward. She shook her head, then felt like an idiot, because of course he couldn't see. "I don't think that's a good idea."

"It's a great idea. I know I moved too fast for you last night, but I won't push you again, I promise. Just…don't shut me down. We could have a quiet evening or something. I'll come to your place."

"No." She didn't want to be all alone with him where her big comfy bed was just a short walk down the hallway if things got out of hand again. But neither could she bear the idea of not seeing him at all. "I suppose we could go to a late movie. Or, I know, we could go dancing." That suggestion ought to discourage him. Men never wanted to risk dancing with a professional. And if he reined in whatever this thing was going on between them, it would let her off the hook.

He surprised her. "Yeah, sure, we could do that," he said easily. "But you gotta do me one favor, all right? Ride to work with your friend this evening. At least let me see you home myself."

Since visions of being alone with him again in the parking garage had her heart thundering like crazy, she agreed, then qualified it by adding cautiously, "But only if I can catch Carly before she leaves to run her dogs. She's often in and out and hard to get a hold of. Either way, I'll see you tonight. Same place by the elevators in the main salon." She hung up before she could change her mind, then wondered if she was making a huge mistake.

If so, it was too late to do anything about it, so she put it out of her mind, and she was finally starting to settle down again when her doorbell rang. She went to answer it, smiling to see her petite next-door neighbor Ellen Chandler on the other side.

"Hello, darling," the older woman said. "I'm sorry to show up unannounced like this. Have I come at a bad time?"

"Not at all." Charmed as always with the retired librarian's manners, she stood back to let her enter, happy for the distraction. "Please, come in." She found Ellen's company soothing, and she loved the way the fifty-nine-year-old often spoiled her with some of the best home-baked goodies she'd ever tasted. She gave the foil-covered plate in Ellen's hands a covetous glance.

Ellen caught her at it and extended the plate. "For you."

"Thank goodness! For a second there I feared I was just a pit stop on your way to deliver it to someone else." Grinning, she took the plate and headed for the kitchen. "I'll put the coffee on. What did you make me this time?"

"Nothing special." Ellen followed her around the breakfast bar that divided the small, cheerful room from the main living area. "Just a few snickerdoodles and chocolate drops."

Treena guffawed. "Nothing special, she says." Pulling off the foil, she breathed in the rich, home-baked aroma. "Ohmigawd, Ellen. I think I love you."

"That's why I keep baking for you, sweetheart. You're so easy."

"Yes, ma'am. But I'm not cheap."

When Ellen laughed it was a deep, rich, surprisingly bawdy sound at odds with her short salt-and-pepper hair and neat-as-a-pin gray tank top, trim belt, and walking shorts. "Some might say that's debatable if I can buy your affection with a plateful of cookies."

"Hey, I'll have you know it's a cumulative effect. It took a *lot* of platefuls to get me to this point."

"Well, that's a relief—I'd hate to think you were selling yourself short." She straightened a magnet on the refrigerator, then looked over at Treena. "So tell me about this new man in your life. A hottie, I believe is how Carly described him."

The smile slid from Treena's face and her hands stilled over the coffee fixings she was assembling. "Carly talks too much."

Ellen's brow wrinkled. "Oh, dear. Was I not supposed to bring him up?"

"No. It's fine. I'm being rude—I'm sorry." That seemed to be her favorite new phrase. "It's just that I'm a little confused about my feelings for Jax at the moment, and I don't think I'm quite ready to talk about it."

"Then we won't. Did I tell you I've been debating joining a tour for that trip to Italy I've been wanting to take?"

Treena studied the petite older woman for a moment, then released the tension that the introduction of Jax into the conversation had settled in her shoulders. She shot Ellen a smile and resumed getting their coffee ready. "You have got to be the politest person I've ever met."

"Yes, well, what can I say?" Ellen shrugged. "Early training digs its roots deep."

"It's very nice. I've never known anyone quite like you. So what's the debate?"

"I don't want to go to Italy by myself. But I'm not sure I care to travel with a bunch of strangers, either. Then there's the being-at-the-mercy-of-a-tour-group's-schedule factor."

"Yeah, it's that last thing that would stop me," Treena agreed and asked the other woman to grab the cookies. She poured two cups of coffee and carried them to the small dining room table. "Strangers, you can always get to know. But I'd want to be able to explore all the sights on my own timetable." She reached for a cookie. "Don't any of your friends want to go? I know I'd go with you in a heartbeat if I had any vacation time coming." She smiled ruefully. "Well, that, and if it were even remotely in my budget."

"I took an early retirement and most of my friends are still working. And the only one of them I can actually imagine living with day in and day out for three straight weeks is Lois. In fact, we've sort of dream-planned this trip for years, and this fall was going to be the time when we actually took it. But her daughter in Minnesota found out two months ago that after years of trying she's finally pregnant, so Lois is saving up her vacation time instead to go help out after the baby is born." Ellen raised one delicate-fingered hand and sipped her coffee. "I'll probably just postpone the trip until next year when she's free to join me."

"You must be so disappointed, though. I'm sorry."

Ellen flashed her an affectionate smile and reached across the table to pat her hand. "You're a good girl."

"Can I have that in writing? My parents are positive my job is a one-way ticket to hell."

"Ah." The older woman nodded wisely. "I imagine it's hard for them to realize their baby dances topless in one of the shows."

"Um, no, that would merely be the clincher. They've pretty much reserved my handbasket for the trip without ever having learned that part."

Someone pounded on the front door and they both jumped. Treena got up to answer it, stopping to peek through the peephole first to see who it was. "Ah, Mack," she said. He was the neighbor who lived on the other side of her.

Ellen made a small hissing sound of disapproval, but Treena ignored it and opened the door. "Hey there," she said to the burly man on her threshold and cocked an eyebrow. "Is the building on fire?"

"Nope. But rumor has it your libido is. Hear you've got yourself a hot new guy."

"Boy, that Carly's sure been a busy little beaver, hasn't she? I can see I'm going to have to talk with her."

"Now, don't be mad, sweetheart. She's just excited for you." He sniffed the air. "Is that coffee I smell?"

"It is. And some truly divine cookies to go with it." She opened the door wider and stepped back. "Come join us."

"Us? Who's us?" He stepped over the threshold, five feet nine inches of raw energy that stopped dead when he saw Ellen sitting at the table. "Oh, hell. It's you." He thrust a weathered hand through his curly gray hair and glowered. "I should have known. Don't you have a home?"

Ellen took a dainty sip of her coffee and gave him a bland look. "I could ask the same of you, Mr. Brody."

"Mack," he snarled. "How many times do I have to tell you to call me *Mack*? Is that so fricking hard to remember?" He hooked his thumbs in the back pockets of his Levi's and muttered, "Hearing myself called Mr. Brody makes me feel like a goddamn old man."

She looked him up and down and raised perfectly groomed eyebrows.

"Yeah, so, big deal," he growled. "I'm no spring chicken." He crossed to the table where he pulled out a chair, spun it around, and straddled it. Stacking his sinewy arms upon the top rail, he propped his chin atop them and returned her perusal. "But then neither are you, Miz Librarian."

Treena sighed. She adored both her neighbors but when they got together it wasn't pretty. "If you two are going to spar, take it outside," she ordered. "I'm not in the mood."

"Whoa." Mack turned to look at her. "What's got your undies in a twist? One would think you weren't getting any." He jerked his chin at Ellen. "Now, if it was this one I'd understand—"

"That's *enough,* Mack," Treena snapped, and Ellen pushed her chair away from the table and rose to her feet.

"I have to go."

"Ellen, please, don't rush off." She started toward her but the older woman smiled determinedly.

"Thank you for the coffee, darling. I'll talk to you soon." She nodded at Mack without really looking at him. "Mr. Brody."

A second later she was gone.

Seriously irritated, she turned back to Mack. "Are you happy now?"

Mack jerked his frowning gaze from the door. No, he wasn't happy. He hadn't been since the day more than a year and a half ago when he'd taken one look at Treena's new neighbor and fallen headfirst in lust for the entire tidy little package even though he'd received nothing but cool-eyed disdain in return.

"I don't know what's the matter with you two." He heard Treena chastising him as if from a distance, but he tuned her out. What was he doing fantasizing about a frozen-lipped little librarian? Like most guys, sex was pretty high on his list of gotta-haves, and age hadn't slowed down that particular need a whole helluva lot. He was a handyman by trade since retiring from the aircraft industry, and that meant he was good with his hands. His wife, Maryanne, God rest her soul, had always thought so, anyway.

But he knew that even if he was God's brand-new shiny gift to women, little Miss Ellen would hardly notice, and even if she did, the result would probably be about as much fun as fiddling with a piece of sheet metal. The woman was colorless, for God's sake. He'd rarely seen her smile, and he'd *never* seen her wear anything that wasn't a shade of gray or black or tan or that taupe color.

"You always start talking like some randy old goat," Treena said, "and she invariably goes from sweet and funny to stiff and cold. And then there I am, stuck in the middle. How does that old song go? 'Clowns to the left of me, jokers to the right'?"

He'd expected that during the year Treena had sublet her place, the two of them would run into each other less. But he'd discovered that exchanging stiff little nods in the hallway was ten times worse than exchanging insults in Treena's cozy little apartment. He admitted that while Ellen remained cool on the outside, he noticed that her cheeks heated up a little, and her pretty hazel eyes flashed fire when they sparred. He enjoyed seeing that.

He'd gone too far today, though. She'd refused to look at him after he'd said what he had, but he'd seen the hurt on her face anyhow. And now he felt like shit for being the one to put it there.

"I'm sorry I busted up your hen party," he said in self-disgust, ignoring Treena's sudden silence and look of surprise. Shaking his head at himself, he climbed to his feet and headed for the door. And for the first time in his life, he felt like the old man Ellen had implied he was.

Six

Jax came back from Los Angeles with a feeling of accomplishment in his chest and a sizable wad of cash in his pocket. He had the taxi driver drop him off at Bellagio, and grinned at a young bride and groom in full wedding regalia when they crossed his path several minutes later in the area where Bellagio gave way to Caesar's Palace. He'd seen more wedding gowns in the past few days than he'd seen in his entire life.

He headed for Appian Way with the vague intention of buying himself something to celebrate today's success. Once upon a time, he'd been a lousy dresser, but when he was sixteen and a junior at MIT he'd discovered the value of a good jacket. Once he'd learned a designer sport coat, a silk T-shirt and a pair of jeans would work for damn near any social situation, he'd never looked back. Every now and again he enjoyed adding to his collection.

Trying to remember where he'd seen Bernini's, he

sauntered past an upscale jewelry store near the fine Italian apparel store, then abruptly stopped.

A woman swore and careened off his side. He reached out to steady her and even remembered to apologize, but it was an automatic reflex, for his mind was engaged elsewhere. Staring up at the casino's enclosed, temperature controlled sky, currently fading from its bright high-noon mode into the golds of afternoon, he reflected that for a supposedly smart guy, he could be one hell of an idiot.

Hadn't he tossed and turned until the wee hours after that case of blue balls Treena'd given him last night? Hadn't he sworn at the end of it that he'd learn to play the game as well as she did? Well, this was his opportunity. She was a high-maintenance showgirl who'd married a rich old man. No wonder he was getting nowhere with her—he hadn't coughed up the proper incentive.

Turning on his heel, he headed back to the jewelry store.

He expected to walk in, grab something with a lot of spangle, and walk right out again. Instead, he found himself spending more time than he would have believed possible searching for just the right piece because he couldn't remember ever seeing her wear jewelry—sparkly or otherwise. He didn't know if that was because she didn't wear it, or because she did and he'd simply overlooked it.

He dismissed the rings, because he didn't know her size and he imagined nothing would bust a mood faster than asking a woman to give back the gift she'd just received so it could spend a week in the shop being adjusted. Earrings were out, because he didn't know whether or not her ears were pierced. He looked at the case of gemstone pendants and bracelets, but nothing seemed quite right, and he was on the verge of leaving when a necklace behind a bunch of larger pieces caught his eye.

He gestured to the saleswoman who'd been hovering a few feet away and she opened the case and pulled out the piece. It was simpler than the others he'd been inspecting. Instead of diamond piled upon diamond, it consisted of a single delicate platinum chain, from which a tiny pavé diamond pendant was suspended. It was shaped like an evening bag and reminded him of the one Treena had knocked off her chair the other night.

It was perfect. The piece was dainty, it had meaning, which women always seemed to get off on, and it was…holy shit…just this side of four thousand dollars!

With a mental shrug, he pulled out the roll he'd won. What the hell. Easy come, easy go. He informed the woman the sale was hers—provided she could expedite the rest of his requirements.

She leaped into action, and fifteen minutes later, he walked out of the shop with a tiny gift-wrapped package in his pocket.

He went to Bernini's next, but discovered he was no longer interested in looking at jackets. So he headed back to his hotel.

He tried to reach Treena on his cell, but no one answered at her place. Belatedly, he remembered her telling him about a rehearsal this afternoon for a new number that was being introduced into the show. So instead of going up to his room when he reached the Avventurato as he'd intended, he found himself trying the ornate doors of the showroom where *la Stravaganza* was staged.

They were locked. Rolling his shoulders, he turned away. It hadn't been a well-thought-out decision in the first place.

Then one of the doors suddenly banged open behind him, and he swung back. A harried-looking young woman barreled out of the auditorium and headed with long, purposeful strides toward the casino. Jax dove for the door, hooking its handle with a fingertip just before it slammed shut again. He slid into the showroom.

"And, *rock,* two, three, four, five, six, seven, eight," a female voice called out, and he paused at the back of the immense room to stare at the lighted stage.

At least a dozen women and four men were dancing in sync with directions being snapped out by the young woman who'd made such a production out of Treena's age on her birthday. Jax swung a chair away from one of the tables at the back of the darkened room and straddled it, looking among the dancers for the woman who'd drawn him here.

She wasn't difficult to spot without the showgirl headgear. Her colorful hair was pulled up in a ponytail high atop her head, shining beneath the lights and floating like a cloud on the wind, a dawning sunrise of color above the drab charcoal-colored getup she wore.

He noticed that there were as many styles of workout gear as there were dancers up on the stage, and that some of the outfits barely covered the essentials. He saw bouncing breasts in tiny tops, G-strings, naked abs and chests, bare feet and high heels. A woman with a long braid wore a crop top and fishnet stockings with minuscule panties built in, and one guy up there danced in nothing more than a loincloth. Treena's tastes, on the other hand, apparently ran toward old ratty leotards under T-shirts with the sleeves and bottom halves hacked off.

He shifted in his seat. Her gear was a world removed from the costumes she wore in the shows or even last night's dress. While her breasts were fully covered, her legs were bare. They were sleek, toned, and they exposed a yard of creamy skin from her scuffed black, medium-heeled Mary-Jane-like shoes clear up to the high-cut leotard. And when the line of dancers turned and shimmied with their hands on their knees, he couldn't help but notice that she had a world-class ass, with a thumb-print dimple where her thigh flowed into her hip.

So, big surprise, genius—look around you. They're Vegas dancers, for chrisake. A great body is the name of the game.

Even so, except for his one brief assessment of dance attire he barely spared a glance for the other females up on the stage.

"Ric," Julie-Ann suddenly barked. "Do you think you could shake a little *life* into your sorry ass? And you, Treena—let's see some energy in that high kick. We're professionals here, so if you two would be so kind as to quit dancing like a couple of first-year students, maybe we'll all luck out and actually come across that way in tonight's show." She strode to center stage and stopped in front of the chorus line, where she turned her back on them to face the showroom. "Now watch and I'll show you *again* what I want. Try to get it right this time." She began moving her feet in rhythm with her snapping fingers. "And *two*, two, three, four—"

A guy Jax could only assume was Ric flipped her off behind her back, but also launched into the routine with the rest of the line and was dancing flat out by the time she turned around to inspect them again. They all looked very professional to Jax, so he couldn't see what her bitch was.

On the other hand, what did he know? He wouldn't expect Julie-Ann to understand the nuances of poker, and he freely admitted he didn't know squat about the shades and graduations of professional dancing, either.

They all looked damn good to him.

After only a few additional snarled remarks from Julie-Ann and one more run-through, the session broke up. Jax watched Treena yank her butchered T-shirt off over her head as she walked over to a pile of gym bags at the back of the stage. She pulled out a towel and blotted herself dry as she looked up at Carly who stood over her chatting while taking swipes at her short blond hair with her own towel. A couple of other dancers that he recognized from her birthday party joined them. Finally, Treena stuffed the towel into her bag and pulled out what looked like a thirties-era fringed table shawl. Rising to her feet, she folded the rose-strewn black material into a triangle and tied it around her hips. Then, even as she and Carly continued talking to their friends, they began backing toward the wings. He wondered if they'd leave through a rear exit and was debating whether or not to call attention to himself when they suddenly rerouted for the edge of the stage. They hopped off and started up the aisle toward the exit behind him.

When they were almost parallel with the row of tables where he sat, he rose to his feet. "Treena."

She stopped dead. "Jax? Ohmigawd. I thought you were going to be in Los Angeles today."

"I was."

"How did you get there and back so fast?"

"Learjet."

Carly raised her brows. "Well, ooh, la, la."

He laughed. "Be a lot more impressive if it were mine. But it was sent for me."

"Like I said."

"How did you get in here?" Treena asked.

"The door was open."

Both women gave him skeptical looks and he grinned. "Okay, I caught it before it closed when some woman left in a big hurry."

"Mary," Carly said, and Treena nodded.

"She's the assistant company manager," she explained to Jax and pointed out an older woman he hadn't even noticed seated at one of the banquettes down front. "That," she said, "is Vernetta-Grace, the chief manager. Be very glad she didn't see you sneak in. You'd probably be cooling your jets in the county clink about now if she had."

"Not a happy proposal," he said gravely.

"Not happy at all." She gave him a crooked smile. "What are you doing here?"

"I knocked 'em dead in the game today, and thought it would be nice to see you in the honest-to-God daylight. Do you have any free time? I imagine it's too late for lunch, but maybe we could grab a cup of coffee or something." He looked at Carly. "You're welcome to join us, too, of course," he offered, counting on her turning him down.

She flicked him a knowing grin. "Thanks, I'd love to." *Shit.*

"But I've got babies to feed and water."

Ex-cellent. Still, he knew his eyebrows had shot up in surprise. "You have kids?" She didn't look like the maternal type.

Both women laughed, and Carly said, "Pets. I have several pets."

"Oh." He shook his head. "Obviously I'm confused. I thought you lived in the same complex as Treena."

"I do."

"Ah. There's no covenant limiting the number of pets each unit can keep, I take it."

"Well, actually," Treena said, and Carly shrugged.

"There is," she said, "but right now the apartment next to me is empty, and the rest of the neighbors have been great about my babies, so it's never been an issue. And really, they're very well-behaved. Well, Rufus, my newest, is still getting used to the place, so he gets to barking sometimes when I'm not there. He's also got some obedience issues, but everyone's been very patient while I work on getting him trained. Speaking of which." She hiked the strap of her dance bag higher on her shoulder. "I'd better get moving. Do you still want a ride to work tonight, Treena?"

Turning golden brown eyes on him, Treena quirked a questioning brow.

"Oh, yeah," he assured her. "This isn't a date; that's still on for tonight. This is just a quick cup of coffee."

"In that case, yes," she said to her friend. "I'll need to get a few things together." The corner of her mouth quirked in self-deprecation as she cut him a sideways glance. "For my hot date."

"Yeah, yeah, rub it in for those of us who have no social life." Then Carly turned a stern look on him that he found at odds with those breasts and legs and that funky hair. "Have her home by six-thirty, Gallagher."

He nodded solemnly. "Okay, Mom."

She laughed. "Be good, kiddies. Play nice." She strode to the exit and pushed through the ornate double doors.

He turned back to Treena. "Are you hungry?" he asked. "Because it occurs to me my lunch hour and yours might be on two different timetables."

"No, I'm fine. A cup of coffee sounds great, though." She, too, hiked her bag up. "Would you like to get away from the strip for a while?"

"Yeah, that sounds like an excellent plan—all the noise around here can really wear you down. Direct me to a nice quiet coffee shop."

"What strikes your fancy? Starbucks, Java Hut, Miss Italia? We're not in the same league as a certain coffee town up north that shall remain nameless, but we still have our share of national franchises to pick from, as well as a number of nice independents."

"I'm not fussy—you choose." He reached for his cell phone. "I'll call for a car."

She snorted. "It's a coffee date, Gallagher. Hail us a cab."

Pulling his attention away from her lips, he realized she was serious. It caught him by surprise, and he had to slap his poker face in place to prevent her from noticing. He'd pegged her as a woman who would expect to travel first class. Always.

And who says she doesn't, bud? Face it, she knew how to play him. "You trying to save me money, lady?"

"Oh, absolutely. I wanna be sure you have plenty of coin to buy me the biggest, priciest mocha Frappuccino on the menu."

"Let me guess." He looked her over, studied that athlete's body with its zero superfluous fat. "I bet you order it short, skinny, hold the whipping cream, am I right?"

"You wish, pal. Get ready to lay down some cold, hard cash for a venti extra mocha, extra cream."

He emitted a rude sound. "You didn't get that body drinking thousand-calorie drinks."

"Hey, I burn a lot of calories in my line of work. It's when I quit doing this for a living that I'm going to have to start watching what I eat. That's one of the reasons I'm having so much trouble keeping up with the troupe now—because I was away from it for almost a year."

They hit the street and were immediately swept apart by the pedestrians crowding the sidewalk. When they came together again at the corner, Treena laughed.

"Whew. You'd think this place would be a ghost town in the summer, wouldn't you? But not even bake-your-brains-out heat can slow the Vegas tourist machine."

He stared at her, all easy in her skimpy leotard and hip-hugging shawl, grinning up at him with those golden brown eyes the color of honey in the sunlight, while a trace of perspiration began dewing on her upper lip. His own body felt stiff and jerky as he abruptly turned away. He stepped to the curb, thrusting his arm in the air when he saw a taxi cruising down the strip.

Celine Dion's voice soared in the air as the cab veered over to the curb, and Treena's head came up as she sauntered over to join him. "Oh, look," she said, "it's the fountain show at Bellagio." She gave a good-natured shrug. "Well, it's the tip of it, anyhow. What is that, the theme song from *Titanic*? I *love* that song." She began to sing along as he held the door for her.

Jax stared at her. Her left thigh appeared through the widening gap in her shawl while she slid across the seat, but it was her complete lack of self-consciousness that really grabbed him.

He'd worked like a dog to weed self-consciousness out of his own system, but it was something that never completely left him. While he'd come a long way from the days when his father's constant pushing propelled him into extreme shyness, he would never in a million years burst into song in a less-than-perfect voice on a crowded city street.

His expression must have been as poleaxed as he felt, because she bent that slight smile on him and said, "I know. It loses a certain something when I sing it."

"No, you sound great." But inside he was shaking his head. Jesus. What was his problem? Shoving away the old familiar sense of inadequacy that had surfaced full-blown, he told himself it was allowing the sight of a little female flesh to turn him into a fool that sent uneasiness gnawing at his gut.

Yeah. That was it. He didn't usually act like a hormone-crazed adolescent when presented with a glimpse of leg.

There was sure as hell no mystery why his old man had fallen for this woman, though. She was a walking, talking aphrodisiac.

He had to remain immune to her charms. "So tell me about this trouble you're having keeping up with the troupe," he invited after she'd given the driver their destination. The cab took off like a rocket, and he settled into the corner to give her his full attention. "Did you keep eating like a trucker without your show to keep you in fighting trim or something?"

"No, I actually did order short, skinny, hold the whipping cream then. But my husband took sick early on, so I didn't go back to work after the honeymoon like I'd planned. And I wasn't able to take the classes I needed to stay on top of my game."

His heart thudded the way it always did whenever he thought of his father battling cancer. "How early on are we talking?"

"Pretty much immediately." She was quiet for several minutes, then shrugged as they pulled up in front of the coffeehouse. "He tried to hide it at first, but it soon became apparent he was very ill."

Jax wasn't very proud of himself for wondering how his father's illness had affected their sex life. But he was discovering that he didn't like the thought of her getting naked with the old man. His feelings were most likely some competitive, knee-jerk juvenile thing he hadn't entirely outgrown. Or maybe they were simply brought on by watching the ends of her shawl shimmying around her legs as he followed her into the coffeehouse.

He swallowed hard.

She grabbed a table while he placed their order with the barista. Fingering the tiny jeweler's box in his pocket as he waited for the drinks to be prepared, he wondered if he should give the necklace to her now or wait until this evening. Giving it to her now seemed like a good idea, because then she'd have the rest of the afternoon and part of tonight to consider all the myriad ways she could show her appreciation.

The instant he brought her Frappuccino and his cup of coffee to the table, however, he found himself returning to their previous conversation. "Help me understand why not taking a bunch of classes while you weren't working made such a big difference."

"It's the use-it-or-lose-it principle. I imagine you need to play poker on a regular basis to stay competitive, right? Well, I was away from a show that I was accustomed to dancing in five nights a week—four of which had twice-nightly performances. That's nine times a week, Jax, not counting classes and practice sessions like today's when there's a new routine to be learned. And as it's been pointed out, I'm not as young as I once was."

"You know my feelings on that."

"Yes. And flattering as it is to have you believe I'm in as good of shape as a twenty-five-year-old, the sad truth is I'm not. I fatigue easier, I wind easier and I've gotten more injuries since I've been back than I've ever had in my life. I'm taking classes almost daily, trying to catch up, but I'm scared to death it's not going to be enough and I'm going to fail the annual audition week after next." Then she straightened in her seat and gave him a big, bright, stage-worthy smile. "But you don't want to hear my problems. So. Tell me about your work."

He *didn't* want to hear her difficulties. Hell, he hadn't thought she could even have problems, and her unexpected vulnerability shook him up.

The last thing he could afford around this woman was to feel sympathetic.

Still. He was passing himself off as an urbane man, and at the very least she probably expected him to know how to segue into a few amusing tales of life on the pro circuit smoothly enough to forestall her embarrassment.

But while he had all sorts of usable talents and excelled at a number of skills, human relationships that weren't basically superficial had never been his strong suit. He merely touched his fingertips to her free hand and said clumsily, "I'm sorry you're having a rough time."

She gave a choked laugh and set the cup she'd been about to sip from back on the table. "Oh, God. You are so nice."

"No, I'm not," he said flatly to counteract the unfamiliar feeling crawling through his gut.

Guilt.

She blinked at his tone, and he modulated it when he said, "Believe me. I'm not." Then he changed the subject. "So I'm guessing you didn't get to take the classes you needed because you were busy taking care of your husband?" Damn. Was it possible he'd misread the situation from start to finish?

"I do sound like a martyr, don't I? Saint Treena." She snorted. "No, we had a nurse to help. It's just—"

The guilt disappeared, and he tuned out the rest of what she had to say. Of course they'd had a nurse to do the real work. Treena had probably been too busy shopping to concern herself with the now-lamented classes or a pesky little thing like a dying husband.

Who was it who'd said there was a sucker born every minute? It wasn't the first time he'd caught himself being manipulated by her. Hell, it wasn't even the second or third time. Shelving his misplaced self-recrimination, he began mentally laying down plans for tonight's date. He'd had enough of this waiting around for her to give him permission to act bullshit.

It was time to turn up the heat.

Seven

Ellen threw her towel over the back of a lounge chair, dropped her key on the table next to it and walked over to the pool. It was the height of the afternoon heat and like mad dogs and Englishmen, she didn't have the sense to stay out of the sun. She simply loved to swim, and through trial and error with various other forms of exercise she had discovered that it also benefited her most. Climbing up on the low spring board, she took two steps out into the broiling sun, bounced on the third, and then dove in. The water was lovely and cool as it closed over her head.

Slicing like a javelin through aqua silence, she surfaced halfway down the pool. She hadn't, she assured herself stoutly as she headed for the shallow end with smooth, steady strokes, picked this particular time of day because she knew Mack Brody would never choose the hottest hour of the afternoon to clean the filters or do whatever it was he did that kept the pool functioning problem-free. It had nothing to do with that.

Really. Nothing at all. He didn't intimidate her.

Reaching the end of the pool she performed a shallow racer's turn and headed back toward the other end. Midway through her lap, she caught a blur of movement whizzing overhead as she turned her face to the side to draw in a breath, and for a moment she faltered. A second later something hit the water with a huge splash, and she scrambled to get out of the way.

"Rufus, no!" Carly yelled. "Oh, Ellen, I'm so sorry."

Dropping her legs to tread water, Ellen turned to see Rufus paddling like mad in her direction, his black and brown fur sleek from the water, his mouth open in a big doggie grin. She had to smile at the sheer joie de vivre he managed to project.

Clearly, Carly wasn't as amused. "Heel!" she yelled. "Dammit, you worthless mutt, come here!" When Rufus continued to ignore her, she leaped into the pool after him.

Ellen laughed aloud. Carly's skimpy workout gear was the next best thing to a bathing suit, so she couldn't truthfully say her young friend had jumped into the pool fully clothed. Carly had, however, forgotten to kick off her little canvas ballet slippers.

Life was so much more interesting than it had been before she'd moved into the complex and met Carly and Treena. She adored both of the young women, and was tickled on a near daily basis by their impetuosity, their friendliness and their easy laughter.

And as a diversionary tactic, Carly's gambit worked spectacularly. With a joyous woof, Rufus changed direction midpaddle, making a beeline for his mistress. The showgirl laughed and sidestepped his furiously churning paws. Grabbing him by the scuff of his neck, she guided him over to the side of the pool and with a hand under his belly boosted him up onto the concrete apron.

"You really are worthless," she said fondly, and hiked herself up to sit on the tiled edge, water squishing out of her soaked workout gear. "Great," she muttered as the dog shook chlorinated water all over her. But she gave his head an affectionate scratch when he flopped down beside her.

"What's going on here?"

Recognizing the gruff voice calling out the question, a dirty word flashed across Ellen's mind. It was such a truly nasty one that never before in its entire long, misbegotten existence had it made its way into her vocabulary—and for a moment she was ashamed. But just for a moment. Because of all the bad luck! She'd thought she'd been able to avoid Mack Brody this afternoon.

"Are you letting that mangy mutt swim in my clean pool, Carly?"

"Sorry, Mack." She smiled wryly. "It wasn't intentional—he just got away from me." She slung an arm around Rufus's neck. "He's a stubborn little cuss—aren'tcha bud? Or maybe headstrong is a more accurate word."

"Try brainless."

Carly laughed. "Oh, yeah. That's a definite possibility. However you define him, he's taking longer to train than any dog I've ever had." She gave the mutt a tender look, and Rufus panted up at her with happy, clueless devotion in return. "But he'll get there. It just takes longer with some."

Ellen shot the sweet young woman and the older man surreptitious glances. Carly, even in her bedraggled wet clothing and ruined slippers, looked fresh and sexy, but Ellen would give Mack credit for never once looking at any of the young females in this building with even a hint of old goat lasciviousness.

Still, there was no way she intended to get out of the pool in front of him while the pretty dancer was there. Mack had a way of making her feel like a sexless old crone at the best of times. The last thing she thought she could bear was a comparison between Carly's perfect figure and her own month-and-a-half-away-from-her-sixtieth-birthday body.

She resumed her interrupted Australian crawl to the deep end of the pool.

Stiffness rendered her strokes awkward at first, but once she'd performed the flip-turn at the blue-tiled wall she lost her self-consciousness and settled down to swimming some nice steady laps.

Still, it wasn't until Carly and Mack's voices had long faded, leaving nothing but the lap of water against her ears and the whisper of wind through the palms that she swam to the ladder and pulled herself up. Pausing on the top rung, she tilted her head to tap water out of her ear.

"About damn time you finished."

She jerked around so violently she nearly slipped off the ladder. Peering into the shadows beneath the palms, she saw Mack sitting on the same lounge chair where she'd dropped her towel. He scowled at her and raked her from head to foot with his deep brown eyes.

She wanted desperately to sink back into the water to avoid his insolent inspection, but pride got her moving. Her heart skipped a beat as she hauled herself the rest of the way up and stepped out of the pool onto the apron. Painfully aware of the lost muscle tone of her inner thighs and the slight rounding of her tummy beneath her navy swimsuit, she raised her chin to meet his stare head-on.

Mack was every bit as old as she was, if not older. How woefully unfair was it then that he looked so much fitter in his neatly pressed khakis and white polo shirt? There was simply no justice in the world.

She swallowed the bitter fact, however, and managed a courteous nod. "My apologies, Mr. Brody. I didn't realize I was holding up your work." Biting back a satisfied smile at the irritation she saw flash across his eyes when she used his last name, she tried to tell herself it was petty to be so pleased at his aggravation. Yet she didn't plan to deprive herself of the pleasure. "If you'll just toss me that towel, I'll get out of your way."

He snatched the towel up off the hard plastic seat and rose to his feet. Striding over to her, he thrust it out. "Here." His dark eyes gave her another quick up-and-down. "Cover up. You're dripping all over the damn place."

She caught his gaze lingering for the briefest second on her small breasts. God. Men. Even when they thought someone was a dried-up old prune, they couldn't resist ogling the goods.

Well, let him look. That was one attribute that was still reasonably perky. A primitive urge washed over her with abrupt white-hot intensity. Thinking of all the insulting assumptions he'd made since the day Treena had introduced them, she had a sudden wild urge to demonstrate exactly how misguided he was about the sexuality of librarians in general and her own in particular.

She did no such thing, of course. Plucking the towel from his outstretched hand, she wrapped it around her waist, thanked him sedately and, stopping only long enough to collect her key, she headed for her unit with all the dignity befitting an almost-sixty-year-old.

Standing backstage later that evening as they waited to go on, Treena laughed at Carly's story of Rufus in the pool. The mutt's antics delighted her, but hearing Ellen and Mack mentioned in the same sentence brought back memories of Mack's behavior in her apartment. She recalled the thought she'd gotten at the time watching them. "So, what did Mack and Ellen have to say to each other this time?"

"Nothing." Carly looked at her in surprise. "I mean, Ellen just went back to doing the laps Rufus interrupted, and I'm not sure what Mack did after that. I talked to him for another minute or two, then I took Idiot Dog in and changed out of my soggy clothes."

"He was still there when you left, though?"

"Yeah. I think he sat down to wait for her to finish so he could, I don't know, clean the pool or something."

"Uh-huh." Treena's hunch strengthened, and she shot her friend a wry glance. "Because he does that so often in the middle of hundred-degree afternoons. You wanna know what occurred to me today?"

Carly raised her brows in assent.

"I think he's got the hots for her."

"Get out!" Carly laughed, but sobered when Treena's immediate response wasn't to crack up. "Are you serious?"

"Yeah. I am." Pulling her right knee up and hugging it to her chest, she slowly straightened her leg until it stretched straight up, toes pointed, over her head. Balancing on her left foot, she flexed the right one and told her friend about that morning's exchange in her apartment. "You should have seen his face, Carly, when I came down on him for his behavior." She lowered her leg, then repeated the hamstring stretch with the left. "I have a feeling, though, that it wasn't my wrath that got to him. I think it was knowing that he'd genuinely hurt her feelings."

"I think those two get off on hurting each other's feelings." Then enlightenment dawned. "Ahhh. Shades of junior high school, you think?"

"Yes. The old switch and bait—tweak the braids of the girl you wanna kiss, so she doesn't figure out she's got the power."

"Yeah, they hate it when a woman's got her hand firmly on the joystick, don't they?" Carly said. She laughed. "Well, actually they like that part. It's knowing she has control of it—and therefore of them—that makes 'em crazy."

Treena nodded, although she couldn't truthfully say she had an abundance of experience with that particular power. "I'm not sure what Ellen's feelings are in the matter. She plays her cards much closer to the vest than Mack does."

"Yes, she gets a lot of mileage out of acting all cool and refined, which probably contributes to the driving him bananas factor." Carly grinned. "She loosens up a lot more when it's just us girls, I've noticed."

"Yes, I've noticed that, too." The audience out in the auditorium laughed at the comedian's closing joke, and thunderous applause broke out. "Sounds like Harry's in even finer form than usual tonight," she observed as the two of them walked over to join the other dancers lining up in the wings. "So, what do we do? Anything?"

"Well, I'll tell you right now that I'm not willing to tackle Mack."

"I know. Even thinking about saying, 'You dying to do the hootchie-kootch with Ellen, Mack?' makes my mind—" She shook her head in hopeless bafflement. "God, makes it simply…"

"Boggle," Carly supplied.

"Big time."

"You'd think it would be easier with Ellen, though, wouldn't you?" Carly demanded. "I mean, what woman doesn't want to hear some guy's hot for her? But—"

"It's that generational thing."

"Exactly! I sure can't conceive of telling *my* mother that some guy's itching to get his hands down her shorts." Her laugh went a little wild. "But then you've met my mom—we both know she'd prefer to pretend I was delivered by the stork…with none of those messy, undignified bodily fluids involved."

"Whereas my mother's grounded firmly in reality. Sex, however, is not a subject to be discussed with one's daughters, as far as she's concerned. I think the sum total of The Talk with me and my sisters was, 'Boys only want one thing. Don't let them have it.'"

"Ellen is a lot more approachable, though," Carly said.

"Yes. Definitely."

"So…"

"You and I will stay as far away from her and Mack's sex lives—or the lack of one—as we can get. Am I right?"

"Oh, yeah. Right as rain, toots."

"Okay, then." The comic exited stage left, and the music introducing the troupe swelled. The chorus line began moving forward as those in front swept onto the stage. Treena turned to give Carly one final look before she ran toward the spotlight. "Sure glad we got that worked out."

Shit.

Jax looked around the popular nightclub and shook his head. This hadn't been one of his brighter moves; that was for sure. The place was upscale, and God knew it was jumping. It had a reputation as one of *the* top Las Vegas clubs. Lights were low, voices were loud—and the hip-hop music currently blaring out of the speakers had him on the verge of a headache.

He and Treena sat in the spacious main room, not far from one of its two bars and its sunken, circular dance floor. By taking a professional out to dance when he himself was far from the suavest dancer in town, he'd intended to show her what a good sport he could be. Not to mention get his hands on her during the slow dances. But now he realized his plan was just plain nuts.

There hadn't *been* any slow dances, it wasn't a quiet place by any stretch of the imagination and it sure wasn't romantic. Hell, it wasn't even new to her. The bouncer at the door had recognized Treena and waved the two of them to the front of the line…and then added insult to injury by giving them the locals' discount on the cover charge when he'd planned to impress her by buying the VIP package.

He looked at her across the table. She seemed happy enough with the place, jiving in her seat and sipping a Cosmopolitan as she watched the frenetic action out on the dance floor. When she glanced away from it and caught him staring at her, she grinned.

His mood instantly lightened, and he couldn't help but grin back. Still, he leaned across the table. "It's too loud in here!"

Cocking a hand behind her ear, she leaned toward him. *"What?"*

He laughed, even though he didn't think she was kidding. "I said it's TOO LOUD!"

She nodded and rose to her feet, picking up her tiny purse and tucking it beneath her elbow. Grabbing her drink in one hand, she offered him the other and jerked her head toward a doorway at the far side of the room. She moved close enough for him to catch a whiff of her shampoo when he sidestepped the table to join her and, tilting her head, she brought her lips to within a hair-breadth of his ear. "Come with me."

He followed her as she turned to weave her way through the close-packed tables.

A few moments later they were being seated in an

open-air patio that looked out on the busy Strip. Traffic roared past and the club's music could still be heard, but it was at a much more manageable decibel level.

"Thanks, Cath," Treena said to the young woman who had procured them a place. "You're a peach."

"You bet I am," the waitress replied with a cheeky smile. "And I expect your tip to reflect that."

"This is much better," he said as Cath sashayed away. He tilted his head in her direction. "Where do you know her from?"

"She used to live in our complex until she and Danny got married. He's the guy at the door."

"Small world."

"Well, small town, anyway. Sooner or later—if you live here long enough—you keep bumping into the same locals. Which, incidentally, I find majorly cool to be considered these days, even though, like most people who live here, I'm originally from somewhere else. Both Danny and Cath grew up here, however." She gave him a sudden bright-eyed look over her cranberry-colored drink. "Hey, maybe you knew them!"

Yeah, him being so close to the hip crowd in those days and all. "I think they're younger than I am."

"Oh, I suppose they are. But wouldn't it have been something if you'd all gone to the same high school together?"

"Yeah. Something." Reaching across the table, he took her hand in one of his and reached into his pocket with his other. "Do you remember me telling you at the coffee shop this afternoon that I'd had a particularly good day at the tables?"

"Of course."

"Well, I got you a little something to celebrate."

"You're kidding? You got me something?" Laughing, she sat up straighter. "What is it?"

Pulling the tiny jeweler's box from his pocket, he slid it across the table.

She simply stared at it.

Tipping his head to gaze at her in puzzlement, he gave it a gentle nudge, pushing it closer to her. "Open it."

Still she hesitated, then finally reached out and picked it up. Slowly, she opened the lid. And sucked in a breath.

"Oh, my God." She looked up at him. "It's beautiful. Exquisite." She bent her head to study it. "Oh, my heavens, it's my little purse!" she said in delight. "How did you ever find something so perfect? It's just lovely. Thank you so much." Snapping the case shut, she slid it back in front of him. "But I can't take it."

"What?" He snapped erect, his pleasure in her reaction forgotten beneath the sudden cold slap of rejection. "Of course you can!"

"No," she insisted softly. "I really can't."

"Why the hell not?"

She touched gentle fingertips to his fisted hand. "Because it's much too much."

"I don't get it. You were tickled to be getting a present. You can't deny it—I saw the way you perked up."

"For heaven's sake, Jax." She pulled her hand back. "I thought it was going to be a four-piece box of Godivas! Or a gift certificate for a couple of venti mocha Frappuccinos. Not jewels!"

"It's just a little necklace."

"This is good jewelry, from the looks of it—in fact, I'll eat my shirt if those aren't real pavé diamonds."

"So?"

"So, I haven't known you long enough to accept it." The look she bent on him was suddenly fierce. "Just because I'm a showgirl doesn't mean I'm for sale."

"I never thought that you were," he lied. His heart beat all out of proportion to the situation—after all, it wasn't as if a million-dollar tournament were on the line here. Opening the lid again, he pushed the tiny box back in front of her. "But you have to accept it. Please. Look at the back."

"Oh, God, please tell me that you didn't have it engraved." She picked up the minuscule diamond purse from its velvet-and-satin bed and turned it over. Holding it close to a little candle-shaped light on the table, she bent over it, then sighed. "You did. *2 Treena*," she read. *"4 making me laff."* Her rigidly set shoulders slumped. "Oh, Jax."

"I would have spelled everything correctly, but it's a little piece and it wouldn't fit."

"Jax, I can't—"

"I'm not asking for anything in return," he insisted, and surprisingly, in that moment he actually meant it. "I just had an amazing day at the tables, and I saw this on my way to buy myself a new jacket and thought of you. Don't read anything into it that's not there," he said, abruptly relinquishing his own much-anticipated plan to climb into her bed that night.

The fact that he was more concerned about making

her smile again than fucking her made him straighten in his seat as uneasiness crawled up his spine.

Then he shoved it aside. So, hey, big deal. He'd made a tactical error with the necklace, but if she wanted to pretend she was the girl next door, he could do that. In fact, it was to his benefit. After all, it would save him money, and that was always appreciated. He watched her replace the necklace in its box and gaze down at it with an expression that seemed to mix longing with repugnance. Finally, she closed the lid and pushed the tiny case into her purse. Her reluctance was palpable, however, and it was clear to him that she was keeping it only because the engraving made returning the piece impossible.

A *big* tactical error, and he needed to remedy it, pronto. "When's your next day off?"

She glanced up cautiously. "Tuesday."

He quickly ran his agenda through his mind. "Perfect. I'm scheduled for a game at Binion's, but that's not until seven. You want to do the tourist thing with me and go out to Hoover Dam?"

"Have a non-Las Vegas date, you mean?"

"Exactly."

She gazed at him for a moment, then gave him a slow smile. "Sure. That would be nice."

"Excellent," he said. "Consider it a date then."

Her smile widened, and he felt the knot in his gut relax.

Not that he really cared about her feelings or needed her approval, he assured himself quickly. Hell, no. What he felt was relief over the fact he was getting his program back on track.

The little voice in his head that demanded he acknowledge the core truth of a situation started jangling, but he ruthlessly ignored it.

For once in his life, he had no desire to analyze the heart of an issue. So maybe he was stretching the facts a little to suit his purposes.

He could live with that.

Eight

Getting ready for her date Tuesday morning, Treena bent to work a strappy sandal onto her left foot while still squeezing her right upper lashes between the rubber crimpers of her eyelash curler. The multitasking worked such a treat that she switched to the opposite side, curling her left lashes while reaching cross-body to slide the sandal's back strap up over her right heel. Once she had finished applying her makeup, she turned to her jewelry box. Pulling open one of its drawers, she stared at the necklace Jax had bought her.

She had such mixed emotions about it. On the one hand, it was possibly the most perfect gift she'd received. On the other, it was the kind of thing a Stage Door Johnny bought a showgirl when he wanted to get his hands down her knickers.

She fingered the necklace's delicate chain, rearranging it into different configurations on the drawer's forest-green felt lining while she debated whether or not to wear it on her date. Finally, she picked the piece up and carried it over to the mirror. Leaning forward, she hooked it behind her neck, finessed the pendant into just the right placement, then stood back to check out the result.

She'd dressed for the Hoover Dam tour in an above-the-knee khaki skirt, low-heeled sandals, and a burnt-orange tank top, and she half expected the necklace to be too dressy for such casual attire. In a way she'd hoped it would be, since that would at least relieve her of having to make a decision.

But it wasn't. Although the little pavé handbag glittered in the muted sunlight slanting through the blinds, it was a dainty enough piece to wear dressed up or down. She sighed, checked the way it hung above the hint of cleavage reflected above her tank's scooped neckline, then dropped her hands to her sides. All right, then. It stayed.

The doorbell rang, and she shoved the drawer closed and grabbed up her tube of sunscreen, shoving it into her tote as she headed for the tiny entryway. She pulled open the door, expecting to see Jax, but it was Carly who stood on the other side.

Her girlfriend zeroed in on the necklace. "Oh, good. You decided to wear it," she said, and walked into the condo. "You gotta give the Incredible Hunk points for having a good eye. That is so you." She caught Treena sneaking a peek at the mantel clock and gave her a wry smile and a friendly nudge with her elbow. "Don't worry, I'm not trying to horn in on your date. I just wanted to catch you before you left to ask if I can borrow your car this afternoon. I picked up a screw in one of my back tires, and the guy at the station said it could be up to three hours before they'll get to it. If it's sooner rather than later, I'm set. But if they actually keep it that long, I've got a conflict because Rufus is scheduled to have his shots brought up to date at one-thirty." She blew out a gusty sigh. "Why is it again that I thought bringing that mutt home with me was a good idea?"

"Well, lemme see. Could it be because you're a soft-hearted sucker who's constitutionally incapable of leaving a stray on the side of the highway? And that you love him to death?"

"Oh. Yeah. Thanks. He's been such a pill lately that I tend to forget that last part."

"And yet you wouldn't change a flea on his furry little body." Treena dug her keys out of her bag, but then dropped them back into its inside pocket and went to the kitchen for the spare key instead. "I hate trying to wrestle the house key off the ring. I can never seem to do it without snapping a nail." Coming back, she tossed the spare, with its attached keyless remote, to her friend. "Here."

Carly snatched it out of the air. "Thanks. I'll have it back before you get home from your date." She nodded at Treena's medium-sized tote. "Got your sunscreen in there?"

"Yes, Mother."

"Water?"

"Oh. No. Thanks for reminding me." She strode into the kitchen and grabbed a couple of bottles out of the fridge. "This should be enough to get us started."

"You think?" Carly gave her a wry smile. "I know I started this by asking, but you're headed for a tourist trap, toots. It's not like there won't be lots and lots of places to buy stuff." She reached out and gave Treena a quick, fierce, one-armed hug. "You have fun."

"I intend to, since I'm blowing off a practice session at the studio to go play."

"Good for you. You've been knocking yourself out with all those classes and studio sessions—you can afford one day off. Speaking of which, I'll get out of your hair. Thanks for this." She waved the key ring. "It saves me having to make a bunch of complicated arrangements to fit everything in today." She headed for the door.

Treena accompanied her and jumped in surprise when Carly opened the door and they found Jax standing on the other side with his hand raised to knock.

He dropped it to his side and gave her a quick up-and-down. His gaze lingered for the briefest instant first on Treena's necklace, then on her bare legs, but it was the way his gaze ultimately rose to her face and stayed there that she found most flattering.

"Wow," he said. "You look great."

"Thanks. So do you." And he did. It was the first time she'd seen him without one of his designer jackets. Dressed in a tight T-shirt and jeans his shoulders looked wider and his legs seemed longer. The sum total, she decided, made him look somehow tougher, less civilized, than she previously imagined.

"Yes, we *all* be pretty," Carly said and performed a tap sequence that culminated in a slow twirl with her hands spread, palms up, to display her baggy faded shorts and grape-juice-colored sports bra.

They laughed, and while Jax assured Carly that she, too, looked damn fine Treena was relieved that her friend had thrown a breaker on the electric tension circuiting through her. It had been a long, long while since she'd felt this sort of high-voltage sexual awareness for a man, and she was having a hard time remembering how to conduct herself.

On the other hand, the great thing about being in Jax's company was that in the end she invariably found it easy just being herself. Greater yet was the way he seemed to appreciate that, to genuinely like the real her. For if that wasn't one of the sweetest feelings in the world, she didn't know what was.

He ushered her out of the apartment and through the complex grounds to the sidewalk. When he stopped a few moments later in front of a red sports car with a black convertible top, all she could do was stare at it in amazement. "Wow," she breathed. "Is this yours?"

"I wish." His eyes crinkled as he gazed down at it with the same sort of adoration Carly showed her pets. "I rented it."

"I don't think I've ever seen one of these before. What is it?"

"A Viper SRT-10." He ran a reverential hand along one sleek, glossy bumper. "Isn't she a beauty?"

"I'll say. But it must be costing you a fortune. I don't know why I didn't think to offer the use of my car today."

He gave her an indecipherable look. "I can afford it, Treena. And I thought it might be a treat. For both of us."

She grimaced. "I'm sorry—I'm screwing this all up, aren't I? I'm just so used to watching my pennies that I tend to forget not everyone has to. What I meant to say was, what a smokin' car! Are you going to put the top down?"

"Would you mind? I know not all women enjoy the wind messing with their 'dos."

She made a rude noise and dug a small gold-patterned bandana out of her tote. Finger-combing her hair into a ponytail at her nape, she said, "Here, hold this together for me for a sec."

Jax reached around her to grasp her hair in both fists before she could present him with her back, and she quickly twisted the scarf into a rope. He stood close, and their arms rubbed together as she raised her own to knot the bandana around her ponytail. God, his chest looked as if it had been chiseled out of granite, but his inner forearms felt smoother than satin as they glided against hers. Plus he smelled like a million bucks, all laundered cotton and clean, healthy man. Her heart hammering in her chest, she slowly raised her gaze to find him standing very still as he stared down at her.

"Um...there," she said and stepped back before she could do something demented like take a big juicy bite out of his bottom lip. "That oughtta keep it out of my face." She scrambled into the car, breathing shallowly to avoid pulling any more of his intoxicating scent into her lungs when he climbed in the driver's side. It felt lodged in her senses as it was.

She pulled a tooled-leather visor and a pair of sunglasses out of her bag and slipped them on. Feeling a bit more armored, she turned to look at him.

He was watching her, a small smile kicking up one corner of his mouth. "You got the kitchen sink in that bag, too?"

"Everything but, pal." She pulled out one of the bottles of water. "Want a drink?"

"Nope. But I'll take one of these." And leaning over, he hooked his fingers around the back of her neck and tugged her close to kiss her.

Her mind shut down as blood departed her brain to pulse crazily in her lips. The water bottle thunked forgotten onto the plushly carpeted floorboards.

He kept the caress soft and brief, and straightening back into the driver's seat a moment later, he licked his lips. "Just thought I'd get that out of the way so I don't spend the whole day dwelling on it. I like to believe I could've carried on a rational conversation either way, but the sad truth is, if *I-shoulda-kissed-her* is wailing away in the back of my mind our entire date, chances of that are probably pretty slim."

Her response sounded mortifyingly like, "Ulp." Which only went to show that while *he* might be able to carry on an intelligent conversation, her own abilities were in serious doubt. She was grateful when he donned his sunglasses and turned away, reaching for the ignition key. The car roared to life and loud rock and roll blared from the stereo.

He shot her a grin as he turned down the volume. "Sorry about that. This is the kind of day, the kind of car that just makes me want to tool around with the top dropped down and the tunes cranked up." He lowered the convertible top, and intense heat beat down on them.

"Whoa. Maybe this isn't such a brilliant idea, after all."
Reaching across the gearshift, he skimmed his fingers
down her forearm, and his hooded gaze behind golden
brown lenses followed the movement. "You've got the
kind of skin that looks like it'd burn real easy."

Why did she feel as if he'd just stroked something a
lot more intimate than her arm? She cleared her throat.
"I don't tan worth a damn, that's for sure. But I slath-
ered up with SPF 45, and I have more in here." She patted her tote.

"You sure?"

"Yes." Awareness throttling back, she ran an appreciative hand over the butter-smooth leather seat. Seeing
the water bottle on the floor, she leaned to pick it up,
giving him a crooked smile. "This is just too fabulous
to pass up."

"Yeah." He flashed her a grin. "So we better get
going, then, before we fry." He put the car in gear and
accelerated away from the curb.

Hoover Dam was only about thirty miles away at the
Nevada-Arizona border, and Treena spent most of the
trip enjoying the wind in her hair as she watched Jax
drive. He was a good driver, fast but not careless or run-
up-your-tail impatient. His grip was easy on the wheel
as they roared down the road, and she found her gaze
returning again and again to his hands.

She liked them a lot. They were long and strong-
looking, with clean nails, largish knuckles, and soft
veins that roped the backs just below the skin. They
looked very…masculine. Competent. And she kept
remembering the feel of them—slightly rough of skin,

but gentle in her hair and firm and sure on the back of her neck.

"You said you're used to watching your pennies," he suddenly yelled over the rushing wind and the CD that she'd turned back up because playing it at high volume seemed to give him so much enjoyment. "Didn't your husband leave you any money? No insurance or anything?"

"No." Having no desire to impart this particular information at the top of her lungs, she reached over and turned down the music. "Big Jim's illness ate up his fortune," she told him. "Doctors, drugs, hospitalization—they're all prohibitively expensive these days, even with Medicare. And maybe because he was a big, healthy man before the cancer, he'd never carried medical insurance for himself. So by the time he realized just how ill he was, he was no longer insurable."

"I'm sorry. That must have been tough, especially if you went from being wealthy to not so well-off in a short period of time."

She shrugged. "I wasn't wealthy before I met him, and I didn't really have time to grow accustomed to having discretionary income after we got married. So I don't miss it all that much." Except for the loss of her own savings, which had gotten gobbled up once Big Jim's money was gone. That, she missed a lot, because its loss had spelled the death of a long-held dream and toppled the sense of security it had taken her years to build in the first place.

Jax took his eyes off the road for a moment to glance at her. Could that truly be what happened to the old man's fortune? Had illness eaten it all up—or had

Treena helped the process along with unlimited spending sprees? He hadn't caught more than a glimpse of her condominium when he'd picked her up, so his first visit there hadn't exactly gained him a wealth of information. He had a feeling she wasn't telling him the whole truth now. He also had to admit, however, that when she'd said earlier that she should've offered him the use of her car, it had caught him by utter flat-footed surprise that she wanted to save him the expense of renting one.

Of course that could've been nothing more than a clever ploy. After all, she'd made a production out of not wanting to accept the necklace, too, yet he hadn't failed to notice she was wearing it.

Something primal and possessive had washed over him when he'd seen it dangling around her neck. But that wasn't the issue under consideration.

He shot another glance at her, trying to pull the truth from her by sheer force of will. But when her sincere gaze from behind her sunglasses met his squarely, he turned his attention back to the road.

She could be telling the truth, he supposed.

Or she could simply be a dynamite actress.

How was he supposed to know? For a guy who made his living in part by following his own instincts, he sure as hell didn't trust them right this minute. Because all he had to do was look at her and his hands itched to feel the softness of her hair again, to reach out and touch the surprisingly cool sleekness of her skin. He was supposed to be so damn brilliant, but dump sex into the mix and it made even the smartest men stupid. Brains went soft when bodies went hard.

Not a winning combination.

"I'm sorry," he said once again, because he had to say something—and because it was true. He and the old man had hardly communicated for the past couple of decades. But he sure as hell wouldn't wish that kind of illness on anyone.

She touched his wrist. "Do you mind terribly if we don't talk about him today?"

"No." In fact, he was dead relieved at the opportunity to change the subject. "Of course not. I shouldn't have brought him up in the first place." He looked at her and told himself it was time to turn on the charm. "So. You ever been to the dam?"

"No. And isn't that something? I've lived here thirteen years and have never done a fraction of the tourist things that people come to Las Vegas to do. I haven't been to the top of the Eiffel Tower at the Paris, or seen the Liberace museum. I missed my chance at Siegfried and Roy while there still *was* a Roy. And I've never been to Hoover Dam. How about you?"

"I went once, but it was on a high school field trip, and I was so busy lusting over Carol Lee Sweeny that I don't remember much about the tour."

Treena laughed. "I bet she dug the hell out of that."

"No, she was too busy mooning over the baseball team's star pitcher to know I was alive." *What the hell?* He was supposed to be charming her, but instead he found himself revealing his loser moments. Carol Lee's attraction to a guy who was everything he wasn't had only magnified his father's expectations of him. He'd also been so far out of his social element that he hadn't had a chance in hell of gaining any girl's attention in his class, let alone the reigning beauty's.

"You're kidding me. I always thought jocks were a bunch of meatheads. Still, I can commiserate with the unrequited crush thing, because I remember what that felt like. For me it was Jeremy Powers. He was president of the science club." She flashed him a grin. "I liked the brainy ones."

Then what the hell were you doing married to my old man? he wondered, but merely said, "Oh, mama. Where were you when I was seventeen?" Which was just about the time he'd finally felt ready for girls—upon graduation from MIT.

"Probably applying acne cream to my chin on my way to dance class, where I worked like a dog while dreaming of being a famous dancer somewhere far, far away from Palookaville, Pennsylvania. Oh, look!" she exclaimed as they neared the dam. "We're here. I bet I've driven over Hoover a dozen times or more, but I always forget between times how immense it is."

Downshifting a few minutes later, he whipped the Viper into the multistoried visitor center parking garage and drove up to the third floor. There he headed for the corner farthest from the dam but closest to the road and lucked into a parking spot with a premier view.

When they climbed out of the car, he pointed out the attraction: a large metal tower that soared in front of them. Six cables stretched from it across the canyon. "That's the largest, oldest operating Cableway Crane system in the world," he told Treena as he escorted her down to the road level, where they headed for the tour center.

Before they reached it, however, he herded her toward the rock wall to the right of a row of palms. "You're not an acrophobe, are you?"

"Beats me, since I don't know what that is."

A smile tugged the corner of his mouth at her honesty. "Are you afraid of heights?"

"No. Not as long as there's a...*whoa!*" She stared all the way down to the distant bottom of the canyon. "That is one hell of a drop." She took a step back, knuckles bloodless where they gripped the top of the wall. "I don't usually have a problem with heights as long as there's something solid between me and the ground. But this—*whew!*—it makes my head feel kind of whirly."

"Allow me to help you with that." He wrapped his arms around her waist and hugged her back against his body, inhaling the beachy scent of her sunscreened skin. He gave her hip a little stroke.

"My, my, aren't you the heroic one." She shot an elbow into his stomach and stepped away from both him and the wall when he grunted in surprise and turned her loose. "I don't believe you just used my moment of wooziness to grab yourself a cuddle. And here I thought you were the original Mr. Suave."

"What can I say?" He gave her a faux innocent look. "I started life as a geek—"

"You did not!"

"Yeah, I did." He told himself to shut up, but there was simply something about Treena McCall that set his lips to flapping. "And this place brings back memories. I had a make-up-for-my-lost-opportunity-with-Carol-Lee moment."

She sputtered out a short laugh. "Well, hey, lucky me. I get to be a stand-in for a girl who thought bonehead jocks were the epitome of cool."

He looked at her, standing there all tall and luscious, and thought that between her hair blazing in the sunlight and her creamy skin, she looked like some wet dream version of the girl next door. "Trust me, honey," he said drily. "There's not a man on this planet who'd consider you a stand-in for anyone. C'mon." He took her elbow and steered them to the top of the escalators. "See that cactus garden over there? Did you know the film crew that made the National Lampoon Vegas Vacation movie put that in because they wanted it to look more 'desert-like' for the scene they shot here?"

"More desertlike than what? We're in the middle of the Mojave."

"I know—don't you love it?" He laughed with genuine amusement. "They also weren't overly concerned that the Mojave has never had this type of cactus. But look, if the irony of that doesn't float your boat, over there by the canyon wall is the mascot's grave. Now *that's* a guaranteed chick-pleasin' tearjerker of a story."

She quirked a brow at him. "About…?"

"About this little black puppy who was found under the porch of one of the dam workers' houses and became the mascot for the entire construction site. He met an untimely death in 1941 when the truck he was sleeping under rolled over him. All work was suspended for the day and a tomb was erected over the site. Is that a tear I see in your eye?" He gave her a hopeful look. "You wanna use my handkerchief? Need a hug, maybe?"

"Where do you get all this stuff?"

"The Great Gallagherini sees all, knows all."

She gave him a cool-eyed look and raised both eyebrows this time.

"Okay, fine, I went to their Web site last night and downloaded the self-guided tour." He crossed his arms over his chest. "Spoilsport."

"And did what with all that information after you downloaded it? Made crib notes?" She grabbed his wrists and uncrossed his arms, turning his hands over as if expecting to see detailed notes written on his palms.

"No," he said with great dignity. "I memorized it."

She looked at him thoughtfully. "I imagine a good memory would be a useful tool for a poker player, wouldn't it?"

He, too, could play the raise the eyebrow game.

"Not giving away your corporate secrets, huh? Well, okay. But something tells me you've got even more trivia where the movie and puppy stuff came from, don't you?"

"Oh, yeah. We haven't even reached Safety Island yet, with its winged statues, the floor design and the horoscope and compass dedication plaques. Then there's the old Exhibit building."

"Ooh." She pinched the little pavé diamond pendant between her thumb and finger and slid it slowly back and forth on its chain while she looked up at him with that faint half smile that drove him crazy. "I think I might be getting a little…excited."

"Yeah?" He stepped close, bowing his head to bring his lips next to her ear. "Then you're gonna love what I have to say about the bas-relief on the Nevada elevator tower," he murmured. "Did you know they depict the main five reasons for building Hoover Dam?"

He knew he ought to be more on guard with this woman, but what the hell. It had been a long time since he'd had the opportunity to flirt like this—and even longer since he'd felt this carefree. And for the next couple of hours he planned to make the most of it.

Because, come hell or high water, at the end of the day he had every intention of being inside her condo, the great baseball search begun.

What was the harm in enjoying himself along the way?

Nine

The High Scaler monument outside its namesake café was a tribute to the men who had hung hundreds of feet in the air on the side of Black Canyon, knocking away loose rock with jackhammers and setting dynamite charges during the construction of the dam. The statue struck a chord with Treena, and as she and Jax roared back through the barren landscape toward home, she twisted in her seat to gaze at the scaled-down replica that was wedged into the tiny space behind Jax's seat. "That is so great. I can't believe you bought it for me."

"I could tell you really liked it." Jax shrugged and took his gaze off the road to shoot her a puzzled glance. "Better than the necklace, I think."

"Oh, no, the necklace is gorgeous." She curled her fingers around it. "But the High Scaler—I don't know, it reminds me of the steelworkers back home. Not that my dad or uncles did any high work. But the hard hat and rough clothes, the everyday Joe face, and especially the way the skin is cleaner and lighter around the eyes where the goggles have been pushed up—man, that is so home."

"I guess I was under the impression you couldn't wait to kick the dust of your hometown from your heels."

"The town, absolutely. But not the people. My mom and pop and sisters may never understand my need for a different life from the one they know, but they'll always be my family." It struck her even as she said it, however, that her feelings toward them had changed substantially over the years. "Or maybe it's just that I'm finally growing up," she said with slow thoughtfulness. "Because you're right that when I was a kid I wanted nothing more than to get as far away from them as possible. I think I feared that if I didn't I'd be stuck in that life forever— and it sure wasn't what I wanted for myself."

A breath of laughter escaped her. "It's still not. I'm sure my folks don't approve of what I do, but I've never thought for a minute that they love me any less. I'll tell you something, Jax. I've been around the glitz of Las Vegas for so many years and met so many phony people that I've come to appreciate my family for being so genuine. They say what they think and they do what they say—and it may have taken me a while, but I've learned to value how rare that is. In the end honesty and integrity are probably two of the most important qualities in life. So this—" She reached back and ran a finger along the slab of sheer rock face from which the high scaler was suspended. "This will be like having a little piece of them with me. Thank you so much."

Jax's face was unreadable when he took his eyes off

the road to look at her, but he shook his head as if she were utterly beyond his comprehension. Pulling her knee up on the seat, she swivelled to look at him. "Don't you have family like that somewhere?"

"No." He hesitated, then said, "My mom died when I was—" He cleared his throat. "Before I hit puberty. My father was one of those guys who lived for his job, so he was never around much when she was alive. That is, he probably was, but not during my waking hours. Then when he inherited responsibility for me…well, we didn't get along. We had two very different ideas of what I should do with my life."

"And what does he think of what you do now?"

"I don't know. He died a while ago."

"Oh, Jax, I'm so sorry. What about brothers or sisters?"

"I don't have any."

Unthinkingly she reached out and gave his shoulder a squeeze. "It must be tough knowing you're all alone. I can't honestly say I see my family very often, but it's comforting to know they're there."

He shrugged. "You seldom miss what you've never known—and frankly I don't know squat about Brady Bunch-style families."

Heat seeped through his T-shirt from the hard muscle beneath her hand, making her aware that she'd been absentmindedly petting him. She drew it back and cleared her throat. "No aunts, uncles or cousins, then?"

"Nope. My mom was an only child. I think my father had some family, but if so they either lived a long way away or he didn't get along with them, either, because I sure never met any."

She noted his grip growing tighter on the steering wheel the longer they talked. And since he plainly longed to change the subject, she complied. "So tell me about this geek thing."

For the briefest instant he looked horrified. But his expression changed so quickly that she suddenly wasn't sure whether she'd actually seen what she thought she had.

"Trust me," he assured her drily. "You don't want to know about that."

"Yeah, I do. Because I'm having a really tough time imagining it. You seem so at ease and debonaire, like someone who's never had an uncomfortable moment in his life. Yet you say you started life as a geek, which must have been tough."

His laugh was short and humorless. "You could say that."

"Did the other kids make fun of you?"

"Not really. Well, some of them did, I suppose, but not many whose opinions I actually gave a damn about. I think I told you I got my growth early, so it's not like I had to deal with that getting stuffed in a garbage can thing that some of the scrawnier misfits were subjected to. It was just…" He shifted his broad shoulders. "Remember what you said the other day about football at your school? Mine was like that, too—except it wasn't only football that was God. Basketball and baseball got their turns. Which suited my dad right down to the ground. Or would have, if I'd been the jock he wanted instead of a kid who got off on playing chess and figuring out math equations."

Treena blinked. There was a faint trace of bitterness

in his voice and, surprised, she considered him. His usual elegant slouch was nowhere in sight as he sat stiffly upright in the low-slung car, and his wonderful hands were now so inflexible on the steering wheel that his tendons stood out from his knuckles to his wrist. This was obviously a sore subject for him. Reaching across the console once again, she touched her fingertips to his forearm.

It was rigid as steel.

She gave the warm, unyielding limb a gentle rub. "Jax, you don't have to talk about this if you'd rather not."

He flexed his shoulders again, this time in a dismissive shrug. "It's no big deal."

"Right. That's why you look as though you'd rather stick a needle in your eye than continue the conversation." She gave his arm a squeeze. "Forget I brought it up, okay? We haven't really known each other long enough for you to feel compelled to share memories you find painful. You can tell me when you're ready. Or never tell me at all. The last thing I want to do is ruin your day."

"You're not." The tension slowly melted out of him and he gave her a rueful smile. "You couldn't. If anyone's thrown a damper on this party, it's me. I'm sorry. I don't usually act like a twelve-year-old whose machismo has just been threatened."

Oh, man. She really liked this guy. She liked his sophistication and his willingness to suspend it and act a little silly. She liked the glimpse of vulnerability he'd displayed over the whole geek business. It opened the possibility that like her, he, too, had felt like a misfit, even if he'd been too big to physically torment. She always found it interesting to see just how far people had come from the bad old days.

Jax had obviously come miles.

Just as obviously, he didn't want to discuss the journey. And since there were some parts of her own life history she preferred not to dwell on, she felt compelled to honor his wishes.

Settling back in her seat, she unhurriedly crossed one leg over the other and said airily, "So…how about those bas-reliefs on the Nevada tour elevator, huh? Wait 'til I tell Carly that hunky guys are carved right into the walls. We'll probably have to make a pilgrimage to see them, just us girls."

He glanced at her in obvious surprise, but when she met his gaze with a level, oh-so-innocent one of her own, his lips suddenly quirked. "You will, huh?"

"Umm-hmm."

"Well, hell, as long as you're going to make the trip, maybe you should bring paper so you can make some rubbings."

A laugh bubbled out of her, but she nodded, as if actually considering the suggestion. "Maybe. I won't tell her the part, though, where you could have posed for the relief depicting Power." She studied him from beneath her lashes. "Of course, I'd have to see you without your shirt on to know that for certain."

The suggestion coming from her own lips brought her up short. She *never* indulged in sexual innuendo, because when it came to her own sexual shortcomings she didn't fool herself. She knew perfectly well she was unlikely to follow through to anyone's satisfaction on her implied promises. And nobody liked a tease.

Unfortunately, it was too late to warn Jax that he was destined to end up frustrated and unfulfilled. The look he turned on her was warm enough to melt rock. "That can be arranged."

A little thrill of pleasure shot through her. But before she could analyze it—much less decide what was going on with her own uncharacteristic behavior—they arrived back at her condominium complex.

As if it were the most natural thing in the world, Jax drove through the gates of the complex and parked in a visitor's spot. Climbing out of the car when he opened the door for her moments later, she abruptly decided that, right or wrong, she wasn't ready for their day to end. She reached for his hand and linked their fingers together.

"I had a really great time today," she said huskily. "And I'd love to make you dinner to thank you for it, if you've got time before your game."

Jax ignored the unexpected twinge of guilt that stabbed him and smiled down at her. "Are we talking home cooking here?"

She nodded. "But before you get too excited," she said with a small, crooked smile, "be warned it's only spaghetti. I'm not a bad cook, but I'm a long way from a great one."

He pulled their linked hands to his lips and kissed the tips of her fingers. "That sounds great." Belatedly, her mention of his scheduled game sank in, and he glanced at his watch. "If you don't mind that I have to leave by six-thirty, that is."

"Not a problem. We'll just eat a little early."

They walked through the landscaped grounds past decorative ponds and fountains and several pretty three-story, white stucco, red-tile-roofed buildings until they reached the one that housed Treena's condo.

"I meant to tell you when I picked you up how nice this complex is," he said as she let them into the building. "It really is beautiful. The waterscapes alone are amazing."

"Aren't they wonderful? I love the place." Bypassing the elevator, she led him to the stairs. "It's the first home I've ever owned all on my own."

Paid for with the old man's money, no doubt, he thought cynically, but for some reason his mind immediately rejected the thought. He was usually pretty good at reading people—and she wasn't behaving the way he'd expect a gold-digging showgirl who'd married an old man strictly for his money to act.

Not that she couldn't still be playing him. God knew his judgment got seriously whacked whenever he was in her company, because she had a way of commanding his full attention to the detriment of everything else going on around him. Just look at the way he'd almost told her how old he was when his mother had died, when he knew that, as big a disappointment as he'd been to his father, the old man might have at least mentioned that much about him to his new wife. Such sloppiness was anathema to everything his math-and-logic-trained mind believed in.

Yet despite all the analytical reasons to the contrary, the longer he was around Treena, the more he began to doubt all the assumptions he'd made about her up to now.

Then again, sport, maybe they're right on the money, he thought when they entered her apartment. Giving her furnishings a quick but comprehensive survey, he saw that for the most part she had a cozy mix of overstuffed chairs that had probably been picked up for a song and reupholstered on the cheap—a coffee table that while beautifully refinished, still looked more rummage sale old than antique find-of-the-century, and girly touches such as bright silk pillows, candles in bronze holders, and a large Moroccan mosaic mirror over the mantel of the small gas fireplace. But mixed among them were a few really good pieces—a mahogany credenza with inlays, a couch that had probably cost a pretty penny, a painting on one wall that looked as if it might be valuable, and an area rug on the hardwood floor that he'd swear was a Tabriz.

He looked around for the World Series baseball, but if she had it displayed anywhere it wasn't in the living room.

"Nice place," he said and watched Treena drop her tote on the credenza. "You really like color, don't you?" It was everywhere: in the Italian villa, gold walls, in the muted rug, and in the art and other vivid accessories that served to pull the room together.

"What was your first clue, Sherlock?" She laughed, a deep, throaty chuckle, and carried the High Scaler replica over to the fireplace.

Although her tone was teasing, he answered seriously as he watched her take down a large vase of dried grasses to make room for the sculpture on the mantel. "Your clothes. I've noticed that except for that killer dress you wore to dinner at the Commander's Palace, you're not exactly a basic black kind of woman. Instead you wear colors I wouldn't normally expect to see on a redhead." Looking at her orange top, he mused, "By rights they ought to clash, but somehow it all works."

"Glad you approve." But her reply was vague because she was obviously focused on getting the sculpture's placement just right. She stepped back to eye it critically, reached out to angle it a fraction of an inch toward the center of the mantel, then backed up several feet to get a different perspective. "There," she finally sighed after a few additional tweaks. "Perfect." Then she smiled at him over her shoulder, turning the full wattage of her attention back on him. "I can't thank you enough for this."

And that was what really got him. She genuinely seemed to wring more enjoyment out of a statue that reminded her of the men back home than the much more valuable diamond pendant. If she'd wanted to put on an effusive act, the smart money would have been on doing so over the necklace—not some hunk of rock, wood, and mold-cast bronze that had cost a fraction of the jewelry's price.

But since he could hardly demand to know why she was messing with his head this way, he flashed her his most charming smile and said, "Feeding me a home-cooked meal is thanks enough."

"Come on, then, and I'll get it started." She pointed to a bar stool at the counter as she walked around to the kitchen side. "Grab a seat. You want a glass of wine?"

"I'd love one, but I'd better not. I make it a policy never to drink within four hours of a game."

She nodded. "I can see where keeping your wits about you might be a good idea."

"Only if I want to stay in the game," he said lightly, pulling out a stool at the breakfast bar separating the living area from the kitchen and hitching a hip onto it.

But she seemed able to see through him to the truth. "You take your work very seriously," she said approvingly. "Is that why you keep your hand in with these other games you've been playing, instead of waiting for the actual tournament to start?"

"Yeah. It's kind of like your dance classes—it keeps my skills lubed up."

"I hear that. So, wine's out. How about a club soda, then?" She stretched to open a cupboard.

"That would be great."

She pulled one out of the refrigerator and poured it into the glass she'd fetched. "Ice?"

"No. Thanks." He looked at the bright pottery on the counter and the color-coordinated but mixed pattern towels looped through her refrigerator door handle and hanging from a towel bar. "I know I commented on your affinity for color, but I don't think I said how much I like the way you've fixed your place up." And he did. There was something very homey and welcoming about it.

Her smile lit up the room. "Thanks. I've done it a little at a time."

It was the perfect opportunity to find out how long she'd owned the place—and if his father had, indeed, had anything to do with its financing.

Before he could inquire, however, she handed him the highball glass of club soda and gave him a quizzical look. "Playing in a professional poker tournament must require an enormous amount of concentration," she said as she reached for a bottle of Merlot and poured herself a long-stemmed glass. She nodded at the club soda he'd picked up. "Not to mention discipline."

"You have to keep your mind on the game," he agreed and watched the taut pull of her khaki skirt over her world-class ass as she stooped to pull a pan from the drawer in the bottom of her stove. "*You'd* be a definite distraction to have around."

She flashed him a smile over her shoulder and rose with the pan in hand. "Why, you ol' sweet talker." Slipping the pan onto a burner, she sipped at her wine and began assembling ingredients from her cupboards, laying them out one by one on the counter.

He watched her work with pleasure. He might have had an agenda when he'd angled for an invitation for a home-cooked meal, but he sure as hell hadn't exaggerated how much he longed for one. "This is heaven," he said with genuine contentment. "I can't tell you how sick I am of eating out."

"So you've said before. I doubt you and I will ever see eye to eye on that score."

"Tell you what: I'll take you out until you get your fill of restaurant fare. I bet it won't take as long as you think." He observed her as she checked over her array of ingredients then grabbed a package of hamburger from the freezer and threw it in the microwave. "Can I do anything to help?"

"No, you relax. You can help me build the salad a little later on. I just want to get this sauce started so it can simmer a while." Pouring some olive oil into the pan, she turned the burner on under it, then reached for an onion and a green pepper and proceeded to chop them up with more enthusiasm than expertise on a Lucite cutting board. As she finished preparing the sauce, fragrant steam soon rose to flush her face and tease corkscrew-tight little ringlets away from the bandana tying her hair back. Jax found himself shifting on his stool. Who would have guessed a Betty Crocker moment could be such a turn-on?

Treena suddenly looked up, and for a second he thought she'd somehow read his mind. But she merely said, "You want to turn on the stereo? It's in the armoire over there, top section."

"Sure." He rose off the stool and headed for the indicated piece of furniture. Opening its top doors, he discovered a DVD multichanger on the shelf and several stacks of CDs. Selecting a few, he popped them in the player, used her remote to program a random, all-play mode, and hit Play. Strains of Dire Straits' "Brothers in Arms" soon filled the room.

She smiled at him. "That's quite different from what I expected, judging from what you played in the car."

"Hey, there's driving with the top down music, and then there's music to cook by."

She laughed and then disappeared from sight, and he heard her rummaging around in one of the lower cupboards.

"Oh, I don't believe this!" she suddenly exclaimed.

"What's that?" He walked back to the counter and leaned over it to peer down at her.

Crouched in front of a narrow open cupboard, she glowered up at him. "I had all the fresh stuff that I'm usually out of to make the sauce, but I forgot to replace the damn spaghetti when I used up the last box." She surged to her feet. "I'm going to have to run to the store."

"Maybe Carly has some," he said, then could have kicked himself. This was the perfect opportunity to take a look around for the baseball.

Treena laughed in his face. "Carly's cupboards have the finest dog and cat food money can buy, but they seldom have anything in them that's fit for real people to eat." Coming around the counter, she grabbed her wallet out of the tote on the credenza where she'd tossed it and pulled out her keys. "Make yourself comfortable. I won't be long." And a second later, she was gone.

He simply stood there for a moment, staring at the door that had banged shut behind her. Then he made a conscious effort to snap his sagging jaw shut. But, good God almighty. The woman was a firecracker.

Having his imagination segue into the red-hot question of how that might correspond to action with her in bed sure as hell wouldn't get him any closer to finding the baseball, so he shook off the graphic images that had exploded full-blown in his mind and headed across the room. He had a finite amount of time to search, and shoving aside the inexplicable discomfort he felt about pawing through her stuff, he plotted a mental diagram of her apartment. Considering he didn't see the ball out here, the smart thing would be to start in her bedroom. But this burglary business wasn't exactly his usual milieu, and he couldn't quite get past his unease at going through her personal belongings. He decided to search some of the apartment's less intimate areas first.

He started with the beautifully inlaid credenza, sliding open the rounded front panel. The craftsmanship of the piece was exquisite, and it must be worth a small fortune. It contained nothing more than china, however, and he closed it again. The small bookshelf held books and girl-type pretties, and he passed it by. He opened the sections of the armoire that he hadn't already seen and found a TV and a VCR in the middle compartment and tapes, a set of candlesticks and two vases in the bottom.

Since there was no sense in rising to his feet merely to have to squat again a couple of feet away, he crab-walked toward the tiny cabinet she used as an end table.

He was just reaching for the decorative pull on its door when a key turned in the lock.

Ten

Treena let herself into the condo and headed through the archway into the living room. "Hi, I bet you didn't expect me back this quic—"

The sight of Jax's muscular butt, thrust up in the air where he knelt at the end of the couch, severed her power of speech. He was twisted from the waist, his right shoulder dipped to the hardwood floor to fit his arm biceps-deep beneath the little cabinet she'd picked up at a Palm Springs flea market and fixed up for an end table.

"Do I dare ask what you're doing?" she finally managed, as her gaze ping-ponged between his rump and the slice of flesh above his waistband where his sky-blue T-shirt had separated from his jeans.

"Hang on a second—there!" Pulling back, he flipped over and rolled to sit on that very fine butt, holding up a gold-rimmed black coin draped in a dust bunny. "I dropped George—my good-luck two-pound piece— and he ran for the hills."

She crossed the room and took it from his fingers, blowing off the streamer of dust. "Well, this is embarrassing. Now you know I don't move my furniture to clean."

"Yeah, that's a real priority in my life. I don't know if we can still be friends after this."

"Hey, *I,* at least, don't name my money."

He climbed to his feet and reached out to turn the coin in her hand. On the back, in a bold relief of gold against black, was a man on a horse, thrusting a sword into a dragon. "It's a 1987 St. George and the Dragon."

"Thus George, I'm guessing. I also imagine he's worth more than two pounds."

He grinned at her. "A bit. It's the luck he brings me that's his real worth, though."

"You're superstitious?" She probably shouldn't have been surprised, but it wasn't a label that ever would have occurred to her to pin on him.

He smiled. "Well, I've got something of a split personality when it comes to that. The math lover in me believes in numbers and nothing but. Yet I'm a gambler—and by nature we're a superstitious lot." Plucking the coin from her hand, he kissed it, rolled it in a nimble display across his knuckles from index to baby finger and back again, then dropped it into his pocket. "Therefore George here always accompanies me when I play." His gaze went to her empty hands. "So where's the spaghetti?"

"Oh!" She smacked her palm off her forehead. "I lent my car to Carly earlier. It was supposed to be back in its spot by now, but I guess she ran into trouble." She crossed to the answering machine on the end of the breakfast bar and sure enough it was blinking its red message alert. "I didn't even look at this when we got back." She pushed the Play button.

The first message was from the studio offering her a newly opened time slot the following morning. The second was from Carly.

"Treena, I'm sorry!" she said. "Rufus got away from me when we were leaving the vet's and I'm hunting him down. God, who knew one mangy mutt could disappear so fast? I swear this dog's going to be the death of me— he's more trouble than Buster, Rags and Tripod put together! Oh, for— I just ran over the damn curb." Her stressed sigh came clearly down the line. "I suck at this multitasking crap so I better hang up before I kill somebody. I'll get your car back as soon as I can. I'm really sorry. I hope this hasn't screwed up your plans."

Treena laughed. Then she considered her predicament. "Okay," she said slowly. "Let me think. I suppose I could go ask Ellen if she has any spaghetti."

"Or you could take my car." Jax tossed her the keys.

She caught them out of pure reflex but simply stood clutching them in her hand for a moment as she stared at him. "Are you serious? You'd let me drive that marvelous car?"

"Sure." He shot her a look from those blue eyes. "That is—you *will* bring it back, won't you?"

"Oh, absolutely." She headed for the entryway before he could change his mind. Pausing with her hand on the doorknob, she shot him a grin over her shoulder. "In a week or two."

And knowing the value of a good exit line, she sailed out the door.

Jax watched her go, shaking his head. Then he went back to the work she'd interrupted.

That had been close. Too close, and with renewed determination he headed for her bedroom, telling himself firmly that he couldn't afford to be squeamish.

But he stopped short in the doorway, as surely as if he'd run up against a stone wall. Man. The scent in here was elusive and girly and without conscious thought he dragged in a deep breath, inhaling appreciatively through his nose.

He ordered himself to snap out of it. He couldn't afford to be sidetracked. Crossing the threshold he glanced around, noting the bright silks and altogether feminine look of the room. Then he shoved his impressions aside for more practical concerns. Focusing on her closet, he decided to start with that, and opened one side of the mirrored slider.

He had to breathe shallowly as more of that incredible scent wafted out. He was behaving like a callow fourteen-year-old.

That shook loose a bitter laugh. Treena had said today that he always seemed so at ease and debonaire, but he worked like a Trojan to protect that image. Not that it was a sham. The confidence of having done something well for the past twelve years *was* ingrained in him by now. He'd established a good life for himself. He'd moved beyond his childhood problems, yet just about the time he grew cocky enough to believe that stupid kid desperate for his daddy's approval was gone forever, his insecurities would return. The disappointments of a somewhat-less-than-functional childhood still managed to stage the occasional hit-and-run visit on his adult psyche.

And nothing could shoot his normal self-assurance to hell faster than knowing that he was never fully braced against it, knowing that he had waited too long to tell the old man exactly how he felt and now it was too late to rectify any of it.

"Jesus," he muttered. This was the *last* train of thought he ought to be pondering. He had to quit moping around like some sorry-ass kid and focus on what needed to be done.

The baseball was what mattered, so he picked a spot to start searching and got busy. Given the ball's worth, he doubted Treena would just toss it in the bottom of the packed closet. But he'd start there all the same and work his way up. Squatting, he began sifting carefully through the clutter on the floor.

It was filled with shoes. Red shoes, black shoes, blue shoes, green; they came in all shapes and styles: high heels both of the spiked and the chunky-heeled variety, ballerina-type slippers, sandals, wedgies, and flats. There were also a few handbags and a box that contained some hand weights and some other assorted odds and ends. Mostly, though, it was a jumble of shoes.

And definitely no baseball.

After double-checking to be certain he'd left the clutter the way he'd found it, he rose to his feet and reached for the nearest box on the overhead shelf. It was filled nearly to the brim with loose photographs, and he carefully sifted through the pile, working his hand down to the bottom of the carton to make sure the ball hadn't been buried beneath several inches of snapshots.

It hadn't.

He replaced the box and reached for the next one. Removing the lid, he saw that this one, too, had photographs in it, only this batch were all matted and framed. The one on top was the same professional head shot of Treena that his father had sent him. The one that showcased the slight half smile he now knew was pretty much her default expression. Looking down at it, he remembered the day the photo had caught up with him— it had shown up a good month or two after it had been mailed, arriving in a padded envelope covered with forwarding stamps.

He watched his thumb brush back and forth against the glass-covered quirk of her lips for another moment, then tipped the frame on end against the side of the box and reached for the next. This one was smaller, a framed snapshot, and he lifted it from the dimness of the box and turned it toward the light.

He froze, his mind a sudden hot jumble of broken words and scrambled thoughts. His heart pounded with slow, sickening thuds, just the way it had done in the chest of that poor, inept eleven-year-old standing so stiffly within the drape of his much larger father's arm when the photo was taken more than twenty years ago.

He remembered that day. A humorless laugh burned his throat, because *remembered* was such a pallid word. The day was etched in his mind in acid. Big Jim had yelled invective and instructions from the sidelines of a softball game Jax hadn't wanted to play in the first place but had participated in at his father's insistence. After the game was over the old man had slung an arm around his shoulders like they were the best of buds while another father snapped their picture. Then, just when he'd thought the whole torturous ordeal was finally over— that he couldn't possibly be humiliated any further— Big Jim had hauled him off to the pizza parlor where Jax had let him down *again* with his losing struggle to interact with other players who hadn't wanted him on their team any more than he'd wanted to be there.

What the hell was that photograph doing here, all framed and matted? As he pawed through the other photos in the box it quickly became apparent all of them had once been his father's. Staring down at this picture, he saw in his younger self every single bit of the wretched awkwardness he had worked so hard to eradicate.

So, get over it, he ordered himself sharply. *Christ Almighty, you're not eleven anymore. It was a long time ago, a lot of water under the bridge, spilled milk, yesterday's news—*

The absurd host of clichés served to steady him. With a slight smile he began straightening the rifled mementos.

Then another worry assaulted him and his hand stilled within the box. Even though he'd taken care not to disclose anything that might fire off a synapse in Treena's brain and link him to Big Jim's son, he'd never genuinely worried about her making the connection between his younger self and the man he'd become. He'd changed so much since he'd left Las Vegas that he doubted the few people who'd actually known him back then would recognize him now. The only thing at all distinctive about him was the shade of his eyes, and how likely was it that anyone meeting him for the first time would think to associate the blue eyes of a stranger to those of a long-gone kid?

Never in his wildest dreams had he ever imagined the old man would keep a picture of him on display. After all, this was the relative who hadn't even bothered to come watch his seventeen-year-old graduate with honors from MIT.

Retrieving the framed snapshot once again from the box, he took it over to the window and unwound the blinds a fraction of an inch to study it by the harsh light of the afternoon sun. And by increments, the tension in his shoulders eased.

He wore a baseball cap in the photo, and between that and the thick lenses of the glasses he'd worn before undergoing laser surgery, his eye color didn't even show. The geeky shirt and the jeans that were nearly an inch too short for his then still fast growing legs told him he'd been an even lousier dresser than he'd thought. Smiling, he closed the blinds again, replaced the photograph in the box and put it carefully back where he'd found it. It would prove harder to erase the host of questions its unexpected discovery raised in his mind.

But he squared his shoulders. This waltz down memory lane wasn't helping him find that ball, and as that charmer Sergei had reminded him, the clock was ticking.

He was reaching for the next box on the shelf, a lidded, heart-shaped floral number, when someone pounded on Treena's front door. He nearly jerked the box off the shelf and, sucking in an angry breath, he grabbed its tilting front tip to stop its downward trajectory. He pushed it back in place. *What the hell is the matter with you?*

Usually he had nerves of steel. But ever since he'd connected up with a certain white-hot redhead, his much lauded steadiness seemed to be unraveling faster than a ball of yarn in a kitten's paws. He gave the closet a quick once-over to make sure nothing was glaringly out of place, and slid the door closed. Smoothing his hand over the front of his T-shirt, he watched his features adopt their expressionless game face in the mirrored slider, then stepped back and turned his back on his reflection. The caller pounded again, and he strode out to the tiny entryway.

Opening the door, he found a short muscular man with steel-gray hair standing on the other side.

Impatient dark brown eyes regarded him with suspicion. "Who the hell are you?" the man demanded. "Where's Treena?"

"I'm Jax. Jax Gallagher."

"Ah. The new boyfriend."

His eyebrows shot up in a silent demand to elaborate. Is that what she was telling people he was? Inexplicably, his ego swelled.

A moment too soon, as it turned out. "Or so Carly's been saying, anyway. I'm Mack." He didn't offer his hand. "The guy who makes sure the girls' dates are good enough for them. What took you so long to answer the door?"

He gave the man a cool smile. "I was tossing the joint."

"I'll take that as gospel until the day comes that I know you well enough to tell if you're serious or just being a smart-ass. If you even last that long, that is." Suddenly he inhaled sharply through his nose. "Whoa. Treena's making spaghetti?" He took a purposeful step forward.

Jax had the impression that Mack would have no compunction about mowing him down if he didn't step aside, even though Jax was more than a head taller than the older man. And since he wasn't here to get in a pissing match with one of Treena's friends, he shoved his hands into his pockets and stepped back. "Come on in," he said drily.

Mack either didn't hear the irony or he chose to ignore it. He looked him up and down with steely eyes. "So, where did you say Treena is?"

"I didn't. But she ran to the store to get something for her dinner."

"And you didn't bother going with her? What are you, one of those bums who lets the women do everything?"

Having a guy old enough to be his father find fault with him right out of the gate rubbed an exposed nerve, but he said evenly, "She took off the first time before I could even offer."

"The first…?" Mack nodded. "Ah. Sure. Carly's got her car. I thought she planned to be back with it by now, though."

"Apparently her dog staged a getaway from the vet, and she's out looking for him." His brows furrowed above his nose before he could prevent them, but he smoothed them out pronto. "I suppose you think I oughtta be out helping *her* look, too."

The other man laughed. "Hit a sore spot with that, did I?" The idea clearly pleased him.

Jax shrugged. "It's not like I'm not used to old men finding fault with me—my father never hesitated to say I wasn't worth much, either." Shock sizzled down his spine. He couldn't believe he'd just said that. He'd always been the Sphinx where his private life was concerned. Now suddenly he was Chatty Cathy? What the hell was this town doing to him?

Before he could even consider trying to backpedal, however, Mack sobered. "Now, that I'm sorry about, because I can't wrap my head around laying that kind of garbage on a kid. I raised two girls, and they were the apples of my eye. Still are. Unfortunately they live in North Dakota and New Hampshire these days, but I've got the girls here to practice my protective impulses on."

Without further ado, Mack headed for the kitchen, where he pulled a couple of beers out of the refrigerator. He offered one to Jax, but shrugged without comment when he shook his head in refusal. The older man simply returned it to the fridge, then twisted the cap off his own bottle.

"Carly's strays are her problem," he said. "The truth is, they're usually not much of one, but Rufus is proving difficult. My money's on her, though. She'll get him whipped into shape one of these days." He strode into the living room, flopped down on one of the upholstered chairs and looked at Jax when he sat in the chair opposite him. "So why didn't you go with Treena the second time?"

"Because she wanted me to stay here. Mostly, I think, because she wanted to drive my rental."

"Why? What's so great about it?"

"It's a Viper SRT-10."

Mack sat upright. "No shit? And you let her drive it?"

The incredulousness in the older man's voice sent unease crawling through his gut. "Yes. Why? Is she a lousy driver or something?"

"No, she's a good driver. But a *Viper.* I've only seen one once, but it was a beauty." He took a pull on his beer and grinned. "You might as well turn down the heat under the sauce, boy. She may or may not have your car back some time this week."

Jax felt a smile tug the corner of his mouth. "That's what she said."

"And you probably thought she was kidding." Mack shook his head. Then he leaned back in his chair once again, cradling the beer bottle against his flat stomach, and regarded Jax with level eyes. "Carly tells me you're some kind of gambler?"

"I'm a professional poker player," he agreed and braced himself for the older guy's condemnation.

But Mack merely asked, "And you can actually make a living at that?"

"Yes. A pretty good one."

"Huh. It's a different world than when I was your age." Jax shrugged.

Surprisingly, Mack laughed. "I know. It's the standard old fart speech. When I was a kid—" his voice went stentorian "—ice cream cones were—"

"A nickel a scoop," Jax supplied, amused in spite of himself.

"Heard that one already, huh? Well, I'll make you a deal, son. I'll refrain from dragging out the rest of my When-I-was-youngs—and, trust me, I've got a million of 'em, so this is no small deal. I'll even back off on my protective shtick where Treena's concerned…as long as you agree to treat her right." Then the warmth bled out of his dark eyes. "You hurt her, though, boy, and I'll hunt you down like a dog."

His gut went hollow, because that was exactly what was going to happen. He didn't give a damn about Mack's threats. But although he hadn't worried about hurting Treena when he'd first set out on this quest, the idea of it now was beginning to bother him.

A lot.

But he gave the older man a steady look. "What if *she's* the one who ends up hurting me?"

"Then I'll assume you were begging for it."

His mouth twisted beneath the sudden stab of bitterness. "Of course. Why worry about a little thing like fairness?"

"I never claimed I wasn't partisan. I'm on her side, all the way."

"Well, as long as we understand each other."

"My thoughts exactly."

A key turned in the dead bolt, breaking their damned-if-*I'll*-be-the-first-to-look-away locked gazes.

"Honey, I'm ho-ome." Treena's voice preceded her

into the room. "I want you to know I was a good, good girl. I really wanted to take that car down to L.A. for a test spin, but I wrestled mightily with my conscience and resisted." The sound of keys disengaging from the dead bolt and the door closing accompanied her words, then she appeared in the archway, her arm hooked around the paper bag riding one hip. Golden brown eyes widened for an instant as they took in Mack's presence, then a warm smile lit her face. "Well, hi there. I didn't expect to see you here."

"I smelled spaghetti cooking and came to investigate. Young Gallagher here insisted I stay for dinner."

Treena's surprised gaze whipped over to lock with his. "You did?"

He snorted. "In his dreams. But ancient as Old Mack is, he's far from feeble—and I couldn't budge him."

"Ancient, my ass," Mack grumbled. But he gave Treena an affectionate, wheedling smile. "A hot dinner sure sounds better than the cold, stale sandwich I was planning to have."

"Please," Jax muttered. "You're breaking my heart."

But Treena laughed. "Mack, won't you stay for dinner?"

"Why, thank you, sweetheart. I'd love to."

"You're kidding, right?" He couldn't hide his dismay as he saw his chances for a little one-on-one with her go up in smoke before his eyes. "You can't possibly have fallen for a con that weak." But when they both turned to look at him, she with a chastising gaze, Mack with a smug one, he knew he might as well give in gracefully. So he did.

Sort of. "Fine. He stays. But he's doing the dishes."

The doorbell rang, but before anyone could move to answer it the door opened with a bang. There was a scramble of nails on the tiled entryway floor, then Carly and a black-and-brown dog exploded into the living room.

"God, what a day!" She crossed to the couch, collapsed in a sprawl of long legs and shoved the dog away when he tried to climb up onto her lap. "Get down, you fleabag! You're on real shaky ground here—I'm talking one nudge away from euthanasia." But when Rufus's tail thumped enthusiastically against the hardwood floor, she gave his ears an absentminded scratch. "Hi, Mack. Hi, Jax." She looked up at her friend. "Treena, I'm so sorry about keeping your car this long."

"Not a problem. I got to drive Jax's Viper."

"What's a viper? No, wait, is that the red sports car I saw down in the parking lot?" At Treena's nod, she gave him an approving look. "Whoa. You have serious great taste in rides."

"Thanks. I'd love to be able to tell you that it's mine, but I just rented it for the day."

"Still classy either way." She inhaled. "Oh, my God, is that spaghetti I smell?"

"Yeah." Treena blinded Jax with her smile before saying to her friend, "Wanna join us?"

"You know it, toots." She slowly straightened. "But I'll decline. I don't want to horn in on your date."

"Wish your buddy here felt the same way," Jax said.

"You mean Mack's staying?" At the older man's decisive nod, she smiled brilliantly. "In that case, why not? After the day I had, a meal someone else cooked sounds so divine, I can't even begin to tell you." She surged to her feet. "I'll just go put Rufus in the apartment and feed the rest of the babies." Grabbing the dog by the collar, she detoured by the breakfast bar, where she picked up the bottle of wine. "I suppose it wouldn't be cool to drink this straight from the bottle. But if you don't mind, I'll just pour myself a glass for the road. A *big* glass," she muttered. "I earned it."

The late afternoon passed into early evening in a blur of noisy conversation, tasty food, and flowing wine. A tidy little woman named Ellen, who turned out to live next door, joined them, as well, and Jax was tickled to note she took the burden of Mack's scrutiny off of him. From the moment she walked into the living room, bearing a plate of cookies, Mack turned his attention to her.

The older man's gaze tracked her every move as she greeted Treena and handed over the heaping plate. When she came into the living room where they were seated a moment later, he gave her a comprehensive once-over, and the introduction to Jax was barely out of the way before he said, "Festive as ever, I see. You ever considered dressing in something besides basic crow? You make Heckle and Jeckyl look flamboyant by comparison."

"Who?" Jax asked.

Ellen's pretty smile dimmed and her cheeks went pink, but her chin shot up. "Mr. Brody is referring to cartoon characters from the '60s, Jax. But as usual his lips move without actually saying anything worth hearing." She turned back to Mack. "Heckle and Jeckyl were magpies, you old fool, not crows."

It went downhill from there, and Jax sat back, sipped his club soda and watched. He continued to observe them with fascination during dinner.

While he was hardly the biggest ladies' man in the universe himself, he had Mack beat all to hell. For a second he even considered pulling the old guy aside to give him a pointer or two on improving his mating technique. God knew his current one sucked.

But it wasn't his problem, and it was time for him to leave, anyway. He found himself curiously reluctant to go, but he pushed his chair back and rose. "I'm sorry," he said when conversation at the table abruptly died and everyone stared up at him. "This has been great, but I have to get ready for my game."

"Ah, so that's why you haven't been drinking, huh?" Mack said at the same time Carly wished him good luck.

"It was nice to meet you, dear," Ellen said. "Be sure to grab a few cookies for the road."

Treena rose to her feet, as well, as he took the older woman at her word and filched a couple cookies off the plate. "I'll walk you out."

She stole several glances at him as they headed toward the door. "I'm not sure whether to apologize or congratulate you on your forbearance," she admitted.

She felt guilty for the way she'd let herself be surrounded with her friends to avoid the possibility of intimacy with Jax. She'd given in to a cowardly impulse because there was just something about this guy that made her ache to present her best, and her abilities in the bedroom didn't do that. She knew men looked at her, heard what she did for a living, and made huge assumptions about her sexuality. But no matter how great it started out, it always seemed to end up a big, fat disappointment for all concerned—and it was usually her fault because she just couldn't seem to let go and really cut loose. She didn't want to see the same disappointment on Jax's face that she'd seen on others.

She wondered what he thought of the afternoon's impromptu gathering, but couldn't tell from his noncommittal expression. So she tried to find out in a more roundabout manner. "This isn't exactly what you signed on for."

"Don't worry about it," he said easily, stopping at the front door to look down at her. "I had a good time. Well, the jury is still out on Mack, since one look at me and he turned into a junkyard dog. But Carly and Ellen are great, and the meal—that was sheer heaven, Treena. My only complaint is that—with all the others here—I had no chance to do this."

His long-fingered hand wrapped around the back of her neck. With a tug, he tumbled her against his chest and lowered his head, stamping his mouth firmly over hers.

Like their kiss in the parking garage, it only took one touch of his lips, one confident sweep of his tongue across her own, for her brain to go into meltdown. Wrapping her arms around his neck, she kissed him back, and between one pounding heartbeat and the next her entire world was reduced to hot, seething sensations and swirling colors. She pressed closer.

Then his hands, strong and firm, gripped her forearms and deftly disengaged her hands from where she'd plunged them into his soft, thick hair. He moved her back a step.

She might have been embarrassed, might have felt the slap of rejection, except that she could see his chest rising and falling beneath the snug blue T-shirt as his breath heaved in his lungs.

"Holy shit," he said hoarsely. "Ho-ly—" He cut himself off and took a step back, as well. One hand reached for the doorknob, while the other raked his sun-streaked hair back from his brow. "Jesus, Treena, you're more potent than a straight shot of bourbon. It's going to take me every minute between now and the start of the game to get my head on straight." He opened the door and stepped through, but paused on the other side to look at her. Suddenly, he leaned back in and pressed a quick, hard kiss on her lips. "I'll call you," he said.

Then he turned and strode away.

Pressing her fingers to her lips to retain the feel of his kiss, she leaned out into the hallway and watched him until he disappeared down the stairway. Then she closed the door and leaned back against it, smiling dreamily at the High Scaler on the mantel, which she could just see through the archway. Perhaps there was a guy on Planet Earth with whom she could cut loose.

Eventually, when it began to sink in that she couldn't simply prop herself against the door for the rest of the night, she smiled goofily. Then, drawn by the clink of dishes and animated voices coming from her small dining table, she drifted back to rejoin her guests.

Eleven

Ellen didn't slam the door behind her when she returned to her apartment later that evening. She'd lived far too many years with her husband, Winston, who had liked things on an even keel, to radically change her behavior at this late date. She closed the door with deliberate gentleness.

In her mind, however, she banged it so hard it rattled the windows, shivered the timbers, and shook the entire building on its foundation. "Dress like a crow, my sweet fanny!" She strode straight into her bedroom and over to the mirrored doors of her closet.

Fine, she thought fiercely as she checked out her reflection. *I wore black tonight.* Big deal. It was a good, basic color, the foundation of every woman's wardrobe. One could dress black up or down. Still, she had clothes in lots of other colors. Sliding open the doors, she rattled hangers one by one along the bar, taking stock.

She had black, black, navy, black, brown, black—

aha!—*taupe* and *beige*, navy with white piping, black, forest green, black and brown, *golden* brown, and… black. She also had several crisp white blouses of various styles interspersed. Her shoulders sagged. Oh, dear. She'd never realized her wardrobe was quite so…dark. So unstimulating.

The doorbell rang and, grateful for the interruption, she abandoned the closet. Opening her door, she was surprised to see Treena standing on the other side. "Well, hello there. It seems like an age since I've seen you."

Treena laughed. "I know, long time, no see." She extended the cookie plate. "I just wanted to return this while I was thinking about it. Otherwise it's bound to sit on my counter gathering dust for the next week or two."

Instead of accepting the dish right away, Ellen stepped back into the small entryway and invited Treena in. "And, really," she insisted when her young friend complied, "you didn't have to wash it."

Treena's mouth quirked. "I'd hardly call it washing—it was more a matter of rinsing off a few crumbs. Believe me, a lot more effort went into making the cookies than washing the plate. Your baked goods are always so yummy."

Ellen closed the door, took the plate, then led Treena to the living room where she invited her to take a seat. "Speaking of yummy," she said as she continued into the kitchen with the dish, "your Jax is very attractive."

Delicate color bloomed in Treena's cheeks. "Well, I don't know if he's *my* Jax, but he really is a treat for the eyes, isn't he?" She collapsed gracefully onto the chintz divan. "I can't figure out why that is, exactly. It's not like he's movie-star handsome or anything. Taken one by one, his features are fairly average, but there's just something about the total package. It's largely his attitude, I think—the cool assertiveness, the confidence. Combine that with the features that are outstanding: that great body, the nice hair and those truly gorgeous eyes—" she flashed a sleepy smile "—and 'yummy' is an excellent word."

Then she collected herself and straightened up on the couch. "But back to the cookie plate," she said briskly, nodding at it in Ellen's hand as she was about to set it atop the stack in the cupboard. "You do know, don't you, that I'm not the one who actually washed it. You must have noticed Mack doing the dishes."

Ellen released the plate faster than she'd shake loose a rabid toad. Luckily it was close enough to the stack that it only rattled a little. "Don't speak to me of that man. He said I dress like a *crow.*"

"Yeah, that was pretty low. You shut him up pretty fast, though, when you informed him Heckle and Jeckyl were magpies."

Yes, she had. She noticed, however, that Treena wasn't exactly jumping in to defend her style. "Do *you* think my clothes are drab?"

"I think they're…elegant. And, um, classic."

"But drab," she insisted, realizing to whom she was speaking. She walked over to the couch. "Of course you do—you love color. In fact, you're pretty much the queen of color."

Amusement deepened the ironic tilt of Treena's lips, scoring a tiny groove in her cheek next to the corner of her mouth. "I suppose I am. And okay, I admit I'd like to see you in more than your usual blacks and earth tones. But it's not like I'd want you to quit wearing those." She reached for Ellen's hand, urging her with her soft grip to sit next to her on the sofa.

She complied, and Treena's eyes held a gentle smile in their honey-brown depths as they studied her. "There's no need to change your basic style," she reiterated. "Because it is definitely you: elegant and sort of posh. But a discreet use of color would really accentuate your classical pieces, with the added bonus of supplementing the outfits you already have. You've got such lovely skin and that dramatic salt-and-pepper hair. And hazel eyes offer so many color combinations that it opens up all sorts of possibilities for accessorizing. A lavender tank top or blouse, for instance, would look great with most of your shorts, as well as with your dark suits. So would a soft coral. And sea-foam green, or sage, or an old gold like my living room walls would bring out your eyes."

The younger woman suddenly sat upright. "Oh! I have a brilliant idea." She jiggled Ellen's hand as her cheeks flushed with enthusiasm. "Tomorrow Carly and I have a mutual day off. I have studio time booked in the morning, but then we're going shopping. Come with us."

Ellen pulled back slightly. "Oh, darling, thank you for the offer. But I don't think so."

"Why not?"

"Well—" she waved a hand at the dancer "—look at you. Then look at me. Not only am I old enough to be your mother, we have totally different body types. Not to mention that our sartorial choices are polar opposites. I doubt we shop at the same stores."

Treena laughed, and it was so deep and infectious that Ellen couldn't help but smile in return.

"We aren't going to Spandex R Us," the redhead said. "Come with us. I bet we can find you a few pieces that will satisfy all our tastes." She gave Ellen's leg a poke. "Unless…you got a hot date?"

She smiled. "No."

"Then what have you got to lose? At the very least you'll have a few laughs with us."

"Yes, that's something I'm definitely guaranteed with you and Carly. But shop for bright clothing? Winston would roll in his grave."

"Why, was he a big fan of funeral weeds?"

For some reason when Treena poked fun at her colorless wardrobe, it struck her as funny, and a burble of laughter rolled up her throat. It was nothing like the way she felt when that testosterone-laden, socially challenged Brody man did the same thing. "He was, yes. Winston truly believed black was *the* classic color—that one could never go wrong with it."

"What a fun guy," Treena said drily.

A smile curled Ellen's lips as a host of memories flashed across her mind. "Oh, he had his moments."

Her friend grimaced. "I'm sure he did, and it was insensitive of me to imply otherwise about a man I never even met. I just think unrelenting black is kind of, well, dull, and it's time we glammed you up a bit. C'mon," she urged. "If not for me, then think of how bent out of shape it will make Mack."

She'd been wavering, but Brody's name made her snap erect. "You think I want to give that rude man the satisfaction of thinking anything he said drove me to change my style?"

"Oh, trust me, Mack's got such a lust on for you that if you flash a little color, maybe a hint of cleavage at him, he'll be lucky if he has a functioning brain cell left to ask if anyone got the number of the train that hit him." She laughed, deep and bawdy, as if someone had just told her a deliciously dirty joke. "I'm betting it'll be all he can do to remember his own name, let alone that anything he said may or may not have instigated a couple of changes in your wardrobe."

A lust on? Treena was mistaken. Ellen smiled wryly. Ah, to be at an age again where everything boiled down to sex.

Nevertheless, her heart picked up its beat, and feeling suddenly, inexplicably lighter than she had in quite some time, she said slowly, "Well, I suppose it wouldn't hurt to pick up one or two colorful pieces. Not that I care what that old goat thinks," she hastened to add. Okay, that was a big fat lie, but she refused to regret it—let alone take it back—for she didn't see the point of making herself look foolish in her young friend's eyes.

"Of course you don't," Treena agreed. "You're doing this strictly to give yourself a lift. If Mack has a problem with black, let him get himself a hot pink shirt."

"Yes," she agreed fervently.

"So, we're in accord, right?" Treena climbed to her feet. "I'll call Carly and let her know you're coming with us. I think, in the interests of time and to avoid having to deal with too many cars, I'll just take the bus to the studio. Carly already said she'd drive, so you two can pick me up at ten-thirty." She strode for the door. "Oh, this is going to be fun. Wear comfortable shoes. We're gonna shop till we drop."

And before Ellen could have second thoughts and perhaps recant her decision, her friend had breezed out the door.

Treena was less than thrilled to arrive at the studio the following morning and discover Julie-Ann there, but after exchanging curt nods they staked out opposite ends of the long narrow room and quite effectively ignored each other. She found the younger woman's choice of music obnoxious, but Julie-Ann had gotten there before her, and the unwritten rule in these situations always favored the first to arrive.

With anyone else Treena would have hammered out a musical compromise, but she didn't even try with the young dancer. This was her final day off and she had zero desire to start it off with a pissing match. So she let it go with a mental reminder to bring her Walkman next time.

Within moments, she was so deep into the practice session, she barely even remembered that the other dancer was there. She ran through one series of steps after another, constantly changing combinations and monitoring herself closely in the mirror. By the time Carly and Ellen arrived she was fairly satisfied with the morning's session. She completed her final set, picked up her towel and, dabbing the sheen of sweat from her face and chest, walked over to join her friends, smiling at the physical disparity between them.

Carly easily exceeded six feet in her high heels, and her spiky blond hair made her look like some Valkyrie warrior goddess—an image that was enhanced by the hammered gold bracelet circling her upper arm. Cream-colored sharkskin slacks and an electric blue halter top clung to her lush curves. Next to her Ellen was a petite, elegant sprite in a black silk suit and sensible pumps.

The elegant sprite broke into applause and smiled radiantly at her. "I know you're a dancer, of course," she said. "But I tend to forget from day to day exactly how much talent that encompasses. It is *such* a joy to watch you in action."

"Good improvement on your high kicks," Carly agreed.

Ellen beamed. "It's been a long time since I've watched the two of you dance together. I'm definitely going to attend your show again soon."

"Why wait?" Carly said. "We'll give you a little demonstration right now."

"In your street clothes, dear? I couldn't ask that."

"It's no biggie." Carly kicked off her shoes and unzipped her pants, peeling them off. She handed them to Ellen, who looked as if she couldn't decide whether to be horrified or fascinated by the younger woman's total lack of self-consciousness as Carly stood easily before her in nothing more than a pair of panties and a tight top.

"I'm going to take a wild stab here and guess you don't control the music today," Carly said in a low voice to Treena as she stepped back into her heels. Then raising her voice, she said, "Julie-Ann! Can we borrow the stereo system for one song?"

"Certainly," Julie-Ann said with such saccharine good will it made Treena's teeth ache. She came over to join them as Carly headed across the room to select music. "Hello," she said to Ellen and stuck her hand out. "I'm Julie-Ann. I'm the captain of Carly and Treena's dance troupe."

Treena was saved from having to make polite, insincere conversation when the intro to one of their regular show numbers began. Excusing herself, she met Carly out on the floor. They turned as one to face Ellen—just in time to hear Julie-Ann say, "I'll just go join them. Then you'll really have a treat."

Shit.

Before the young woman could make good on her intention, however, Ellen put a hand on her arm. "No, keep me company, dear. You can explain what the steps are as the girls do them."

"I can't decide," Carly muttered. "Which is worse, do you think, having Julie-Ann join us or having her critique our performance to Ellen?"

Treena shrugged but said under her breath, "I'd rather have her bad-mouthing us to Ellen, who thinks we're great unconditionally, than up here showing us up with her perky-ass high kicks." Raising her voice again, she called, "Restart the music, will you Julie-Ann? We'll take it from the top."

The younger woman shot her a venomous look, but crossed to the stereo.

On the downbeat they launched into the routine, and

for a few shining moments Treena recaptured the joy that dancing had given her before her eleven-month hiatus had turned everything she'd taken for granted into such a struggle. Ellen was an enthusiastic, uncritical audience who made her want to deliver her very best, and dancing with Carly was always fun. From their very first audition together, she and Carly had connected not only on a personal level but on a professional one, as well. It was as if each could predict the other's next move before she even made it, and they flowed through the number now in perfect unison. When they brought it to a conclusion with splits on the floor, their hands flung theatrically overhead, Treena felt a twinge of regret that it was over.

Then Ellen heaped effusive praise on them, and grinning, Treena stood and toweled off for the second time while the older woman continued to exclaim over how spectacular she and Carly were.

"Yes, that was really quite nice," Julie-Ann chimed in. "It's a shame you couldn't have seen Treena dance before she left to get married, though." She gave Ellen a look brimful of faux sympathy. "I'm afraid she lost her edge during her time away."

Die, you bitch. Before Treena could decide if she actually wanted to articulate her thought out loud, Ellen was patting Julie-Ann's hand.

"That's all right, dear. She has something infinitely more valuable."

Julie-Ann's eyebrows shot up. "What's that?"

"Loyalty. Manners. And much too much style to ever denigrate another dancer's abilities." With a graceful gesture to Treena and Carly, who stared at her mutely in the wake of her soft-voiced salvo, she politely herded them ahead of her across the floor and out the studio.

The door swinging shut behind them broke their stunned silence, and both dancers whooped.

"Oh, wow." Treena gasped, and Carly grinned at Ellen as they clattered down the stairs.

"Remind me never to piss you off," the blonde said gleefully. "You slipped that knife in so slick and clean, Julie-A is probably just now getting around to realizing the blood's starting to pool at her feet."

"Oh, yeah," Treena agreed. "You are *good.*"

Ellen shrugged. "One doesn't work in a library for thirty-odd years without learning a thing or two about handling people. That was a beautiful performance you two put on for me, and I wasn't about to let some self-absorbed young woman trash two of my favorite people after they'd given me one of the nicest presents I've had in recent memory." But her eyes widened in sudden horror as she looked at Treena, who had already descended the stairs and was waiting for her to pick her cautious way down to join her. "Oh, darling, I'm so sorry! I hustled you out of there so quickly you didn't even have time to change."

She looked down at her sweaty leotard, bare legs and character shoes, and shrugged. "Not a problem," she said, pulling her fringed scarf out of her dance bag and tying it around her hips. "I've got clothes in here and I'll change in the car. Carly should probably put her pants on, though. Thong panties and heels on the street might attract a little attention."

"Then again," Ellen said drily, "this is Vegas."

"So, maybe not," Carly agreed with a laugh. But she stopped to kick off her heels and don her slacks.

It set the tone for the day. They laughed as Treena dressed behind the car in the parking garage and laughed some more while she applied makeup and arranged her hair as Carly drove them to The Boulevard, Nevada's largest shopping mall. They were laughing still when they made their first stop at The Petite Sophisticates.

"Oh, look at this one," Carly said, pulling a periwinkle crepe-de-Chine camisole off the rack for Ellen to admire. "This would look beautiful with the suit you have on."

Treena looked up from the rack she was perusing and nodded agreement. "As well as with a lot of your other pieces."

Carly held the cobwebby garment against her own full breasts. "Man, would you look how tiny this thing is? I feel like Gulliver in the land of the Lilliputians in this store."

"Oh, now here's something." Treena extracted a pumpkin-colored suede shirt-jacket and brought it over to Ellen. "I know it's probably too hot right now to think of long sleeves, but look at this with your coloring."

Carly joined them. "Wow. It makes your skin look like pure cream. Don't you have a beige tank with a mock neck?"

"Yes." Ellen took the shirt and carried it over to a mirror. She held it up to herself, then set her purse down and pulled the shirt-jacket off the hanger to try it on.

"I thought so. That would look really hot with the jacket and a pair of jeans," Carly said. "And, oh, look at you. It looks fabulous with the black, too."

Ellen laughed. Really hot. That probably wasn't a phrase most people would associate with her.

"Here." Treena brought her a medium-length strand of chunky stones in cream, orange, verdigris-green, pale gold, and silver-blue that she'd picked out from a display on a nearby counter. "Try this with it."

Ellen put on the necklace and studied the overall effect in the triple mirror. The girls were right—the shirt-jacket's color truly did make the most of her complexion. Plucking up the tags dangling from a button, she twisted them around to read. "It's washable," she said in delight. "I'll take it."

She threw herself into the project after that, forgoing all her previous reservations and grabbing every colorful piece that grabbed her attention. Entering the dressing room a short while later, she hung an armful of clothing from the hooks on the walls and tossed a stack of soft T-shirts and tank tops on the bench. The selections were a mishmash of her style and taste and that of the dancers, and she reached for one Carly had selected first. She inspected the sage-green sleeveless tunic with its back tunnel drawstring, then pulled it on and buttoned it up the front.

The girls had insisted she model every number for them and she soon had three piles: the thumb-downs, the maybes—most of which she figured would end up with the rejects—and the definite buys. Whirling back into the dressing room after modeling one they'd all rejected, she said, "There's only one left, then I'll buy you two lunch. This shopping is hard work."

She pulled the periwinkle camisole that had been

Carly's first selection over her head and tugged it into place. Looking up from her adjustments, she saw her reflection in the mirror and froze. "Oh, my."

It was the sexiest garment she'd had on since she couldn't remember when. Not in a see-through or plunged-to-the-waist kind of way, but simply by flattering her coloring, making the most of her curves while disguising her flaws, and caressing her flesh like titillating fingers. It displayed a hint of cleavage before cupping her breasts, and it made her feel beautiful just wearing it.

"Ellen, you still with us?" Treena called.

"Yes. I'm just…um. Yes."

"Well, come on out and show us the final number," Carly said.

"I don't think I should display this one outside the dressing room. It's that camisole you picked."

Carly laughed, and Ellen jumped to hear her voice right outside the dressing room door. "No one's in the store but women, little lady," she said in an atrocious John Wayne imitation. Then her voice went back to normal. "In fact, there's no one here right now but us three and the salesclerk. So come on out."

She opened the door and stepped out.

"Oh, wow," Carly breathed. "Treena! Come see!"

Treena materialized from around the back side of the triple mirrors. She stopped short and stared. "Oh, Ellen," she sighed. "That is simply fabulous on you."

"Isn't it wonderful? I feel so pretty in it."

"Not to mention sexy as hell," Carly added. "You know what?" she demanded with a wry twist of her lips. "Pretty soon the only one not having sex in our little threesome is going to be me."

Ellen's heart skipped a beat at the mere thought of being held again, of being touched. She stood transfixed until Treena said, "I'm not having sex."

Carly made a rude noise. "Yet. But we all know it's just a matter of time." Her smile turned wistful. "I love sex and, boy, has it been a while since I've had any. I really miss it."

Ellen happened to be looking at Treena and caught the funny little nose wrinkle she made, as if she neither loved nor missed the act herself. But that couldn't be right. Still, intrigued, she said to Carly, "Would you mind seeing what other colors this comes in, darling?"

The moment the tall blonde disappeared from view, she turned to Treena. "Did you decide you're not that crazy about your Jax, after all?"

The dancer's eyes rounded. "Oh, no, I'm pretty crazy about him. Why would you think I wasn't?"

"When Carly mentioned sex you got this look on your face. I thought perhaps things were cooling off between you." Then a vision of Treena's face, the way it had looked when she'd returned from walking her young man to the door last night, flashed into her mind. "But that doesn't make sense. You looked as though you'd been kissed to within an inch of your life when you came back to the table last night."

"I had been. And I *love* the kissing part. The whole necking and petting part." Then she blinked and shot Ellen a glance as she flushed a painful-looking red.

But not what comes after? Ellen opened her mouth

to query the young woman further, encouraged by the fact that Treena looked at her as if she weren't totally adverse to the idea of discussing the matter further.

Then Carly strolled back into view with several more camisoles, and her young friend stiffened and said under her breath, "Please, I don't want to talk about this right now, okay?"

"Of course." She reached out and gave the redhead's hand a gentle pat. "But being a retired librarian is rather like being a pit bull. Neither species lets anything go once we've sunk our teeth into it. So resign yourself, darling. You and I *will* talk. Soon."

Twelve

Jax rolled his shoulders, then lifted his hand to tap out a rhythm on Treena's door. He supposed he should have called first, but he wanted to take her for a drive and he was afraid announcing his intentions might give her the opportunity to say no. He didn't know why it meant so much to him that she go. His head insisted it was strictly to get his agenda rolling, but his gut seemed to have a different theory.

One he didn't particularly want to study too closely.

A moment later the door opened and Treena stood on the other side clad in a faded aqua sports bra and low-riding cutoffs that were worn nearly white at the seams. Her face was scrubbed clean. For just an instant she stared blankly at him. Then she blinked, and a smile curved her lips, lit up her eyes. "Well, hi there."

"Hi, yourself. Sorry I didn't call ahead, but I thought maybe we could—" He broke off, staring at her nose.

"Hey. You've got freckles." Only a few, but he'd never noticed them before.

She rubbed her fingertips across the bridge of the object under discussion. "Oh, God. You caught me without makeup." Then she shrugged and stepped back. "But that's what you get when you don't give me warning. Come on in. I was just cleaning the place up."

"Need any help?"

"I bet you think I'm gonna murmur a polite 'no thank you,' don'tcha?" she said as she led him to the kitchen. "Well, more fool you, baby—I grew up with sisters who were always trying to wiggle out of their share of the work around the house, so I learned early to take my help where I can find it. Grab the dust mop out of the closet there. You can sweep up the dust bunnies on the living room floor while I finish dusting the furniture." She shot him an ironic smile over her shoulder. "Feel free to move the furniture. I know neatness ranks right up there on your list of essentials." She strode into the living room.

He eyed the roll of her hips as he strolled after her, floor duster in hand. Music poured out of the stereo in the armoire, and the swivel in Treena's walk grew more pronounced the closer she came to the source, her hips swinging in time to the music. She sank into a straight-back crouch in front of the credenza, her butt bumping and gyrating in sync with the bass backbone of the jazzy tune. He watched for a minute, mesmerized, then turned his attention to the floor.

Flipping the dust mop over, he studied it for a second, then attached the disposable cloth to the rubber pad and flipped it back and began gliding the appliance along the hardwood floor. It slid easily into narrow spaces and beneath low furniture, and he grinned at the back of Treena's head. "This thing is pretty cool."

She twisted to look at him and the corner of her mouth tipped up. "Yeah. It's one of those things that makes you wish you'd invented it, doesn't it? Simple, effective and bound to make millions."

He eyed her thoughtfully. "What would you do if you had a million dollars?"

"Buy a studio," she replied promptly.

He stopped pushing the dust mop around the floor to stare at her. "Like—what?—Warner Brothers?"

She laughed so hard she plopped over onto her butt. Raising her feet, she spun on her rear to face him. "No, I think I'd probably need more than a million for that. I'm talking about having my own dance studio. A little place where I could teach classes and rent rehearsal space."

"You want to be a *teacher*?"

"Yes." Clearly, however, he'd sounded every bit as incredulous as he felt, for she gave him a crooked smile and said, "I know it probably doesn't sound all that exciting to a guy who's traveled the world, but I like teaching dance and—believe it or not—I'm good at it. I was saving up for my own place, but then…well, things happened."

He wanted to ask what things, but she cocked a slender eyebrow at him and demanded, "What about you? What would *you* do if you had a million bucks?"

"I actually won one point three million at the Aviation Club de France in Paris two years ago."

Skintight

Her jaw dropped open.

"Before you get too impressed, though, know that doesn't make me a millionaire. I had to give almost half of it back to Uncle Sam for taxes."

Treena snapped her mouth shut. "Oh. Well, gee. Poor baby. Only six or seven hundred thousand dollars for a single night's work?"

"Four days' work, sweetheart. Four *long* days. Not to mention travel time."

"Hell-o! To *Paris*."

"I can see I'm not going to get any sympathy for the long, hard, nerve-racking days I put in, am I?"

She snorted, but then looked at him with bright-eyed interest. "What was the most you bet on a single hand in that game?"

He didn't even have to think about it. "One hundred and ninety-two large."

"Large being…?"

"A grand."

Her jaw dropped. "As in *dollars*? You bet one hundred and ninety-two thousand *dollars*?"

He grinned at the look on her face. But that win was a good memory, and he said, "You should have seen it, Treen. I went 'all in,' which means I pushed all of my chips into the pot."

"Oh my God," she moaned.

"That's a favorite tactic of the Europeans, but I'm usually a fairly conservative better, and the players on the circuit know it. So it worked in my favor. My stiffest competition in that hand was an Australian named Benny. He actually had a better hand than mine, but he folded because he thought I must have something massively great to be betting it all." A big smile stretched his lips at the memory. "There was three hundred and seven thousand dollars in that pot."

Treena shook her head. "I can't even imagine. I would have been sitting in a pool of sweat." Her voice squeaked on the last word, but immediately recovering her poise, she cocked an eyebrow at him. "So. Wanna be a silent partner in a nice dance studio?" Without giving him a moment to decide whether she was serious or not, she demanded, "What did you buy yourself with your windfall?"

"A new suit. Well, the jacket, anyway."

"A suit jacket? That was it?"

"Hey, it was a really nice jacket." When she continued to stare at him as if he were crazy, he shrugged. "There wasn't actually a helluva lot I wanted. But I did take the Eurostar over to London for a few days."

"Oh, my God." Lounging back on her elbows, she stretched her long, bare legs in front of her on the hardwood floor. "Paris, London, the *Eurostar.* I could listen to this all day. You're my Living Vicariously guy. Tell me everything you can remember about the things you saw."

So he did, and as he regaled her with tales of London and Paris he had a tough time believing anyone could fake the level of enthrallment that she displayed. Although she kept trying to dust, she would invariably turn around and stare at him with bright, fascinated eyes as he described a district or a landmark. He tried to chase dust bunnies, but she kept asking questions that made him cross his arms over the dust mop and talk some more.

Finally he couldn't take it any longer. She was so enthusiastic that he had to touch her, had to feel for himself the heat that came off her skin, that emanated from
her personality. He crossed the room, where he
squatted, scooped his arms under her thighs and behind
her back, and surged to his feet.

A startled whoop escaped her, and she clutched his
shoulders. "What on earth…?"

He rocked his mouth over hers.

"Oh," she murmured beneath his lips. And kissed
him back.

He knew this wasn't the best idea in the world, that
he should be going about a more cold-blooded seduction, should be deliberately driving her out of her mind
while keeping a firm lid on his own emotions. But like
a rock tossed into a well, he sank without a trace. Her
lips were soft and sweet, her mouth was hot and tasted
of coffee and Treena and red-hot desire, and he couldn't
get enough—not nearly enough. Without breaking the
kiss, he strode over to the couch and dropped down
upon it, his long, tall dancer a warm welcome weight
in his lap.

They kissed for minutes, for hours, for God alone
knew how long. Eventually he lifted his head and gazed
down at her. "Man," he said. "You do something to me."
And that was the X factor in his game plan, the contin-
gency he'd hadn't planned on.

"Tell me about it," she agreed with a breathless little laugh. "You do something to me, too." Then, hooking her hand around the nape of his neck, she tugged his
head back down so she could kiss him once again.

He took it like a man, went without a fight, his right palm spreading over her throat, his thumb and fingers grasping her jaw while he widened his mouth over hers. Tongue slid against tongue and they both groaned.

Treena felt herself losing control and tried to grab hold of it before it escaped completely. The only trouble was Jax could kiss like no one she'd ever met. Minutes passed and every so often a neuron would suddenly fire off in her brain, reminding her to rein it all in. Yet she'd immediately be lost once again beneath the sensations bombarding her from every angle.

When his hand trailed down her throat and onto her chest, she returned to her senses. She didn't so much stiffen as collect herself from her complete sprawl across his lap, but her compacted position halted the downward trek of his fingers.

It didn't, however, stop his talented lips from pressing and rubbing against her own, nor his supple tongue, which flicked across hers in a teasing foray that was boldly dominant then infuriatingly elusive. With a frustrated moan, she grabbed his head and held him in place as she locked her mouth on his.

So involved was she that she barely noticed his hand as it moved to cover the thrust of her breast until he pinched her nipple between his thumb and index finger.

She inhaled sharply as lightning speared from the point of contact to nerves deep between her thighs. But before she could decide whether it was the best feeling in the world or perhaps the scariest, his hand was gone, his fingertips lightly tracing the outline of her sports bra.

He raised his head and gazed down at her. "You've

got the silkiest skin," he murmured, giving her a sleepy smile. Hooking his fingers around one of the garment's straps, he slid it off her shoulder. "Your body is so fit and hard, but your skin is soft. Incredibly soft. Incredibly smooth." Bending his head, he gently bit the flesh he'd just exposed. "I want to touch every square inch of it."

Oddly enough, Treena thought that was beginning to sound like a really good idea.

Jax had slow hands, and he didn't seem to suffer from the usual need to push them straight up her blouse or down her pants. She knew he was aroused, for she could hear the harsh rasp of his breathing, feel the hard prod of his erection nudging her hip where it curved into his lap. But he continued to alternately nip at her shoulder, then lick the tiny indentations he created there.

He took his time with the process, too, interrupting himself only to press kisses up and down her throat. And where his lips weren't, his hands were. His fingers brushed down her arms, along her neck, across her collarbone. Occasionally they wandered onto the washed-out aqua lycra covering her breasts, but always they steered clear of actually touching her nipples again.

Until Treena reached the point where she could concentrate on nothing else. Wriggling on his lap, she grabbed a fistful of his sun-streaked brown hair and guided his mouth back to hers. The next time his hand encroached upon her sports bra, she turned into his touch, nudging her breast into his palm.

Yes! Triumph detonated in Jax's chest, and he smiled against Treena's lips. God, he'd never worked so hard for a woman's response in his life—let alone felt such appreciation upon finally getting it. He'd felt her withdraw earlier when he'd slid his hand onto her tit, and he'd backed off, determined to demonstrate a little finesse.

Only he'd found himself caught in a web of his own making.

Part of him wanted nothing more than to strip her bare, to bury himself deep inside of her and satisfy his burning need to get off once and for all. But the rest of him really enjoyed stroking her, feeling the plush satin of her skin beneath his hands, the light wash of goose bumps that rose in the wake of his fingertips when he touched a particularly responsive area.

He couldn't decide who this woman was. Was she the hot-blooded good-time girl who'd given as good as she'd got upon the hood of her car and who came close to letting him go the distance on the first full day of their acquaintance? Or was she the leerier, more cautious woman of today?

For a while, that evening in the parking garage, she'd been as hot as he had been—he didn't doubt that for a minute. But she'd broken it off all the same, and he realized she'd displayed some of the same confusion and wariness she was exhibiting today.

He didn't have time to figure it out now, for up until this point his brain had been keeping pace with his hard-on for control of his body, and perhaps logic had even been winning.

Suddenly, though, all thought was being left in the dust.

If Treena was acting he didn't care. The breathy moans of surprise she made when he pinched her nipple between his fingers went straight to his cock. It, in turn, pushed insistently against the solid curve of her hip, shifting and prodding her as if wondering where the hell the entrance to paradise had gone.

Her old aqua sports bra had to go, and he slid both thumbs beneath its abbreviated hem and pushed it up over her breasts. He half thought she might stiffen up on him again, but he was the one who froze when he saw the pale curves he'd uncovered.

They were just as he remembered them from the night he'd stared holes down the neckline of her sexy black-and-gold dress. Only this time he got to see them in their entirety, and they were all gently rounded and creamy, her nipples the color of warm cinnamon, hard and tight and pointed straight at him.

It was Treena who crossed her hands over her chest and peeled the garment off over her head.

"God," he said, and his voice sounded as if it had been shredded with a cheese grater. "They're even prettier than I imagined."

Her mouth quirked up on one side. "Yeah, why is it tits are such a magnet for men? Even the two gay guys in our troupe comment on them."

"It's because we don't have any." His fingers stole along her diaphragm to cup the underside of her left breast. "If we did, we probably wouldn't get a damn thing done for messing with them all day long. They're just so aesthetically pleasing." He gave her breast a slight shake, then sighed in pure pleasure at the resultant jiggle. "Action and reaction," he muttered, then looked up at her with a sheepish smile. "This has got to be the most rewarding reaction of all."

Her eyes had started drifting shut, but she widened them for a moment. "Careful. I just got a glimpse of that geek factor you warned me about. I mean, please, action and reaction? It's a boob. It's got jiggle." She flashed him a smile. "Still. The reaction's not too shabby from this side of the road, either."

"Yeah? Let's give that a closer study." He bent his head, but on his way from her chest to the spiky little nipples calling his name he got sidetracked. "Hey, you've got two, four, six, *seven* freckles," he said counting the tiny specks sprinkled across her modest cleavage like a curmudgeonly serving of vanilla bean in ice cream.

"What is it with you and freckles? That's the second time today you've commented on them. Are you a fetishist or something?"

"I never thought so." He grinned up at her. "But it's like stumbling across sudden treasure, so maybe I am." He leered at her. "Show me a freckle, and I'll show you uncontrollable lust."

"Ooh." She wiggled against his hard-on.

He drew in a sharp breath. "Okay, that does it. No more Mr. Nice Guy." He pushed up her breast, lowered his head and locked his lips over her nipple. It poked his tongue, and he pressed it toward the roof of his mouth and sucked.

"Oh, my gaaaw—" Her head dropped back, which shoved her breast deeper into his mouth. He licked, and she inhaled sharply. He blew against her damp nipple, and she shivered. He sucked, and she went insane.

The latter reaction was his favorite. He liked her panting and blurry eyed, and he forgot all about his own need for release as he set about seeing just how far he could tease her before she fell off the end of the earth.

He released her breast, pleased when she promptly placed her own hand beneath it and lifted it to his mouth. Her other hand speared through his hair.

He smoothed his freed fingers down her diaphragm, over the smooth skin of her abdomen, down to explore the deep dimple of her navel, lower still to tease beneath the waistband of her cutoffs, which rode the swell of her hips. His erection beat time to the "Hallelujah Chorus" when her legs fell apart.

This position wasn't working, though, and he eased her off his lap and onto her back on the couch, turning to lie on his side beside her. She blinked up at him and, propping his head in his hand, he smiled at her flushed cheeks, slumberous eyes and swollen mouth. "You comfy? That was getting a little awkward." Without awaiting an answer, he lowered his head and kissed her again.

She moaned softly and ran her hand down his chest. Fingers plucking at the fabric of his T-shirt, she made a dissatisfied sound and disengaged her mouth. "No fair. I'm topless and you should be, too."

He wrestled his arms out of the shirt and pulled it off. It was still covering his face when her hand spread against the bare swell of his pectorals. Then he felt her shift, and a moment later her mouth replaced her fingers. He yanked the enveloping folds of the shirt over his head.

It felt so good, but fearing for his control, he sank his hands into her hair and, wrapping the soft curls around his fists, pulled back until her lips left his chest and she looked up at him. "I've been thinking about this from practically the minute we met," he admitted. "And we don't want it to be over before it even begins." Exerting force to bring her face closer, he bent his head to reach her lips, but it was a futile attempt, for they were no longer on an equitable level.

She laughed and scooted up, her breasts rubbing against his diaphragm before flattening against his chest. Curving her long, strong arms around his neck, she kissed him.

And just like that, heat flared between them again, burning even hotter than before.

He tightened his fist in her hair and kissed her more roughly, reached deeper with his tongue in a bid to lick up every single flavor. Need rode him hard, and he swept his other hand down to her breast, then ripped his mouth free an instant later and, disentangling her arms from around his neck, he slipped down the couch to replace his kneading fingers with his lips. His freed hand insinuated itself between her legs, and he curved his fingers and pressed his palm against her mound.

"Oh, God, Jax." Treena's hips bucked into his touch. She slicked her hands across the width of his shoulders, squeezing the rounded muscles where they flowed into his arms when he rubbed the seam that ran between her thighs. He took his hand away, and with a shaky little exhalation she smoothed her hands over his chest.

But he wasn't finished, not by a long shot. Releasing her nipple, he turned his head to watch himself unbutton her cutoffs and pull down the zipper. The low-cut jeans immediately sagged open, the two sides falling apart to display lacy purple panties. He eased his fingers beneath the scalloped waistband and watched his hand disappear. His fingertips slid over a small, silky V of hair, then glided between plump lips of baby-smooth skin that was slick with desire. A sound suspiciously close to a growl escaped his throat, and he kept pushing downward until his middle finger found the opening it sought and entered her.

"Oh!" She reached for his zipper, as well, but between his finger striving for her G-spot and his palm flattening over the slippery pearl of her clit, she kept fumbling the task. She continued to clamp the small golden tab between her fingers even as it became evident her impending orgasm rendered her unable to recall what it was she was supposed to do with it once she had it in her grasp.

He could wait. Barely, it was true, but still, he could do it. He wanted her to come first; then, like the Marines, he was going in. The mobility of his hand was restricted by her cutoffs, but her arched back thrust her breasts ceiling-ward, and he hunched over to lap one stiff, straining nipple.

And that did it for her. She was amazingly tight around the single finger he'd buried in her, and the hot satin vise snugged around it clamped against his forefinger's breadth over and over again as low, breathy wails stuttered out of her throat.

"That's it, sweetheart," he whispered, looking up at the pure bliss on her face. He scraped his teeth over her nipple and felt another, harder contraction tug at his finger. "That's it. Come for me. Ah, Treena, yes! God almighty, that's a thing of beauty."

She collapsed a moment later, all the tension that had arched her body like a hard-strung bow fully released. He felt amazingly great for someone with a raging hard-on who hadn't got his, but there was just something so satisfying about having gotten her off. Or—perhaps more specifically—having watched and felt her getting off. Besides, his time had come.

He eased his finger from her body and his hand from her pants and stretched to kiss her, smiling against her lips at the laziness of the kiss she returned. When the girl came, it clearly depleted every store of energy she had. Reaching one-handedly into his hip pocket, he extracted his wallet and fumbled out the condom he'd been carrying in it ever since he'd met her. "You okay?" he whispered, removing her hand from where it rested limply against his fly.

She blinked. "Um-hmm." But she didn't move, merely blinked some more. "I don't seem to have any bones in my body."

He laughed. "Take your time. I'm not planning to start without you."

Her eyes widened and her gaze flashed downward to where his erection pressed against her hip. "Really?" She seemed surprised by that, and as if not quite trusting the veracity of his words, she struggled to get all her limbs moving at the same time. "Oh, man." She fumbled the condom from his fingers. "Here. Lemme give you a hand with that. Get this show on the road." She reached for him.

Jax intercepted her hand. "Whoa. Slow down. There's no rush."

She looked confused and he studied her, trying to figure out what the hell was going on. She acted as if this was some huge new marvel she'd never experienced, and damned if it didn't feel new to him, too. How did she get him so mixed up, he barely knew up from down?

Not that this was the time to think about it. That became crystal clear when Treena brushed her hand against his erection. He jerked, his dick suddenly insistent as her fingers stroked his erection once again. The lady was clearly in the mood for action.

He lowered his head again to give her a let's-kick-this-up-a-notch kiss.

Things were just beginning to heat up nicely once more when the phone rang. Treena's lips stilled beneath his for an instant, then she relaxed against him. Looping one arm around his neck, she unzipped his fly with her free hand and reached into his pants. He sucked in a fierce breath at the feel of her hand wrapping around him.

The phone stopped ringing and the machine kicked on. Treena's message murmured in the background. Then Carly's frantic voice interrupted his mindless haze of pleasure.

"Oh, shit, oh, shit, you're not there. I cut myself washing dishes, and oh, God, Treen, it's bleeding like crazy and I can see the *bone*."

The next thing he knew Treena's hand was gone, his ass was kissing the hardwood floor, and she was bounding off the couch, leaping over his prone body. She hit the floor running, one hand clutching her sagging cutoffs as, swearing like a trucker, she sprinted for the phone.

Thirteen

By the time Treena snagged a nurse who had paused at the E.R. desk to make a notation on a chart, the sun was definitely headed for the horizon. "Excuse me," she said to the woman. "Can you give me some idea when they're going to get Carly Jacobsen in? She's been waiting for over two hours."

"Sorry, miss, it's been a busy evening. We triage for most life-threatening traumas first."

"But she cut herself to the bone. She's bleeding!"

"Let me see." The nurse came around the desk and followed her over to where Carly and Jax sat waiting. Squatting in front of the injured woman, she gently peeled back the cloth Carly had pressed to her wound. "Oh, boy. Washing a glass, were you?"

"Yes. How did you know?"

"We see a lot of these." She covered it back up and rose to her feet. "But you've stopped the bleeding yourself, so I'm afraid you'll just have to wait to have it stitched up until a room is clear. There's been a turf war and the cops brought us several gangbangers who are also bleeding. Only their wounds were caused by knife and gunshot wounds." She gave Carly's arm a little pat and turned on her rubber-soled heel and strode away.

"I'm sorry," Treena said, looking at her friend, who had tipped her head back against the wall and closed her eyes. She reclaimed her seat beside her.

"It's okay, Treen. She's right. This may be a big deal to me, but it's hardly in the same category as a gunshot wound."

"Does it hurt?"

"No, it's kind of numb right now. I'm just hoping they get me in before the numbness wears off."

"They will," Jax assured her, speaking for the first time in quite a while from the other side of Treena.

She turned to him gratefully. "See. So says a guy who's probably been in hospitals all over the world."

"Well, that might be overstating the case a bit, but I've had an encounter or two with the sort of injuries that start out numb then hurt later—and the numbness usually lasts until the anesthesia kicks in."

He gave Treena a do-you-think-she's-buying-it grimace, and she knew he was just making it up as he went along. But it seemed to be working, for Carly nodded wearily without opening her eyes. She even smiled slightly.

"That's good to know," she whispered. "I'm a baby when it comes to pain."

"Then you'll want to be sure to ask them to prescribe

something you can take before the numbing agent wears off," Jax advised gently.

His thigh brushed Treena's as he settled back in his chair and her nipples immediately beaded and she went all tight and achy inside. That was a first, she thought. She didn't usually feel this way about a man after making out. But then she'd never experienced anything quite as intense as the time she'd spent on the couch with Jax. Nor had men ever stuck around long once she'd disappointed them. And if they didn't take off, *she* wanted nothing more than to run for the hills. She'd certainly never actually anticipated round two.

She reached out and took Carly's free hand in her own, lacing their fingers together in hopes of anchoring her thoughts in something more appropriate to the situation and setting. But she couldn't seem to quit sneaking sidelong glances at Jax. Before the phone had blasted everything else from her mind, she'd been in post-orgasmic bliss. She'd had her hand boldly down Jax's pants and for the first time in ages she'd felt the throbbing heat of a hard penis beneath her palm.

Then she'd been jerked from the boneless, lethargic haze of her own pleasure into Carly's kitchen, with its trail of browning droplets spattered across the light vinyl floor between the sink and the phone. Her friend had been on the verge of hysteria, the dogs and cats had all been milling about adding to the confusion, and she'd had next to no time to pull her scattered wits together. Only Jax's calming presence had helped ground her as she'd settled Carly down and pressed a clean towel to her deep wound before bundling her friend into Jax's rental car for the drive to the hospital.

And now that she had the leisure to sort through her emotions, she couldn't. So many scrambled through her system. She felt satiated, because she had never experienced an orgasm that was even close to the one Jax had given her. Guilty because she'd left him high and dry. Sorry, considering how great the preliminaries had been, they had missed the main event. Worried that it would have been every bit as disappointing as she'd come to expect if they *had* brought it to the conclusion they'd been steaming toward before the interruption.

Finally she regretted that poor Carly had to sit in a crowded emergency room so long with a sliced up hand, and she was ashamed that her friend's welfare wasn't even close to the top of her concerns.

"Omigawd, the babies!" Carly's eyes abruptly snapped open, and she raised her head away from the wall, tension radiating from the suddenly stiff set of her shoulders. "I was going to feed them as soon as I finished the dishes, but seeing my own blood drove it clean out of my head. They're probably climbing the walls by now."

Treena rose to her feet. "I left without my cell phone, but I'll find a land line and call Mack to see if he'll feed them for you."

"Ask him if he'll take Buster and Rufus out to do their biz, too."

"Gotcha."

"Here." Jax stood, as well, and pulled his cell phone from his pocket. He held it out to her. "You don't have to look for a phone. You can use mine."

"Even better." She studied his face, which was momentarily close enough to her own for their breaths to commingle, and her heart performed a slow roll in her chest. He hadn't whined once about being so abruptly cut off just when he was about to reap his sexual reward. He had been, in fact, nothing short of wonderful. But he'd also been much quieter than usual, and she wondered what he really thought about all that had happened today. Operating on impulse, she stretched up to plant a quick kiss on his lips. "Thank you," she said, settling back on her heels. "For everything." She took the phone. "I'll just take this outside where it's quieter."

She talked to Mack minutes later and once she explained the situation he was ready to take care of the babies that very minute. With an admonishment to tell Carly not to worry about a thing, to simply take care of herself, he rang off, leaving Treena smiling.

He was a good friend.

And thinking how comforting a good friend could be in a situation like this, she dialed Ellen. The older woman was the closest thing she and Carly had to a mom—at least in this state. Moreover, Ellen *knew* Carly as Carly's own mother did not, and Treena felt a sudden desire to touch base with her.

The accident spilled out of her the moment Ellen picked up and Ellen's response immediately soothed her jangled nerves.

"Oh, darling! How awful for her—and for you, too. Where did you take her? Desert Springs?"

"Yes."

"I'll be right there."

"You don't have to do that." She tried to sound as if she actually meant it, but in truth Ellen's stated intention sounded like the best idea she'd heard all day.

"Of course I do."

"We could be here all night," she warned Ellen. "They don't consider her injuries real high on their list of priorities."

"I don't care how long it takes," Ellen said. "Hang tight, sweetheart. I'll be there in ten minutes. Twenty tops, if traffic is bad."

The phone went dead.

Treena turned to go back inside, then realized she needed to call work and let them know what was going on. It was unlikely she'd be able to make the eight-o'clock show—and God knew she wasn't in the greatest mental shape for it even if she could get there in time. But one didn't simply blow off a performance in *la Stravaganza* and expect to remain employed. Stepping away from the automatic door, she keyed in the general manager's number.

A few minutes later she disconnected, and with Vernetta-Grace's advice to take the rest of the night off, she went back through the E.R. doors, hit anew by the scents and sounds of humanity awaiting help. Codes were called over the loudspeaker, children cried or ran around unchecked, and adults yelled for attention or simply slumped quietly in their institutional chairs, as they waited to be taken back into the mysterious depths of the E.R.

She took her seat between Carly and Jax once again. "Mack said to tell you he's 'on it' and not to worry about anything except getting yourself fixed up."

"He's such a sweetie."

"Yeah. And Ellen's on her way."

"Oh, bless her, bless her, *bless her!*"

Treena laughed. "Now Carly, don't hold it all in where it can fester and spread its poison. Tell us how you really feel."

The blonde smiled wanly. "You know that I regress when I'm sick or hurt. Well, I really need a mommy fix right now. Oh, not *my* mom's brand of mothering. But Ellen is just what the doctor ordered." Her lips, more accustomed to smiling than sneering, curled witheringly. "Or would be, I'm sure, if I could only get in to see one."

"Ellen's the best," Treena agreed. She gave her friend a gentle jostle with her elbow. "Hey, maybe she'll bring cookies."

She didn't, but she did bring immediate comfort. Striding into the E.R. waiting area a brief while later, Ellen promptly zeroed in on their little threesome. Clad in one of the colorful tops she'd bought during their shopping spree yesterday—this one a pretty purple with enough gray in it to accentuate the silver in her salt-and-pepper hair—she swept up to Carly and leaned forward to give her a careful hug. As she straightened she brushed a spike of the younger woman's hair back from her forehead. "Are you all right? You're terribly pale."

"I'm kinda freaked," Carly admitted. "But I'm not too bad, really. It doesn't hurt, and Jax says it probably won't if they give me something to take before the numbness wears off. Anyhow, I'm doing okay as long as I don't think about it too closely. I don't like blood, and I *really* don't like seeing skin split open to reveal the inner workings. Especially my own."

"I'm sure you don't." Ellen took a seat on the other side of her. "If you'd cared to view that sort of thing you probably would have become a nurse instead of a dancer."

"Exactly!"

Treena had known Ellen would be the antidote they needed. The older woman brought a natural warmth and bedrock common sense to every situation.

Jax suddenly climbed to his feet, and she swung around to stare up at him.

"Look," he said, thrusting his hands in his pants pockets as he looked back at her. "As long as Ellen is here, would you mind if I took off?" He glanced beyond her at the retired librarian. "That is, if you don't object to seeing them both home?"

"No, of course I don't."

Treena climbed to her feet, as well, feeling uncharacteristically awkward, as if she were suddenly all arms and legs without a flexible joint between them. Damn. He *was* angry with her. He'd simply been too well-mannered to leave her and Carly to cope on their own.

"Don't look like that," he commanded and, wrapping his fingers around her arm, led her beyond earshot of the other two women.

She stood stiffly within his grasp. "You're mad at me."

"No. I'm not. I know what you're thinking, but this has nothing to do with what happened—or I guess more accurately what didn't happen—earlier. It's just that tomorrow is the first day of the tournament, and I need to psyche myself up for it."

"Oh, my gosh, is that starting already?"

"Yeah. And my process before it begins is to spend a quiet evening dealing with everything that's been going on in my life so none of it's on my mind when I play."

"Uh-huh," she said, and she couldn't prevent the slight edge of cynicism that crept into her voice. "So what were you doing at my place, then?"

"I never intended to stay there long. I just thought maybe we could go for a ride or something. Blow the cobwebs free." He rubbed his hands up and down her arms. "Believe it or not, jumping your bones wasn't in my game plan. And I really didn't plan on this." A tip of his head indicated the teeming waiting room.

Even though she suspected it made her pathetically needy, she was nevertheless soothed by the explanation. It robbed her of the fear that, once again, her sexual performance had driven a man away. "Okay, then." She tried to step back, but his hands tightened on her arms, and she tilted her head back a bit to look up at him. "Good luck on getting your karma in tune, or whatever. And good luck tomorrow, too."

"You wanna wish me luck?"

"Of course."

"Then I'll take this." He lowered his head and kissed her. She was barely able to stand on her own two feet by the time he raised his head again. "For luck," he said, then smiled down at her. "I love seeing that look on your face."

"Hmm?" She blinked up at him, then made a concerted effort to focus. "What look?"

"That blurry-eyed, 'Do me' look."

A sputter of laughter escaped her, but she jabbed stiffened fingers into his hard gut and faked outrage. "My God, nothing wrong with *your* ego, is there?"

"Ego's got nothing to do with it. I just recognize the signs when I see them. And, honey, you've got more postings than a military installation. Do me," he crooned softly in her ear. "Do me, do me, do me."

She bit the inside of her cheek to forestall the grin she felt building. "Be sure to turn that fat head sideways when you go through the doors," she advised. "We wouldn't want you to give yourself a concussion trying to get it through the exit head-on. Though come to think of it, you're in the right place for it." She stepped back to study him. "Still, you've seen how long it takes to get attention for anyone who's not bleeding to death, and sitting around while your brain swells against your skull probably won't improve your game any."

He laughed. "Man, you don't give an inch, do you? I'll call you as soon as I can."

And before she could muster a single reply, he pulled her to him for another hard kiss, then turned and strode away.

She watched him disappear through the glass doors then wandered back to the area where they'd been waiting. She was almost there before she realized Carly was no longer in her seat.

"Did they finally call her?" she asked, flopping into the chair beside Ellen.

"Yes, once I had a little talk with the triage nurse about this hospital's so-called fast-track policy for the less acute care patients."

"You are so amazing. How do you know all these things?"

"A million years' worth of swimming through the public library system. I know how to research and I worked with the general public for so long that I've gotten pretty good at dealing with problems." She smiled. "And the fact is that Carly should have been sorted to the fast-track area the hospital's so proud of when she first came in. Only the E.R. had several things hit at once around that time, so she sort of got lost in the shuffle."

"But I talked to a nurse not too long ago, and she took a look at Carly's wound. Shouldn't she have directed us to the right place?"

"Apparently after she checked her out she did see to it that Carly's chart was moved to the right stack. I just got it moved up a little."

Treena slumped down and rested her head on the smaller woman's shoulder. "You're my hero."

Ellen laughed. "And my rates are reasonable, too." They were quiet for a few minutes, then she said softly, "Speaking of which, you said something intriguing yesterday about your preference for foreplay over sex. Would you care to tell Dr. Ellen what you meant?"

Treena slowly sat back up while she battled a knee-jerk impulse to say she'd rather not. The fact was, though, she truly *would* like to talk to another woman about it—and as close as she was to Carly it was just too embarrassing to admit she wasn't all that crazy about one of the very things her friend professed to love most. Maybe if she'd come clean about it years ago, she wouldn't feel so awkward admitting it now. But she'd let the omission go on much too long, and now she didn't know how to confess without sounding like an idiot. Or worse, like a big, fat liar.

With Ellen, on the other hand, she didn't have more than a decade-long history of dodging the truth. Plus, the older woman was the least judgmental person she knew, and she turned in her seat to face her. She opened her mouth, then closed it.

"This is embarrassing," she muttered.

"Ah, darling, no." Ellen patted her hand. "The last thing I want is to embarrass you."

"Oh, trust me, you haven't. I embarrass myself." She shrugged. "I'm thirty-five years old and presumed by many a man to be the last of the red-hot mamas. That has more to do with me as the dancer than me as the person, I know. But still. When men take me out, they think they're going to get the night of their life. In reality, I stink at sex."

Mack came to an abrupt stop. *Whoa. This is not a conversation I want to be involved in.* Glad he'd come in through the main hospital entrance and not the E.R. doors where the two women would be more likely to spot him, he stepped back to put a pillar between himself and their line of vision. He watched Ellen reach for Treena's hand as he tried to decide whether to leave, make a noisy entrance or wait them out.

"Whenever I hear a woman claim full responsibility for bad sexual relations," Ellen said drily, "I have to wonder if she's truly at fault, or if it's simply her choice of partners that stinks?"

"Probably a combination of both," Treena admitted. "I've certainly run into my share of guys who immediately expect stuff from me that I might be willing to do if I knew them a little better. But mostly it's me, I'm afraid. Like I told you yesterday, I love the kissing and the petting part. But when it comes to the main event, well, I'm sort of a control freak."

"You like to tell them what to do?"

Treena made a sound that was half snort, half rueful laugh. "No, they'd probably get off on that. I really, really dislike *losing* control. No doubt my unwillingness to truly cut loose is rooted in all manner of Freudian crap that would single-handedly put some shrink's kid through college. But I already know the underlying reason."

"Which is?"

"I learned young that in order to get where I wanted to go, I had to depend on myself. I guess I'm afraid if I ever put myself in someone else's hands everything will go to hell." She shrugged. "The bottom line is I slam the brakes on whenever I feel like I'm too close to losing command of my senses."

She swivelled in her seat to face Ellen. "But you know what? I have a feeling that it might be different with Jax. Things are already...different." Color washed up her face. "He makes me feel things I didn't think I was capable of feeling. And he sure makes me forget about keeping the lid on. In fact, if Carly hadn't called when she did this afternoon—" she hesitated, slanting a peek at Ellen "—well, let's just say this conversation might have been moot. Long story short: he'd just given me one of the greatest moments of my life. And we were about to test my He-could-be-the-exception-to-my-freezing-up-in-the-main-event the-ory. Instead he ended up with the short end of the stick."

Okay, way too much information. Mack took a step forward with every intention of announcing himself and stopping this. It was too discomfiting by half to listen to, too close to overhearing the details of one of his daughters' sex lives for his peace of mind. He stopped himself, however, because he knew Ellen would put a halt to it at any minute. And there was no use embarrassing the two of them with his presence.

But all she said was, "Is that why he lit out of here so fast when I got here? Was he upset about being left hanging?"

"No. I mean, that's what I thought at first, too—that maybe, even though he'd been such a rock for us, he was secretly resentful. But he insisted it was strictly because he had to get ready for the first day of his tournament, which starts tomorrow. But, Ellen? For the first time in forever I'm seriously toying with the idea of getting down and dirty with a man. This is a big step for me, and God knows I've got enough other problems in my life already to make me think twice. So am I crazy to be considering taking a chance on him?"

Mack folded his arms over his chest, prepared for Ellen to tell Treena to keep her knees together, to save herself for marriage.

"Well, let me see if I have this straight," the former librarian said. "You had an orgasm today? And that's un-usual for you?"

What are you, nuts? You don't query young women about their orgasms!

"Yeah. At least of a partner-induced variety."

"Then, darling, I'd say you'd be crazy if you *didn't* take the chance."

He felt his jaw sag.

Treena leaned closer to the petite woman. "Can I ask you something personal?"

"Sure. I've been prying like mad into your personal life—I think it's only fair to reciprocate."

"What do *you* think of sex? Like, um, what was it like with, you know, your husband?" She made a sound of disgust. "Good God. I sounded less like a stammering adolescent when I actually was one."

"Probably because you hadn't yet been disappointed in that department and so had nothing to lose. But as for your question, sex with Winston was fabulous. He could be a real stick-in-the-mud in day-to-day matters. But close those bedroom doors and he was a wild man. God, I miss making love with him. He wasn't my first, but I knew from our initial time together that he'd be my last—at least until death did us part. Have you ever heard that lady in the drawing room, whore in the bedroom adage? Well, Winston was my banker in the living room, stud in the bedroom. I loved the juxtapostion of those two sides of his personality.

"Lord, that man introduced me to positions and—well, you don't want to hear that. But if I had only one wish, Treena, it would be that you experience something even *half* as wonderful. So my advice? You go for it with your Jax."

"I just might do that." Then Treena giggled, a sound Mack didn't think he'd ever heard out of her before.

Ellen smiled at her fondly. "What's so funny?"

"Well, I was just thinking. Mack seems to have this image of you as some stereotypical librarian. I'm not sure where he got it, because you only have to spend an hour in your company to know it's about as far from the truth as a person can get."

"Not to mention an insult to librarians everywhere," Ellen said acerbically.

"Still, wouldn't you just love to be a fly on the wall if he could hear you now? You have to admit you're much stiffer around him, but if he ever heard the real you I bet he'd have a heart attack."

His head thunked back against the post, and he rubbed his hand over his chest. *Close enough, kid,* he thought.

Close enough.

Fourteen

The huge ballroom that the hotel had allocated for the tournament was in its familiar state of first-day madness when Jax arrived the next day. The games were scheduled to begin at 6:00 p.m., and a roar of voices bombarded him when he sauntered through the doors at five. All seats were drawn at the beginning of a tourney, and officials were still in the midst of calling out names over a loudspeaker, which someone then posted on a big dry-erase board. With the number of tables they had to fill, it was a time-consuming procedure.

Most of the noise filling the room came from the players milling about waiting to see what their table assignment would be, which position they'd draw, and who'd they be playing their first game against. Anyone able to pay the ten-thousand-dollar entry fee could play, and hundreds of professionals and amateurs did. The latter group in particular had grown in leaps and bounds in the past few years, thanks in part to the popularity of televised tournaments on cable TV.

At the moment the room sounded like the Tower of Babel, but Jax knew once the games began, it would quiet down. At the end of each day's play, tables would be eliminated and physically broken down and removed until, eventually, the defining games of the tournament—the ones that the public usually saw on television—would be moved into a smaller room. It was the coveted inner sanctum that each and every one of them aspired to reach.

Looking at the number of players that had turned out, Jax knew that wasn't going to happen anytime soon. The tournament ran five days, and it would take the first four to weed out all but the final table. And since he wasn't one to speculate on what the future had in store, he'd simply live with the current noise level. He avoided in particular any conjecture about where he'd be at the end of the tournament. Fortunes could and did turn on the flip of a card.

He went over to check out the board to see if his first table had been posted. When he didn't see his name, he wound his way through the crowd to get a cup of coffee from the courtesy table set up against the far wall.

Sipping his drink, he moved a few feet away and leaned against the back wall to watch the crowd. A kid who was probably in his midtwenties but looked considerably younger stood a few feet away, sweating profusely as his glance darted from face to face and table to table like a hummingbird on speed. He appeared to be seeking something, but his gaze never rested on any one thing for long. A young woman postured down by the end of the table, assuring all who would listen that they might as well toss their money into the pot right now and spare themselves the humiliation of being beaten by a girl.

He'd lay odds neither would progress beyond today, but then again, you never knew. It didn't pay to underestimate the competition. Anyone could knock you out of the game at any time. He'd blown pros out of the water as an amateur himself, and he knew it could damn well happen to him if he didn't give the game and every player he played against the respect they deserved.

Hell, it could happen even if he did.

Anticipation began building in his gut. God, he loved this game. Winning was the goal, of course, but win or lose, he enjoyed damn near everything about poker. He loved the logic of its mathematical probabilities and the capriciousness of chance. He loved the occasional bluff when his brain insisted he should fold but his gut had other ideas and he enjoyed even more manipulating his opponents' bets toward a larger pot when he was dealt a solid hand.

He was ready for the games to begin.

Two large bodies suddenly appeared against the wall on either side of him. He knew those ugly faces and with a silent curse he waited for Moscow's version of Elvis to appear. "Hello, Sergei," he said calmly, even though he didn't yet see the man.

"Hello, Jax." Kirov materialized in front of him, resplendent in a silver-shot navy jumpsuit, a white silk scarf draped around his neck. Like any great star, he pretended not to notice the curious stares that were sent his way. "You are ready for the tournament?"

"Yeah. I was just thinking how much I'm looking forward to getting my hands on some cards. You?"

"The same. Just as I am looking forward to taking possession of my baseball."

Shit. His gut began to roil, but he regarded the other man with his most noncommittal poker face. "Do we really have to go through this routine every time we run into each other?"

"Of course not. Was just thinking—it would be a shame if something happened to—oh, I don't know… your hands, perhaps…should you—how do you say it?—go back on deal."

The ape-resembling Ivanov brothers on either side of Jax each took one of his hands in their own. The movement was subtly executed, but the end result was no different than if they'd muscled him for the entire roomful of people to see. The pressure they exerted on his thumbs sent pain radiating up his arms. Breathing shallowly, he had to concentrate in order to say calmly, "When have you ever known me to default on a bet?"

Kirov gazed at him a second. "Never," he finally admitted and gave the merest of nods.

His henchmen dropped Jax's hands and stepped away.

"Good luck in the game," Sergei said. And with a spin that made his scarf flutter, he walked away, his ever-present goons flanking him.

"Yeah, you, too, asshole," Jax muttered, massaging his hands. What he really wished for the Russian at this moment involved hot irons and castration tools, but he'd give the guy this: his little show of force highlighted the fact that Jax had been handed the perfect opportunity to look for the baseball last night, and he'd let it slip right through his fingers.

He was in big, big trouble, but what had he done after he'd left Treena at the hospital? Gone straight back to his room exactly as he'd said he would even though it had been an ideal chance to go through her place. Carly's phone message had so rattled Treena that he was pretty sure she hadn't even bothered to lock up. She'd simply raced off to her friend's apartment, and he'd followed.

And what was the story with that? All of his plans were turning to shit, and the reason for it could be placed squarely on the fact that he was getting much too involved with a certain redheaded dancer.

That wasn't supposed to happen. He wasn't supposed to be fascinated by Treena or her merry little band of friends.

Yet somehow he was.

Involvement wasn't his strong suit because he'd always felt different, as if he didn't quite fit in. He'd given it his best shot in the early years and played nice with others, but it had never seemed to get him anywhere. Maybe things would have been different if he'd stayed in one place long enough, but the old man's restlessness after his mother's death had taken them to whatever town hosted the current failing company Big Jim had bought. They'd stayed just long enough for his dad to rebuild and sell it, then they'd move on again. They hadn't landed anywhere permanent until Jax was twelve and a half and attending his second high school. That's when his dad had suddenly, inexplicably settled on Las Vegas.

By then, however, Jax had given up trying to fit in. He'd skipped too many grades, had too little in common with his peers, and he finally admitted he was one of those people who simply didn't belong. Anywhere.

Yet when he was around Treena, it was as if she *made* him belong. And it felt good.

And that had to be all wrong. He decided the sexual pressure was getting to him. She was playing him, and sucker that he was, he was falling right in with the program.

Yet he wasn't all that sure anymore that she had the boundless sexual experience he'd first assumed. He'd questioned it last night on her couch, and her covert glances and uncertainty in the E.R. had made him even more unsure.

A true player would have solidified her position with him. He'd let her know he'd won more than a million dollars in France—a gold digger would have rushed to fuck his brains out and let Carly go hang. She sure as hell wouldn't have dumped her potential sugar daddy on his butt and left him with a raging hard-on while she went to play Nurse Nancy with someone who quite frankly had all sorts of alternate people she could have called for help. He couldn't figure the woman out at all. His instincts said she was just what she seemed. Sexy, yeah, but also nice. Maybe even special.

But his brain, which had made its mind up ages ago, insisted she was something else entirely.

Either way, he'd gotten himself into one mother of a

mess, and the only way out was to get his hands on that ball. Kirov's thumb-bending demonstration had driven home the fact that he'd better get his act together. Not only would his professional reputation be in shreds if word got out he'd defaulted on a bet, but his continued physical well-being was clearly in a precarious position, as well.

The idea of stealing from Treena, however, no longer felt so hot. Not that it was really stealing, he reminded himself with a scowl. He was just retrieving what was supposed to be his.

The situation, which hadn't exactly been wonderful to begin with, was beginning to have No Win written all over it in big neon letters.

He'd have to put it out of his head for now, though, if he was to play his best today. He couldn't afford to dwell on something that he hadn't the least chance of controlling—at least not until today's leg of the tournament was over.

He might as well go check out the board one more time to see if his seat assignment had been drawn yet. The microphone had fallen silent, he realized, so the officials should be finished. And not a moment too soon, if you asked him.

He needed to get his head in a place where he had some confidence he actually knew what the hell he was doing.

The last person Ellen expected to see on her threshold later that evening was Mack Brody. So when she answered the summoning knock to find him in the corridor outside her door, she was momentarily dumbstruck.

He stood there with a hip-shot, cocky posture, his shoulders slanted and his left thumb tucked into the key pocket of his jeans. His right hand was hidden from sight behind his back. It was such a cock-of-the-walk stance that her lips started to curl up in an involuntarily appreciative smile.

It died a quick death when he snarled, "What the hell are you doing answering the door without checking your peephole first? Haven't you listened to a *thing* I've told the girls?"

She swallowed a sigh. Just once it would be nice not to start off on the defensive with this man. Last night when he'd shown up at the hospital shortly after her heart-to-heart with Treena, he'd seemed different. He'd been quiet and low-key, and she'd caught him a couple of times gazing at her with a thoughtful expression on his face. Not a single negative word had passed his lips, and it had been a really nice change. For a short while she'd been treated to the sweet personality he normally reserved for Treena and Carly.

But here he was, reverting to type once again. Yet even now, before she could form, much less utter, a single response, he managed to confound her once again.

"I'm sorry," he said gruffly. "Believe it or not, I didn't come to pick a fight." Whipping his arm out from behind his back, he thrust a colorful bouquet of flowers at her. "Here. I came to give you these. And to apologize."

At first she was too surprised to take the proffered flowers. The little surge of shock quickly passed, but even as it faded she decided she deserved a tiny bit of fun at his expense. Tipping her head to one side, she suctioned her palm against her ear. "I seem to be hearing things. It almost sounded as if you said you came here to—" She raised her eyebrows at him inquiringly.

"You're going to make me repeat it, aren't you?"

A smile of pleasure wanted to curl her lips but she rubbed them together to suppress it. "Indeed I am," she said primly once she was certain she wouldn't grin at him like a loon. "You say you're here because you want to…?" She twirled her hand, encouraging him to fill in the blanks.

"Apologize. Okay? I came to apologize." He pushed the flowers against her midriff. "Would you take the damn things?"

"You're such a charmer." But she accepted the flowers, gathering them in to cradle against her breasts as she watched him run the fingers of his freed hand through his curly steel-colored hair. It stood up messily in their wake.

To her surprise, he nodded briskly and said, "I know. Sometimes I find myself saying things I had no intention of saying. Words just seem to come out of my mouth before I give them any thought."

Gee, you think? But she bit her tongue against voicing the flippant thought. "Only sometimes?"

"All right, with you, I'm guilty of messing up all of the time." He rolled his burly shoulders in a tough-guy shrug. He looked her in the eye. "Maybe you intimidate me—you ever think about that?"

"Oh, sure, often." She would have snorted if she hadn't been raised to be a lady. But it was at times like this that her upbringing had its drawbacks.

"Yeah, well, maybe I am intimidated. I'm just a meat-

and-potatoes kind of guy—not a man of culture like the ones you're probably used to." Hooking his thumbs in his jeans pockets, he rocked back and forth on his heels. "Look, the fact of the matter is, you and I got off on the wrong foot pretty much from the first day we met—and that's my fault." He nodded at the bouquet. "The flowers there are my way of saying I'm sorry, and that I'd like it if we could call a truce. Maybe try to start over again as two reasonable adults or something."

Her heart picked up its pace at the thought, but she gave him a suspicious glance. "Why the sudden change of heart?"

"A number of things. I've said some stuff to you I'm not proud of, behaved with a rudeness that I've never shown another woman in my life. Plus, watching you with the girls last night made me realize how wonderful you are with them. I'm amazed you never had kids of your own."

An old, familiar pain slapped at her. But it was a weak blow and its sting faded almost immediately, as most of its power to wound had dissipated over the course of the years. "I would have loved to have had children, but Winston and I weren't blessed with any."

Winston. Mack barely controlled a grimace. His only consolation these past many months that he'd spent struggling with his unrelenting attraction for Ellen had been the natural contempt of the physical man for his noncallused, pencil-pushing brethren. He might find himself behaving like a twelve-year-old with his first crush, and Ellen might look upon him with such scorn it made him feel like the dirt on the bottom of her shoe.

But at least he wasn't an asexual banker with a namby-pamby name.

He'd known that feeling of superiority was a spurious thing at best. It had nevertheless given him immense comfort, and now that comfort was gone. It was hard to feel superior after overhearing tales of Winston's sexual prowess.

Mack had always considered himself pretty damn adept between the sheets himself, but he hadn't been kidding when he'd told Ellen he was a meat-and-potatoes man. All those Kama Sutra positions seemed like overkill to him. Just give him plain old vanilla missionary, woman-superior or doggie style—with some long, lazy foreplay thrown in to mix things up—and he was a happy man. But not only did Ellen like sex, which blew him away in and of itself, she apparently liked it upside down and fancied up, as well.

Now, however, probably wasn't the best time to ponder that too closely. So he shoved his jealousy aside to return to the conversation at hand. "Not being able to have kids must have been tough. I can't imagine my life without my two girls."

"It was difficult. For years I would have given anything to get pregnant, but eventually I simply had to resign myself to the fact that it wasn't going to happen." She lowered her head to smell the bouquet in her arms, then gave him a tentative smile over the blossoms. "I should put these in water. Would you like to come in for a cup of coffee?"

"Yes, please. That would be nice."

He entered her apartment for the first time and looked

around as he followed her to the kitchen area. The condo was tasteful, formal and full of books. "Terrific place," he said, taking a seat at the breakfast bar and swiveling his stool to look from the kitchen to the living room and back. "It looks like you—all sort of refined and elegant."

She paused in the midst of retrieving a vase from an overhead cupboard to shoot him a wary glance. Then she set the vase gently on the counter she continued to regard him with cool eyes. "Is that another way of saying I have boring librarian tastes?"

"No! I wasn't taking a shot. I told you I'm sorry for that. I just meant it's real pretty in here. The stuff in my place works like clockwork and it's comfortable and suits me well enough. But it's pretty utilitarian compared to this."

She poured them both a cup of coffee and set out cookies on a plate decorated with a white paper doily, the same sort of special touch, he noted, that she always added to the plates of goodies she brought to Carly and Treena.

"In that case, thank you," she said. "And I must say I'm not surprised your things work with precision. It's plain to see from how well-run everything you handle in this complex is, that you're quite handy to have around."

He watched as she sipped her coffee, pulled a pair of gardening sheers out of a drawer and turned on the faucet. Thrusting the flower stems beneath the running water, she snipped off their ends with economical efficiency, then arranged them one by one in the vase. Her cheeks were flushed to match the soft peach-colored top she wore.

"I like your shirt," he said. "It's a pretty color." It was the first time he'd ever seen her in something that wasn't a neutral color. No, wait, come to think of it, she'd worn a colorful top last night, as well. He'd just been too blown away by the discovery of her sexuality to pay it much attention.

Glancing up, she shot him a grin. "Thanks. I went shopping with the girls and bought much more than I ever intended."

Her smile shot fire straight to his groin, but he swallowed hard and said, "Yeah, I know from experience that young women can make you squander more of your money than you ever thought possible. I don't think I ever had two bucks to rub together until my daughters got married. Before I gave their hands in marriage to their young men I had to take them out of my wallet first."

She laughed in delight and he felt relieved that he was holding up his end of the conversation. It was hard to tell, because his throat was tight with longing, and his mind refused to settle on the words coming from his mouth. He wanted to kiss her, but he could just imagine how *that* would go over, so he sat frozen, gripping the seat of the stool hard enough to leave imprints in the brass-studded maroon leather.

What was it about her, anyway, that messed him up so badly? He'd always been a confident guy who had felt absolutely no need to apologize for his lack of a higher education or his blue-collar background. But she turned him upside down. He wanted to get close to her, but he kept sabotaging himself. Hell, he'd just wasted a year and a half letting concern over her opinion drive him into behaving like an idiot, had allowed her upscale demeanor to make him question his own worth. Every chance he'd had to get to know Ellen, or to let her learn a little something about the real *him,* he'd managed to screw up left, right and sideways.

Now, even with his newborn determination to acquit himself more responsibly, he was hesitant to make a move. Nothing like a little performance anxiety to stop a guy in his tracks.

He felt his ire rise and tried to tamp it down. He had nothing to apologize for in that department. Maryanne had certainly never complained. Of course, Maryanne had been one hell of an earthy woman.

But then, so was Ellen, if what he'd gleaned from last night's overheard conversation was true. He set his cup down a little harder than necessary and met her startled gaze belligerently. "I like my sex straight up."

She froze. "*Excuse* me?"

Straight*forward*, he should have said. Shit. Straight *up* made it sound like he liked a good strong erection. Which he did, of course, but that was probably way more information than she'd ever thought to learn about him. Oh, Christ. When was he going to learn to keep his big mouth shut? As if she wanted to hear *anything* about his sexual preferences.

Unfortunately it was too late to just drop the subject now, for although her cheeks looked as if they were on fire, she pushed the last flower into the vase, then set the arrangement aside. She reached for her coffee, but the cup rattled in its saucer and she set it down untasted.

Clasping her hands tightly on the counter in front of her, she gave him her undivided attention. "What, exactly, does that mean, you like your sex straight up?"

Encouraged that she didn't add, *and why on earth would you think it concerns me?* he leaned forward. "It means I like long, slow kisses and deep, hard loving— and unlike your late husband, I only utilize a handful of positions."

Her jaw dropped. Her blush deepened and her hazel green eyes turned molten. Then the latter narrowed as the part of his speech concerning her just-had-it-all sainted husband apparently sank in. "How would *you* know what positions Winston liked?"

"I overheard part of your conversation with Treena last night."

"You eavesdropped on a private conversation?"

"No. I—"

"You *eavesdropped*?" She pushed upright and rounded the end of the counter. When she stopped in front of him, her back was ramrod-straight and her hands were white-knuckled fists upon the gentle curve of her hips.

He didn't like being accused of something he hadn't done—or at least he hadn't deliberately set out to do, and he stepped off the stool to confront her right back. "Don't you look at me like I was skulking around just waiting to hear all about your sex life! Until then, I didn't even know you had one!"

Seeing her flinch, he grabbed hold of his temper and hung onto it for dear life. Dammit, it was time to behave the way he kept telling himself he would. He blew out a breath and said in a more moderate tone, "I'm sorry. I didn't say that to embarrass you or hurt your feelings. It's just…I came in through the hospital in time to hear Treena say she stinks at sex. Well, that froze me in my tracks, let me tell you. It was way too much like hearing one of my daughters, and trust me on this: sex is the *last* word you want to hear coming out of your kid's mouth."

"So why didn't you make your presence known?"

He rubbed his fingers over his chin. "I was going to. I debated between that or leaving and letting you handle it. But you started talking, and I was so blown away that I just stood there. Then I did go out the way I'd come in and came back in through the E.R. And I've been trying to forget what you said, but it's like your words were burned in my mind. I can't get them out of my head."

"So—what? You thought you'd just stop by today to see if I was in the mood for a little loving? Now that you're pretty sure I'm not a dried-up old prune after all?"

"No! Damn. I meant everything I said. I have been rude, and I have been wrong, and I wanted you to know I'm going to do better. I want to start over."

"Well, I want you to leave."

His heart sinking, he reached out to touch her face. Her skin was cool and soft. *"Ellen,"* he said, and the pleading tone in his voice didn't even register. His pride wasn't uppermost in his mind at the moment.

She stepped back as if she'd been burned. "Now. Please."

Reluctantly, he dropped his hand, studying her closed

expression. "Fine," he finally said. "But don't think we're even close to done here." And with a little shrug, he turned and strode to the foyer. Hesitating at the entry door with his hand on the knob, he looked back over his shoulder. But Ellen was out of his range of vision and since she couldn't have been clearer about her desire for him to leave, he let himself out.

Clearly he stank at this courting business, but there had to be books on the subject, sites on the Internet, people he could talk to about improving his technique. Hell, simply having a technique would probably be a start. He stalked back to his own apartment, routed but not vanquished. If he didn't know anything else he knew this one thing.

Come hell or high water, he *would* get better at this. He planned to kiss that woman—and soon.

Or die trying.

Fifteen

Carly banged through the front door of Treena's apartment, her hair stuck up on one side and flattened on the other. Her diaphanous flowered skirt floated behind her on the current created by her long strides, and with so many colors in its pattern Treena was amazed that her friend had managed to pair it with the only navel-baring halter top she owned that clashed with them all.

"Hey," she said mildly.

Carly whipped around from her headlong dash to the living room and strode straight over to her, holding up her hand to display her fingers. They were puffed up to twice their size. "I'd planned on getting back to work tonight, but look at these!"

Treena peered at them. "Still swollen, huh? They look better than they did yesterday, though." At her friend's unimpressed snort, she smiled. "Sorry, stupid response." She gave Carly a warm hug and a sympathetic moue. "Poor baby." Then she stood back to examine her. "Although if I were you, I'd be more concerned about your fashion statement."

Carly laughed. "No kidding. I never realized how many things you need two hands for, and at least the skirt and top didn't need to be tied, buttoned or zipped. And look at my hair!" She swiped at it with her good hand. "I can't do half the stuff I'm used to doing."

Treena peered at the abused fingers. "Do they hurt?"

"Not anymore. But they look like little fat sausages, and they're useless!" Then Carly visibly drew herself together. "Maybe I'll go in to work anyway. I mean, there's a chance no one will notice, right?" As if expecting Treena to argue with her, she added defensively, "It could happen."

Treena just looked at her.

The blonde's shoulders slumped. "Yeah," she agreed glumly. "I guess I knew that. Hard to change costumes and attach headgear with one hand. Shit." She stalked into the bedroom and flopped onto her back across the bed. Grabbing a bright silk throw pillow, she hugged it to her breast.

Treena ambled into the room after her, intending to step carefully until her friend's sulky expression eased a bit. But Carly looked over at her and hitched a shoulder.

"What the hell," she sighed. "It's a day off."

"And that's always nice."

"Yeah. If not exactly the way I'd have chosen to spend it."

"Still, a day to laze around with the babies isn't a bad thing."

"That's true." Carly brightened. "Maybe I'll use it to

work with Rufus. The situation with him is getting ridiculous. So far it's boneheaded dog ten, boneheaded human zip."

"What are you going to do if he doesn't shape up?"

"I don't know." Carly stared up at her with worried eyes. "I don't even like to think about it."

Treena joined her friend where she was sprawled across the width of the bed. Turning her head on the mattress she assured her, "It's bound to click soon."

"I sure hope so." Then some of the gloom left her expression. "Hey! Did I tell you I'm getting a neighbor?"

"No. They finally sold that unit next to yours?"

"Subleased it according to Mack. I'm still undecided how I feel about it. Part of me likes the idea of having someone next door again. But I also kind of got used to the quiet and the privacy." She essayed the equivalent of a facial shrug. "I guess it'll just depend on who moves in."

"Mack give you any hint who that might be?"

"Some guy named—get this—Wolfgang Jones."

Treena pushed up onto one elbow and gazed down at Carly with a puzzled frown as an elusive memory tickled the back of her mind. "Why does that name sound familiar?" she asked. Then it clicked. "No, wait— I know who that is. He works at the casino."

"At *our* casino? Avventurato? You're kidding me. So why don't *I* know him?"

"He's security. Handles the money and watchdogs the rest of us less trustworthy employees."

"Ahhh." It was shorthand for *say no more.* The men— and one woman—who handled the protection and transportation of the millions of dollars that flowed through the casino on a daily basis, rarely if ever mingled with their fellow employees, since they were also charged with monitoring the rest of the staff, from kitchen workers to dealers to the entertainment division.

"If he's the one I'm thinking of—and I'm pretty sure he is—he stopped me once on the casino floor to check my bag."

"Describe him for me. I can't place him."

The doorbell rang, and Treena climbed off the bed to go answer it. "Tall," she said as she headed for the door. "Aryan. Killer cheekbones."

She opened the door, and her heart rolled over like a trick poodle to see Jax standing on the other side with his legs planted shoulder-width apart, his hands crossed behind his back. "Well, hi there. How goes the tournament?"

"I'm still hanging in. That's always a positive sign." Dipping his head, he pressed a soft kiss onto her lips. Raising it a moment later, he smiled lazily at her. "Hello to you, too, sweet stuff. I brought you something." His gaze moved beyond her. "Hey, Carly. How's the hand?"

She glanced over her shoulder to see her friend strolling down the hallway from the bedroom. "Sucky," Carly replied.

"I'm sorry to hear that." Jax looked at the tousled blonde with a bemused expression. "Interesting getup," he said as he stepped into the apartment.

"*You* try pulling yourself together with one working hand." Then she waved it aside. "Did I hear you say you came bearing gifts?"

"Yes," Treena demanded, "what did you get me?" A

sudden thought struck her. "Please tell me it's not encrusted with diamonds."

"No, ma'am. No diamonds. Never again. I learned my lesson on that score."

"Yeah, how dare you spend a small fortune on her," Carly said.

"Ha ha." But she didn't spare her traitorous friend more than a glance before she reached out and poked Jax. "So?"

He grinned at her. "So, pick a hand, any hand."

"Ooh, choices. I love choices." She tapped his left arm.

He whipped it out from behind his back and presented her with a small gold box wrapped with a gauzy white ribbon. A color-coordinated silk flower was tucked into its bow.

"Godivas!" She plucked the box from his fingers. "Thank you! I *adore* Godivas. They're my favorite chocolates in the world."

He brought his right hand out from behind his back, as well, and offered her the small plastic card he held.

"What's this?" She plucked it from his fingers.

"A gift card for a couple of vendi Frappuccinos, extra mocha, extra cream."

"You *doll!*" She planted a hot, fierce kiss on his lips.

"Okay, this is obviously my cue to exit," Carly said. "But break open that box of chocolates first. I haven't had a Godiva in a dog's age."

She selected one from the box Treena held out to her. "Thanks. Now I do believe I hear a mutt calling my name. So long, kiddies. Don't do anything I wouldn't do." Popping the truffle in her mouth, she strolled out the door.

Treena turned to Jax. "Let's take these into the kitchen and eat 'em all, whataya say? You want a cup of coffee to go with yours?"

"No, thanks. I wouldn't say no to another one of these, though." And fast as a striking snake he pulled her to him, bending his head to plant a sizzling kiss on her lips.

Chocolates clattered to the floor as she wrapped her arms around his neck and kissed him back. His arms were strong and warm, his mouth was hot and sweeter than Godiva's finest, and she pressed close needing more. Wanting more.

Wanting it all.

Oh, God. She wanted *everything*. Heart pounding with trepidation, with excitement, she pulled her mouth free and stared at him. His eyes blazed back at her.

And the truth sank in. For better or for worse, she, the girl who would just as soon say no, wanted to say yes to lovemaking with Jax. It might turn out to be yet one more mistake, but she couldn't allow fear of failure to hold her back. Not this time, with this man. He made her feel different than she'd ever felt with any other guy, and she wouldn't be able to live with herself if she refused to take a chance on him, on herself, out of fear of screwing it up. She simply had to hope things would actually work out this time.

Reaching up, she rubbed her thumb over the tiny bit of moisture still clinging to Jax's bottom lip, then stepped back. Taking his hand in her own, she turned toward her bedroom.

"Wait," he said and squatted to scoop the fallen choc-olates up off the floor. He tossed them into the open box, dropped the box onto her entryway table, then reached out to retrieve a slightly flattened milk chocolate truffle. He popped it into her mouth and scooped her off her feet and into his arms.

She laughed, but the dual sensations of chocolate melting on her tongue and his hot tongue slipping into her mouth a second later changed her amusement to a husky moan. Time dissolved, and before she knew it he was lowering her onto her coverlet.

"God," he said hoarsely, coming down on top of her. "I've been dying for this. For you." He speared his hands into her hair and held her in place while his mouth returned to ravage hers.

Heat saturated her lips, her nipples, between her legs, until she couldn't think. For just a second, with some hazy intention of locating her absent brain cells, she struggled to break to the surface of this churning pool of arousal. Then Jax's chest rubbed more urgently against her breasts and his erection bumped the bundle of nerves hiding behind the crotch seam of her cutoffs—rocking her into a fine madness. And she gave up her already nebulous purpose without a second thought. Plunging her fingers into his hair to hold him in place exactly as he held her, she wrapped her ankles around his calves to keep him from pulling back.

Apparently that wasn't in his game plan, however, for with a very male sound of appreciation he opened his hard thighs between hers, spreading her legs wider. He settled deeper between them. Then he slid his right hand from her curls. Reaching to loosen her left hand from its grip in his hair, he linked their fingers and brought their joined hands down to the mattress next to her head. He repeated the action on the other side, then slid their clasped hands against the coverlet until their arms extended straight overhead. Her breasts arched into the hard press of his chest.

Their lips slowly separated by increments, clinging together until the very last instant when he raised his mouth from hers and looked down at her with eyes that had darkened to midnight. "I've got you in my power now, me pretty," he said in a voice so raspy it strummed nerve endings from her nape to her tailbone.

But while his voice was like liquid foreplay to her ears his words roused unfamiliar emotions. Competitiveness surged to the surface. Perhaps she should demonstrate that she, too, possessed power. Being completely, carnally captivated for perhaps the first true time in her life didn't mean she was without resources of her own.

"In your power, huh? You think?" She rubbed the soles of her feet up his calves, to the backs of his knees, to his outer thighs. The action spread her own thighs wide, and tilted her pelvis up. That in turn caused the rigid length of his penis to settle hard between her legs.

They both sucked in a simultaneous breath.

"Maybe not," he croaked. Eyes dreamy, as if he'd never felt anything so marvelous in his life, he oscillated his hips.

"Omigawd." Her newly birthed competitiveness died. "Oh. My. *God.*"

"Oh, yeah," he agreed fervently and lowered his mouth to kiss her jaw and the tender skin just beneath it. "My sentiments exactly."

She tugged her hands against the grip pinning them to the coverlet. "I want to hold you," she panted when he didn't immediately release her. She gave another tug. "Please."

He unlinked their fingers and trailed his down the inside of her forearms, along the vulnerable skin of her inner elbows, up her arms to her shoulders and inward to her neck. Then sliding his hands into her hair, he gripped her head and held it steady as he pressed kisses beneath her chin and down her throat.

Treena stroked her fingers over his wide shoulders. Hard muscle gathered and bunched beneath her touch, and fine wool caressed her flesh as she stroked her hands down his back. Her palms itched to trace the shape of his butt, but between the disorienting sensations burning along every nerve and his jacket vents flapping in her way each time she attempted it, she couldn't quite manage her goal. She plucked at the lush fabric. "You've got on way too many clothes."

Still kissing her neck, his hair softly brushing the underside of her jaw, Jax pushed up on his palms. She slid the jacket off his shoulders, but it would only go so far and no farther, and her feet flopped from his thighs onto the mattress in frustration. With a grunt, he reared back to kneel between her sprawled legs and whipped the coat off, tossing it toward the nightstand but clearly unfazed when it slid onto the floor. Color burned high across his cheekbones as he stared down at her, and his breathing was audible in the silence of the room.

"Lose the shirt, too," she commanded.

He yanked the pristine white T-shirt off over his head.

Treena stared at the view his action exposed and felt a blowtorch of lust consume every last drop of moisture in her mouth.

Jeez, girl, she commanded herself, *get a grip. It's not as if you haven't seen that chest, those abs, before.* She had, of course, just the day before yesterday. Still, the impact didn't lose a thing upon second viewing.

Staring at his abdomen, she reached out and massaged her fingers over each individually defined muscle from his diaphragm to the belt of his jeans. She shivered at how much she wanted him. "How does a sedentary card player get such a nice body?"

"Huh?" He'd hunched over to unbutton her top and, glancing up at her, he slowly blinked. "Oh. Gyms. Being a nerd as a kid made working out something of a religion."

"Hallelujah," she murmured. For if one's body was one's temple, his was St. Patrick's Cathedral, the Sistine Chapel and Westminister Abbey all rolled into one. Beautifully crafted of muscle and bone, it lacked the Neanderthal bulk of the competitive bodybuilder. Rather, lean muscle and sinew formed sculpted planes across his chest, ridged his stomach, rounded the hard mounds of his shoulders and biceps. And he was smooth-skinned all over, with only a feathering of silky brown hair gracing his forearms, tufted in his armpits.

She reached up with both hands and drew her fingertips across the blades of his collarbone, down the slight swell of his pectorals. She circled his flat nipples, rubbing her thumbs over the velvety copper-colored aureolas, flicking the minuscule nipples with her nails.

When he swore and started fumbling to unfasten the

buttons on her top faster, she laughed. For all her bravado of a moment ago, she'd never experienced anything as powerful as what she was feeling at this moment.

Then he spread her top apart and said a reverent, "Oh, man," as he stared down at the breasts he'd bared.

She wasn't overburdened with modesty—she couldn't be and dance in the type of revue she did. Yet when other men had uncovered her breasts in the past, there had been a lewdness to their gaze that had made her feel exposed. She'd felt as if they were so busy congratulating themselves on bagging a showgirl that they couldn't be bothered to share a tender moment with her.

Jax looked at her and seemed to see *her.* So she wasn't embarrassed that she hadn't donned a bra today, didn't feel the need to cover herself up. Because he looked at her breasts as if they were Mona Lisa's smile.

"You have got to have the prettiest tits I've ever seen," he said.

Okay, not exactly poetry.

He seemed to realize it, too, for color washed up his throat. "Sorry. Breasts, I meant. You've got the most perfect breasts."

"Thanks. They're on the small size, which is okay with me but almost got me scratched from the callback list when I auditioned for my job at *la Stravaganza.* The dancers there are more like Carly—a little bustier."

"But yours have got such gorgeous shape."

"Yeah. Which is why I squeaked by." And she laughed, because over the past few years she'd come to think of her body as more a machine that needed maintaining in order to keep her employed than a sexual entity. But she felt sexy at the moment. She felt gorgeous, as well. The latter had far more to do with the way he stroked her, however, both in the physical and the mental sense, than anything she'd ever seen in a mirror.

Eyes intent, he circled his fingers in ever narrowing lazy eights around her breasts, from the perimeter inward to the centers. A hot shot of electricity zinged straight to that sweet spot between her legs, but just as she was holding her breath, feeling his fingertips drifting nearer and nearer her nipples, which jutted up eagerly for his touch, his hand slid away and he rocked back on his heels between her legs.

A soft moan of disappointment escaped her, but he appeared not to hear.

"So pretty," he murmured, stroking his forefinger down the middle of her forehead, along her nose to her lips, over her chin. He continued down her throat to her sternum and along her diaphragm and abdomen to the low-rise waistband of her cutoffs, pausing only long enough to tickle her navel with his fingertip. Then, as if he'd forgotten where he'd been heading, he took a moment to straighten the strings that comprised the straggly hem of her hacked-off jeans.

He was slow and thorough as his fingers worked their way to her inner thighs, brushing up beneath the ragged hem to fish out errant strands of unraveled cotton. With meticulous precision, he tugged each one in a ruler-straight arrangement against her thigh before sliding his fingers beneath the hem once again to hook yet more tangled threads. He neatened both hems at once, and

Treena moved her legs restively when his warm hands came in particular proximity to the sensitive creases where her legs joined her torso. She willed those maddeningly elusive hands higher—just a little bit higher—and eased her thighs farther apart to encourage him.

He ignored the silent invitation.

She glanced up at his face to see if he had any idea how aroused she was getting, but the fan of his lowered lashes hid his eyes as he stared down at his handiwork with apparent absorption. When his forefingers suddenly brushed the edges of her panties and she made a breathy yearning sound, however, a slight smile curved his lips. And she realized he knew *exactly* what he was doing to her.

The idea that he was toying with her awakened her sleeping competitor.

"So this is Date with a Geek, huh?" she asked, reaching up to slip the metal button at his waistband free of its buttonhole. "I like it. Who knew your tidy streak could be such a turn-on?" She unzipped his fly, purposefully brushing her fingers down the hard bulge beneath it as the metal teeth disengaged.

He looked up, his eyes a blistering blue. "I'm a full-service kinda guy," he said in a voice that was easy, almost amused. "Your smallest wish is my command." But his hands, turning from soft and lazy to hard and gripping on her thighs, gave him away.

Her mouth quirked. "So, are you as hot as I am?" And, oh, God, she *burned*, aroused far beyond what the nearly platonic touches he was presently bestowing upon her warranted.

"Hotter." He dove atop her, catching himself on his

palms at the last second to avoid crushing her with his full weight. Lowering his head, he slammed his mouth down on hers.

This kiss was hard, desperate, on the edge of control. Treena wrapped her arms around Jax's neck and exerted steady pressure, wanting, needing, to feel his weight. He came down on her, more than two hundred pounds of aroused male, and she sighed in appreciation at the feel of skin on skin, scratching her nails down his smooth back.

He growled deep in his throat and rolled them over.

Finding herself suddenly on top, she sat up, her head dropping back when his big hands came up to cup her breasts. She rocked against his erection and abruptly found herself much closer to attaining satisfaction than she'd guessed. She shifted slightly and bit back a whimper. *There. Oh, God, there.* Her breath grew choppier.

Then he was lifting her off of him and standing her on the floor, and she moaned her frustration.

"I know, sweetheart, I know," he said in a gravelly voice. "But I want you naked. Now." And kicking off his shoes, he planted his heels and raised his hips to shove his own jeans and boxers down around his ankles. As Treena stripped off the rest of her clothing, he bicycled his feet to kick free of his pants. And suddenly there was almost six and a half feet of aroused, naked man on her feminine coverlet.

She paused with her cutoffs halfway down her thighs to stare. He looked like some sultan surveying the harem girl he'd ordered bathed and sent to his tent as he lounged back against her bright pile of silk pillows, all wide shoulders, muscular limbs and potent thrusting sex.

He wrapped his hand around the latter and stroked it slowly as he stared at her. "Get. Naked." There was no mistaking the command in his voice.

Unable to take her eyes off his tan hand and the long, thick penis it fondled, she pushed her shorts down the rest of the way and stepped out of them.

"The panties, too."

She pulled the strings that tied the two triangles together at either hip and the scrap of lingerie fluttered to the floor.

"Now come here."

It abruptly occurred to her that her much-coveted control was nowhere in sight at this moment. But for once she didn't care. Excitement thrumming through her, she took the step that brought her back to the bedside.

He crunched up off the pillows and reached out to grasp her wrist, yanking her onto the bed beside him. She stumbled forward on her knees and the room twirled as he caught her around the waist and rolled to lie her flat on her back. Before her head could quit spinning, he'd propped himself alongside her and was stroking the flat of his hand down her stomach toward the minute patch of her curls.

"I only got to feel this before, didn't get to see it." His voice was a deep rasp that abraded her senses. "But I've thought about it, imagined it. And it's even smoother, prettier than anything I conjured in my mind." His fingers separated the plump lips of her sex and slipped up and down the slippery tissues. "Ah, God, so wet." His gaze had been following his fingers, but now he looked up into her eyes. "This must be the Brazilian wax job I've heard so much about."

She nodded, beyond words as a long finger slowly entered her. She inhaled sharply and let her knees fall open wide. "Oh, Jax, please."

"You like that?" He eased the finger out, pressed it back in.

"Yes. *Please.*" She could see by his face that he was prepared to tease her further, but she was no longer willing to lie still for it.

Reaching out, she latched onto his penis.

It was his turn to inhale sharply, and she rolled toward him to plant a kiss on his chest. As she marveled at how natural it felt to slide her hand up and down the rigid shaft in her grasp, he snatched up a condom he must have taken from his pants when he'd removed them. He ripped the package open with his teeth.

"Gimme." She thrust her free hand out and he slapped the rubber in her palm. They both watched as she rolled it down his length, then stared at her fingers, wrapped tightly around the base of his erection, once he was fully armored. She slid her hand up his shaft to the mushroom-shaped head then squeezed him through her fist back down to the base.

And he broke. Rolling on top of her, he kneed her legs apart and kissed her with such hot intensity as he aligned himself with her opening that she feared there might be nothing left of her but an amorphous little puddle by the time he was done. He ripped his mouth free and stared down at her as he slowly pushed inside, and it was then, looking into his blue, blue eyes, that Treena realized she had feelings for him that she'd never in her life felt for another man. She hesitated to give those feelings a name, but she knew she couldn't hold anything back from him.

She had to give this thing between them everything she had.

Then he was as deep inside of her as a man could go, and she had a feeling that, even without the new emotions boiling through her, it would have been impossible to hold back. One minute he was buried to the depths, hot, huge and hard, and the next, before she even had a chance to acclimate to the intrusion filling her, he was sliding out again. Then he eased back in.

And out.

And in.

Friction set nerves afire and she raised her hips and pushed back against every forward thrust, grasping his hard buttocks and clinging when he withdrew inch by maddening inch. Her knees fell farther and farther apart as she began to feel a coiling tightness deep inside of her. "Oh, God, Jax. Oh, God."

He rose up onto his knees and began pushing harder, faster, his hands grasping the front of her thighs and pulling her into him. She made a high-pitched noise unlike any other she'd ever made in her life, but that iron-hard heat stretching her, incinerating her, bumped up against something inside of her with every inward thrust of his hips, and she found it impossible to keep quiet. Dear God, she was close…so close.

"Look at you," he crooned, sliding his thumb and forefinger into her wet folds and finding her clitoris. He trapped it between his fingers and delicately rolled. "Look at you with your pretty hair and your pretty lips and your pretty, pretty—hah!" His breath exploded from his lungs as she clamped down around him with a single hard, sharp contraction.

She hadn't been prepared for it any more than he had. There was just something about him getting verbal that really seemed to set her off. And it was hardly a monster orgasm, more like a single yank on the cords of a drawstring purse that snapped it closed. Almost immediately, however, she felt the real deal building inside of her, and she knew it was going to be bigger, brighter. Longer.

He shuddered through that brief fist of muscle clamping around him then went right back to it, talking to her again, driving her higher with his body, with his words. "That's it, sweetheart," he growled as his thrusts began to slap his pelvis against the spot where they joined, his testicles grazing her bottom. "Come for me. I want you to come all around me, all over me. I want to watch that pretty—"

Hearing failed and thought fled as a hidden land mine deep inside of her tripped. Her world blew apart as screaming sensation tore through her body in an explosion that she thought just might bury her in the resulting rubble. Instead, she flew to the sky on it, rolled with it in a free fall back to earth. Her body shuddered and quivered. And all the while that secret sheath between her legs clamped over and over and *over* again against the marvelous, beautiful invader treating her to the sensation of a lifetime.

"Christ!" Jax snarled. "Oh, Christ, oh, Jesus, oh, *fuck*, Treena, I'm going to, oh, God, I'm gonna—" His teeth clenched and his hands gripped her thighs hard, yanking her to him and holding fast as he thrust deep one last time.

She watched as his orgasm claimed him, saw his eyes screw shut, his lips draw back from his teeth as he groaned low and long, and it ripped another climax from her. Reaching for his wrists, she found she didn't quite know what she'd intended to do with them once she had them, so she merely sank her nails into the warm skin and anchored herself.

After the last aftershock had rippled through her body she went limp, her arms and legs splaying helter-skelter against the coverlet. A second later Jax toppled like a felled tree, his weight driving her body into the mattress and her breath from her lungs. They lay there, plastered together chest to knees for several silent minutes while perspiration cooled and heartbeats slowed.

Finally, he eased his chest up slightly and turned to kiss the damp tangle of hair sticking to her temple. "You still breathing?"

"Uh-huh."

"Am I?"

A laugh bubbled out of her. "Hard to tell without a mirror. I'd run get one, but I'm not sure I can walk." She tried lifting one arm but was simply too lethargic to follow through and it dropped back onto the bed from the meager two-inch elevation she'd managed. "What did you do to me? I seem to have turned into a jellyfish." She'd never felt so relaxed in her entire life.

"Tell me about it." He rubbed his chin against her curls. "I sure hope you enjoyed yourself, because that may've been my final performance. It was one for the record books—and for that I thank you. But I think you may have just killed me."

There was one part of him, however, that still had life in it, for when she stretched luxuriously beneath him a minute later, interesting things began to happen. His penis, which had begun to soften inside of her, suddenly pulsed. Then it grew harder. Within seconds it was plainly *very* happy to see her.

"Then again," he said, raising his head to give her a crooked grin, "maybe not."

Sixteen

A light slap on Treena's sheet-covered bottom startled her out of a sound sleep. The hand that administered it stayed to soothe away the slight sting and that felt good, so she didn't bother opening her eyes to see why she was being manhandled. Instead she settled more firmly into her comfy spot and let the tides of slumber begin to suck her out to sea once again.

"Up and at 'em, babycakes," Jax's voice commanded. "You're sleeping the day away."

"Yeah?" she mumbled into her pillow. "Wha's your point?"

"That time's a-wasting."

She yawned, which caused her to suck in a mouthful of feather-plumped Egyptian cotton. Coughing, she spit it out. "If you hadn't kept me up half the night doing a marathon session of the hootchie-kootch, this wouldn't be a problem. But you did and I'm tired. Go away."

His laugh stroked its way down her spine, and the mattress next to her hip suddenly depressed as he sat. "Hootchie-kootch, huh? I like that."

She heaved a big sigh into her pillow. "You're not going to let me sleep, are you?"

"Nope."

She rolled onto her back and pried her heavy eyes open, gazing up at him.

Ah, man, no one should look that good at the crack of dawn. Peering at the bedside clock, she saw it was almost noon but dismissed the fact as a minor detail. Close enough, considering Jax had gotten even less sleep than she had, if his well-groomed appearance was anything to go by. His eyes were clear and bright as a newborn's after a satisfying nap, his jaw had a freshly shaven satin sheen, and his still pristine white T-shirt clung like a second skin to that beautifully proportioned upper body. Sitting there hip to hip with her, he looked every bit as loose-limbed and relaxed as she felt.

Except she had the feeling that instead of looking like a god, she more closely resembled the wrath of one.

He brushed a curl away from her left eye. "Get dressed, sleepyhead. Much as a hot young thing like you would probably prefer spending the entire day wrecking your bed with me," he said, treating her to a virtuous smile, "I'm not that kind of man."

She guffawed. "Yes you are."

Laughing, he got up off the bed and reached down to pull her to her feet. "Okay, I'm exactly that kind of man. But the weather's broken, it's a balmy eighty-three degrees outside and I thought we could take a picnic out to Lake Mead. Maybe rent us a little sailboat."

Disappointment filled her. "Oh, Jax, I'd *love* that. But I've got studio time scheduled for two o'clock, and I can't afford to blow off practice."

Disappointment flashed in his eyes, as well, but all he said was, "When's the audition for your show?"

"Next Tuesday. And I'm frankly worried about it, so I need every session I can cram in between now and then." Passing the audition had been her driving force these past four months, but she found herself stepping close to wrap her arms around Jax's waist. Stroking her cheek against his warm chest, she looked up at him. "I'm sorry."

"Hey, this is not a problem." Wrapping her in his own arms, he propped his chin on the crown of her head. "Today's the first nonblistering Saturday I've seen since I've been in town, so the lake's bound to be a zoo anyway. We'll just push out our plans to next Wednesday instead. After you've nailed down another year's employment and I've won the tourney we'll both have all the time in the world to enjoy ourselves."

"You're a real glass-half-full kinda guy, aren't you? I'd give a bundle to be a fraction so confident."

He squeezed her. "You're gonna blow 'em out of the auditorium."

Dear God, she loved this man. The truth of it burned through her, warming her clear to the tips of her fingers, to the ends of her Scarlet Passion painted toes. She'd known it deep in her heart last night but hadn't been ready to fully acknowledge her feelings. Because on a logical level, it was just too unlikely for words, wasn't it? She and Jax had known each other for less than two weeks, so how could she possibly think she was in love with him?

Yet she thought precisely that, and she simply couldn't deny it any longer. The way she felt was so much more than simple lust, so far beyond sex, no matter how unexpectedly marvelous last night had been, that it wasn't even funny. And she needed to acknowledge these feelings—if only to herself—had to admit that this sensation warming her from the inside out was love. Heady, scary, genuine love for one particular man.

Pure and simple.

Except, of course, that nothing ever was that simple. She didn't, for instance, intend to burden Jax with her feelings. They *had* only known each other for a very short time, and the last thing she wanted to do was send him hotfooting it away from her because she'd freaked him out by becoming too serious way too fast.

She needed to keep it light. Extracting herself from his arms, she stepped back. "We still have a couple hours before I have to be at the studio," she said. "You wanna go take a swim in the pool?" Then with a wry twist of her lips she amended, "Or in my case, a splash and a wallow?"

"You don't swim?"

"I do…just not very well. I never had formal lessons, but my uncle Frank taught me and my sisters sort of piecemeal at the town pool. I can get from one end of a lap to the other, and I don't even look too terribly awkward doing it. But I'm not a strong swimmer. So mostly I just play around." She shot him a cocky smile. "Still, I've got stylin' in my bikini down cold. And I can hold down a lounge chair with the best of them."

"Hey, we all gotta have our strengths. Now, me, I do a mean cannonball." He hesitated, then said, "I don't have trunks, but I noticed some stores not far from here. Why don't I go pick something up while you get into that bikini?"

"Deal."

He headed for the bedroom door but turned back before he reached it. "Just one more thing before I go."

"What's that?"

He crooked a finger at her. "Come closer. I can't tell you from way over there."

Smiling, she crossed the room to stand in front of him. "What?"

He hooked his arm around her waist, pulled her to him and kissed her. Raising his head a moment later, he said softly, "Good morning."

"Good morning to you, too." She cocked her head to one side. "I didn't even think to ask, but do you want breakfast or a cup of coffee or something?"

"Nah, I'm good. I made myself a piece of toast while you were sleeping."

"Then I'll make myself a slice, too, and be ready when you get back."

"I'll be as quick as I can."

He was gone less than a half an hour. When he got back he changed into his new suit in the bedroom and rejoined Treena in the kitchen where she was throwing sunscreen and bottled water into her tote. Coming up behind her as she bent over to see if there was anything that could remotely be considered a snack in the fridge, he snugged up behind her and leaned forward to kiss her neck.

A shiver shimmied down her spine, and she turned in his arms to kiss him on the lips. Happiness welled so fast and furiously inside of her she feared it might spill over in the form of tears. Pulling back, she grasped him by the biceps and pushed him an arm's length away to check out his new bathing trunks.

He'd donned a pair of black baggies with a band of blue-and-purple palm fronds around the hips. "No Speedo for you, huh?"

"Please." Looking pained, he made a disparaging noise. "Real men don't wear Speedos."

"Real men beat hairy chest and drag real women off to cave by hair," she said.

He grinned at her. "All right, smart-ass, *I* don't wear Speedos."

"Fair enough. You look mighty fine in your surfer boys, by the way." And he did, particularly since that was the only stitch of clothing in a long, naked expanse of Jax. She reached out and snapped the waistband riding low beneath his navel. "I especially like the way you color-coordinated the accent band with your eyes."

He tossed his sun-streaked hair and gave her a vacuous smile. "Absolutely, dude. Fashion coordination is, like, too bitchin' fer words."

She laughed. "Perhaps you should have gone with the Speedo after all. I think the baggies already melted a few brain cells."

They headed down to the pool where they staked out a couple of lounge chairs in the shade of a nearby palm. There were surprisingly few people in the enclosed area, only a young mother who was packing up a rambunctious little boy even as Treena and Jax spread their towels out on the chairs, and two twentysomething women. The latter ogled Jax until Treena turned the evil eye on them in silent warning. With twin shrugs, they turned back to the conversation Jax and Treena's entrance had interrupted.

Jax snagged her hand as she was pulling her bottle of sunscreen out of her bag. "Let's go in the pool," he suggested huskily. "If I get started spreading lotion all over you I can't guarantee I won't drag you back up to your apartment."

Looking at him standing there with the sun shining in his hair and sheening his lightly tanned shoulders, she was tempted to thrust the bottle of sunblock into his hands, then race him back up to her bedroom. But she also wanted a chance to simply play with him, to further test the compatibility they'd been building without the sexual component clouding the issue. So she dropped the lotion onto the small table next to the lounges. "Let's see that cannonball, sport."

"Damn," he breathed. "I was hoping you'd insist on full SPF protection." Stepping close, he ran a fingertip down her arm. "After all, you've got all that sensitive skin."

A quiver dusted her nerve endings, and she leaned toward him.

With a soft-spoken curse, he stepped back. "This trying to be a new-age enlightened guy is harder than it looks. I hope to hell that water's cold." And taking several giant steps, he leapt high and tucked himself into a tight ball. His full two-hundred-plus pounds hit the water with a force that generated a splash so huge it drenched Treena from head to foot and even spattered the two women sitting quite some distance away.

Shrieking in outrage they jumped to their feet, slapping at the water sprinkling their hair and suits as if it were toxic waste. When Jax shot to the surface a moment later, tossing his wet hair out of his eyes, they sent him a collective look that should have sent him straight to the bottom of the pool, sliced, diced and julienned. When he remained cheerfully afloat, they gathered up their belongings and stormed out of the pool enclosure.

He looked from their stiff retreating backs to Treena's drenched figure. "Uh, my cannonball must be even more killer than I remembered."

She threw back her head and laughed. "Oh, God, it was beautiful."

He gave her a puzzled look. "You're not mad, then? You don't mind getting soaked?"

"Seems like the whole point of going to a swimming pool to me." Her laugh deepened. "Whataya wanna bet, though, that that was the closest those women's suits ever came to chlorinated water? Ah, me." She wiped her streaming eyes. "They were not happy campers. Guess they won't be giving you the eye any longer."

Like every man she'd ever known, he came to attention at the news of being scoped out by a good-looking woman. He glanced from the now empty gates back to Treena. "They were checking me out?"

"Big time. But, tough luck, buddy, because you just officially drowned any possibility of ever scoring with either of 'em." Then, still grinning, she launched herself at him from the side of the pool.

He caught her and they both went under. As if remembering her warning that she was an unsure swimmer, however, he promptly brought them back to the surface.

She wrapped her legs around his waist and leaned back. "Hey, there, big boy," she said, lying back in the water and spreading her arms to keep afloat. "You sure know how to clear a pool. I *like* that in a man."

"I like you in a woman." His hands tightened on her hips, holding her to him. "And nice as it is to have pretty women notice me, I'm not interested in anyone else."

"Glad to hear it, because I intend to keep you very, very busy." Then, unhooking her legs, she used her feet to push off his chest and shot backward toward the shallow end of the pool.

He gave chase, and they spent the next twenty minutes frolicking like a couple of kids. They played tag and leapfrog, swam between each other's spread legs and took turns standing on their hands underwater for the other's amusement.

The tone changed when Treena said, "No, wait, I can do better," and performed her second handstand. This time she concentrated on the placement of her hands, pretending the floor of the pool was just another dance floor. Once focused, she executed perfect form, hands firmly planted against the concrete, feet together and toes pointed, a slight arch in her back for balance.

Then, knowing she was showing off shamefully, but unable to resist, she separated her legs to splits position. She felt Jax's hands skim her thighs at the same time she began to run out of breath and went into a back bend, her left leg continuing over until her foot touched bottom. Planting it, she followed through with the right foot and raised her upper body out of the water, flinging her arms over her head in triumph. "Ta-da."

Jax stepped close, his fingers reaching out to stroke down her throat. "Treena is a very, very flexible girl."

Heart beginning to pound at the heat pulsing out at her from those intense blue eyes, she said through a suddenly tight throat, "Yes, she is."

"All that flexibility is giving me ideas." He lowered his mouth to her ear. "Hot. Raunchy. Ideas," he whispered. Raising his head he looked her in the eyes. "And unless you want to be nailed against the wall of this very public swimming pool in about, oh, say, the next thirty seconds, I think perhaps we should retire to your place."

She dropped her gaze and stared at a droplet of water rolling from the hollow of his throat, between his collarbones and onto his chest. Without stopping to think, she leaned forward and licked it up. Then she looked up at him.

And was amazed that the water around them wasn't boiling.

She leapt for the concrete steps at the shallow end of the pool. "Last one there's a weenie!"

She didn't doubt for a minute that he could overtake her if he chose, but he stayed just behind her, and excitement thrummed in all her pulse points at the sensation of being pursued. She felt his hot breath on her neck as she reached her front door, and he lightly sank his teeth into the angle where it flowed into her shoulder as she fumbled the key in the lock. A second later they stumbled into the apartment.

He slammed the door closed behind them and reached for the fastening on her bikini. The two pieces hit the tiled entryway with a wet plop. A second later his trunks squelched down next to them and he crowded her up against the door. "Let's see that leg thing again," he invited, patting his left shoulder.

She slid her foot up his chest until the back of her leg was flush with his abdomen and chest, smiling on the rush of power that his harshly indrawn breath brought her. She felt his erection rub against her stomach, then he was bending his knees and aligning the broad head of his penis with her opening. He started pushing it slowly inside of her and she winced slightly.

He pulled out. "You're not ready yet."

She started to apologize, vaguely embarrassed that she wasn't fully lubricated, but he wrapped his hand around the back of her neck and tipped her chin up with his thumb, then brushed its pad across her lips to shush her.

"You've got nothing to apologize for," he said. "It's *my* lack for rushing things. Foreplay is our friend. I got excited and forgot that for a minute." Sliding his thumb away, he bent his head and kissed her lips sweetly. Then he sank to his knees in front of her, and her raised leg bent at the knee as it lowered until the sole of her foot rested against the rounded muscle of his shoulder.

Seeing where that placed his eye level, she moved to

hastily lower her foot, but he wrapped his fingers around her ankle and held it in place, grinning up at her. "Close your eyes if it makes you nervous, buttercup, but don't lower that foot. We're about to play a little catch-up in the excitement game here." And lowering his gaze, he simply gazed at her exposed sex for a moment before bowing his head to kiss it.

At the first touch of his lips, the first gentle lap of his tongue, Treena's head thunked back against the door. Her supporting knee threatened to give out on her and, reaching down, she grasped Jax's hair in both hands, forcing his head back. "I'm caught up," she breathed as he licked his lips. "Oh, my God, I am *so* caught up."

"And yet I'm not quite done," he murmured. "I love the way you're so smooth. And the way you taste, so salty and sweet. I could just eat you all day long."

"Ohmigawd." Her fists tightened in his hair as he proceeded to follow through on his statement. Within moments, her hips began a subtle rocking motion, and mere seconds after that, it seemed, she started to babble. *Oh, please, oh God* and *Jax* appeared to be her entire vocabulary.

Seconds after that, she exploded.

She shuddered through a series of lesser orgasms once the first big one had died away. Finally, limp with pleasure, she started to slide down the door.

But Jax scooped her up in his arms and headed toward the bedroom swearing beneath his breath. "There goes my against-the-door fantasy," he mumbled as he dropped her onto the bed. He snatched his discarded jeans up off the floor and started rummaging through the pockets. "Where's that condom? I'd sure as hell make a lousy Boy Scout, because this ain't exactly prepared. There it is. Come here, you little devil." Tossing the jeans aside, he turned back, ripping the foil packet open with his teeth. He stopped midrip, however, when he saw her rolling from the far side of the bed. "Where you going, Treen?"

"The front door's not the only one in the joint," she informed him. "We've got another right here." And heart pounding at her own daring, she closed the aforementioned portal, leaned back against it and slowly, very slowly, raised her right leg until her toes pointed straight overhead, hoping to heaven she didn't look like some crazed calendar girl wannabe.

That fear disappeared when he breathed, "Ah, man," and crossed the room to her in a few ground-eating strides. Slapping his hands against the door on either side of her head, he leaned into her until they were body to body, just the way they'd been out in the entryway. He looked deep into her eyes. "You are, without a doubt, the sexiest woman I've ever known."

"You make me feel sexy. That's something I've rarely felt with other men."

He stilled. Then he gazed into her eyes as if trying to read the fine print in their depths. "Are you serious?"

Swallowing hard, she nodded.

Something indefinable flickered in his eyes. "Not even with your husband?" Grimacing as if a bitter taste had invaded his mouth, he shook his head. "I'm sorry, it's none of my business. What's past is past. The important thing, right here, right now, is you and me." And lowering his head, he kissed her. So very, very tenderly. Pulling back, he hooked a drying curl out of her eye and lightly pushed it back into what she feared was a growing mass of frizz. The fleeting thought of looking like a redheaded version of the Bride of Frankenstein didn't have its usual galvanizing effect, however, because the look in his eyes held her enthralled.

He handed her the condom, and she rolled it down his length. Then he squatted slightly to align everything and eased into her.

"God." The word was not a blasphemy but a prayer. Slowly, gently, he rocked his hips. "I feel like you're my Christmas present and an early birthday present all rolled into one."

She sucked in a breath as he stretched up inside of her. "You have a birthday coming up?"

He nodded, bent his knees to withdraw a little farther, carefully thrust a little deeper.

Her eyes drifted shut as he hit her sweet spot, but she pried them open a second later. Her breath was choppy, however, when she forced out, "When?"

"Huh?"

"When's your birthday?"

"Soon." He made a sound deep in his throat, and his hands wrapped around her head, his fingers tunneling beneath her hair to caress her nape, his thumbs bracketing her cheeks. He kissed her as if she were the most fragile thing on earth and continued to rock slowly in and out of her. Within moments, however, the mood changed from languid and easy to quick and impatient.

Rapidly followed by hot-as-sin desperate.

He hit high inside of her with every thrust and within moments she felt the pressure begin to build. And build.

Until finally it detonated.

She cried out as sensation whipped and sparked and lashed like an out-of-control fire hose inside her. The high-pitched sound that purled out of her throat was absorbed by Jax's mouth locked over hers.

Then a groan rumbled deep in his chest. He surged upright one last time, lifting her clear off the floor, and she grabbed at his shoulders, wrapping her unsupported leg around his waist.

He ripped his mouth free, and knotting one hand in her hair, he cupped her throat with the other. "Oh, Christ," he panted, his mouth a bare inch from hers. "You're the one, you're the one, you're the one."

Then his eyes glazed and he growled long and low as if he felt the flames of hell licking at his feet. Treena felt him pulsing inside her, however, and knew pain was the last thing he was feeling. She dropped her head to his shoulder and inhaled the scent of him, of her, of the two of them together. And when he collapsed against her a moment later, pinning her to the door, she wrapped him in her arms.

You're the one.

Okay, it was probably just sex talk, but she hugged his words to her breast all the same. Because she'd never been "the one" for anyone before. Even Big Jim, who had treated her nicer than anyone else in the world, had admired her more for the status she brought him with his friends than as his one true soul mate. She was pretty sure, for him, that designation had gone to his first wife. But Jax Gallagher said she was *the one*.

And even if he didn't truly mean it, she couldn't recall one other moment in her entire life when she'd felt as good as she did right then.

Seventeen

I'm fucked. Sitting against the studio wall watching Treena put herself through her paces a short while later, Jax hungrily followed her every move while his normally facile mind scrambled for a way out of the corner he'd painted himself into with her. But nothing came to him; not one damn thing that might salvage their relationship once the truth came out. And it would come out; he didn't doubt that for a moment. *I am so fucked.*

As his gaze tracked her routine from high kicks to crossovers to what she'd informed him were step ball changes that provided the transition to some slow, sexy move she'd refused to identify because she said she had to concentrate and couldn't answer all his questions, the irony of the mess he'd gotten himself into didn't escape him. He'd never even *had* a relationship with a woman before—not one, at any rate, that had lasted for more than a night or two. So didn't it just figure that the first woman he'd forged a connection with, the one person to click with his own personality so effortlessly that getting close to her had actually been easy, would turn out to be the only person he'd lied to from the moment they'd met? She'd talked about her family as if she valued honesty and integrity above all else, and he was Mr. Lying Through My Teeth.

What a mess.

He'd give his left nut to still believe she was the golddigging tramp he'd been so certain she was before he'd gotten to know her. Maybe then he wouldn't feel like such a low-down rat. Because as much as he liked her, as much as he could *see* her seamlessly integrated into his future, he still intended to relieve her of the baseball.

Only now he knew how she felt in his arms. He had burned into his brain the wonder with which she'd greeted his lovemaking—as if no one had ever taken the time to make it really good for her before. He'd experienced her inner heat, all slick and tight around him. He knew the sounds she made when he satisfied her.

He also knew that with the sale of the damn collectible she'd have a healthy cushion for her studio should she somehow flunk the upcoming audition. Watching the fluid expertise with which she practiced, he couldn't quite visualize that happening, but he understood that her confidence about the outcome wasn't as assured as his own.

The music stopped and a moment later Treena strolled over to where he was sitting. Blotting perspiration from her throat and chest with a small hand towel, she dropped to a spread-kneed squat in front of him and nearly blinded him with the brilliance of her smile. His heart slammed up against the wall of his chest.

"That was the best, most relaxed practice I've had in months." With a throaty laugh, she walked her fingers up his thigh. "Too bad I didn't know about this sex therapy business sooner. I'd be so much further along."

"Nah. It probably wouldn't have done you any good," he assured her easily, "since it only works with me." He felt anything but relaxed, however, when he privately acknowledged that he didn't like the idea of her doing the—what had she called it, again—the hootchie-kootch?—with anyone but him. Didn't like it one damn bit. Pressing his spine against the wall, he sat a little taller. "Treena, have you saved any money at all for that studio you want to open?"

She blinked at the abrupt change of topic; then her eyes went serious and she plopped down on her butt in front of him. "Yeah, I did. If you count the interest, I had almost sixty thousand in CDs."

Relief washed through him to think that at least his betrayal wasn't going to leave her destitute. Then the past tense she'd used sank in. "Had?"

She hitched one shoulder. "I cashed them in to pay for that nurse for Big Jim I told you about."

Shit. Shit, shit, shit, shit, shit! He felt his corner shrinking smaller and tighter around him. "You had her help 'round the clock?"

"His help. And no, we couldn't afford that. But David filled in the graveyard shift while I slept."

Double hell. Okay, there had to be a solution. He'd *pay* her for the baseball. Sure, why not? He should have planned that from the beginning anyway, and it would be the best thing for both of them. She'd get cash for her studio and he'd get to keep all his bones in their original, unbroken state.

But if she'd been unhappy about accepting an engraved diamond necklace from him just how likely was she to accept a huge chunk of cash? He looked into her trusting, smiling golden brown eyes. Oh, man.

He was so screwed.

Ellen halted at the top of the swimming pool ladder when she saw Mack sitting on the lounge chair where she'd tossed her towel. "Déjà vu," she murmured calmly, but her heart rapped out a beat that was anything but placid. It took all her willpower not to look down to assure herself the movement wasn't visible through her suit. Drawing in a calming breath, she stepped up onto the pool's apron.

Mack climbed to his feet, sweeping up her towel as he vacated the chaise. He strode over, clad in his usual khakis and a chocolate-brown polo shirt, to offer the terry to her. Discomfort at once again finding herself half-naked while Mack was fully dressed began itching along her nerve endings, particularly when his intent gaze made one swift, comprehensive pass over her figure as she hurriedly swung the towel behind her and wrapped it around her waist to disguise her tummy and less-than-perfect thighs.

The barefaced approval in his dark eyes, however, went a long way toward vanquishing her budding self-consciousness. "That sure is a pretty suit," he said.

She smiled in pleasure, glancing down at the crimson-and-black tank. "Isn't it great? I just fell in love with it and was thrilled to pieces when it actually passed my checklist."

He cocked his head. "You have a checklist? What's on it?"

"That it not ride up in back, pull down in front or have straps that slip off my shoulders. Any suit will do for lounging around in a chaise, but swimming demands more stringent criteria." That this one had covered all of hers and was pretty to boot struck her as the next best thing to a miracle.

Mack studied her. "The way it makes your cheeks pinker than a girl's doesn't hurt, either."

Delight sent yet more color throbbing in her cheek's apples. "Why, you honey-tongued devil. I didn't know you had such compliments in you."

"I haven't exactly shown you my best side," he agreed. "But trust me, I look at you and there's a whole slew of 'em where that one came from." The grin he flashed almost stopped her heart. "So, are you still mad at me?"

"I should be." But once she'd cooled down she'd had a difficult time thinking beyond the stunning knowledge that if what Treena had said was true—and Mack's own behavior the last time she'd seen him seemed to indicate that it was—he wanted her.

The thought wasn't exactly conducive to lowering her silly heart's thunderous beat to a more manageable level.

"I'm sorry I listened to a conversation you had every right to assume was private," he said with gruff-voiced sincerity. "But I swear to God eavesdropping wasn't my intention."

She nodded. "I believe you."

"You do?"

"Yes. You're too straightforward to be skulking around trying to catch wind of my deep dark secrets."

He flashed that smile again. "Do you have many more of those I should know about?"

She gave him a repressive look. "As if I'd just blurt them out if I did."

"How about if I ply you with liquor? Any chance of hearing them then?"

"You're such a funny fellow." Her tone indicated he wasn't, of course. But it was all she could do not to grin at his wagging eyebrows.

He quit wiggling them to crook one at her inquiringly. "Funny as in none of my business or as in you aren't going to tell me, blurting or otherwise?"

"Take your pick."

"Okay. It's none of my business. So if I promise not to try teasing any more information out of you, would you—" he cleared his throat as ruddy color flowed up his jaw "—do me the honor of going out to dinner with me tomorrow night?"

She hesitated a moment purely for the rare pleasure of seeing him squirm. Then she managed a reasonably serene smile that hid the fact she felt giddy as a young girl. "I'd like that very much."

"Yeah?" He laughed as if genuinely relieved she'd accepted his invitation. Then briskly rubbing his hands together, he said, "What kind of food appeals to you?"

"Oh, gosh, I like just about everything. Except Indian. I'm not a big fan of curry."

"I hear that. I'm mostly a meat-and-potatoes man. But I like Italian and Chinese, too," he hastened to assure her, as if worried she might find his tastes plebeian. "So I'll figure out somewhere nice and make us a reservation. Seven o'clock okay with you? Or maybe you'd prefer eight?"

"Actually, if you don't mind terribly, I'd prefer something a little earlier. I've never been a big fan of the fashionable hour. I tend to get grumpy if I haven't eaten by six-thirty or so."

His eyes lit up. "You really are a woman after my own heart. I like to eat at six, myself, but I thought you might go for a more sophisticated hour."

"No, that was always a problem for me when Winston and I used to attend charity events. They always ate so late that by the time I got my dinner I was no longer feeling very charitable." Gratified by his laughter, she rewarded him with her warmest smile.

He took a step back and stuffed his hands in his pockets. "So, uh, I'd better go and see about getting us a table somewhere. I'll be by to pick you up tomorrow at five-thirty."

She watched him walk away, her gaze lingering on his very nice backside. He really was exceptionally fit for his age, and she loved the fact that he wasn't super tall. She'd had her share of cricks in her neck from evenings spent staring up at some six-footer.

She pressed her fist to her chest to contain her racing heart. She had a date. Lord have mercy, she hadn't dated since 1975—what on earth would they find to talk about? They had nothing in common.

Well, except for their mutual fondness for the girls. But how much conversation could Treena and Carly take up? Oh, God. She'd be spending a couple of hours in Mack's company, without either of the dancers to act as buffer. It would be just the two of them. The thought terrified her.

At the same time, she'd hadn't felt so excited in years.

Treena couldn't deny it. She felt like pretty hot stuff when she strolled into the poker tournament that evening beneath the drape of Jax's arm. She'd never been one to get all excited about the status of the people she hung out with, but she couldn't help but notice, as they made their way through the Bellagio ballroom that hosted the games, that in this milieu Jax was well known. Perhaps even a star. His name was a murmur in several of the groups they passed, and it fueled her excitement at the prospect of finally getting to see him play. She wouldn't be able to observe the entire evening's tournament, but at least she could watch for a short while before she had to head over to the Avventurato to get ready for the show.

She nudged him in the side with her elbow. "So, you're a pretty big fish, huh?"

His mouth crooked in a self-deprecating smile. "In a really small pool."

"And modest, too. Be still my heart."

"Hey, whatever gets me in your pants," he said wryly, and she laughed.

"Hello, Jax," a sultry voice said, and they both halted. Treena craned around to see a beautiful woman walking up to them and shot Jax a questioning glance.

He shrugged as if to say, "Beats the hell out of me."

The approaching woman was petite, blond and built, clad in a low-cut, hell-red spandex halter dress that was short on material and long on titillation. She walked right up to them, then ignored Treena as if she weren't there. "My name is Sharon," she purred. "I'm a huge, huge fan."

"Glad to hear it," he replied easily. "Poker's a great game."

"*You're* a great player." Reaching out, she rubbed her manicured hand down his jacket lapel.

Treena felt her jaw sag. For God's sake! Was she invisible, or something?

Jax's hand tightened on her shoulder as if to assure her she wasn't, and he eased them back a step.

His fan's hand dropped to her side. Apparently undeterred, however, she smiled up at him. "May I have your autograph?"

"Sure." Setting Treena loose, he reached in his jacket's interior pocket and brought out a chrome and black pen. He looked at the other woman. "Do you have a piece of paper I can write on?"

"No. But you can use this." And reaching behind her, she unhooked her halter top, peeling down one strap to expose all but the nipple of her right breast. A man passing by careened off another in a group of them standing with their drinks suspended and their mouths agape as they stared at the lush flesh she exposed.

"I don't think that's a great idea," Jax said coolly, repocketing his ballpoint. "As you can see, I'm with someone."

The blonde glanced at Treena, then dismissed her with a shrug as she refastened her top. Fishing a plastic key card out of her purse, she slid it into Jax's breast pocket behind his silk pocket square. "I'm staying here until next Wednesday if you get bored," she said. "Room 1218." She gave Treena a second glance. "I'll do her, too, if that's your thing."

"Ew," Treena protested, but the woman had already turned and was strolling away, her hips swiveling as if she heard a bump-and-grind drumbeat the rest of them could not.

Treena watched until Jax's new fan was out of sight, then slowly turned back to him, trying to erase the lines of distaste from her expression before she looked up at him. Suddenly his comment about whatever it took to get in her pants didn't seem so funny.

She realized just how much of her small-town upbringing still lingered in her, but then again she was pretty sure the blonde's boldness had been over the top even for Las Vegas. "Well." She cleared her throat. "That was…interesting. Does this sort of thing happen to you often?"

"I've been offered a couple of room keys before," he admitted, his expression noncommittal. "But I've never run across anyone quite as blatant as she was." Hugging her to his side, he smoothed his free thumb over a wrinkle still lingering between her brows. "I'm sorry."

It might not be fair, but a tiny part of her did hold him accountable. Still, making a face, she conceded, "It's not as if you asked her to come over. I've just never experienced anything quite like that before." She studied him. "It makes me look at you in a whole new light."

It was his turn to grimace. "Swell."

For no reason she could think of, other than the fact that Jax's groupie had all but presented herself to him on a silver platter, Treena's thoughts segued to something he'd said earlier while they were making love. "So, you have a birthday coming up, huh?"

He stared down at her as if she'd suddenly spoken in Swahili. "How do you jump from room-key-offering women to my birthday?"

"It's not that big a leap, Romeo. She all but wrapped herself in a big gold ribbon for you, and that reminds me of presents, which reminds me you said you have a birthday coming."

"You are one scary woman, Treena Sarkilahti."

"McCall," she corrected him. Then she grinned. "But thank you. So when did you say it was?"

"I didn't."

"Then this is your golden opportunity to do so, pal. Give me a date and I'll throw you a party."

"God, no." He shuddered, looking legitimately horrified. "I'm not big on that sort of thing."

"In that case I'll only invite a few friends."

He rubbed his hand up and down her upper arm. "I'd really prefer you didn't."

"Fine." She blew out a put-upon sigh.

Jax merely smiled. They'd begun to walk away from the spot where the woman had accosted him but now Treena stopped, and the sudden cessation of movement swung him around until his arm was still slung over her left shoulder but he was facing her. Flashing him a smile filled with promise, she leaned in to kiss his smooth jaw, then murmured in his ear, "Give me a date and I'll give you a *very* special present on your birthday." Her lips curved up when she felt the subtle tremor that passed through him.

"Now that's tempting," he admitted. Stepping back, he slid his hand down her arm and grasped her fingers. "But, honey-plum, you treat me to many more of those 'special presents' and my heart just might explode beneath the strain."

He couldn't believe how much it bugged him that there was so much he couldn't tell her for fear she might learn he was Big Jim's son. One of the things he couldn't say was that his old man had pretty much put him off birthday parties for life. His dad had been big on huge theme parties that had been more about the type of boy he'd wished Jax to be than the real Jackson McCall.

On the plus side, however, he had to admit he was having fun watching Treena come up with ways to coerce his birth date out of him. He hadn't really analyzed it before, but being with her made him happy.

But right now the tournament was about to begin, and he couldn't afford to think about anything else. "I've gotta go," he said, taking a long last look at her golden brown eyes, that warm smile and crazy-curl hair. "Give me a kiss for luck."

She promptly grasped his shoulders and planted a warm one on his lips. He sank into its sweetness and heat and almost got sucked in to the point that he forgot where he was and why he was here. Luckily, she stepped back before he could start waltzing her toward the nearest supportive surface.

Oblivious to his lapse in concentration, she smiled and reached up to wipe her lipstick off his lips. "Knock 'em dead, cowboy," she whispered and pressed a key into his hand. "Meet me at my place after you've won tonight's game." Spinning on her heel, she headed for the place where he'd shown her she could sit and watch.

He turned in a daze for the reader board that would tell him which table he'd be playing today.

He got his head screwed on in a hurry when he saw that Sergei was one of the players at the table he'd been assigned. Great. He couldn't afford to lose today's game in particular, or the pressure to produce the baseball would really intensify. Blowing out a breath, he shook out his hands, found his table and took a seat.

Then he searched the crowd for Treena. He located her and went over to where she'd sat down. Grasping her hand, he pulled her to her feet. "I don't know what I was thinking," he said as he led her back through the tournament room. "This isn't the final table—you don't have to watch from the gallery. You can stand back here if you want." He positioned her behind his chair. "See the game a little more up close and personal."

She gave him a pleased smile, but then looked around. "You'd better sit down," she whispered. "Everyone else is seated."

"Yeah. I'll see you later, huh? At your place?" He still hadn't quite absorbed the fact she'd given him a key.

"Yes. Now, go, go!"

He took his seat just as the final warning was announced. Nodding to the other players, he slowly inhaled, breathing in the scent of green felt and stacked chips to help him settle into his zone.

The game began and the button, which signified the deal although an actual casino dealer was used, went to the player two chairs to his right. That put Jax in the large blind position and sliding on a pair of dark glasses, he shut out all other considerations and focused, because the large blind and the small blind, which was the seat between him and the dealer, were the two lousiest positions at the table. It obligated him and the other player to bet six thousand and three thousand dollars respectively to guarantee a pot, regardless of the cards they drew.

And his hold cards were clunkers. They didn't improve appreciably when the flop cards were turned over, and grateful for the accrued winnings from previous days that provided him with a cushion, he studied the table presence of the remaining players.

He'd played before with Sergei and with Ben Janeau, so he was familiar with their methods. But he didn't know the man on the button well enough yet to determine if the pulse beating in his throat stemmed from the excitement of holding a great hand or from a not-quite-sure-of-himself bluff. Nor, as he watched the woman at the other end of the horseshoe-shaped table, did he understand yet the significance of her fingering her bracelet before she placed a bet.

He lost the hand, but gained the satisfaction of putting together a couple of the players with at least some of their body language tells. And as he anted up for the next hand, he settled into his seat, the rest of the world beginning to recede. He lost his awareness of Treena and all the other onlookers standing behind him. The clang and clatter of the room muted.

Until finally all that was left was him and the game.

Eighteen

"You should have seen it, Carly," Treena said in the dancers' dressing room later that evening. Leaning in to the lighted mirror, she carefully fit the first number's towering headpiece over her hair. "They bet as much as a hundred and thirty grand at a pop while I was watching—and apparently the pots grow larger as the game goes on. God, I wonder how Jax is doing since I left? His stack of chips was one of the biggest on the table when we arrived, and a guy next to me told me that's because while everyone starts out with the same amount, the current table stakes are the accumulated winnings since the beginning of the tournament."

"So, you probably wanna avoid playing strip poker with the man," Carly advised drily.

She laughed. "Probably so." But heat tickled deep inside at the idea. "On the other hand, it might be kind of fun." Then she remembered the way the evening's game had begun and frowned. "He started out losing right away, though. My chatty friend said that's because Jax was in a lousy position because of some rules I frankly didn't listen to all that closely, except to learn that it had to do with being obligated to place a bet even if you were dealt cards that would ordinarily cause you to fold." She shrugged. "Apparently those positions change after each hand. It's confusing—something to do with a button and the dealer. I was too nervous about all the money changing hands to really pay attention. But I wish you could have seen Jax. He sat there in a pair of shades like some mafia don or something, all cool and steady as an iceberg." Her eyebrows drew together. "Is that mixing my metaphors? Language Arts was never my strong suit in school."

"Beats the heck outta me. You'd have to ask Ellen."

"You know what I mean, though, right?"

"Sure." Carly nodded sagely. "He turned you on."

"Big time. That's where that strip-poker-possibly-being-fun comes in." Leaning toward her friend, she lowered her voice. "I know it's all very unliberated of me, but I can really picture him ordering me out of my clothes and telling me exactly what he'd like me to do." She blew out a breath and fanned herself. Her reflection in the mirror displayed flushed cheeks even through the heavy stage makeup. "Good grief. I can't believe I just said that." Nor could she believe she'd gone from thinking sex was for the birds to getting all tight between the legs at the thought of Jax giving her sexual orders. She realized that the scenario playing in her head was fairly mild as carnal experimentation went, but it signaled a complete change in attitude for her.

"At least you actually have a chance of fulfilling a fantasy or two," Carly said wistfully. "Hell, plain old vanilla, nonverbal *missionary*-style sex sounds good at this point."

"Well, hey, maybe you'll hit it off with your new neighbor. If I remember correctly, he was—well, I suppose handsome isn't precisely the word—but definitely one of those 'Got Testosterone?' kind of guys you go for."

Carly grinned at her description, but said regretfully, "Unlikely, toots. As convenient as it would be to have a nooky man right next door, those security types aren't exactly known for fraternizing with the rank and file." Then she visibly cast off her discontent. "But what the hell—I'll just have to find someone who's not so fussy. I've gotten myself in a rut, that's all. But I intend to climb right back out of it." She checked her dramatic makeup one last time in the mirror, then rose to her feet, all long legs, tall headdress and extravagant tail feathers. "Maybe not tonight or, unfortunately, even tomorrow. But soon, for certain."

"Yeah, your dry spell's about to end," Treena agreed loyally. "I feel it in my bones."

Carly kissed her bunched fingertips then flicked them open, sending the kiss winging in Treena's direction. "From your lips to God's ear, sister."

Jax let himself into Treena's condo just before midnight. "Hey," he called out softly. "You home?"

There was no answer.

Navigating by the light of the moon that filtered through the venetian blinds to cast achromatic stripes across the hardwood floors, he made a circuit of the apartment to satisfy himself she wasn't simply in one of the other rooms but hadn't heard him. When he was sure that wasn't the case, he went back to the living room. He'd only been alone in the condo that one time and knew if he were smart he'd take advantage of Treena's absence to get cracking on his search for the baseball.

Instead, he flopped down on the couch and spread his arms along its back, his legs stretched out in front of him. Looking around, he marveled at how different the apartment looked in the moonlight. Except for one fruit-filled, colorful pottery bowl highlighted by the dim spot-light of a Tiffany-shaded accent lamp on the counter, all the colors in Treena's apartment were leached of their usual bright hues by the silvery illumination that turned everything to an indistinguishable, impersonal gray. If he didn't know better, he'd swear he'd landed in some stranger's house by mistake.

But of course he did know better. And any minute now he was going to haul his ass up off this comfy couch and start tossing the joint for the cursed collectible.

He just needed a second to give his strategy some thought.

Before he could drag his butt up off the couch, how-ever, he heard Treena and Carly laughing out in the hallway. And his heart lifted.

He assured himself the phenomenon was strictly re-lief that he'd held off on his search. He'd never find what he was looking for if Treena came in and caught him red-handed going through her stuff.

Then he snorted. Because he knew perfectly well that he was full of shit.

Carly's voice grew fainter as she continued up the stairs to her apartment, and a moment later he heard Treena's key in the door.

"Hey," he said softly, and smiled when he heard her startled squeak.

She appeared in the archway, a pleased smile curving her lips. "You *are* here. I thought I must have beat you home."

Home. God, it had been such a long time since he'd possessed a place he could call home that the mere word did something to his gut. He couldn't afford to consider what the root of that "something" was, though, so he shoved down the desire to explore the feelings it conjured and simply smiled back at her. "Yeah, I guessed as much. Sorry if I startled you—I wanted to warn you before you walked in and saw some shadowy man sitting on your couch."

She strode over and mounted his lap like a cowgirl climbing onto a paint, nimbly swinging her leg over to straddle his hips. She wiggled herself to a comfortable position upon his burgeoning erection. "Hmm. Doesn't feel all that shadowy to me. It feels, in fact, downright substantial. So what were you doing sitting in the dark?"

"Decompressing from the game."

"Oh!" She sat up straighter, which pressed the softness between her legs harder against his straining dick, making him groan. Looking down at him, she started to rise up off his lap. "I meant to ask right away, but I seem so easily sidetracked these days. Mostly by this, you devil." Reaching between her legs, she gave the hard-on tenting the fly of his jeans a brief stroke. Then she took her hand away. "How did the game go after I left?"

He grabbed her hips, hauling her back down to her rightful place. And grinned. "I won."

She whooped and wrapped her arms around his head, hugging his face to her shallow cleavage. "Oh, Jax! *Congratulations.* Man, I take back every bit of my lack of sympathy when you tried to tell me poker could be a stressful job. I couldn't imagine it at the time when I tried reconciling the kind of money you make for the short amount of time it takes you to earn it. But after watching you—" she heaved a sigh, which pressed his nose deeper between her soft breasts "—I don't know how you can do that night after night without having a heart attack. I nearly had one just watching how much cash you bet on every hand."

He laughed and worked his tongue into the low neck-line of her backless halter top—the same one she'd been wearing the first night they'd met. He lapped her cleavage from sternum to clavicle.

"That's it?" Gripping a handful of his hair, she pulled his head away, leaning back in his lap to stare down at him. "That's your answer to my very genuine apology? To lick my boobs?"

"Well…yeah. They're very lickable." He gave her a double wag of his eyebrows. "Salty and sweet as a world-class margarita."

"Oh, for crying in a beer." She shook her head in faux disgust. "You're such a guy."

"And this would be a bad thing?" Pulling free of her

grasp on his hair, he buried his face back in her cleavage. He dragged his hands forward from their spread-fingered grip on her bare back to frame the sides of her breasts. Pressing them together, he reveled in the feel of their silken inner curves against his cheeks. Her flesh caressed his beard-shadowed skin as he nuzzled her, and he ensnared her beaded nipples between his fingers and gently compressed them through the thin crepe that poked out over their impudent thrust.

She sucked in a sharp breath and arched her back. "Ohmigawd," she whispered. Rocking slightly upon his erection, she inhaled deeply, as though seeking to control her feelings. But her exhalation was a long, shaky sigh, and her head fell back as if it were suddenly too heavy for her slender neck to support.

Hungrily he stared up at the vulnerable arch of her throat, the sensuous droop of her mouth and the shadowy fans her golden red lashes created against her flushed cheekbones. And his heart performed an unfamiliar, almost painful clench, as if suddenly squeezed in the bench-vise grip of an unseen giant.

Treena open her heavy-lidded eyes and gazed down at him with an expression that nearly incinerated him on the spot. "So," she said in a husky voice. "If you're not all burned out on cards, how would you like to indulge in a little game of strip poker?"

They were lethargically assembling breakfast late the following morning when someone knocked on the front door. Treena looked up from the stove where she was turning bacon to glance over at Jax, who stopped slopping pancake batter around a pottery bowl to quirk his eyebrows at her. "Will you get that?" she asked. "I'm afraid to leave this."

"Sure." And propping the wooden spoon he was using against the bowl's festively hued rim, he slid from the bar stool and padded barefoot to the entryway.

"Well, hi there," she heard him say an instant later upon opening the door. "You're the last person I expected to see, given I've never been here when you haven't just let yourself in."

"Hey, I knock," came Carly's voice. "Well, sometimes, anyway. Treena here?"

"Yeah, c'mon in. She's in the kitchen. Excellent timing, by the way—we're getting ready to put breakfast on the table. I don't know what Treena's philosophy will be on feeding your two friends, though."

She barely had a chance to wonder who Carly might have brought with her when Rufus came charging around the corner. Her throw rug on the hardwood floor where the kitchen and living room met accordion-pleated beneath the pup's exuberant onslaught, and with a startled yip the black-and-brown mutt scrambled in place on the fabric bunching beneath his paws, which caused it to contort even further. Then he sprang free, but his balance didn't improve appreciably when he landed on the tiled floor.

He skidded across the kitchen like a sailboat without a rudder, sliding past her to thump up against the cupboards.

Treena laughed so hard she slid down the stove to an ungainly heap on the floor. Lifting her head to wipe her streaming eyes she saw Buster, who had followed more decorously in the younger dog's wake, plopping his slightly overweight butt down on the Rufus-crumpled area rug. His tail thumped twice against the floor.

She tried to get a grip, but each time she came close to gaining control the look of shock on Rufus's face as he'd sailed past her would flash across her mind's screen once again. And off she'd go on another wild ride through Hysteriaville. It didn't help when Rufus scrambled past her with an almost human look of sheepishness on his furry face to join Buster on the crumpled rug. Panting, he leaned heavily against the older dog.

Jax's legs appeared in front of her just as she was sure she was finally getting control of herself. Over the sound of her own intermittent snickering she dimly heard the click of a burner being turned off. "Oh, God, the bacon," she said, and for no good reason she could think of the idea of it burning to a crisp while she laughed like a loon cracked her up all over again.

"She's easily amused," Jax said, presumably to Carly, although her friend was nowhere she could see. He crouched down next to the dogs in the kitchen opening. "I gotta hand it to you," he said to Rufus, ruffling the dog's ears. "That was one spectacular entrance." Then he turned to Buster. "You're a bit more sedate than your little buddy here, aren't you, sport?" He shook the paw that was offered him. "Nice to meet you, too. What did you say your name was again?"

Treena finally got herself in hand and pushed to her feet. Castigating herself for acting like a buffoon, she cleared her throat. "That's Buster."

Jax turned back to look up at Carly as the other

woman rounded the corner. "Interesting dog," he said with mellow amusement. "He looks like something Dr. Seuss might have created."

That nearly reversed Treena's newly regained composure, because it was so wonderfully apt. Buster had long legs and a wide rear, and his splotchy ginger-colored fur was short-haired everywhere except for the wild tufts that sprang up from the crown of his head and formed feathery ruffles around his ankles.

Carly's arctic voice, however, cut through her amusement like a razor through silk. "Oh, that's nice," her friend snapped in a tone that suggested she thought it was anything but. "Do you kick cripples when they're down, too?"

There was a moment of stunned silence. Then Jax rose to his feet and said with cool courtesy, "My apologies. It wasn't my intention to make fun of your dog. I only meant—"

"No, I'm sorry, Jax," Carly interrupted and sighed. "I had no right to go off on you like that. Buster *is* a Dr. Seuss kind of dog, aren't you sweetheart?" The mutt thumped his tail agreeably, and Carly went down on one knee beside him to sling an arm around his neck and give the wild tufts between his ears an affectionate noogie. "Hell, I've said it myself—he's so ugly he's cute."

That satisfied Jax, but Treena, who knew her friend better, wasn't fooled by Carly's sudden breeziness. "What happened?" she demanded.

"Huh? Nothing." She climbed to her feet, dusting dog hair from her palms, and gave Treena an innocent look. "So what's for breakfast besides bacon?"

"Pancakes. What happened, Carly?"

Her friend's jaw tightened and she simply stared at her for a moment. Then with another sigh, she slumped. "I met my new neighbor this morning."

Uh-oh. It clearly hadn't been a positive experience. "And?"

"If I kill him, Treen, will you help me hide the body?"

"Absolutely," she promptly agreed. "There must be a million places out in the desert to dispose of one annoying man."

"Whoa," Jax said, taking a giant step back from them, his hands raised, palms out, as if to ward off trouble. "Remind me never to piss you two off." A look of uneasiness suddenly chased across his expression but before Treena could decipher its meaning he turned to ask Carly incredulously. "How bad can a guy you just met be?"

"Plenty bad." Her pretty features were stiff with remembered affront. "Trust me. He's a buzz-cut, stick-up-the-butt, dog-hating jerk."

Treena zeroed in on the pertinent information in her friend's rant. "He didn't like your dogs?"

"Oh, boy," Jax murmured under his breath, obviously already attuned enough to Carly to realize there was no bigger offense in her book.

"He kept calling Rufus *Dufus*! And he wanted to know why the hell I didn't get him under control." With an indrawn breath that appeared to be one part oxygen and nine parts indignation, her breasts swelled to threaten the stretch of her tank top's fabric. "As if I haven't been knocking myself out trying to do that very thing!" Then she exhaled loudly. "Well, screw him. If that man tries messing with my babies, I don't care if he does have the steeliest buns I've ever seen—he's going *down.*"

Hello. Treena went on alert, even as she slung a comforting arm around her friend to lead her to a stool. *This is interesting.*

She would have sworn there wasn't a guy born who could attract Carly's attention once she discovered he wasn't an animal lover. So the fact that she'd noticed the buns of a man bad-mouthing her dog suggested some *serious* chemistry between her and this Jones character.

Treena, however, knew better than to raise the point in Carly's present condition. Instead she settled her friend in her seat and squeezed her white-knuckled hand. "You just take a couple of deep breaths and have some pancakes and bacon with us. Then I want you to do your best to forget that clown. Maybe he just had a bad day. Or maybe he's always a jerk. Either way, these things usually have a way of working themselves out."

"*Death* has a way of working things out, too. And really, it's not as if it would be murder, or anything. No, no, it would be euthanasia, a genuine mercy killing, considering the man's too stupid to live."

"Be a shame to deprive yourself of a view of that butt, though."

"Yeah." With a regretful sigh, Carly laid her head down on her crossed arms on the countertop. "There is that. It's the only downside I can think of, though."

Man trouble seemed to be in the air. Backstage in the dressing room that night Jerrilyn, whose most recent boyfriend was the World Poker fan who had recognized Jax's name, listened to Carly's rant against her new neighbor. Then the other dancer nodded in total sympathy.

"Wolfgang Jones," she said, nodding. "I know who that is—he's in security, right? I don't think I've ever seen him smile. Great butt, though. And did you get a load of the six-pack abs on him?" She waved the question aside without waiting for an answer. "Never mind. Personally, I don't believe some guys deserve a second chance—much less a third or fourth one." She straightened her fishnets. "Despite that, I gave Donny several, but frankly the boy had nothing going for him but his ability in bed. So, really, I had no choice but to dump him." She shook her head. "I'm sure gonna miss those sessions between the sheets, though."

Eve nodded. "I swear, sometimes, that's the *only* thing men are good for. If I come home from work and find one more stinking pair of socks laying next to the bed or a wet towel tossed on the bathroom floor, my Jeremy is going to be one sorry son of a bitch. Is it too frigging much for him to carry his dirty laundry to the basket?"

"For me it's the damn whiskers in the sink," Michelle said. "There's a whole stack of Dixie cups right next to the faucet—how hard can it be to use one of 'em to rinse his mess down the drain after Gordie's done shaving? But *does* he ever? Oh, no."

Everybody seemed so depressed and anti-men as they left the dressing room for the wings that Treena almost felt guilty for not feeling the least bit down herself. But things with Jax were so great she was still kind of vibrating.

Of course, she didn't have a clue what was going to happen when the tournament ended next week. Would he simply pack up and take off for the next tour in who knew what far-off exotic location?

And if so, would he want her to go with him?

What would she do if he did? As much as she loved him, she'd spent the majority of her life with one goal—to provide herself with financial security.

Not that she was doing so well in that department at the moment, but at least she was drawing a steady paycheck.

And hopefully would still be doing so after this week.

So if she passed the audition could she actually toss her need for security to the wind and follow a gambler from city to city? Could she simply abandon not merely the only career she'd ever known but her dream of establishing her own studio some day?

It wasn't as if the studio was even a remote possibility any longer. So who had the more stable life now—she with her steady paycheck, uncertain future employment prospects and no savings, or Jax with his multi-thousand-dollar wins and losses? Neither of them struck her as overwhelmingly stable.

But that was all smoke and mirrors. She had a feeling that, secure financial future or not, she'd follow him in a heartbeat if he asked her to.

Which of course was the real issue. For when had Jax ever said the first thing to indicate she meant more to him than a Las Vegas fling on this leg of his tour? She honest-to-God felt sometimes that he genuinely did care for her, perhaps even as much as she did for him.

But that was all it was—a feeling. He'd certainly never said one word to indicate it was actually the case.

Well...shit.

She could have gone all night without thinking about any of this. Now she was as depressed as everyone else backstage.

Dancing was suddenly the last thing she felt like doing, but the music introducing the next act swelled out in the orchestra pit. So with a resigned sigh, she pulled herself together and headed for the stage.

Nineteen

Jax couldn't believe what a charge he got out of doing housework. Of course he knew that was because of Treena. Doing damn near anything with her was what got him all jazzed. And since this was her Monday off, he'd offered to help with the weekly cleaning of her condo so they they'd have more time to play outside before her dance class later that afternoon. The equinox had brought weather too beautiful not to take advantage of after the long, hot summer.

They'd decided to divide the final two chores to speed things up, so as soon as he finished dusting the floor in here and she was done in the kitchen they'd be ready to take off.

He was working the duster around the back of the toilet when something bumped the backs of his knees. His legs buckled beneath him and with a grunt he braced his free palm against the top of the tank. Then strong, soft-skinned arms wrapped around his waist.

"Hey there, big boy." Treena rubbed her breasts side to side between his shoulder blades. "Long time no see. So when did you say your birthday was again?" Her voice sounded innocent in his ear, and her body felt like pliable, fragrant heat against his back.

Bracing the duster against the wall, he unwound her arms from his middle and turned. "Why, I believe I told you it was—" grasping her hips he lifted her onto the counter next to the sink and leaned in "—the thir— no…no…wait. Come to think of it, I don't believe I mentioned the actual date at all." Running his hands down to her thighs, he pulled them apart and stepped between them.

"Damn!" Biting back a smile, she thunked him on the chest. Then she gave the abused pectoral a little rub. "But at least I've got a clue now. You said the *thir.* So, the thirtieth, then? The thirteenth? The third? Or crap, it could be the third pick-a-day-any-day of the next couple months, couldn't it?"

He grinned. Treena was constantly trying to wheedle his birthday out of him and it had now become a game of sorts. He might break down one of these days and actually tell her, but for the moment, he was having way too much fun waiting to see what ploy she'd use next in order to discover it for herself. He bent his head to kiss her.

"In your dreams, pal." Jerking back, she slapped both hands to his shoulders and shoved, holding him at arm's length. "Don't even think you have a shot at getting lucky now. In fact you may *die* before you ever get any again." She shot him a smoldering glance from beneath her lashes. "Unless, of course, you want to cough up a date. Then we'll talk."

He trailed his fingers down the side of her throat, smiling slightly when her eyelids went heavy and a soft breath shuddered out of her throat. "Wanna make a small wager as to who can hold out the longest?" he murmured, even though he wasn't all that certain that was a bet he had any hope of winning.

"Nope," she said cheerfully, and slid off the countertop. Then she simply stood there, making no move to get out from between the vanity and his body. She nodded toward the dust mop he'd leaned against the wall. "You about done with that?"

"Yeah. Let me just run it over the spot I missed over there by the tub, then I'm good to go." Grabbing the duster by its long blue handle, he completed the chore even as he stated his intention.

She flashed him such a brilliant smile that his chest constricted. "Great. We're finished, then," she said. "If you'll go put the duster away, I'll slap on some makeup and we can head out. Be careful, though," she warned. "That closet is pretty much a catchall, so it can be a little treacherous to the uninitiated. In fact, just stick it in the front of the closet and I'll put it away later."

"What do you think I am, an incompetent boob? I'll have you know I've got reflexes like a cat. I'm the smoke in the mirror, babe, the shadow in the night, the fog in the—"

"Yeah, yeah, I get it. You're the guy whose machismo has just been impugned."

A smile tugged up the corner of his mouth. "Got it in one, sweet thing." God, he loved this woman.

Everything inside of him stilled. Loved? He was in *love* with her? At the same time that he told himself he couldn't be in love, that it simply wasn't smart given his ulterior motives, he knew it was true. He felt it on a gut level so deep there was no sense denying it.

Even if he didn't have the first idea what the hell he was going to do about it. He stepped back and indicated the mop. "I'll go put this away and leave you to slap on your war paint."

She laughed. "You are such a smooth talkin' guy."

His heart thumping uneasily, he carried the dust mop to the living room closet and opened the door. "Holy shit," he murmured, amazed at its jumbled interior. "Catchall was a euphemism, I take it."

This was full-out chaos, the universe after the Big Bang. Treena's tidy gene clearly stopped at the door to the coat closet. He snorted. Interestingly named space, considering coats were probably the least represented article in the deep, narrow cubicle.

It was filled from floor to ceiling with all sorts of crap—or so it appeared at first glance, anyway. He wouldn't have thought it was possible for Treena to have more shoes than he'd already seen on her feet or in her bedroom closet, for instance, yet several pairs of leather boots were lined up beneath the coats. And not one of them, as far as he could see, was of the useful variety. Hell, you could probably aerate a dozen lawns with the heels on most of these puppies, but step in one pile of dogshit wearing them, and the shoe in question would no doubt get tossed in the nearest garbage can so fast it'd be nothing but a streak of light to the naked eye.

Shaking his head, he looked at the boxes stacked in the back and intermittently along the right wall.

He could barely see the hook on the back wall through all the junk in his path so he started picking his careful way between the piles, trying to avoid precariously mounded odds and ends beneath the hang rod on his left. He veered too near a stack of boxes on his right, and when his biceps brushed against a loose object he felt it shift and fall from atop the stack. Dropping the mop, his hand shot out with more instinct than forethought, and he caught a furled travel umbrella with a bent spoke before it hit the floor. Carefully restoring it to its place upon the top box, he blew out a breath at the near miss and was happy to see that the area directly in front of him opened up to something actually resembling floor space. Retrieving the duster, he took a careful step toward the open area, only to promptly crack his elbow on the sharp corner of something sitting atop the pile to his left.

Things immediately began slip-sliding in the unstable heap and Jax dropped the dust mop once again and grabbed the Plexiglas box that had started the avalanche, slapping it against his stomach to keep it from tumbling away. Swearing under his breath, he braced his shins against the bottom of the pile and managed to rearrange a few things with his free hand. His efforts seemed to halt the mad rush toward the floor, and it wasn't until he was pretty sure he wasn't going to be buried up to his eyeballs in Treena's junk that he actually looked down at the object that had nearly disabled him.

He jerked in shock. The movement caused the pile he'd just saved to flow like lava from its shifting base, but he paid it no heed as he stared down at the collectible that had brought him into Treena's life.

After a moment he roused himself and bent to retrieve the duster and clip it into its holder. Then he simply stood in the recesses and studied his grandfather's baseball in what little light managed to filter back into the corner.

The ghostly echo of his father's voice immediately started issuing orders in his mind. *Goddammit, Jackson, those were easy pop-ups! Pay attention out there—all you have to do is stay sharp in the outfield and you'll start catching them.* He stared down at the ball in its clear box, sick with feelings he'd struggled long and hard to eradicate. Inadequacy, insecurity and a crawling sensation of shame and worthlessness clamored for his attention. The 1927 World Series ball represented the majority of his youth.

And, God, he despised the fucking thing.

So smuggle it the hell out of here today and hand it over to Sergei. Then all your problems will be over, right?

Sure, if he didn't mind the fact he'd be stealing from the woman he loved. If he didn't care that his betrayal would no longer be merely one of intent but firmly rooted in actuality instead.

Shit.

Still, what other choice did he have? He had to turn the baseball over to Kirov.

But he didn't have to do it today.

Jax carried the ball in its Plexiglas container back to

the stack of boxes and carefully set it behind the umbrella. Picking up a scarf from the floor, he released the fingers he'd pinched it between and watched as the satiny fabric fluttered down to cover both items.

Then he shook himself. He still had until after tomorrow night's tournament. Maybe by then a way to tell Treena the real reason he'd first inserted himself into her life would occur to him.

"Hey," her voice suddenly called, and he heard her footsteps crossing the living room. "Did you get lost in there?"

He rammed his fingers through his hair. "No," he called back. "It's like deepest, darkest Africa, but I think I'm finally approaching the Serengeti." He turned and picked his way out of the closet, then stood blinking in the bright light that bathed the living room. When Treena walked up to him, vibrant in a turquoise tank top, matching casual skirt and strappy low-heeled sandals, he draped his arms over her shoulders and bowed his head to rest his forehead against hers. A feeling of peace bloomed within him as all the negative feelings resurrected by the ball's discovery faded away.

"I wasn't sure if I'd ever see you again," he said, and to his chagrin there was a very real catch in his voice. He cleared his throat. *Keep it light,* coached the part of him that had spent a lifetime instructing him in ways not to care when someone he loved found him a huge disappointment. "What with, uh, all the booby traps in there and all."

She started to pull back as if to examine his expression, but he laced his fingers together through the soft cloud of curls at the back of her head. He didn't want her looking at him right this moment, since he wasn't at all sure he had his poker face in place.

She didn't fight his hold but rather rolled her forehead against his and smoothed her hands over his chest. But her voice held a hint of concern when she asked, "Are you okay, Jax?"

Tell her. Tell her now, demanded his accountable adult self. *Maybe she'll understand.*

But maybe she wouldn't, and his self-protective side had been active since he was a kid and was much stronger than his conscience could ever hope to be. So he merely said, "Sure. I was just thinking about Treena Sarkilahti's secret life of sloth."

"McCall," she corrected as she always did when he used her maiden name and this time she did raise her head. She poked him in his abs. "And I'll have you know, Gallagher, that I'm usually pretty neat."

"Uh-huh. Sure you are." He slapped on a look of cool cynicism even as he realized what should have been a no-brainer from the beginning. The reason he never called Treena by her married name was because he couldn't bear the thought of her being wed to his father. He couldn't face the idea of her lying in the old man's arms the way she'd lain in his, all flushed and warm and satiated from his loving.

Pushing the image away, he said, "That closet was a revelation, babe." Then without giving her an opportunity to reply, he indicated the front door with a jut of his chin. "So, you ready to ride?"

"I was born ready," she retorted, and he laughed.

She touched his lower lip and said, "Let me just grab my tote. I've got my sunscreen in it and a bottle of water."

He let her slip away and half of him was pleased he'd eased around a potential land mine. The other half had a different take on the matter, but he stuffed down its objections with the rationalization that blurting out his real identity today would do neither of them any good. They both had a big day tomorrow. She had the audition she'd been working so hard toward, and provided he played well tonight, he'd have a seat at the tournament's final table. Upsetting her now would merely screw things up for both of them.

He knew he had to tell Treena the entire truth, no matter how damning, and he *would* do it tomorrow, just as soon as everything was over. No more excuses, no more prevarications.

Still, that gave him a twenty-four-hour grace period. And until it was up, he intended to avoid *anything* that might put a look of betrayal on her face.

Mack knocked on Ellen's door promptly at five-thirty that afternoon.

"So what are your thoughts on prime rib?" he demanded the moment she opened it. Then he took her in from head to toe and his eyes nearly bugged out of his head. She wore a simple black suit with sheer black hose and sensible black pumps. Beneath the jacket, however, was a silky little purple top. Its satiny sheen made the moisture dry up in his mouth, for it looked like fancy underwear, like something forbidden that offered him a glimpse of cleavage when her suit jacket pulled back as she swung the door open wide to admit him.

"I'm all for it," she said with a smile.

He jerked his attention back to the subject at hand. "I only ask because I made us a reservation at Lawry's The Prime Rib, and if you've ever been there you probably know you can have anything you want—as long as it's prime rib. So in case that doesn't hit your hot button I also made a reservation at Austin's Steakhouse over on Texas Star Lane." He shook his head and stared at her again. "Damn, you look good!"

A delicate rose colored her cheeks. "Thank you. You look very nice yourself."

He looked down at his charcoal suit, white shirt and the silver-gray tie that felt like a noose around his neck, and hitched one shoulder. "Yeah, I'm passable, but you…you look good enough to eat." He nodded at the little top that commanded his attention. "I sure like your whozit there. What do you call that color?"

"Purple," she said, deadpan. But her pretty hazel eyes twinkled with suppressed humor.

He laughed. "Come on, what do you really call it? I know you ladies have fancy names for colors. Like puce. I remember my mother calling something puce once. What the hell is that?"

"A brownish purple."

He shook his head. "Jesus. And this shade?"

"Periwinkle."

"Okay, sure, like the flower. Maryanne grew some of those in the yard of the house we rented before we bought our first home. It's a very pretty color. You look real good in it." He cleared his throat. "So, which restaurant hits your hot button?"

"Lawry's. I've never been there and I love prime rib."

"Hot dawg." He rubbed his hands together. "That's what I had my taste buds set for, too. You mind if I borrow your phone? I should probably call Austin's and cancel the reservation I made there."

He ushered Ellen into the red-carpeted reception area of Lawry's a short while later and admired her by the light of the fireplace while they waited for the hostess who would take them to the main dining room. "Did I mention how pretty you look tonight?" he asked.

"You did, yes." She smiled demurely. "But a woman can never hear a compliment like that too often."

He threw back his head and laughed, then placed his hand at the small of her back as he guided her to the white linen-covered table the hostess indicated. The silky material of her slip-top shifted beneath his hand and her jacket.

They were seated and a waitress appeared at their table to introduce herself as Mrs. Baxter and take their drink order. After she walked away, Ellen smiled at him. "This is very pretty. I love the Art Deco decor."

"Is that what it's called?" He looked around at the coved ceilings, hardwood floors and colorful rugs, before turning his attention back to her. "I like the use of all the wood."

"Isn't it lovely? Oh, and the waitresses' uniforms!"

"Yeah, I read somewhere that they haven't changed the style since the first Lawry's opened in Beverly Hills in 1938." Mrs. Baxter returned with their wine and they both silently admired her crisp old-fashioned uniform that was the same rich burgundy color as the restaurant's velvet banquettes and chairs. It sported a starched white collar and cuffs and a pristine white apron that tied behind her back in a huge bow.

When the waitress had performed the wine ritual and left them once again Mack gave Ellen an inquiring look. "What do you suppose those tall head things they all wear are called?"

"I have no idea, but I remember seeing them on the counter-servers at Woolworth's when I was a girl."

"You know what they remind me of? My nurses at the hospital where I had my tonsils removed back in the early fifties."

"In the fifties, huh?" Her eyes held warm interest as she gazed at him across the table. "How old were you?"

"Just turned ten."

"Was it awful? I had mine taken out when I was fourteen. It was on the first day of spring break and my mother promised me I'd be up and at 'em by the following day, but I was sick as a dog the entire week and furious that I'd missed my vacation."

"I had an easier time of it. I got to eat ice cream and Jell-O for two days, then pretty much bounced back to my usual trouble-making ways." Mack leaned back in his chair. He had been half-afraid they wouldn't have much to say to each other once he finally got Ellen to himself, but he found himself completely relaxed. "So tell me what it was like to work in a library all those years."

Her face lit up. "I just adored it. I enjoyed my coworkers and loved helping people find a novel they'd enjoy or the research material they needed to complete a paper or a project. I loved that each day I learned something new." She sighed with pleasure. "But most of all I adored being surrounded by books."

He grinned. "From the looks of the shelves in your living room, you're still surrounded by books."

"Yes, I admit it, I'm an addict. How about you? Are you a reader?"

"Nothing like you are, I bet. But I like a good Elmore Leonard or Neal Stephenson book. Especially if I've had a particularly busy day. I'm not a big fan of all the reality TV that seems to be the big craze these days, so I find it a great way to unwind."

"And you certainly keep busy." Leaning in, she reached across the table to touch her fingertips to the back of his hand. "It must be very rewarding to be so competent at so many things." The corner of her mouth crooked. "Winston, bless his heart, was a whiz when it came to banking. But when it came to keeping anything running around the house he was utterly helpless. I so admire the way you seem to master every single thing you put your hands to."

I'd like to put my hands to you, he thought. Feeling heat rise up his throat, he tugged at the knot of his tie. *Down boy,* he lectured himself sternly. He didn't want to blow the opportunity he had with Ellen. Focusing on the topic she'd begun, he told her a bit about his background in the aircraft industry and how his father had started him down his current path as a handyman by teaching him how to work with tools.

It was difficult not to think hot thoughts, however, when she fanned herself with her hand a few moments later and said, "This wine has certainly warmed me up," and pulled off her suit jacket, rising to drape it over the back of her chair. He stared at her shoulders gleaming in the muted light as she reseated herself, gazed with covetous eyes at the way the skimpy periwinkle slip-top cupped her pretty breasts.

He felt enormous gratitude toward Mrs. Baxter for her timely intervention when she returned to take their order.

Unfortunately, once he'd allowed sexual thoughts into his mind, they stuck like a freeloading relative to the guest-room bed, and he had to work like the devil to evict them. His choice of restaurant helped, for Lawry's service was a show that provided built-in distractions. Instead of tossing their salads, the waitress spun their mixed greens, shreds of beets, bits of egg, grape tomatoes and croutons in a stainless-steel bowl atop a bed of ice, drizzling in dressing, then serving the mixture onto their plates and presenting them with chilled salad forks. The chef rolled a stainless cart to their table and carved their individual servings from the majestic standing rib it showcased.

Then there was Ellen herself. The more they talked, the more imperative grew his need for a relationship deeper than a quick tumble into the nearest bed—although that desire was rapidly reaching near-addictive proportions. She was smart and funny and a whole lot earthier than he'd ever imagined.

Discovering that their senses of humor often meshed, they laughed frequently. She told him about her canceled trip to Italy and he told her about his one and only vacation in Europe, the excursion he and Maryanne had taken to England and France the year before she'd died. They talked about his daughters and about "their" girls, speculating on how serious Treena was getting about Jax and how long it would take Carly to whip Rufus into shape. The conversation flowed almost nonstop, but even the occasional silences were companionable.

Once they were enclosed in his car heading home, however, all the sexual tension he'd managed to tamp down during the meal returned with a vengeance. On the drive back to the complex he found himself growing more and more edgy the closer they got to home, and by the time they reached Ellen's door he had outright knots in the back of his neck. He wanted in the worst way to push her up against the unyielding wood and put his hands all over that seductive little top.

Instead, he leaned forward and kissed her with the utmost gentleness, taking extra care not to touch her with anything except his lips.

And he did all right, he held it all together, until her soft lips opened beneath his. Then, promising himself he'd take only one little taste, he eased his tongue into the warm, damp cavern of her mouth.

That was a big mistake. His kiss turned fierce, desperate, and he trembled with the effort it took to hold himself back, to not plaster his body against hers and simply take and take and take. He ripped his mouth free and stared down at her, breathing hard. "Well, uh, good night," he said hoarsely, shoving his hands into his pockets to keep himself from pawing her like a rabid dog.

She blinked, then drew a shuddery little breath and opened her purse to retrieve her key. Upon unlocking and opening her door, she looked up at him and bade him a soft good-night.

Then the prim curve of her lips turning into a siren's smile, Ellen reached out, wrapped his tie around her petite fist and hauled him through the doorway into her apartment.

Nobody had to invite him twice and, heart beating fast and furiously, he grasped her fine-boned shoulders. Kicking the door closed behind them, he pulled her into his arms and rocked his mouth over hers.

Twenty

Jax was still asleep when Treena came back to the bedroom after her shower the next morning. They'd certainly been burning their candle at both ends and she knew she'd feel like sleeping for a week, herself, once this afternoon's audition was finally behind her. That was a pipe dream, of course, but she at least intended to sleep late tomorrow morning.

Looking at such a large man sprawled out on his stomach like a little boy made her feel all gooey inside. His arms curved over his head and one knee was pulled up, his thigh free of the covers tangled around his hips. Observing him, so big and male and utterly at peace in her bed not only touched a tender spot inside of her, it managed to settle some of the butterflies fluttering in her stomach over the upcoming audition.

She moved quietly about the room as she pulled fresh undies and a gauzy top and jeans from her drawers and dressed. Then she headed back to the bathroom to apply her makeup.

Jax still hadn't stirred when she returned to the bedroom, so she set about gathering her stuff together for the tryout. Forgoing her usual ratty leotard, she packed fishnet stockings, an almost new double-cross halter top and a pair of V-front boy-cut shorts into her dance bag. She polished her black T-strap shoes and placed them in the bag's end pocket. *la Stravaganza* didn't require its dancers to audition in full makeup and costume like some of the shows did, but she'd learned over the years that putting an extra effort into her appearance paid off. The choreographer and GM who conducted the tryouts paid attention to that sort of thing.

And this year she needed all the help she could get.

She spotted Jax's wallet on the floor by her vanity chair as she passed by on her way to grab an additional pair of stockings. Pausing to pick it up, she tossed it atop his jeans on the little chair and had taken several steps away before she suddenly came to a halt. She glanced over her shoulder at the leather billfold, then over at Jax, still deep asleep.

And she grinned. "Driver's license," she whispered gleefully.

Whipping around she retraced her steps and dropped to a squat in front of the chair. She picked up the wallet and with one final glance over her shoulder, flipped the tri-fold open.

Jax's license had been issued in Massachusetts, a state she'd hadn't even realized he'd ever lived in, and it occurred to her there was a lot they'd never discussed.

He'd taken a good, if slightly sober-faced, picture and his birthday was—aha!—October third.

"Gotcha." She smiled at herself, tickled to have won the ongoing game between them. Now her biggest decision was whether to let him know right away that she knew exactly when he was going to turn thirty-four or to wait for his birthday and surprise him. The fact that he was slightly younger than she was didn't bother her, though she was surprised.

As she happily considered her options, her gaze drifted across the name on the driver's license. And her stomach dropped. Her smile froze. No. No, that couldn't be right.

But reading it again, she saw that, indeed, the license had been issued to Jackson Gallagher McCall.

The man she'd fallen in love with, the man she'd trusted, the man she'd been weaving goddamn *fantasies* of a rosy future around was Big Jim's son. Something almost audible reverberated in her head.

She thought it must be the sound of all her dreams caving in.

Jax jerked awake as someone yanked urgently on his left biceps. Blinking groggily, he struggled up on his right arm. "Huh? What?"

He saw Treena bent over him. She slapped at his head, his neck, his shoulders with both hands then wrapped them around his upraised biceps again and tugged, obviously trying to pull his two hundred and eighteen pounds out of bed. "Get out," she yelled. "Get out of here now!"

"Honey?" He sat up. "What's the matter? Is the condo on fire?" But he knew that wasn't it. He was waking up fast now and beginning to realize she wasn't concerned for his welfare.

She was furious with him, and there was only one reason he could think of for that. Acid poured into his gut and his heart started banging like a loose shutter in a hurricane against the wall of his chest.

"Oh, God." She laughed, but it was an arid, humorless sound. "What's the matter? What's the *matter?* I thought I knew you, but I didn't know squat. And I want you out of my house, Jackson McCall." She spat his name as if to get it out of her mouth before its corrosiveness could eat through her tongue like acid. *"Now!"*

Shit.

"How did you find out?" he croaked.

Wrong question. He knew it the instant the words left his mouth. Dodging the fist she sent hurling his way, he said hastily, "That's not what I meant! Listen to me, Treena. I was going to tell you myself tonight, I swear."

"Liar!" She came at him, murder in her eyes and her hands an erratic blur as they smacked at any part of him she could reach. "You goddamn liar!"

Jax surged to his feet and wrapped his arms around her, pinning her hands to her sides. She bucked and fought, and this wasn't some delicate little English flower he was wrapped around. Treena was tall and strong and mad as hell, and he had to plant his feet, tighten his hold and hang on until she wore herself out.

It took a while but finally she went limp. His heart

just broke when he felt scalding tears trickle down his chest, and he pressed his cheek to the top of her head, where he swore he could feel steam escaping.

"I was going to tell you tonight," he reiterated, his voice hoarse with the urgent need to make her listen to him—to make her believe. "When I first met you I didn't plan to tell you at all. But then I fell for you. God, I fell for you so hard, and I didn't know what the hell to do—so I kept putting off telling you who I was. But I swear on my mother's grave that I'd made up my mind to tell you tonight. I just didn't want the knowledge of my identity to foul up your audition."

Her head snapped up so fast she damn near shattered his cheekbone, and he bit back an oath as pain radiated out from the point of contact.

She glared at him through narrowed lashes. "Oh, trust me, you son of a bitch, I'm going to pass that audition. You will *not* screw that up for me, too." Her heart pounded against his diaphragm. "How long have you known who I am?"

He was tempted to lie and say the morning following her birthday when she'd first mentioned Big Jim's name. But he had to tell her the truth. He owed her that.

And, God, so much more. "Before we met."

The pain that flashed across her face nearly brought him to his knees.

"You bastard," she whispered. Her breath sawed in and out of her lungs as she stared at him and her voice was anguished as she demanded, *"Why?"*

"To get my grandfather's baseball."

"Your…what? A baseball?" Incomprehension furrowed her brow. Then her eyes widened. "The World Series ball?"

"Yes. I got myself in a jam, and I need the ball to get out of it with both hands still intact."

It was clear she had no idea what he was talking about, and Jax drew in a deep breath and eased it out again, trying to marshal his thoughts. "Look, all my life I've had the history of Grandpa's baseball shoved down my throat—and the lecture always ended with my father telling me that someday it would be mine. Well, the truth is, I never wanted the damn thing. It seems like all we ever did was fight about my disappointing skill in sports, and that stupid ball epitomized our entire dicked up relationship. So the day I found out Dad was dead I did something incredibly stupid. I allowed my ego to do my thinking during a poker game. The result of *that* brilliant move was that I let myself be maneuvered into putting up the ball for a wager."

"You *bet* it?"

"Yes."

She stared at him as if he were a slug with a mile-long slime trail. "So let me get this straight. You couldn't be bothered to attend your father's funeral but you had time for a card game, where you wagered his most prized possession."

Trying not to let the contempt in her voice get to him, he said levelly, "I received the letter informing me of Dad's death months late because it ended up chasing me all over Europe. And the day it finally caught up with me, I went a little crazy. I was drinking and not thinking real straight."

"So you lost it." It wasn't a question.

"Yes. And the guy I lost it to is threatening to have his goons break all my fingers if I don't give it to him after the tournament tonight."

For the first time she looked perhaps the tiniest bit sympathetic toward him. "Some man threatened to break your fingers?"

He gave a little shrug. "Not in so many words. But he implied it, and having his henchmen bend my thumbs backward made it pretty damn clear." Sucking in another breath, he felt Treena's breasts flatten against his diaphragm and realized he still held her immobile. She seemed to have calmed down enough to abandon her plan to beat him to death and he knew he ought to ease away and set her free.

He didn't. He wanted to hang on to her for as long as he could. He loosened his hold slightly, though. "I honest to God wanted to do this the right way, Treena. When I found out the ball hadn't been left to me after all I authorized my lawyer to make you an offer for it."

"That was *you?*" She stared up at him, dumbfounded. Then a maniacal laugh burst out of her, and it wasn't a pretty sound. It was harsh and loud and went on much too long.

He was beginning to fear what he'd have to do to stop the hysteria when the crazed sound stopped with the abruptness of a needle being snatched up off a record. She looked up at him and his head jerked back at the scorn that flared so hotly in her eyes it had burned away the last of her tears.

"You sorry-ass buffoon," she said contemptuously. "I

wanted to take that offer in the worst way. It would have given me the security I'd enjoyed before I gave up the cushion of my savings—it would have allowed me to start my dance studio should today's audition not go the way I hope it will. The way it *has* to go now."

She wrenched free of his hold and stepped back. "But you know what, *Jackson?* I couldn't sell it. And would you like to know why?"

"Sure." Without taking his eyes off of her, he snatched his jeans off the little chair and pulled them on.

"Because I knew Big Jim wanted it to go to his worthless son. Gawd, don'tcha just love it? Isn't that *rich?* All this time that you were planning to—what, steal it from me?—I was saving it for you."

Crap. His head swam, his usual methodical mind a frozen wasteland.

She laughed bitterly. "The joke was certainly on me, wasn't it?"

"No." Dropping the T-shirt he'd picked up to put on, he ran his forefinger down the soft skin of her cheek. It was flushed and hot beneath his fingertip. "The joke was on both of us."

She made a skeptical sound and knocked his hand aside. "What the hell did *you* lose? I mean, come on! This is pretty much a win-win situation for you. You get your precious ball." For a second she faltered. "Or maybe you've stolen it from the closet already."

"I left it where I found it, Treena."

"Well, hallelujah—you managed to keep your sticky fingers off of it. So, you get the ball, you get to keep your clever hands in one piece, and hey! You didn't even once have to visit your sick father to get your inheritance! You didn't have to go through all that dreary effort of putting yourself out for a man who pined to see you one last time before he died."

It was a direct jab at Jax's hottest button, and all his warmly concerned penitence turned to ice. He stepped back, his spine snapping straight, his most noncommittal poker face slamming into place. "You don't know what the hell you're talking about," he said coldly.

"Oh, don't I?" She thrust her face up under his, poked a long finger into his sternum. "I was there, buddy, you weren't! And it was all *Jackson* this and *Jackson* that. He lived for your sporadic phone calls, bragged to his friends about what a mathematical genius you are. Big Jim was the nicest man I ever met and you never once, in all the time I knew him, came to see him!"

"You're damn right I didn't! I don't know where all that newfound fondness for me came from, but when I was growing up I couldn't do *anything* to make that man proud. And as for his so-called pride in my math abilities—"

"There was nothing so-called about it, *Jackson*."

"Stop calling me that!" He was nearly beside himself, hearing the hated name coming from her lips. "The only person who ever called me Jackson was my father—and that was usually when he was haranguing me for missing some stupid pitch in some stupid game I didn't want to play in the first place. I'm *Jax*. Got it? That's what my mother called me and that's who I am."

"Fine then, *Jax*. Don't you tell me what I know. And I know he was proud of you—leagues beyond what you deserved, if you ask me. I must have heard once a day how you'd graduated top of your class from MIT at seventeen freaking years of age."

"Then why the hell didn't he bother coming to my graduation?" Jax roared.

"He was sick, you ass. He didn't want to take away from your big day."

"Had better things to do, is more like it." He remembered the old man's phone call that day. *"Sorry, kid,"* Big Jim had said. *"You know how it is. Things come up."* "I knocked myself out trying to please that old bastard, but it was an exercise in futility. *Nothing* I did was good enough for him."

She nodded. "Your father admitted he made a lot of mistakes with you."

"Ya *think?*" he said with bitter sarcasm. "He didn't understand the first goddamn thing about me."

"That's probably true. From what he told me, your mom was really good with you and he didn't know much about kids at all. So when she died and you were this frighteningly bright kid who didn't like any of the things he did, he didn't have the first idea what to do with you."

His stomach rolled and pitched queasily. "But that didn't stop him from trying to browbeat me into being a clone of Big Jim McCall."

"Oh, grow up," she snapped. "We all have crappy things to deal with as kids. You think my folks approved of what I wanted to do with my life?" She pinned him in place with a withering glare. "Parents mess up. Get over it."

Her contempt lashed him on the raw, and he struck

out blindly. "Screw you. At least you knew your folks loved you. The only time my old man felt affection for me was when I could field a pop-up or score a base run. In other words, goddamn never! Or, oh, yeah—when I was long gone, apparently, and he decided my being a math geek wasn't such an embarrassment to him after all. Well, where the hell was he to say, 'Everything's gonna be all right. I'm proud of you' when I was fourteen and on my way to a university where the next youngest student was at least old enough to drive? I knocked myself out for his approval and he made me feel like the world's biggest loser for my efforts. So, honey, he may have talked a good game to you but take it from someone who was there. His parenting skills were more than 'messed up.' They were nonexistent."

"At least he didn't lie through his teeth!" Storming over to the coat closet, she wrenched the door open and disappeared inside. A horrendous racket ensued as she banged around. "At least he never made you fall in love with him then ripped your heart out and stomped it into the ground!" She reappeared, scarlet-faced, with the Plexiglas box gripped between her white-knuckled hands.

Jax froze, all his ire draining away. Aw, crap. He'd messed up so bad, and he had to fix it. He stepped forward to say he was sorry, to make her realize how much he loved her, too.

Before he could even open his mouth, however, Treena slammed the box into his stomach. Sheer reflex made him grab it.

"Here. Take your goddamn ball and go. For whatever faults your father had, he was honest. He had integrity."

She herded him toward the door but stopped just shy of it to look him squarely in the eye. "And Jackson, or Jax or whatever the hell you're calling yourself? He was twice the man you are."

"No." Nausea rushing up his throat, he hunched over as if she'd just kicked him squarely between the legs. For a second he was eleven, twelve, thirteen years old again where his reality was the knowledge that he might be book smart, but nothing he did would ever measure up to larger-than-life Big Jim McCall.

He swallowed the sickness the best he could and reached out to touch her hair. "Don't say that," he whispered. "Please, Treena, don't tell me that."

Her face was stony as she ripped open the door. She thrust an arm out, her index finger pointing rigidly to the corridor. "Get out of my house. I never want to see you again."

Unable to discern the least bit of indecision on her face and hurting so badly he wasn't sure he could draw a full breath, he trudged out the door.

It slammed behind his back the instant his bare heels cleared the threshold.

Treena slid down the door until her knees were wobbling in front of her eyes. Wrapping her arms around her shins, she buried her face between her knees and cried, huge, wracking sobs that threatened to tear her lungs out of her chest, to rend her broken heart from its mooring. She cried until she had no tears left. Then she curled limply on her side in the fetal position.

She had no idea how much time had passed when a

sudden knock erupted like a gunshot on the panel above her head. Her heart jumped in shock but she stayed where she was, willing whoever it was to go away. The knock came again, then the door opened, stopping abruptly when it hit her body.

"What the hell?" Carly's voice said. "Treena? Are you in there? We should take off pretty soon for the audition."

Right. The audition. A thin thread of determination found its way through her despair and Treena pulled herself up off the floor.

Carly fell into the apartment. She swore, righted herself and took a long, hard look at Treena, who figured she must look pretty bad because her friend's face paled.

"Oh, my God," Carly said. "What happened? What did that bastard do?"

Twenty-One

The mattress dipped next to Ellen's hip and she smiled as Mack leaned down and pressed his lips to the back of her neck. With a hum of pleasure, she arched like a cat beneath the sensations he invoked.

"Hey, sleepyhead," he murmured in her ear, then changed the angle of his head to kiss the nerve-rich curve where her neck flowed into her shoulder. He stroked her hip through the blankets. "It's almost eleven—I bet you haven't slept this late in ages." With one last kiss, he pushed back from the bed.

Missing his nearness, she rolled onto her back and stretched luxuriously, feeling a deep feminine satisfaction when his dark chocolate eyes went almost black. "That's true," she agreed and sat up, tucking the sheet beneath her armpits. "On the other hand, it's also been an age since I've participated in such vigorous activity."

He laughed and handed her a robe. That's when she realized he must have been back to his apartment already this morning, because last night's suit and tie had been replaced by his usual neatly pressed chinos and a black T-shirt. But she forgot all about his clothing when he flashed her the sweetest smile she'd ever seen on his craggy face.

"You sure look pretty in the morning," he said. "And I'd like nothing more than to tumble you onto your tidy little backside and love you silly one more time." His smile turned wry. "But I'm an old guy and you wore me out. So, how about I feed you instead? You hungry?"

Her stomach growled as if on cue and they both laughed. Pulling on the robe, she rose from the rumpled sheets and tied the chenille belt around her waist. "It's a little late, I suppose, to pretend I couldn't eat a thing."

"I'd be real disappointed if you did. Breakfast is almost ready."

Delight bloomed. "You *made* it? Oh, my gosh. You're a regular Renaissance man."

His eyebrows elevated. "Now that's something I can honestly say I've never been called."

"It's what you are, though. I have yet to see anything you're unable to do. You keep this entire complex running, you cook, you're *very* good in…well." Cheeks heating as she glanced at the bed, she cleared her throat.

He grinned and slung his arm around her waist, guiding her from the room. "You're very good in…well, too." Splaying his workingman's hand possessively over her hip, he gazed down at her with warm eyes. "I have to tell you, Ellen, that last night was the best time I've had in years."

"For me, too."

He halted in front of the bathroom and she thought he was going to kiss her. He did, but it was a butterfly peck on her lips, there one second then gone, with only a whisper of sensation left in its wake. When he raised his head he tipped it toward the bathroom door. "Would you like a minute in the…?"

Lord, she was crazy about this man. "Yes, please. In fact, give me a few minutes and I'll join you in the kitchen."

"You got it. What would you like to drink with your omelet?"

"Tea, please. If you'll just turn on the kettle, I'll select which kind when I get there."

She used the facilities, washed her hands and face and brushed her teeth. As she attempted to bully her hair into something that resembled an actual style instead of the obvious case of bed head it was, she thought about the man in her kitchen.

And she smiled. Mack might prefer a select number of positions when it came to lovemaking, but that certainly hadn't detracted from the quality of his work. She got dreamy-eyed just thinking about it. The first time had been all hot, frantic passion. But the second time had been slow hands and dark words and a fever that had built and built until she'd thought she'd spontaneously combust. And he was a postcoital cuddler. She grinned at her image in the mirror. A postcoital cuddler who cooked.

Life didn't get much better than that.

She saw when she rejoined him that he'd used her best everyday dishes and set a pretty table. It even included a motley arrangement of flowers, which he must have picked from the grounds and jammed into a water glass.

He handed her a mug of steaming water as he passed her on his way to the table with a short stack of buttered toast. She quickly chose an Irish Breakfast blend out of her selection in the cupboard and glanced at Mack over her shoulder as she brewed her cup of tea. "What can I do to help?"

"Come take your seat. I just have to grab the platter out of the oven and we're in business." He pulled out a chair for her and ran callused fingertips over her bare skin where the collar of her robe slipped as she sat.

She shivered in pleasure. Winston had possessed banker's hands—all smooth skin and manicured nails, and for more than two decades she'd loved their touch. She'd had no idea until she'd felt Mack's hard-textured hands on her last night that rough-skinned fingers could contribute such an exciting level of tactile eroticism to the senses.

He served them omelets rich with green onions, tomatoes and cheese, along with fried potatoes and toast. Their conversation was desultory as they made inroads into his fare.

Ellen finally pushed her plate back and sighed. "Oh, my," she said with utter contentment. "That was a treat."

He accepted her compliment, but then gave her one of his no-nonsense looks. "You know, I've been thinking."

She planted her chin in her palm and smiled, enjoying simply looking at his solid shoulders and lived-in face. "And?"

"And I think we get on well together. *Very* well."

"I think we do, too. It's pretty amazing, really, considering all the fussing and fighting we did up until a few days ago."

"Yeah, well." Dull red climbed his strong neck. "Much as I hate to admit it, I have to take the blame for most of that. The first time I saw you I thought you were the prettiest thing I'd ever clapped eyes on and wanted you on the spot. But instead of saying so, I regressed to grade-school behavior. It must be clear to you by now that my courting skills began and ended with Maryanne. I met her in the sixth grade and married her right out of high school."

"No kidding?" The knowledge startled her. "I had no idea you'd married that young."

"Yeah. We managed to defy the failure-rate statistics for teenage weddings and had a marriage that actually grew stronger over the years instead of falling apart by the time we'd reached our midtwenties." He gave his head an impatient shake. "But that's not what I wanted to talk about. Like I said, you and I mesh really well together. I think we ought to make this relationship permanent."

She straightened in her seat. "As in *get married?*"

"Sure. Why not? It's a great idea."

"It's an insane idea. Mack, we've had *one* date."

"And look how well that turned out." He pushed his plate aside and folded his forearms on the table, leaning toward her with a winning smile. "I considered just living together, but I've got two impressionable daughters to think about."

"Who, if I remember correctly, are thirty-six and thirty-three years old." But she couldn't prevent the smile that curled her lips. He looked so good, sitting across from her with his strong arms resting on the table and his dark eyes intent on getting his way. But it was his you-gotta-love-me grin that really grabbed her heart.

"Okay, so they're not exactly babes in the woods anymore," he admitted. "Still, I'm sure they'd much rather see their old man duly wed than living in sin with the last of the red-hot librarians." His smile turned downright cocky. "And admit it. You're tempted."

"The crazy thing is, I am. But I'm a cautious woman by nature and—"

He snorted. "Oh, yeah, I could tell that by the way you hauled me in here by my tie last night."

Although she felt her cheeks flame again, she knew this particular heat was generated by a covert pride, not embarrassment. She had to admit she'd considered that a pretty hot-mama move, herself.

Still. "That was an impulse—and an extremely uncharacteristic one, I might add. Also, while I might have been a bit precipitous jumping into bed with you, I definitely don't leap into marriage with someone with whom, up until a few short days ago, I've done nothing but trade insults."

"But you're not blowing off the idea entirely, right?"

She gave him her most demure smile. "Let's just say I'm not dismissing the possibility for some future date."

"Some *near* future date," he promptly stated. "Neither one of us is getting any younger."

"No, we aren't. Which to me means we're mature enough to get to know each other before we go rushing off to the Chapel of Love. So convince me a permanent relationship would be a smart move on our part, then we'll talk timing."

"All right, now we're talking my language." Rubbing his hands together, he rose to his feet and came around to pull out her chair. "Let's step into your office and I'll give you a quick lesson on how a master negotiator operates."

"Or a master operator negotiates," she suggested drily. Heat started building deep inside of her, but she gave him her don't-mess-with-the-librarian face. "This 'office' would be my bedroom, I take it?"

He wagged his eyebrows at her.

"You do realize, don't you, that by getting to know each other I meant in more than merely the biblical sense?" Then without awaiting an answer, she demanded, "Besides, what happened to being an 'old guy' that I'd worn out?"

"Well, it's the damnedest thing," he murmured as he hustled her down the hall. "Turns out I recover a helluva lot quicker than I thought."

The music for the audition's final number died away but Treena kept moving to keep her muscles warm until her heart rate decreased. She stepped side to side, alternately shaking out and stretching her arms.

"Thank you," called *la Stravaganza's* general manager from the darkness of the auditorium. The other dancers milled around as they, too, went through their cool down routines. Treena could tell the ones who weren't familiar with the show's procedure, because they tried to peer past the bright lights that flooded the stage, clearly expecting to hear an immediate verdict from the judges. Treena, knowing Vernetta-Grace's spiel by heart, headed for the dressing rooms, and Carly fell into step beside her.

The GM's voice followed them backstage. "Those of you who already dance for *la Stravaganza*," she called in her usual brisk, no-nonsense tones, "may expect a letter informing you whether your contract will be renewed on your station by the end of the last show Thursday night. If we require anything further from the rest of you, we'll contact you by phone Friday morning."

"Thank you for participating and have a good day," Carly recited in crisp unison with Vernetta-Grace's dwindling voice as she and Treena headed down the backstage corridor.

They were the first ones in the dressing room and all the energy Treena had summoned to get her through the tryout dribbled away like water through a preschooler's hands. Only sheer stubborn pride had kept her moving for the past hour and a half—she'd worked too damn hard to let some man torpedo everything she'd been killing herself to achieve. So she had emptied her mind of everything except the performance she needed to give in order to pass the audition. Now that it was over, however, she could barely hold her head upright, and the dam she'd hastily erected to keep the pain of Jax's betrayal at bay was springing leaks faster than Hans Brinker's dike.

Still, she felt a wisp of pride as she turned to look at her friend. "I think I did it," she said wearily. "I think I passed."

"I know you did," Carly said. "You were amazing—and I don't just mean because of the extraordinary circumstances."

"I hurt in every muscle in my body, though," she admitted. "What I wouldn't give for a good night's sleep." Her eyes burned from all the tears she'd cried earlier, but when she looked at her reflection in the mirror she was surprised to see that the ice-bath therapy Carly had insisted upon before they'd left home had actually done the trick. It had involved Treena plunging her face into a bowl full of ice water while her friend held her hair back, but between that and the tea bags she'd pressed to her eyes while Carly had driven them to the Avventurado, her swollen face and bloodshot eyes had been reduced to a manageable level. Extra makeup had taken care of the rest—or so she preferred to believe.

Catching a glimpse of Carly stripping out of her crop-top next to her elicited a sudden sharp tug to her conscience. *Good God, Treena, have you had one thought today that included anyone other than you?*

"I'm sorry," she said contritely. "I didn't even ask how you did." In previous years she'd had a good idea of how everyone had performed at an audition, but today it had been all she could do to focus on her own performance.

Her friend looked up from peeling down her tights with the tiny built-in panties and grinned. "I aced it, girlfriend, and so did you. But you know who didn't?" A deep-throated laugh slid out of her. "Our good pal Julie-Ann."

Surprise filtered through Treena's general misery. "You're kidding."

"I'm not. Oh, it was nothing dramatic like her blowing the thing all to hell and gone. But she was a far cry from her usual standards, and I gotta tell you, toots, it was a joy to see. Did you notice the brunette with the jazz-baby haircut? About twenty-two, maybe twenty-three years old, wearing a red unitard?"

She shook her head.

"Well, the girl was dynamite, and I think it occurred to little Miz Julie-A for probably the first time in her life that maybe she'd be wiser to look to her own laurels rather than spending all her time ragging on the older dancers in the troupe. Because if there's one given you can count on in this biz it's that there will always be a new crop of younger, prettier, *better* dancers out there ready and willing to take your job."

Treena didn't even pretend patience for Julie-Ann's woes. "What did the self-absorbed twit think, that she'd be the youngest dancer in the troupe forever?"

"I doubt she's ever thought about it, period. Julie-baby hasn't had her teeth kicked down her throat as often as the rest of us have yet, and self-absorbed is the word for her. But I think she caught a glimpse of her future seeing Red Unitard dance circles around everyone. And let me tell you, toots, it shook her right down to the ground, because you can be sure Vernetta-Grace is going to hire the girl if there's an opening, and just knowing that is giving J-A a taste of what it feels like to have someone breathing down your neck." Carly smiled with sheer pleasure. "You gotta love karma."

She went on to critique other performances, but Treena quit listening. Dancers began filtering into the room in twos and threes, laughing and talking and making plans to blow off some steam now that the audition was behind them, and the cheerful din unleashed all the wretchedness she'd been holding back. She tried desperately not to give in to it but knew she wouldn't be able to stave off the misery for long. Hell, she'd deem it a success story if she could simply keep from falling apart until she got home.

Not wanting to be pulled into any of the conversations going on around her, she finished changing, then shoved her damp dance togs into her bag and leaned over to interrupt Carly, who was happily dissecting the audition with Eve. "I'll wait for you outside the showroom."

Telling the other dancer to hang on a sec, Carly dug in her bag until she came up with her key ring. She handed it to Treena. "Take the car. I'm going to stick around and grab a drink with Eve and Michelle."

Eve leaned around Carly. "You oughtta come, too, hon."

"I don't feel too good, Eve. I think I'm gonna just head for home."

A stricken look flashed across Carly's face and she shook her head. "I'm sorry, Treen," she said under her breath. "I forgot everything else for a minute in the euphoria of having the tryouts finally over for another year. I'll drive you home." She reached to take back the keys.

Treena whipped them out of reach. Oh, God, she didn't want that. She'd actually felt a moment's relief knowing she'd soon be alone. She didn't want to see anybody, have to talk to anybody. "Don't be silly," she said and hoped she didn't sound as desperate to escape as she felt. Grabbing her dance bag, she rose to her feet. "Go and have a good time—I'll be fine. I'll see you all later," she said to the room in general, then left before anyone could stop her.

She didn't draw a steady breath until she hit the darkened auditorium and felt she could safely quit worrying about breaking down in front of everyone she knew. They were her friends and would be staunchly on her side, but she'd never been comfortable with flopping her emotions down for wholesale consumption. No comfort awaited her in the usual slice-and-dice the troupe indulged in when a man broke the heart of one of their own.

She was almost home free, however, and her heartbeat finally started to settle down as she pushed through the showroom doors. She might make it back to her nest without a meltdown after all.

"Treena."

Ice slithered down her spine, and she jerked. *Nooooooo!* Dammit, she wasn't ready for this! But there was no mistaking that voice and blast Jax's black soul, the last man she wanted to see was here whether she was prepared to deal with him or not.

Jax knew even as he straightened that this wasn't going to be easy. His emotions had been all over the map since the moment she'd shoved him out her apartment door and slammed it shut behind him.

When he'd first walked away he'd simply felt defeated and ashamed. But as he'd driven back to the Avventurato defensiveness had begun to kick in. Hey, he'd *planned* to tell her the truth, hadn't he? That ought to count for something. And she didn't know what the hell she was talking about when it came to his father. By the time he'd stalked bare-chested and barefoot through the hotel to reach his room he'd been determined to turn the goddamn baseball over to Kirov, win the final game tonight and get the hell out of Vegas.

Instead, he'd removed the baseball from its Plexiglas holder, locked it in his room safe and gone down to the casino to play some cards. When things went to hell, he'd always found that gambling took his mind off his troubles.

Not today, though. He lost hand after hand, but that wasn't the worst of it. The worst was how damn alone he felt in the crowd. It shouldn't have bothered him, for it was certainly nothing new. Yet, in the short time he'd known Treena he'd grown accustomed to feeling like he belonged to someone. He discovered he cared a lot.

Desperate to know how Treena's audition was going, he couldn't concentrate worth shit on the cards and finally cashed in his few remaining chips and headed back up to the room. He knew what he had to do.

So here he was, with a gift bag in one hand and his other hand stuffed in his pocket, and Treena was blowing right past him as if he were invisible. He made a move to block her.

She jerked violently out of his path. "I don't want to talk to you."

Careful not to crowd too closely, he turned and walked alongside her. "Please. I'll only take a minute of your time."

She ignored him, but he matched his stride to hers until finally she stopped and turned to face him, her normally warm eyes ice-cold and the hands that had patted and stroked him fisted so tightly on the strap of her dance bag that her knuckles were white. "What do you want, Jackson?"

"I'd like for you not to call me that," he said, but immediately shook his head. "But that's not why I'm here. How did your audition go?" Her pretty eyes had a bruised look around them that made his gut churn.

She looked at him as if he were a bug that needed squashing and said frigidly, "I'm probably still employed."

"Good. That's good." They'd always talked so easily and it killed him that every word between them now was stilted and strained. He cleared his throat. "When will you know for sure?"

"Thursday night. Now, if that's all…?"

He supposed he had hoped somewhere deep inside of him that if he could just see her, could just talk to her one more time, she'd somehow find it in her heart to forgive him. It didn't take a keen eye to see that was a futile wish. So he stuffed down all his raw emotions and thrust the gift bag out at her. "Here. I want you to have this. Sell the damn thing when you're ready and buy your studio." He could at least give her that much.

She took the bag because he'd shoved it into her hands but didn't bother looking inside. Instead, she searched his face. "You're giving me your grandfather's baseball?"

"Yes."

"Why? I thought the guy you lost it to was threatening to break all your fingers if he doesn't get it tonight?"

He hitched a shoulder. "That's my problem." Then

the myriad ways in which he'd screwed up with her rose like a tsunami in his soul and he added flatly, "Let him. It's probably no more than I deserve." An abrupt, humorless laugh exploded from his throat. "I thought I was so fucking smart. I was going to be James-frigging-Bond and seduce my way into the showgirl's house, steal Grandpa's ball and disappear with the breeze. I'm good at statistics and probabilities, you know—a regular wizard at figuring the odds. But I made a major miscalculation this time. I didn't take into consideration the impact you would have on me."

All of the emotion he'd tried so hard to suppress exploded and, heart pounding against the wall of his chest, he speared his fingers through his hair and stared down at her.

"I sure as hell didn't count on you," he said hoarsely. "I wasn't prepared for those honest eyes or that great big heart of yours. I didn't know there was anyone in this world who could make me feel as if I'd known her all my life, that a place existed where I'd feel as if I belonged, the way I felt in your home." He reached out, wanting to trace her face with his fingertips, but he didn't think he could bear it if she jerked away from his touch, so he dropped his hand before it made contact.

"I sure wasn't prepared to fall in love," he whispered, and his voice was a raw rasp in his throat. "But I did, Treena. I love you more than my mother, more than my country, more than the air that I breathe. And God, I am so sorry I hurt you, but by the time I realized what I was feeling I'd dug a hole for myself so deep I couldn't figure out how to climb out of it. So you take that." He nodded at the bag dangling limply from her fingers. "You take it," he repeated fiercely, "and get yourself that studio. And I'll get the hell out of your life before I do any more damage."

He wanted to kiss her but knew better than to try. Wanted to touch her, but felt he'd forsaken the right. So he forced himself to turn and walk away and to not look back.

It was the hardest thing he'd ever done.

Twenty-Two

Jax prowled his hotel room like a caged cat, telling himself even as he did that he needed to knock it off. The clock was ticking down toward the final round of the tournament and he had to empty his mind, start getting into his game head. But his emotions roiled and writhed, which made trying to stay still a joke. And even if he could manage to sit for more than a minute at a time without twitching right out of his skin, his mind refused to obey. Images of Treena and snatches of the two exchanges he'd had with her today replayed through his mind. He couldn't make them stop.

His old man had been honest and good, according to her. He wasn't.

Big Jim'd had integrity. He didn't.

She'd loved Big Jim and had been starting to love him, too, until he'd gone and screwed things up.

He hadn't known it was possible to hurt this way and his instinct was to place the blame squarely on his father, to say that this, too, was Big Jim's fault. Except every time he started to do just that, he heard Treena's voice in his head telling him to grow up.

It made him realize that he'd never looked at his convoluted relationship with his dad through the eyes of an adult. But maybe what Treena had said had a grain of truth to it—maybe Big Jim hadn't known what to do with him any more than he'd known what to do with Big Jim.

He was still a lousy father. Jax stopped at the expanse of drapery that framed the wide window and watched storm clouds race across the sky. Then, rubbing the back of his neck, it occurred to him that although his father had dragged him from pillar to post for a couple of years, he'd kept him with him. From that standpoint, he had to admit Big Jim had rearranged his own way of life quite a bit to see that Jax still had one parent left in his. That was worth something. Jax wondered what he would do, given the same situation.

A better job than the old man did, he thought with automatic defensiveness. Turning away from the window, he resumed pacing. *A hell of a better job.*

All the same…taking a deep breath he crossed the room, yanked down the smaller of his two suitcases and retrieved the letter that had trailed him all over Europe before finally catching up with him in Geneva. He took the single sheet of paper from the envelope, then dialed the phone number on the letterhead. After a few minutes' conversation with the law office that had handled his father's estate, he cut the connection and dialed the number they'd given him for Big Jim's oncologist. Expecting to be added to a callback list, he was surprised when the receptionist put him straight through to the doctor instead. As they discussed Big Jim's case, he restlessly paced the length of the telephone cord in every direction that he could make it stretch.

When that call ended, he replaced the receiver very carefully in its cradle and blew out a breath. All right then.

Treena was right.

Big Jim had been diagnosed with prostate cancer shortly before Jax graduated from MIT. Maybe his father *would* have been at the ceremony if he hadn't been recuperating from surgery at the time.

He doubted it, though. It was just as likely the old man wouldn't have shown up regardless.

"Shit!" Snatching up his keys, Jax headed for the door. He needed to take a drive, clear his head, because this was getting him nowhere. One day soon he'd sit down and figure out how to give up his grudge against Big Jim. His continued resentment was pretty damn futile with his father dead and buried. Not to mention that—as Treena certainly made clear—nobody liked a whiner.

Treena. Fresh pain hit him hard, and he slammed out of the hotel room as if he could somehow outrun it.

His feelings for his old man would just have to go unresolved a while longer. Because compared to the loss of Treena, those tangled emotions were chump change.

And he had no patience for them today.

That low-down, dirty gutter rat! Treena glared at the baseball sitting in its Plexiglas container on the coffee table in front of her. Heels up on the couch, she wrapped her arms around her shins and hugged herself into the tightest ball possible while eyeing the collectible as if it were an anaconda poised to constrict the life out of her.

Jackson Gallagher McCall had betrayed her in the worst way a man could betray a woman. He'd taken her trust, her love—pieces of her heart and soul she didn't give lightly, that she had, in fact, given to no man before him—and he'd crushed them beneath his sneakers like so many discarded cigarette butts. The very *least* she deserved in return was to loathe him without reservation.

But had he been content to leave her with even that tiny scrap of comfort? Oh, no. He'd had to go give her the damn ball back. To put his own hide in danger.

He'd had to go and say that he loved her. And to say it eloquently, blast him.

Then walk away.

She felt like breaking his hands herself. How dare he make a selfless gesture while she was still so furious? How dare he sweet-talk her into almost understanding why he messed up so badly? She really needed to hang onto her righteous indignation.

She needed Jax back in her life.

That really pissed her off. She refused to be jelly-spined and helpless. She didn't need a man to complete her life!

I love you. Jax's voice, raw with emotion, whispered through her mind. *I love you more than my mother, more than—*

His words had played through her mind more than once in the past hour and she latched on to them now.

She'd be willing to bet most men didn't compare the way they loved their mothers with the passion they felt for a lover. Ignoring the core declaration itself, still too upset to deal with the way it sent blood rushing hot through her veins, the way it threatened to dissolve her determination to keep him out of her life, she rested her chin in the notch between her knees and chewed on the mother angle instead.

The implausibility of her thoughts caused her arms to loosen their grip around her legs and her chin to lift from its resting place. Her feet slid across the couch and she lowered them to the floor, slowly straightening her back.

Maybe his mother was his only frame of reference when it came to love.

Nearly everyone else she knew had been in and out of love at least once during the time she'd known them— and usually more often than that. But it was possible that Jax had never known true love with another woman.

She may never have experienced a man/woman-type love, but she had bonded to Carly like a soul sister and she loved Ellen and Mack as if they were her own parents. And before the three of them had become part of her life she'd had the love of her family and a few select others. Jax must have friends somewhere, as well, even if he'd never talked to her about them. He must have people who kept him grounded simply by their affection for him.

And yet some of the things he'd said to her outside the showroom this afternoon seemed to indicate otherwise. He'd disavowed the existence of a place where he could feel as if he belonged, had claimed he hadn't known there was anyone in the world capable of making him feel as if he'd known them all his life.

Those assertions had held such power and conviction that she'd hugged them to her bruised heart like a consoling hot water bottle. Since they concerned the way Jax felt about *her,* however, she hadn't stopped to consider what they might say about the larger picture.

Maybe he *didn't* have anyone.

During her brief marriage to Big Jim, she'd bitten her tongue as often as she could manage when she'd seen the defeated look on his face after one of his rare telephone conversations with his son. But the few times she'd snarled over what an ingrate Jackson was, Big Jim had always insisted that he was getting no more than he deserved. "I'm simply reaping what I've sown, sweetheart," he used to say.

She'd found that hard to believe, but she'd concede that perhaps Jax had a tiny basis for his bitterness. She would defend Big Jim to the death, but one thing she couldn't deny was that he had cared way more than he should have about what his buddies thought. And if that had meant pushing a grieving boy in directions he wasn't suited to go then maybe Jax had a point.

The disloyalty of that thought, like a jolt of electricity, catapulted her to her feet. Fuming, she bent down to snatch up the gift bag she'd tossed aside earlier.

She stuffed the Plexiglas-encased ball back into its nest of colored tissue at the bottom of the bag, then disguised it with the additional sheets she'd pulled out of the package earlier.

I love you.

Her shoulders went so hard and tight at his words whispering through her mind that her neck threatened to spasm. She had to start remembering his actions spoke louder than his words.

I love you more than—

Swearing, she snatched up the bag and stomped over to the coat closet. Yanking open the door, she tossed the gift sack into a pile several feet away, then slammed it shut again.

Merely getting it out of her sight wasn't sufficient, however, and she headed for the foyer. She was so damn confused she didn't have the first idea what she wanted. Her nerve endings felt too close to the surface, and even though just a short while ago she could hardly get away from everyone fast enough, now the walls seemed to be closing in on her and she was less than thrilled with her own company. She felt an overwhelming need to get the hell out of here. To go somewhere she could breathe.

She only made it as far as the front door, however, before she stopped with one hand on the knob to look back at the closet.

Damn. She didn't feel right about leaving the ball behind.

"Oh, for God's sake," she said aloud. "You've got real problems—the last thing you need to focus on is the absurd." She'd been perfectly happy storing the ball in the closet since putting it away following Big Jim's death. Even learning the collectible could command a considerable sum of money hadn't given her the urge to find it a safer berth.

Now, though, she knew its existence could mean the

difference between Jax being physically injured or not. Not that she'd decided to give the ball back so he could dodge that particular bullet. There was a part of her that wanted to ride her wave of anger—not to mention the greedy little gremlin inside that insisted she had earned this ball. She'd paid dearly enough for it. Still, she understood the consequences he now faced.

Even if she did decide to give the ball to him, she had no intention of seeing Jax tonight. So what difference did it make whether she left the damn thing in the closet or not?

Yet no matter how hard she tried to rationalize it, she felt an almost superstitious urge to take the baseball with her. She went back to collect it, then stormed over to the front door and yanked it open.

Mack and Ellen stood on the other side.

Both women yelped at the shock of unexpectedly coming face-to-face with the other, and Treena slapped her free hand to her chest. The plate in Ellen's hand dipped, and only Mack's quick, steadying grip around her fingers saved the cookies it held from sliding to the floor.

"Holy sh—" Biting off the expletive, Treena blew out her breath. "You startled me."

"Tell me about it," Ellen agreed, reaching out to pat Mack's wrist as his hand slipped away from hers. "I think I just sprouted a few new gray hairs." Then she laughed and fixed her sparkling hazel eyes on Treena as she deftly straightened the jumbled cookies. "Sorry, darling. We thought we heard movement in here and since we're dying to learn how the audition went, we came over to investigate."

We. Looking at them, Treena saw that Mack's non-cookie-rescuing hand rested lightly on Ellen's hip. She noted, too, that the petite librarian leaned just the slightest bit against the stocky man at her back.

Her happiness for the couple was genuine if a bit envious. It was nice to see love working out for someone.

"Were you on your way out?" Mack asked. "That's a relief, because to tell you the truth, hon, I got a little worried when we heard a door slam in here. I figured if everything had gone well you and Carly would be out celebrating 'til the cows came home." A groove furrowed between his eyebrows as he leveled his dark-eyed gaze on her. "It did go well, I hope."

And because she loved him for worrying about her and Carly every bit as much as he would his own daughters, she smiled. It was the first time she'd felt her lips curve up since she'd opened Jax's wallet that morning.

"We won't know for certain until Thursday night, of course—but both Carly and I think it went very well. And I am on my way out. Some of the dancers are having drinks at the casino to celebrate." She felt no compulsion to add that she hadn't made up her mind yet whether she'd actually join her friends or not.

"We won't keep you, then. We just wanted to hear how you did and to give you these." Ellen handed her the plate of cookies and stood on tiptoe to kiss her cheek. "Congratulations! We knew you'd pass."

"Damn straight," Mack added.

"Aw, you guys. Thank you. You both mean so much to me." And damn it, their kindness brought tears to her

eyes. That's *just* what she needed to round out her day—
to break down in front of them.

"I'm surprised Jax isn't here," Mack said. "You tell
him yet?"

The tears dried up quickly and she silently blessed
him for invoking the Antichrist's name. "He was actually the first one I told," she answered honestly. "He was
waiting for me outside the showroom." She'd have to
tell Ellen and Mack the truth about Jax soon, she knew.
But not today.

She simply could not face it today.

After talking with the older couple a moment longer,
she watched them disappear into Ellen's apartment.
Then, suppressing a pang of the poor-pitiful mess
brought on by their obvious happiness when she felt so
wretched, she set out for her car.

By the time she reached the Avventurado a short
while later she'd decided she'd rather take her chances
being miserable in a group than be on her own one minute longer. Left to her own devices her thoughts kept
spinning like a cartoon Tasmanian devil, and the day
was difficult enough already without that added aggravation. Perhaps company would focus her mind on
something other than herself.

She went straight to the dance troupe's favorite little
bar in the heart of the casino—the same place she'd celebrated her thirty-fifth birthday. When she didn't find
Carly and Eve there, she left to check out the other Avventurado watering holes.

Her friends weren't in any of them, either, and twenty
minutes later she was back in the bar where she'd begun.

A waitress she knew breezed by with a laden tray and Treena flagged her down. "Hey Carol, have you seen Carly tonight?"

"Yeah. She and half the troupe were in earlier. I think I heard them say something about catching the Thunder from Down Under show."

Crap. Thanking the cocktail waitress, Treena looked around for a clock. But this was a casino, so of course there were none. And truthfully, even if she had time to make it to the Excalibur before the show started she wasn't in the mood to watch a group of Australian hunks whip a crowd of females into a frenzy.

Maybe this was a sign she should just go back home, after all. She clearly wasn't going to be satisfied no matter what she did—when she was alone she wanted company; when she had company she wanted to be alone. Newly determined to ride out the remainder of the evening in the comfort of her own bed, she headed for the exit.

When she hit the street, however, she found herself walking up the strip instead of collecting her car. Lightning cracked across the sky and dark clouds boiled out over the desert to the east. It was all flash and fire that didn't produce a drop of rain, and a short while later, she entered Bellagio.

She stopped just inside the lobby doors. *Oh, God, Treena. This is not a good idea.*

It was, in fact, a spectacularly bad one, but the sudden compulsion to see Jax's final game was stronger than her sense of self-preservation. So she headed with a purposeful stride past the flashy Dale Chihuly hand-blown glass flowers ceiling, past the conservatory and botanical garden to wend her way through the complex hotel to the big ballroom where Jax had taken her the other day. When she arrived at her destination a few moments later and reached for the handle on one of the tall double doors, however, she found the room closed up tight.

"No." Certain that couldn't be right, she set the gift bag on the floor and used both hands on both handles, rattling the doors furiously when they remained firmly locked. Panic danced a jittery little jig in her stomach. "No!"

"May I help you, miss?"

Skin hot, breath short, she whipped around to see a middle-aged black man approaching. He wore the Bellagio maintenance department uniform, and she snatched up the bag and strode over to meet him, struggling to compose herself as the distance between them narrowed. Good God. How had Jax turned her into someone she didn't even recognize in the space of one day? And what difference did it make if she didn't see him play the last game anyway? It wasn't as if the outcome would change anything between them. Hell, the mere thought of coming face to face with him made her stomach hurt.

And yet…

"I came to watch the final game of the poker tournament but the doors are locked. Is it over already?" Had Jax packed up all his marbles and left town?

"No, ma'am—last I heard there were still three players in the game. Since they no longer need this much space, though, they pulled a wall down the middle of the smallest Degas room and moved the final table into one half. I'd be happy to show you the new location." He led her back down the corridor the way she'd come. "The game's being televised so I'm afraid you won't be able to get anywhere near the actual table. But there's a live feed into a close-circuit TV in the other half where you can watch the action."

Oh, even better. She could satisfy her curiosity about the outcome of the tournament without having to worry about running into Jax.

The maintenance man flashed her a smile that show-cased a gold-crowned front tooth. "I caught part of the game a short while ago. They've got cameras that show you the players' hold cards, so you actually know more of what's going on than you would have if you were watching the game in person." He stopped in front of a door. "Here you go, Miss," he said, opening it for her. "Enjoy."

More people crowded the room than she anticipated, but she picked her way past a row of knees to take one of the remaining unoccupied seats. Heart drumming with apprehensive anticipation, she settled herself, fussed over wedging the bag with the baseball beneath her seat, then slowly raised her eyes to the big-screen TV. Her breath stopped up in her lungs at her first glimpse of Jax.

He shared the screen with two men, but she didn't give the other players more than a cursory glance. Jax sat, his face expressionless and his body still except for one long-fingered hand that riffled a stack of chips. Dark glasses covered his eyes, and all he needed, she thought with forced sarcasm as she stared at the shades' black rims and his dark suit jacket, was a black fedora and he could have passed as a Blues Brother. As she watched, he took several chips off the stack he'd been toying with, then pushed the remainder into the pot in the middle of the table.

"Christ almighty," a man one row forward of Treena and two seats over muttered. "What the hell is the *matter* with him tonight?"

Her skin going cold, she leaned forward and tapped the man on the shoulder.

"Hey!" he snarled. "Hands off." When he turned in his seat to look at her, however, his attitude changed. "Oh. Say. I take it back—you can touch me whenever you like."

"What do you mean?" she demanded. When he gave her a blank look, she prompted, "About Gallagher?"

"Who? Oh! Gallagher." He shook his head in disgust. "He's been sleepwalking his way through the game ever since he sat down. That bet he made just now?" He tipped his head toward the screen. "He drew a seven of clubs and a two of diamonds. He should've folded."

"Maybe he's bluffing. He told me once that he won a tournament in Paris because he's usually a conservative better—so when he went all in his competition folded."

"Well, that's not gonna happen this time," the man said at the same time the television announcer exclaimed, "Whoa! Do you believe that? Smith tossed in his hand."

The man shrugged and gave her a slight smile.

"Okay, it is. But I stand by my earlier statement—Gallagher's playing a crap game tonight. It's like his mind is somewhere else."

The man next to him agreed, but the first man ignored him in favor of giving Treena a slow up-and-down. "So, you know Gallagher?"

"I thought I did," she said bitterly. The man's confused blink made her rein herself in, however, and she amended levelly, "I used to."

"How 'bout that." His gaze skimmed over her, pausing on her breasts for a moment before rising to meet her eyes. "Buy you a drink?"

"I appreciate the offer, but no, thanks." She softened the refusal with a slight smile.

He shrugged and turned back to the screen.

Jax tossed in his cards on the next hand and one of the players went all in on three aces but lost the hand when the last card turned over gave his opponent a full house.

Then there were two players left in the game.

A huge fanfare ensued as three beautiful women wheeled in the million-dollar prize money and built a pyramid of cash on one end of the kidney-shaped table. Treena recognized the tall unsmiling man unobtrusively guarding it as Carly's new neighbor.

The theatrical production underscored the fact that the game was down to the final two contestants. But the guy in front of Treena was right. Jax clearly didn't have his mind on the game and, to the disgust of everyone around her, he kept making one bad move after another. His stacks of chips rapidly shrank down to a single column.

Treena thought his misfortune should have pleased

her no end, that she ought to feel like dancing in the street at seeing him get what was coming to him. Instead it made her stomach knot. Jax was clearly every bit as messed up and unhappy as she, but rather than revel in the knowledge she merely felt colorless and depressed, as if all the joy had been sucked out of her world.

Then he played his last pile of chips. And lost.

She sat there for a moment while all around her people began gathering their belongings and filing from the room. *So what?* she silently demanded as she watched his onscreen image rise from the table and walk out of camera range. *So he lost. Second place still wins him more money than I made in the last four years combined. Go home, have some wine, and think about selling the ball like he told you to. Think about what kind of dance studio you could start.*

But she knew she wasn't going to listen to her own advice. On some level she'd probably known it all along.

Forgetting her intention to avoid Jax at all costs, she fished the gift bag out from under her seat and went to find him.

Twenty-Three

Jax strode out of the tourney room and straight into the crowd making an exodus from the other side of the divider where they'd set up the visitors' gallery. He paused to let a group go by.

One of the departing spectators gave him a commiserating look. "Tough break, man."

Shame, like a shard of glass, pierced his general detachment, but he managed a nonchalant shrug. "Thanks. You win some, you lose some."

A couple of tournament groupies rushed up to him. "Hey, Jax," purred the blonder, bustier of the young women as they sandwiched him between them. "Sign an autograph for us?"

"Yeah, sure." *Shit.* He had to get out of here. But he forced a smile for his two fans, pulled his Cross Matrix from the inside pocket of his jacket and scribbled his signature on the slips of paper the women handed him. Then, he turned and walked directly opposite the way he'd intended to go.

He'd give the crowd streaming toward the public thoroughfare a few minutes to clear before he set out in that direction himself. God knew he was in no mood to chat. He'd never played a lousier game in his entire career, and the last thing he was up for at the moment was to hear a bunch of poker fans hold a postmortem on his lackluster performance all the way to the lobby. Not that he didn't deserve every criticism that could be leveled at him. His party manners simply didn't stretch far enough to deal with them right now.

He didn't have a problem admitting to himself, however, that there was plenty of cause for complaint. Poker demanded strict attention, and he hadn't paid today's game even a fraction of what it required. He'd played, in fact, like an amateur on downers—and all because he couldn't get his mind off Treena long enough to focus.

Damn, he hated the almost grieflike pain that the mere thought of her pumped through his system. Love sucked.

No. He halted midstride. Love was great, and he'd been damn lucky to have a little come his way. He wasn't exactly known for being the happiest man in the universe, but for a brief time he'd been happy with Treena. What sucked was the way he had handled it. And if he'd been reduced to skulking down casino hallways like a damn weasel to avoid having his crappy execution of the final game shoved down his throat, he had no one to blame but himself. He turned on his heel and strode back the way he'd come.

It was high time to stop feeling sorry for himself and face his future like a man.

* * *

Treena thought for sure she'd catch up with Jax in Bellagio's lush lobby, but when she arrived, slightly out of breath, he was nowhere in sight. How on earth had she missed him? A wedding party decked out in all their finery crossed the lobby toward the chapel. Folks checked in and out of the hotel at the registration desk across the spacious vestibule, and a group of women laughed as they sat on the tasseled velvet settees beneath the Chihuly ceiling showing each other their purchases from upscale shopping bags. But nowhere did Treena see a big, broad-shouldered man in an impeccably tailored jacket and broken-in jeans.

She didn't get it. She couldn't have been more than a minute or two behind him.

Her shoulders slumped and she was suddenly so exhausted she could barely hold her head upright. She sank into a nearby chair, the gift bag thumping to the floor at her feet.

She'd always been so pragmatic—yet here she was in blind, optimistic pursuit of Jax. It had seemed like such a swell idea in the visitors' gallery after the game. Now it simply suggested she was a lot more starry-eyed than she ever would have believed possible.

Not for the first time in this very long and tiring day, she realized she didn't know what she had expected—didn't have a clue what she might have done if she'd found him as easily as she'd assumed she would. Why had she taken for granted that everything would fall into place? It was so unlike her and, tired to the bone, she was ready to call it a night.

She was beyond ready. Her feet felt like lead, her head hurt like hell, and she really needed to get off this emotional roller coaster and haul her weary butt home.

Then she saw him. He was strolling her way, easy as you please, from the same direction she'd just come. How she'd gotten ahead of him was anyone's guess, but the sight of him was like mainlining a double shot of espresso, and her tiredness washed away beneath the sudden rush of energy. She rose to her feet.

Before she had an opportunity to let Jax know she was there, however, two men closed in on either side of him, and she sat down again, blowing out an impatient breath. Leaning forward, she tapped her foot against the carpeted floor. Then she forced herself to sit back. His fans looked similar enough to be brothers, and they were intense about whatever they were saying to him. So she'd give them one minute—maybe two if she could stand it—then she was going over there. She didn't know exactly what she'd say to Jax once she was face to face with him, but she was restless and on edge and ready to find out.

Rather than separate, with Jax's fans going one way while he went the other, the three men began walking in her direction.

And Treena realized something wasn't right. The men with Jax didn't look anything like the poker fans she'd seen in the viewing room. These two were huge enough to make Jax look almost slight by comparison; they were beefy in the way of bodybuilders or bouncers and had low, prominent brow bones. Plus they crowded too closely on either side of Jax, almost as if they were shepherding him in this direction. Almost as if…

Oh, crap. It was after the tournament. She didn't know why she hadn't remembered before this moment that the men threatening Jax would be waiting for him.

They were almost upon her, and she wondered frantically what to do. Should she make a scene? Call the cops?

But what if she was reading this all wrong? Talk about typecasting, after all—the two men were just too cliché to be real live villains. If she ended up making a big stink over a couple of dentists from Poughkeepsie, she was going to be mighty embarrassed.

But, oh, God, if she was right and sat here doing nothing she'd never forgive herself. Pulling her cell phone out of her purse, she punched the button to get an open line even as she was opening her mouth to yell the house down. If those were the only two options she had, she would run with them.

Then before a peep made its way past her lips or she managed to punch more than 9-1 on her cell's numerical pad, Jax glanced up, straight into her eyes.

He stopped in his tracks. Almost immediately he caught himself and started to take another step forward. But the two men flanking him didn't wait for him to get going again under his own steam. They jerked him into motion so roughly he stumbled.

And Treena was left without a shred of doubt that her first concern had been correct.

Still, she was relieved to make eye contact with Jax, figuring two heads really were better than one. To her surprise, though, he looked anything but happy or gratified to see her. Instead, he narrowed his eyes and gave his chin a subtle jerk toward the hotel entrance, as if he wanted her to take a hike through it. Certain she must have misunderstood, she shook her head and indicated the two of them, then pointed to the phone in her hand.

No! he mouthed and, abandoning subtlety, jerked his chin forcefully at the door, frowning at her. *Get lost.*

"Look," Treena heard the man on Jax's right say. "The big-shot poker player has palsy like old man." The thick-necked man sneered at Jax. "You're not gonna mess your pants, are you, Gallagher?"

"Maybe is just doing a little Saint Vitus's dance," the man on his left said and the two of them laughed uproariously at their own humor.

Then, with Jax inserted securely between them, they walked past Treena, almost close enough for her to reach out and touch the thug nearest her. As she was deciding how she could best help—with or without Jax's consent—she heard him say in a bored voice, "You two really should take that act on the road. Talent this special has gotta be wasted on Sergei."

Within seconds the three men had crossed the lobby and disappeared from view through the exit to the parking garage.

Treena started after them. She was several strides away from her chair before she remembered the baseball.

Then it sank in. *Dear God. The baseball!* Jubilation filled her. She'd been packing the damn thing around with her all evening, and it turned out to have been for a reason after all. *Screw the dance studio. I've got the means to get Jax out of this!* She ran back and swept the bag up in one fist, then walked briskly toward the door where she'd last seen him wedged between the two rough-looking men.

Entering the stairwell a moment later, she paused to listen. Over the sound of her own heartbeat thumping in her ears, she heard several sets of footsteps climbing the stairs. As softly and quietly as she could manage, she began climbing them, as well. She also brought her cell phone to her ear and punched the talk button. She didn't care what Jax had indicated—she thought it was a good idea to call the police. Just in case.

But there was no dial tone, and pulling it away from her ear she stared down in disbelief at the message on its lighted screen. *No signal,* it read.

Fury, fueled by fear, threatened to buckle her knees. "Useless piece of shit!" she breathed fiercely and, snapping the phone shut, tossed it back into her purse. That would teach her to buy the cheap model. Or maybe it was the cheap service provider. Either way, unless she wanted to return to the lobby, where she'd be more likely to catch a microwave signal not blocked by acres of concrete, she was clearly on her own. Taking a deep breath and swallowing her trepidation, she continued up the stairs.

Jax didn't fight Kirov's hired muscle as they towed him up flight after flight of parking garage steps. He was still sweating bullets over seeing Treena, and the more space he put between her and the Brothers Ivanov, the happier he'd be. He didn't know what had prompted her to act out that little charade in the lobby, but he knew he wanted nothing to do with it. He wasn't even sure what she'd meant when she'd gestured between the two of them and her cell phone. She'd obviously figured out he wasn't taking a voluntary stroll with Sergei's trained gorillas, but what had she possibly thought she could do to improve the situation?

He was the one who'd made this mess—no one else. He'd mishandled the situation from A to Z, from throwing the fucking ball into the pot in the first place to lying to Treena in order to get his hands on it. It was his debt to pay—he didn't want her anywhere within a ten-mile radius of Sergei Kirov. The mere thought of the Russian learning she was in possession of the ball made him break out in a cold sweat.

For the first time he actually blessed the fact he'd driven her away.

He didn't understand why she'd looked so hell-bent on helping him now, but once he'd mouthed *Get lost* at her, he doubted it had taken her more than a second or two to come to her senses…a fact for which he knew he ought to be eternally grateful.

Hell, he oughtta be dancing in the stairwell knowing that Treena was safe. But he was so goddamn lonesome for her that dancing was simply beyond him at the moment.

Dumb and Dumber hauled him out onto the fourth-floor parking area and a lightly accented voice said, "Welcome, Jax," from the shadows. Sergei stepped out from behind the squared off hood of a freakishly long Humvee limousine a few rows over from the stairwell. "So kind of you to join us."

"Yeah," he agreed drily as the two henchmen muscled him over to where the Russian stood. "'Kind' is my middle name. Although I must admit I did plan to send my regrets at first and go get laid instead. It's been a long day, you know? But it turns out I was unable to refuse such a gracious invitation." Glancing at the Lowbrow Boys who had released him but only taken a few steps away on either side, he essayed indifference with a quirk of his lips and added, deadpan, "Imagine my surprise."

Sergei appeared unamused and Jax shrugged. He eyed the other man's dyed-black pompadour and pristine white rhinestone-studded jumpsuit and flowing scarf. "You're looking mighty resplendent."

For just a second, the Elvis buff preened and answered with his favorite King of Rock and Roll impression. "Thank you. Thankyouverramuch." But upon studying Jax's empty hands, the Russian's momentary pleasure turned to a scowl. "The tournament is finished. Where is my World Series ball?"

Jax had thought he was prepared to take his punishment like a man, but still he heard himself prevaricate. "I didn't know you expected it the minute the tourney was over."

"You do not have it with you?"

"No."

Kirov looked him over, then nodded slowly. "I suppose is too much to expect a man to watch so valuable a treasure and play in final game, as well. Which, by the way, you played—how do you Americans say it?—piss poor."

"Not my best effort," he agreed.

"But you now have nothing to distract you. So you and I, we take a little ride. Go collect my ball."

He wasn't big on pain—especially his own—but there was no sense putting off the inevitable. He stuffed his hands in his pockets, rocked back on his heels and looked the other man in the eye. "Well, the ride part is doable. Collecting the ball's gonna be a bit problematic, though."

Kirov went very still, his eyes narrowing. "What do you say?"

"I don't have it. Turns out the ball didn't belong to me, after all."

Dangerous color crept up the other man's face. "And you know this fact how long?"

"A while. But I thought I had a chance of getting it for you, anyhow." He grimaced. "I was wrong."

Kirov nodded to his enforcers and the Russian brothers moved in on either side of Jax once more. They muscled him over to the nearest wall and each pinned one of his arms against the cool cement at his back. Sergei snapped his fingers and a uniform-clad chauffeur got out of the car and walked around to the rear door. Opening it, he rummaged inside, then removed something and brought it around to Sergei.

Jax looked at the cordless nail gun the driver placed in the Russian's hands and felt his gut turn to ice.

Kirov approached him. "You will tell me name of person who has my baseball."

"I can't do that, Sergei."

"Then you pay the price."

He swallowed drily, but managed to sound calm when he said, "You're going to make me pay either way—and since I didn't make good on our bet maybe I deserve whatever punishment you mete out." Except being nailed to a wall. No one short of a baby molester deserved that.

"Tell me what I want to know and I merely have the boys break one or two of your fingers." Sergei hefted the nail gun. "Do you know these nails are capable of penetrating cement wall behind you? No telling how much time before someone comes along and finds you. Then there is the extraction process. Much unpleasant."

Christ. He had to swallow several times before he worked up enough spit to croak, "I won't involve someone whose only crime is to be the ball's legal owner."

Sergei looked at one of his goons and the man instantly flattened Jax's left wrist against the wall and uncurled his clenched fingers with a beefy hand. Kirov pressed the head of the nail gun against Jax's palm.

"I give you one last chance to save yourself."

Jax hoped like hell the Russian couldn't smell his fear. Knowing he was about to be pinned to the wall like a bug to a board had hot lightning zinging through his gut and his knees turning to jelly. But he looked at Kirov and didn't say a word.

"Hey! You! Elvis! Is this what you're looking for?"

Jax's head snapped up. He had thought he couldn't possibly be any more scared.

He was wrong.

Treena stood over by the stairs, her hair ablaze in the neon glow that flooded the opening at her back. She stood in a spill of tissue paper, the gift bag he'd given her turned on its side at her feet. His grandfather's baseball was out of its Plexiglas box and in her hand, and even as he watched she tossed it up and caught it. Then she tossed it up and caught it again.

Rage that she would place herself in this situation when he'd done everything in his power to keep her out of it shored up his weak knees. Forgetting the nail gun pressed to his palm, he surged away from the wall to go hustle her ass the hell out of there. When the Ivanovs slammed him back in place, he ignored them to glare at her. "I told you to get lost."

"Yeah, well, big deal. You've told me a lot of stupid stuff." She returned his glower with one of her own. "I am seriously hacked off at you, Jackson—but I'm also damned if I'll stand by and let some bully with a great Elvis look and a bad attitude literally crucify you."

"This is my World Series ball?" Sergei demanded, and Jax took his eyes off Treena long enough to glance at the avid expression on the Russian's face as he watched the ball flip into the air, then land in her palm with a soft smack, flip up and smack into her palm.

Treena commanded his attention once again when she said with flat finality, "It's *my* ball, buddy."

"And you think I cannot take it from you?" Sergei's voice was a slashing blade of ice. "You do not want to mess with Kirov, lady. I can nail your friend to wall and have my property wrested from your hand in mere seconds."

Treena didn't so much as flinch beneath the Russian's threat. "And *you* don't want to mess with a Polish girl from a financially strapped steel town, mister. Because the instant you make one move in my direction or injure Jax in any way, this ball is history." To demonstrate, she whipped to the right with military precision and thrust her arm out the opening above the balustrade that enclosed the floor's outer wall. She gave one brief glance to the street several stories below before turning hard eyes on Kirov. "Lots of people down there, Elvis. If I drop the ball what do you suppose the chances are that it will still be lying around on the sidewalk for you to pick up?"

"You would never do it," he said confidently. "Is much too valuable."

She tossed the ball up and almost bobbled it in the catch. "Whoops. That was a little close."

Sergei snarled something Jax was pretty sure was an obscenity in his native tongue, then lowered the nail gun and turned to face Treena fully. "What do you want? Money?"

"No. You won the ball fair and square. But Jax bet it to you in good faith, as well. His father always told him it would be his, and it was simply a fluke that it came to me instead. So I'll make you an exchange. The ball for Jax." She glared at the nail gun the Russian held at his side. "Unharmed. I've never heard of such a sick use for a power tool in my life."

Sergei snapped his fingers again and the chauffeur reappeared to take the nail gun. Then Kirov gave Treena an appraising look. "You really think my Elvis look is—how you say it?—grand?"

"*Great.* And, yes, I do."

"Kirov likes woman with taste, style and courage."

"Nice to know my good points are appreciated. So what's it gonna be, Elvis?"

He stared at her a moment, then nodded. "We will make exchange. The ball for Gallagher."

"Good. Meet me in the lobby in five minutes."

"No. We do it right here. Right now."

She snorted. "Yeah, right. *That's* gonna happen. Bring Jax with you or the deal is off." And retracting her hand, she disappeared down the stairs.

Sergei stared at the spot where she'd stood, then turned to look at Jax, respect for Treena still lingering in his eyes. "There is no shame being beaten by that one. She is an Amazon. You are a luckier man than you deserve."

"Yeah," he agreed, beginning to breathe easier now that she was safely away. "Lucky." Treena's luck, however, had run out.

Because the minute he got his hands on her he was going to kill her.

Twenty-Four

"Is honor doing business with you." Sergei Kirov bent and planted a kiss first on Treena's left cheek, then on her right. Straightening, he collected the autographed World Series baseball reverently in both hands, nodded curtly to Jax and left.

She watched him walk away from the semiprivate corner of the lobby where they'd handled the trade. "That man is one seriously scary piece of work," she said, relieved to see the last of him. Overloaded with unspent adrenaline and full of herself, she surged up out of her plush chair. Grabbing Jax's hand—his beautiful, undamaged hand—she hauled him to his feet, as well. She needed more space to burn off all this manic energy, fresh air to clear her head, and after executing a fast boogie that included much exuberant wiggling of her backside, she dragged him toward the terrace doors.

She'd done it! By God, she'd been scared and unsure that she could pull it off, but she'd done it. She was intrepid, invincible, and after barreling through the doors and onto the windswept terrace, she whirled to receive her well-deserved kudos from Jax. Beaming up at him she flung her hands wide of her body. "Well?" *Tell me again that you love me.*

His hands bit into her shoulders as he yanked her up onto her toes, his eyes twin gas-blue flames, his nose inches from her own. "What the *hell* were you thinking?"

More stunned than if he'd smacked her to her knees, she attempted to jerk free of his hold, but his grasp tightened, holding her in place. Her temper spiked. "I was saving your ass, you ungrateful jerk!"

"Who the hell asked you to?" he roared, his fingers biting deeper. "I told you to go home."

"No, you told me to get lost! Don't you try prettying it up now that everyone's safe and sound." Bringing her arms up between them, she snapped them wide, breaking his hold. But she didn't retreat an inch. Instead she thrust her face even closer to his. "And *you're welcome,* by the way." She thumped the flat of her hand against his solid chest. "My God. You don't know the first thing about me if you seriously think I'd walk away when I had the means to keep those cretins from breaking your hands. As it was, I was almost too late. That crazy son of a bitch was about to shoot nails through your palms and leave you pinned to the wall like some low-rent Christ to the cross!" The memory alone was enough to send nausea rushing up her throat.

The tail end of the storm blowing through town on its way to the desert to the east swirled her hair around both their heads, and Jax speared his long fingers into the wind-lashed mass of it, anchoring her curls away from her face. For one hot, edgy second, he glared into her eyes. Then he slammed his mouth over hers, and the next thing she knew he was kissing her senseless.

This was no sweet, gentle caress. It was all teeth and tongue and aggression and, burning like wildfire beneath the sheer thankfulness of feeling his touch on her once again, she kissed him back with equal ferocity.

Seconds later, he ripped his lips free and merely looked at her, his breath sawing in and out of his lungs. "You think I give a good goddamn about that?" he demanded.

She blinked, trying to remember what they'd been fighting about before he'd knocked all thought out of her head by kissing her. Oh. Sure. Kirov. The nail gun.

"You think I *care?*" Both questions were clearly rhetorical for he didn't waste any time waiting for her to answer. "I'm not saying it would've been a picnic, but I would have survived it. I would have healed." His voice turned raw. "What I wouldn't survive, what I could *never* heal from, is having something happen to you."

His fingers fisted in her hair as he stared down at her, his expression fierce, and Treena's heart tried to pound its way out of her breast. "All my life I've been out of step with the rest of the world," he said. "Kids that were my age thought I was a freak. Adults admired my brain but had nothing else in common with me. By the time I reached an age where the gap between twenty-four and thirty-four is a hell of a lot narrower than the one between fourteen and adulthood, I was used to disassociating from people on all but the most superficial of levels."

Holding her gaze, he very gently swept his thumbs across her cheekbones. "Then I met you."

Not only were the knots loosening in her stomach, she was beginning to feel downright fine again. "And you fell in love with me."

"God, yes—like a baby grand from a fourth-story window." He pressed a soft kiss on her lips, then raised his head. Looking down at her with those incredible eyes, so sober and serious, he said, "I want you to forgive me."

For just a moment, the tiny slice of her that felt entitled to savor her resentment clung to the last fragment of it. Then she drew in a deep breath and with her exhalation expelled all her toxic emotions. "Okay."

"And for what it's worth, you did save my ass tonight."

"Damn tootin'."

The raw desperation eased from his eyes and his lips tilted up at the corners. "You were nothing short of magnificent up there in the parking garage," he admitted. "And I thank you for what you did, because I know it took courage. But nitroglycerin in the hands of a toddler is more predictable than Kirov, Treena. And if he'd hurt you because of me and my stupid wager, I don't think I'd ever recover."

She wrapped her arms around his neck. "So what are we going to do about you, Jackson Jax Gallagher McCall?"

"Well, clearly I'm a menace to society. So maybe you should take me home with you. Get me off the streets before someone gets hurt."

"How long do you think you'd need to stay with me?"

"That all depends." He released her hair to slide his hands over her shoulders, to stroke them down her back and cup them around her butt. The wind immediately whipped her curls across their faces again, and he backed her into an area marginally more protected. "You plan on throwing my less than honorable behavior in my face every time we fight?"

"Not forever," she assured him virtuously. "But I did figure I could milk it for a good three or four months yet."

"Then let's say thirty or forty years. We'll renegotiate once you get that milking thing out of your system."

"Done." Then her smile faded as almost painful intensity snuck up and gripped her heart. "I love you, too, you know."

"Yeah. Once I calmed down—which is to say about two minutes ago—I figured that out. You never would have put yourself at risk for me like that if you didn't."

"Just so you know, I don't intend to do that again. But then, you're not ever going to make another stupid bet that would make that necessary, are you?"

"No, ma'am."

He looked so earnest, so solid and *hers* that she just had to kiss him. When she came up for air, she brushed a strand of hair off his forehead and simply looked at him. Soaked him in. Saw his incredible blue eyes, bright with happiness, noted the flush across his cheekbones, admired his strong, slightly overlong jaw. And she realized something momentous. "We're going to have a wonderful time together the next thirty, forty or however many years we negotiate, aren't we?"

"Oh, yeah." Laughing, he picked her up and whirled

her round and around. When they finally came to a halt, he smiled down into her eyes. "You can bet the bank on that, sweetheart."

Epilogue

"Here's to Italy!"

Jax watched martini glasses and beer mugs shoot aloft as Treena, Mack and Ellen responded to Carly's toast with "To Italy!" He added his own voice to the salute and lifted his bottle of lager to clink with the other upraised stemware in the little bar where he'd first seen Treena.

"I think it's so smokin' that you two are taking Ellen's long-awaited trip together," Treena said, smiling at Mack and Ellen.

"Yeah, smokin'," Jax agreed. "But when are you going to make an honest man out of him, Ellen?" He gave Mack an evil smile when the older man glared at him. Mack was still holding a grudge against him for lying to Treena about his identity, and Jax had quit trying to get in the duffer's good graces and started going out of his way to needle him instead.

He'd discovered it was a lot more fun.

"If all goes well between us on this trip, I may well do that when we return," Ellen replied serenely.

"May well…" Mack swivelled in his seat to stare at her, his face alight. "No shit?"

"No…um—"

"Fooling, I meant to say."

She sputtered a laugh. "Sure, you did. And yes. No fooling. We'll see how well we come through three weeks of intensive travel together. If we survive that, we can probably survive anything life throws at us."

"Piece of cake. Hell, we've already survived Jax. Everything after that is gravy."

Okay, Jax thought benevolently, so the old bastard was having as much fun as he was getting his licks in. Treena said Mack would come around, but he wasn't holding his breath. Still, he sort of hoped so, because he admired the guy for the way he looked out for Treena and Carly. And you had to empathize with anyone who loved his woman as desperately as Mack loved Ellen. Jax knew what that was all about.

"And what is it with you two, anyway?" Mack demanded. "You've been shacked up now for three weeks. You gonna get hitched or are you just going to keep living in sin?"

"I vote for sin," he replied coolly, just to see the other man's eyes flare.

Treena reached across the table and patted Mack's hand. "Don't listen to him. Jax has been pushing for marriage daily. I'm the one who wants to give it a month or two before we rush into anything." She grinned at Ellen. "You understand what I'm saying, right?"

"Yes, I do, darling. It's men who are impatient, always wanting everything tied up nice and legal with big red satin ribbons."

"Exactly. What happened to the good old days when they only wanted one thing?"

"What the hell is *he* doing here?"

Carly's voice only went that antagonistic over one person and sure enough, following her hostile gaze he saw Wolfgang Jones, standing motionless and unsmiling, as he listened to two people arguing at one of the roulette tables.

"Uh, he works here, Carly," Treena said carefully.

"Well, I don't like it," the blonde replied flatly.

"Hey, there's a big surprise. Far as I can tell, you don't like him breathing the same air you do."

Carly shrugged. "And your point would be? For God's sake, look at that hair. Who does he think he is, a punk rocker?"

Jax choked, but the rest of the table went dead silent, and Carly pulled her attention away from the big, lanky blonde across the room to look at them.

"What?"

When Treena, Mack and Ellen didn't say a word, Carly turned demanding eyes on Jax. He shrugged. "I hate to break this to you, babe, but you and Jones are sporting the exact same haircut."

"What the hell are you talking about?" She ran her palm over her own spiky blond hair. "We are not."

"You could be twins."

She looked to the rest of them to dispute him. "Somebody tell Jax he's full of shit."

"Oh man, I can't tell you how much it pains me not to jump on that bandwagon," Mack muttered.

"I'm afraid he's right, darling," Ellen said." Your hair is a little longer and it's feathery around your face where Mr. Jones's is more blunt-cut. But basically it's the same look."

"Oh, my gawd." Carly patted both hands all around her hair. Then her chin came up. "Well, that does it. I'm growing mine out."

"So, Jax." Mack cleared his throat. "When are you gonna quit living off Treena and get your butt back to work?"

"Dunno. She's happy to still be employed, and I'm enjoying this life of leisure." He bared his teeth at the older man but it was just for drill; he simply couldn't take this newest shot personally. Mack had built a solid little family of friends with the women at this table, and the guy was merely diverting attention away from Carly to give her a second to recoup.

Forearms braced on the table, Jax leaned over his hands, which were loosely cupped around his beer bottle. "Actually, there's a tournament coming up in L.A., so I might commute between here and there for it. Or maybe I'll stay there the nights Treena works and come home on her days off. We haven't really worked out the details yet."

She looped her arm through his and leaned into him, hugging his biceps to the side of her breast. "Can I tell them our news?"

He got lost looking into her excited face for a second, then shook his head to clear it. "Sure."

She grinned at her friends. "Jax is going to take me to the tournament in Monte Carlo in November if I can get the time off work. How smokin' is *that?*"

Mack gave her a tender smile, and Jax realized his popularity index with the older man had just shot up for making her so happy. "Very cool news, indeed," Mack said, and Ellen, beaming, agreed.

Carly, on the other side of Treena, butted shoulders with her friend. "Sounds like your lifelong dream come true to me," she said.

"I know."

The past three weeks had been the best of Jax's life. Even his and Treena's differing opinions regarding his father couldn't dim his happiness. They were slowly finding their way to a middle ground where they could discuss their opposing views without rancor. So far she'd abandoned the idea that Big Jim could do no wrong; he'd retreated from his position that his dad could do no right. Someday he might even be able to appreciate his father for the man she had known. And Treena's repetitive assertion that his father had been proud of him soothed the deep ache he'd carried inside of him for far too many years.

Then there was the "family" stuff. It was all new to Jax, but he liked it. He liked the way the three women and Mack had built a tight little unit that supported and looked out for its members. Admired the way they celebrated each other's successes and were quick to be there with consolation when one of them had a setback.

And he really liked that he was part of it now. Part of their lives, in on the minutiae that formed their daily existence. He belonged.

Knowing it drenched him in so much pleasure it was embarrassing.

Unmanly.

But still…

He turned his head and pressed his lips to the top of Treena's head in a fierce kiss.

She smiled at him.

"Thanks, honey," he said huskily and bent his head to give her a quick kiss on the lips.

"You're welcome," she replied and caught the back of his head to hold him in place while she returned the kiss with one that lingered just a shade longer than his had done. When she pulled back, she cupped his face in her hands and looked into his eyes, her own full of love. Then she said with utter seriousness, "I'm not sure what for, precisely. But Jax, my love, you are welcome."